Coronation

STEVEN VEERAPEN

First published in 2020 by Sharpe Books.

CONTENTS

Prologue

CORONATION

Westminster Abbey, July 1603

Sweat can come in many forms. There is that born of fear, which nips and tickles the nostrils, sticking to the clothes and coating them in vinegar. There is that born of exertion, which is heavier and muskier, weighing one down under the arms and dampening the small of the back. And then there is that born of heat, which is sour and shining and gathers on the forehead in glistening pearls.

The air of Westminster Hall was heavy with all three, the perfumes of civet, musk and rosewater fighting a losing battle against them.

The bishop of Winchester's cracking voice rose to the curving roof struts, almost drowned out by the insistent pounding of rain and the rushing that seemed to roar through the gutters overhead.

'To princes are given the superior powers…'

Rat-a-tat-a-tat-a-tat.

'Subject to no superior judge to give a reason of their doings…'

Ta-ta-rat-a-tat-a-tat.

'But only to God'

The competing sounds echoed. The nave of Westminster was a sparsely populated flowerbed of red roses, their petals thick velvet and satin and their pricks the sharp minds of the nobility who had been forced into the lifeless desert of London. It was a poor show for a coronation, the small gaggle of colourful attendees drawing attention to the lack of a thick and solemn crowd. It made the event seem hurried, furtive, as his coronation as king in Scotland had supposedly been in his infancy.

I warned him, thought Robert Cecil, lately made Lord Robert Cecil, Baron Essenden.

Cecil sat amongst the flowering of attendees, glittering in his chains of office, and muffled from the foul airs – he hoped – by his thick robes and gown. All that was taking place on and around the altar before the meagre congregation was at his bidding. And it had not been easy. On the death of Queen Elizabeth, plague had returned to London. Hundreds were now dying daily, collapsing in the streets, their houses sealed and quarantined for the requisite forty days. People were told not to meet. Crowds were banned. Playhouses and bear pits were closed. And yet daily the numbers of dead reported to him climbed.

It was almost like it was a sign of displeasure from God. This, at least, he had suggested to the king who now knelt resplendent on the kneeler before the altar next to his hook-nosed wife, was how the people might see it.

'The people, pah!' James had cried, looking down from his horse in the stable at Theobalds. 'I maun be crowned else I am not yet the true king.'

'Your Majesty is proclaimed –'

'Proclaimed! A piece of paper, man, read by secretaries.' Cecil had no reply to that. In England, it was sufficient to be proclaimed king by the great council. Perhaps James's Scotland was not quite so concerned with matters of legal nicety, and preferred symbols instead. 'I maun have the crown and be seen by the people.'

'Better, sir, to wait. The number of dead rise daily. It might … ignorant people might say God is displeased with your Majesty's succession.'

'Then they shall die for slanderous scoundrels.'

'Even so. If we were only to wait a little, until the deaths fall. Then, then might it be said that your coming was a great balm, a restorative after the evil sorrows that attended on the queen's death.'

That shut him up. James had leant back in the saddle, chewing on his jaw and scratching at his scraggly beard. 'Yet … I dinnae like …'

'There is a solution, sir.' The heavy-lidded eyes returned to him. Questing. Eager. Cecil resisted the urge to smile. 'A private coronation. Then you will be, as you say, true and sole king. Traitors like Raleigh who cry for others will be silenced.'

'Raleigh, pah!'

Cecil gave a half-nod. Preparations were already underway to trump up charges against the devious Raleigh and arraign him as a plotter who had hoped to put the king's cousin on the throne. He was a sacrifice in the interests of friendship with Spain, but sacrifices were what a royal secretary must be pleased to make. 'Indeed, sir. Your Majesty will be crowned in all pomp yet in safety. And then we might wait a while until the city is cured of its sickness. And then the public festivities might begin. Of thanksgiving at your royal presence bringing relief to these suffering times. I think,' he added, bowing his head, 'it might start a holiday greater than the late queen's Accession Day. A true triumph for your royal house and its ancient line of kings.'

James had said nothing awhile, frowning at his horse's mane and picking at his lips. 'I can see no flaw in it. Good man. Good man. And this … this is a thing right and proper in this realm?'

Cecil had given an offended little look. 'Of course, your Majesty.'

'Then see to, man, see to. Only one thing. Ane small ane, eh? St James' Day. St James the Greater. Aye, I shall debate it with you anon, man. There is good reasoning in it – the doctors of theology agree wi' me. Prepare your arguments against and we shall make merry enough later. Well, see to.' With that, he had ridden off to hunt.

King James, Cecil had thought – still thought – was a different proposition from Elizabeth. Where once the secretary had been barked at or given sullen silences and sour looks from a prevaricating old woman who wanted nothing changed, now he was led by an avuncular university philosopher fonder of clever argument and getting his own way than people.

Still, the king was new to England and Cecil wise in it. Elizabeth had been old in the ways of England when her secretary was still at his nurse's breast.

Between that conversation and the coronation ceremony, there had been almost no time to prepare anything. The knights of the bath? Given days' notice. Cecil had managed to corral them, though. He had managed to secure an order of perfumes to sweeten the ancient stone and hangings of the church, despite the limits and bans on trade. He had personally instructed the Dean of Westminster, Lancelot Andrews, on which books to consult in learning his role as the king's body servant throughout ('ensure he does nothing that is not forewritten' has been Cecil's advice: 'stick hard by him like a barnacle to a ship'). Likewise, the commission to determine which lord perform which ceremonial function had been formalised with days to spare.

A twinge of pride tingled through him, momentarily blotting the growing pain in his head. The picture of majesty, however muted, that lay before him was all his doing. The earl of Oxford – profligate, fat, and rumoured to be mad – who acted as chief chamberlain was his former brother-in-law and now forced to beg him favours. The big man now stood, leading a pair of other nobles, as the archbishop strode around the altar, theatrically looking into its corners, before crying out, 'and to the nobility and realm of England, I ask this: will you call this worshipful prince the right heir of the realm to have him as your king and become subjects unto him and submit you to obey his commandments?'

'Ay,' shouted Cecil. His small voice was lost in the sea of identical replies.

Then came the symbols and a return of the tiresome bishop of Winchester.

'The sceptre represents righteousness, the oil gladness, and to princes then, as partakers with Christ in the power, honour and justice of his kingdom here on Earth are allowed of God a *sword* in sign of power, a *crown* in show of Glory, a *sceptre* for a token of direction, a *throne* for a seat of justice and judgment.' He drew breath. 'And unction as a pledge of outward protection and inward infusion of grace. Justice establishes the throne and belongs to God, and the laws this king is given to protect are also God's. The inward anointing is the diffusion of heavenly wisdom and courage in the hearts of Princes.'

It was all, Cecil thought, rather impressive in the act. None present, he supposed, had ever seen such a ceremony. He certainly had not. After James had made his oath, clearly and with a sprinkling of Scots, the secretary even allowed himself to enjoy the singing that followed. As he did so, his eyes travelled over the altar, which had been fitted out with a curtained pulpit, twin curtained tiring rooms on either side of St Edward's Chapel, and gilded thrones on the chapel proper, one of them the ancient throne of St Edward, for the new king and his queen.

Behind it all, in Henry VII's Chapel, Elizabeth lay, quietly rotting alongside the bones of her grandparents, unremarked, forgotten, and with no tomb to make a memory of her.

There was a great deal of to-ing and fro-ing on the altar and before it as James and Anne sat. Then knelt. Then stood. She rustled in gold tissue; he bobbed and jerked on his ungainly legs. The choir rose and fell. Eventually, the royal couple attained their thrones on the altar proper, guided by the dean, and the anointment took place – the placing of the sacred oil on five parts of his body. They then retired to the curtained tiring rooms and the congregation waited until they returned, this time re-dressed in cloth of gold, crimson and ermine. They sat once again, looking suitably regal, as the sword was blessed, and they were each touched with it. The old silver glinted in the reflected magnificence of a thousand candles.

Finally, came the crowns. James's was to be the ancient crown of St Edward: an imperial one of wrought gold studded with precious gemstones and jewels, all of which dazzled in the candlelight. Anne was to receive that made for Anne Boleyn as a replacement for when the imperial crown of St Edward became too heavy for her ill-fated head. Blessed by the archbishop, they were placed on the heads of king and queen and, to his surprise, Cecil felt tears start in the corners of his eyes.

He had done this.

He had made this happen.

As the ring was slipped onto James' finger and the rod and sceptre handed to him so that he and his wife might sit in a tableau of majesty, the choir launched into the Te Deum, that ancient song of thanksgiving. The royal couple remaining seated in state, the nobles and clergymen rose to begin giving their homages one by one.

Cecil got up to take his turn at the rear of the procession. Barons were far down the hierarchy of the nobility and that, after all, was all he was.

For now.

A murmur ran through the congregation and, fox-like, Cecil's eyes sharpened and he looked over around those in front of him, towards the altar. The young Philip Herbert, younger son of the earl of Pembroke, had reached the carpet before the king's throne. Rather than making his knee and moving on, he had crept closer.

Dear God, thought Cecil, his back stiffening.

The stupid boy crawled right up to the king. And rather than turning a furious royal frown on him, James grinned like a fond father, took the boy's face in his hand, and drew it up to his own. They kissed, fully and sensually, on the lips.

The collective intake of breath threatened even the stability of the choir.

And it was over, and the dean leading Herbert away, roughly, Cecil hoped, and beckoning the next in line to take a more appropriate turn. Queen Anne sat, staring mutely into space, receiving her obeisance with a studied smile.

This king, the secretary thought as he shuffled forward and took his turn, might be easy to guide. But he might not be easy to control. In her final years, all of Elizabeth's friends had been the ghostly apparitions which lodged in her mind. Managing her had been easier than he had appreciated. Though she might not have trusted him, she had had no one else. James surrounded himself with Scots and handsome noblemen, however. Every one of them provided a living, competing, full-throated voice. He was still thinking it when the parade of fidelity was over, and he regained his seat in the nave.

Finally, the communion service began, the archbishop attending first to the king, who took it with good grace, and finally offering the host to the queen.

Again, something went wrong.

The queen turned her head away, mouthing something. The archbishop pressed on her. And then, in the eyes of the congregation of England's highest men and women, she said, quite audibly, 'NO'.

Cow! cursed Cecil, albeit inwardly. Rumoured a papist and no doubt seeking a way to embarrass the husband who had just mortified her. Queen Anne was going to be a problem – as Cecil had known she would be from reading reports of her meddling in Scotland. Every time he looked at her, with her broken-veined red cheeks and her long nose (all too redolent of the late queen), her gaze said, 'I know you do not like me, secretary, nor trust me. And I neither like nor trust you.' The wretched woman would need watching. Her ladies bribed, her letters read, her friends investigated. More expense. Endless expense.

Perhaps he had not quite appreciated having to deal with just one royal figure. A spasm jolted his back, a hard fist grasping and squeezing the base of his spine. Releasing it. Grasping and squeezing again, more tightly. Sweat prickled on his brow.

As the ceremony drew to a close, Cecil's headache threatened again. The heavy scents of the church, he thought. And, of course, the worry that something far more disastrous might happen. As the king and queen retired to their tiring rooms to change for the banquet waiting at Westminster Hall, Cecil rose from his seat and hobbled towards the altar. No one tried to block him: the dean and archbishop, Oxford himself, gave him tight nods. He returned what he hoped was a friendly smile, before passing them entirely and entering upon the sacred ground, his robes whispering across it.

'Your Majesty,' he said, brushing a hand on the closed curtain.

'Enter, Beagle.'

Beagle. Better than pygmy. Cecil slid the curtain to the side and slid in, letting it fall closed behind him. He bowed as deeply as his heavy robes allowed. 'A triumph, your Majesty.' As he rose, he fixed his gaze on the gauzy ruff just below the pig's bladder face.

'Aye, it was that.' The dean of Westminster had the crown in his hands and placed it on a cushion before picking up a smaller, lighter one. Another man was concealed in the makeshift room: a smiling, jolly-faced fellow in his forties, his furred tippet signalling his trade. In his hands were clutched a bottle and a crystal glass. The contents of the former were already swishing in the latter. James took it from him and gulped deeply, breathing hard. 'You did well, Beagle,' he spluttered. 'And we thank you well for it.'

Hard liquor, thought Cecil. At this time, on this day, and in this place. He inclined his head.

'And I thank you, doctor,' said the king. He turned challenging eyes on Cecil. 'A dram for medicinal purposes.'

'Yes, your Majesty.'

'Well, man, what do you clamour for? Not come to cry upon me for the ardent love shown by young Herbert, eh?'

'No, sir.'

'Good. We shall not be told how to treat our good subjects.'

'No, sir,' Cecil repeated. 'I have come to speak with Dr Gurney.'

'Not caught the pox, have you? I hear the trulls south of the river are hot with it, you naughty lad.' James laughed uproariously, once, twice. Cecil did not make a sound. It had always been axiomatic to him that men who laughed at their own jests, royal or not, ought to have their pockets filled with stones and be dropped into the Irish Sea. His laughter subsiding, the king beckoned for another drink, which the doctor poured him. 'Well, it is none of my concern. Only, doctor, see that the man does not die, eh? We shall have need of him hereafter.'

With the new crown on his head, King James took up his sceptre and, with a face redder than his wife's, he nodded in the tall gilt mirror which stood against one curtain wall. 'Aye. Aye.' His chest rose in a shiver of fur, silk, and cloth of gold. To Cecil, he said, 'Do not think we are unmindful, man. This,' he lifted the sceptre, 'is a burden, and no' a blessing.' His words were given the lie by the look of almost feral triumph that swelled his features. 'Now, we maun be off. Aye, speak to the good doctor here. You look a thing sickly.'

James's words caused everyone in the room to freeze. For a brief spell, they had almost forgotten about the plague that raged beyond the church. To his credit the king seemed to realise what he had said. His jaw worked for a few seconds. 'Aye, see to him, Gurney, see to him.' With that, he let the dean lead him out of the tiring room to head the procession towards the hall.

When they were alone, Cecil gave Dr Gurney a tired smile. The fellow was one of the most experienced royal physicians: a Cambridge man who had studied theology as well as medicine. Both the king and his secretary respected such a store of learning. It was why he had been retained to see to the king's health and complexion on the day he was to be on show to his nobility. 'Medicinal?' said the latter.

'I know his Majesty's tastes and needs, I think. He is an easy patient. Give him what he likes, and his humours are in fair balance.'

'Would that my own were.'

'What troubles you, my friend? Sit.'

Cecil sat on the cushioned stool as Gurney fussed about him. 'Pains. In the head, in the gut. I am wearying more quickly these last months than ever. And my back. The pain in my back.'

'This is no mystery, my friend.' Cecil looked up. Gurney held up a finger, raising his voice as the choir began again outside. 'Overwork.

You must rest.' He frowned at the looked of pained amusement on his patient's face. 'This is good advice I give. You cannot … my friend, you cannot be all things to this realm. Not if you wish to live to see it prosper.'

'Rest. Is there no note of physick you can give me?'

'As a substitute for rest? None so good.' He sighed. 'I will write you something that will bring a good sleep. Do you still sleep ill?'

'Yes.'

'And your urges are as they should be?'

'Quite.' Cecil said this tightly. The doctor need not know of his relations with any of the women he had taken up with privately since his wife's death. 'I must go. I will receive your note later, doctor. With thanks.' He ignored Gurney's arm and hauled himself up.

'It is my pleasure, my friend. I am only sorry I can do little more than give instructions. And you are an easy patient too. Not like some.' He hesitated. 'In fact, I had been meaning to ask you, rather than the king. I have been lately troubled by some patients I see in my private work at home. Most troublesome and strange. I do not like their…'

Everybody wants something, thought Cecil, already moving towards the curtain. 'Thank you, doctor. And I wish heartily that all your patients prove as easy as I. I have no doubt you have much work to do with all that is troubling this city. See you stay away from any that are touched by the pestilence. The king has as much need of you as he does me.' Gurney made no attempt to stop him, nor to press whatever suit he had. Good royal servants always knew what was and was not the proper time to plead favours.

'See me again, doctor. On a better day. When I have *rested.*'

The secretary left the tiring room and moved to join the tail of the procession as it made its colourful and musical way the short distance from abbey church to hall. Already his mind was working ahead. How could such a company be kept safe from the plague on its escape from London? Would the meats and drink and sweets be sufficiently tested? What might king or queen say or do if they drank too deeply of strong wine?

How many had died that day?

And to think this was only the beginning. The crowning of king and queen was done, yes – the need for the religious symbolism satisfied. A piece of theatre to please the king and silence the nobility. The people, when they stopped dropping dead, would require their own shows and entertainments, and there lay the greater task. Until then, the coronation would only be half-done. Still there was much to plan, to organise, to maintain the security of.

Carpenters, he thought. Watchmen. City guilds. Purveyors of silks and velvets. Pageants. Poets and playwrights. Makers of cunning fire-shows. A list would have to be got up.

He did not spare a thought for Dr Gurney's enquiry, and promptly forgot the man's mention of troublesome and strange patients, letting it wash away with his sweat, pain, and rapidly turning mind.

It was an oversight he would soon regret.

1

I sponged the boy's brow with a rag made warm and damp by his perspiration. The intense heat of the room, I hoped, would draw the plague out of him.

And perhaps into me.

Forty days. For nearly forty long days, we had been shut away in our house on Shoe Lane. Though we had a reasonable amount of space – my lodgings consisted of two ground-floor rooms with the ceiling knocked through to give us the rooms above – it is a terrifying thing to be locked up with the plague.

And it had been I who brought it home to my family.

'Leave London' had been the first advice to the uninfected when people had begun to die. I had not heeded it.

'Stay at home and speak with none. Do not meet and do not gather,' had been the second. I had not heeded it. In fact, I had done worse. And in what I had done, in my own foolish recklessness, I had brought the laws of quarantine upon the house.

Worse. You caused the boy's illness.

You will likely have heard of the rules that govern the sickness – they are in every man's mouth before, during, and after the visitations. Imprimis: infection is found. Item: those of the household must remain indoors. Item: a bale of straw must be hung from a window (I supposed that an old broom would suffice). Item: A red cross must be drawn clearly on the front of the closed door (whoever spotted the broom must have tended to that) by the local constables. Item: if one of the said infected household must stir abroad, peradventure for meat and drink, he must carry with him a white stick, that the citizens in good and perfect health might stay apace distant.

With my shard of white-painted window frame, I had gone out on the first day of our confinement and, grudging it, bought us a store of salted meats, dried marjoram and lavender, and tobacco. Then I had paid an old woman I trusted, Mrs Frere, to see that we were delivered fresh ale and beer every few days, the stuff left with a knock outside of the door.

And then we decided against tempting fate by venturing out too much. Instead, we nursed the boy. I had seen the plague before. It visited London in fits and starts, felling a milkmaid here, a vintner there.

To think that it had seemed that just another brief visit of the sickness was in the stars in the weeks and months after Queen Elizabeth's death: reports of a drunk who never rose from his gutter and was swiftly carried away and buried, the marks on his body declaring what ailed him. But then it wasn't just one drunk, but a crowd of men who had been drinking with him. And then their wives, and their wives' friends, and their wives' friends' servants. Talk turned from the death of the queen and the coming of the new king to this new and terrible visitation.

Then the screams had started, at all hours, and always followed by the thunder of running feet. Strange how a scream makes a person run, and a person running makes others do the same.

A sign from God.
God is displeased.
It's the incoming of foreigners.
Scots! Spaniards! Flemings! French!

I did not greatly care where it came from. Rather, I had been concerned that the theatres would close, and I would have to rely on my own little strongbox of money for a while – already depleted from purchasing the leasehold of the rooms upstairs for my extended home. I had gone out less and had even managed to keep David and his sister, my other charge, Faith, at home, God-fearing as they were, until that black Christmas and its promised lights.

Except for that one time, eh? That one time you couldn't resist that led to this and might yet have killed the child.

'Water?' croaked David. He lay on his cot in the first chamber of the house, closest to the heat. We had tried freezing the place over that cold winter, leaving the fire unlit and covering ourselves in blankets, wondering if the cold might kill the pestilence. That had only made him shiver. And so we had decided to try burning it out of him.

I lifted the wooden mug to his lips, and he drank. His face, which was always colourless, contorted in a smile of thanks. David, I thought, looking at him. My boy. And it was a far better name than the one he'd been afflicted with by his natural parents – Puritanical creatures who had cursed him with the name Dust before beginning their journey back to it. Putting my palm to his forehead, I returned his smile. 'No fever,' I said.

In a second, his sister was at my elbow. I looked up at her. So like her brother – the same carrot-coloured hair and profusion of freckles. To her credit, she had not blamed me once for the boy's sickening. Not with her words, at any rate. Yet I thought she did with her tilted green eyes. It might have been my imagination, but something in her gaze and her cool attitude towards me seemed to say, 'you did this. You found my brother and brought him here and then through your own selfish folly you made him ill.' And if she was thinking that, she was right.

'No fever?' She echoed, making a question of it. As though she didn't believe me, she reached down and touched him herself.

'You see? Your old Ned is no liar. The lad just needs rest.' Already his eyelids had slid down, vibrant green replaced by chalky white.

'Is he well then?'

'Yes,' I said. In truth I had no idea, but it seemed the right thing to say. The boy's course of illness had been strange to me. It started the way I knew the plague did: first he had overheated and sweated, shivering at the same time. Then the headaches that were so severe that I relented and began the quarantine. And then the bolts of pain that wracked his body, turning the clock of his twelve backwards and making a mewling babe of him. Yet no lumps had developed anywhere about him. Instead, patches of his skin had reddened, forming rashes, which had lasted a week or so and then faded. Then, finally, he had seemed to sweat and shake the disease out. Now even the quivering had stopped. It seemed to me a likely thing that he would live, though I could not understand how or why, nor why Faith and I had avoided it, save my smoking and her keeping mostly to her chamber, not touching her brother, and washing her clothes, hands, and feet constantly. 'Let him sleep.'

I gave him one last smile. Poor boy, I thought. I barely had had time to get to know him before the world had started to fall apart. Still, he was Faith's blood and so I must love him as well as she did. If he was quiet, well, so had she been, when I'd first found her and for long enough after. If he had shied away from my touch when I'd first reclaimed him, well, that too was natural enough.

Because he can divine your perversity.

I sucked in my cheeks. No, I had come to understand his shyness and fear. When it had been necessary to undress him in the first flush of the sickness, I had discovered livid welts across his back. He had tried to lie down, to hide them, and I did not ask about them. Still, my expression must have turned traitor, for he turned his solemn gaze on me and said, 'Because I tried to write my name with this hand'. I had said nothing. Inwardly, I was relieved that it had only been the rough correction of a minor infraction. I had not adopted a wildcat. I looked at him again and brushed a red strand dampened to brown away from his brow. A kitten, more like. I would whip strength into him by other means if I must. He had not, I must point out, become a son to me. I find it appalling that any man in his middle-twenties should have a full-grown lad, and still worse if that lad should appear in his life aged twelve. No, but as I thought of Faith as a sister, he would become my own brother.

I stood, took her by the hand, and we sat at our table on the other side of the room. I wiped down the mug before refilling it from our water jug and taking a swig myself. My linen shirt had become a second, clammy skin, drawing all moisture from me. 'I think I'll go out today.'

'I'll go if you like.' Eagerness added a note of wildness to her tone. In truth, we needed nothing. Yet the weeks spent almost constantly indoors had become intolerable. At first, we had played games, as we tried to forget David's suffering under his blanket. Then the games had grown stale and, when the boy seemed better, I had taught him how to relieve a man of his property without his knowing – a thing he delighted in more than his sister ever had. But that had been a false recovery and soon he was back under the blankets, shaking again.

I had read to them both from the meagre selection of licensed playbooks I owned. That had been another success. In some of the darkest, weariest nights (or days, for time was liquid smoke), I even considered praying. It is not, as a rule, something I do. Ghostly and half-formed in my mind is the notion that by praying I should remind God of my existence and invite him to take a look at my sins and punish me and mine accordingly.

And so, our little bubble of a world floated in a timeless and terrible eternity, enlivened only by imagining worlds outside of it through the playbooks. Even so, staring at the same walls every day, no news to discuss … it was exhausting for us both. The days had passed, and the weeks, until a month had been swallowed up. It was like being in prison – a thing I knew well enough and hated more. There was the same expanding and contracting of time, as each minute pulsed with the fever. A single day stretched interminably, inviting long sleeps, and yet somehow a week passed in a blink. Even the church-bells, London's timekeepers, had grown unreliable. They chimed at random and in bizarre order, signalling new deaths and reminding us all to stay indoors.

'Like that?' My cheek jerked. She was wearing one of my old wool shirts over her nightdress. In the firelight, her colour deepened.

'No, of course not.'

13

'Go up and change, then. I think we might both go out. One at a time. It's over. Forty days.'

She frowned. Her hand slid across the table, towards one of her account books. 'No. No, it's only been thirty-seven days, Ned. I've been counting. Marking every day.'

'Forty, thirty ... Who the hell cares?' I snapped. I fumbled around the table, found my pipe, and lit it.

'Again,' she asked, wrinkling her nose. Those eyes had something hard in them again, critical. Where was my soft little Faith? What had I done to her, through inviting the plague in on her brother?

'Yes, again, *mother*.' My voice was sharper than I had intended. Since I had begun taking the tobacco daily in our house, I found going without it for too long made me ratty. Faith would not touch the stuff. 'Besides ...' Inspiration hit me as the acrid smoke made a desert of my tongue. 'We do need fuel for the fire.' To my disappointment, we had had to begin burning things. Old clothes I owned that were no longer in fashion had already gone, cheerful blue and green suits blackening as they caught, like pyre-sacrifices to the man I had once been. At the thought, more sweat skipped on ticklish, feathery feet on its path from nape to small. 'It's over,' I said, more gently. 'He's well enough. Anyway, I must have a little movement about me, or I'll become fat and ugly and neither of you will want to look at me, never mind live with me.'

'I don't mean to scold. I just –'

A thump. A scratching. Someone was at the door. I set down my pipe with a delicate tap.

Faith drew in her cheeks. 'We just had ale. Fresh stuff, it's here.'

'That's not one of Mrs Frere's molls,' I said, jerking up from my seat.

Someone was feeling their way around the door, checking whether it was barred or not. The noise ceased, before beginning again at the window. Another, louder, thudding sound, wood against plaster, clipped neatly above our heads.

Thieves, I thought. It was something I'd heard of in the past – the lowest of the low would wait until they thought everyone in a plague house might be dead or too ill to defend themselves, and then they would raid the house. Word of my having enough to buy another floor to my home must have got around, followed by news that me and my family were dying within it.

I snatched up the fire poker that Faith used to stir pot herbs and handed it to her. 'If they get a hand in the window, mouse,' I said, 'brand it good.'

She nodded and I flashed her a smile. Once a shy little thing, she had come into her own since I had liberated her brother and reunited them. At seventeen to his twelve (or so I reckoned), the lioness in her had grown claws and scratched its way out. Any anger she had been hiding in her heart towards me was momentarily focused elsewhere. 'Where are you going?'

I didn't answer. Instead, I slid towards the door of my private chamber. It was my treasure house, my cave of delights, rich with the fruits of years of gathering clothes, trinkets, and useless rubbish. I knew its windows were nailed shut and I ignored it. On its left was bolted a ladder leading to the hole in the ceiling which gave access to the upstairs. Monkey-like, I started clambering up the rungs.

'Eyaah!'

I turned at Faith's strangulated yelp. A hand led an arm in snaking its way through the shutter. Her cry turned to fury and her shriek had force enough to cause its retreat. I returned my attention to the rungs and scrambled up.

Suffocating heat assailed me. My head swam in it as my eyes adjusted to the gloom. Broad rectangles of light cut out of the far wall marked the window and upstairs door. Formerly a separate two-roomed lodging, I had had workmen knock away the exterior wooden staircase. I gripped the sanded floorboards, got to my knees, and felt my way across the front room, listening.

Hollow thumps, like someone rapping on an empty barrel. Then wood whispering against wood.

Someone was out there, despite the lack of a staircase, trying to get in.

The door was, like the one downstairs, barred, but the wooden shutters had no locks. They were opened and closed by means of a hole in the centre, through which one could poke a finger and push or pull. One hole was stopped up by the broom handle, the other by a piece of rag.

I tensed beside the window. The rag fell inward, pushed by the unseen creature who meant to rob us. A rapier of light took its place, ending in a point on the floor. Throwing myself sideways, I punched the shutter. It flew open. The other one went too, banging back inwards as the brush of the broom hit the wall.

Light poured in, blinding and golden, in a vicious rush of cold air. It stung the sweat on my brow, attacked my chest, as I found myself caught in the battle between the sweltering house and frosted city.

Outside, a man wobbled at the top of his own ladder as it stood suspended in mid-air. He looked at me, only his wide eyes visible over a bolt of cloth that protected his nose and mouth. I leant out and pushed. The ladder cut an arc backwards to the street, taking the scrawny thief with it.

At the same time, a scream cut a path upwards. Clutching his hand, the man downstairs skipped away from the house. 'We're not dead here, nor ill, you filthy pieces of shit!' I screamed. And then I laughed. The creatures, still yelping, abandoned the ladder and ran off, away from Shoe Lane and towards Fleet Street.

There it all is. The world of London exactly as you left it and yet changed forever.

'Faith,' I cried, plucking at the dead flowers in the bower I had installed to add merriment in better times. 'Faith!' I turned away from the light, blackened heartsease crumbling in my hand. 'We don't need to go far for fuel. Our friends have left us a store of it in the street.'

The plague outbreak, I thought, had given birth to a new breed of criminal – artless and desperate ones, who had no respect for the dead or the dying. With a shiver, I realised that what lay outside the home that became a prison would be akin to the dearth years of Queen Elizabeth all over again, but with red pustules rather than prominent bones.

I did not then imagine the madder sort of criminal enterprise that the infestation was breeding.

2

You may think it hard to imagine London quiet, but I had known it so before. In the weeks before Elizabeth's death, the great city had held its tongue. Those who could afford to had crept away, and those who lacked the means had shut their doors and windows tight against the terror of insurrection. That had been near a year ago – almost exactly, I thought, a full year since I had been drawn into the affair of the succession.

And again, London had lost its voice.

The hard, heatless sun told me it was early morning. I stood in Shoe Lane a while, blinking, and turning on the spot. The town smelt surprisingly fresh, with a bitter undertone of rosemary and burning. Looking up over the rooftops, the dull sky was stained with a smudge of smoke. The clothes and bedding of the dead being burnt, I supposed.

Predictably, few were about and the lack of people over the previous months had meant a lack of sewage and muck. The sewer channel itself burbled with almost-clean rainwater, unrelieved by bits of carcass or adventurous turds. I kicked the ladder apart – it was a badly made, pegged thing – and passed the pieces in to Faith. When she closed the door, I used my forearm to smudge the cross painted there. It did not disappear but left rusty flakes on the sleeve of my livery, which I'd put on after washing my hands and feet, as much to feel like part of the engine of society again as anything else.

There were a few things I intended to do, and I wished to make the most of my time out in the world again. Finding news was first and I left the lane for Fleet Street, where a couple of men were calling to each other across the gutter. I joined the nearest, maintaining a distance, and offered the universal enquiry: 'what news?'

'The king is at Whitehall. Finally, lodging in the city, so he is.' My new friend was a portly man with a red face and clothing which proclaimed him a tanner.

That must mean the plague was retreating. I ventured, 'the death times stopped then?'

'Ay, friend. The dead back to what they was. Hardly not none dying now.'

From across the gutter, the other fellow, who seemed to be wearing an odd assortment of ill-matched clothes, called, 'ay, the king in

London. Bloody rich man's disease if yer ask me. Comes of all this foreign trade. Makes the merchants wealthy but it's the poor what pays for it.' I touched my cap, which sat awkwardly on my tangle of hair, and he seemed to notice my livery. 'Er … I mean …' The fellow became a blur of dun as he fled.

'There's a busy la –' As I spoke, I had turned to my new friend. He too had gone. I sighed. In the past, I would have been paid well to report such words and the people who spoke them. Yet I found I had no intention of doing so, even for money. They were true. We had all been left to die whilst the wealthy had packed up their goods and found clean air and health and life in the countryside.

I crossed Fleet Street riverward and made for St Bride's, where I ignored the Bills of Mortality – new things, full of lies, which told us the number of dead each day – and continued on past the boarded-up print shop, until I found a cramped but expensive townhouse. It was the home of my former landlord, Frere, and his wife – the woman who had ensured that we did not go without good drink during our confinement. I had no intention of paying her anything, but I supposed a thanks and a promise of future favour would suffice.

Any thought of thanks died on my lips as I saw the door. It hung from one hinge, bent back at a crazy angle, like a marker stone one sees on the road, knocked backwards by a generation of gusts. On it was painted the familiar warning cross.

I hesitated in the doorway. Something was wrong.

A soft rustle of movement from within. Whispering.

Run!

Instead, I pushed the door in further and stepped inside.

The house had been wrecked. Smashed cabinets lay like flotsam in a sea of carnage, their plate and contents gone. It was dark, and yet in the darkness I saw solid black figures drifting wraithlike between the ruins. 'Who goes there?' I did not receive a response and remained close to the door. 'Mr Frere? Mrs Frere?'

This elicited a groan. Someone stepped forward and I made a fist, releasing it when I saw it was a woman. Her cap was a plain thing half-askew, and even in the weak light I could see she wore the dullest of serving smocks. 'Gone,' she said in a mechanical voice.

'The Freres have fled?' I knew they had not. The cross told me they had not.

'Dead.'

'Both?'

'Hm.'

Another figure swirled up behind her, bulkier and taller. 'The master and mistress are dead,' he said in the wheezing voice of age, removing his hat and turning it in his hands. 'My master and mistress both dead.'

'But … but … I've been getting small beer and ale from her. My name is Edward Savage – I live on Shoe Lane.'

Something of authority came into the steward's voice. 'Dorcas here has kept to the late mistress's wishes. She brought you your ale and beer as Mrs Frere directed before … before the house was shut up.'

'What happened here?' I pointed, quite unnecessarily, at the wreckage.

'Scum,' spat the girl, Dorcas.

'Thieves,' added the serving man. 'I regret … my master and mistress were shut up alone in this place when the infection came. We have brought them food and ale each morning, as Dorcas brought it to you. Yesterday we received no answer to our knocking and … and …' The girl sobbed and he put a hand on her shoulder. 'They were borne away, as is right. We came again this morning to freshen the house.' Why? I wondered – and realised they probably had nothing else to do. 'And the house we found in this state of repair. Broken in upon in the night. What manner of man steals from the dead, sir?'

'I don't know,' I said. I did, though. Desperate men. And the dead hardly had need of their goods. 'You must report it. Have the watch out.'

'That we will. It will be our last service to them. They were good masters to us.'

'Yes, she was a good mistress,' was all I would give. 'I'm sorry.' I had begun to back out of the place when Dorcas's voice tugged at me.

'You looking for service, mister?'

'I … I …'

'We don't ask much, sir,' said the old steward.

'I'm afraid … I really don't…'

'Please,' said the girl. 'Please, we don't got nuffink else.'

'Don't beg, Dorrie. We aren't no beggars,' warned her superior, resignation, sadness, and pride raising his voice to dignity.

At a loss, embarrassed, I left what had been the Frere house and emerged back into cloudy February sunlight. I fumbled for my pipe, cursing when I realised I'd left it at home.

A drink then.

If there was one manner of place in London that I knew would have thrived even in the plague times, it would have been the taverns. Even with bans on large gatherings, the tapsters had ways of flouting the laws, and people, I had noticed before our quarantine, had been inclined to drink themselves insensible. Perhaps they thought that they might make as good cheer as possible if they might die soon. Or the dulling of drink might ease the pain of losing friends.

Fancying a walk in the daylight, which was rapidly greying, I began my trek through the city proper, crossing the Fleet Bridge and descending Ludgate Hill. Again, memories of the queen's death-days rose up. Yet there was a clear difference. Then, the people had been quiet, hiding away. There had been no question that they would return to their lives when order was restored and a new monarch crowned. Now they had been stilled by death on a grand scale. Many had fled again, to be sure, but many more would never return. Every few houses along the street had their deadly warnings painted. Men and women in tall black hats kept to themselves, occasionally making wide circles around the odd unfortunate wielding a white baton. My boots slid over weeds and grass which grasped upwards from between loose boards of pavement, Mother Nature being swift to reclaim what we had taken from her and made our own.

As I turned left to cut up a lane towards Watling Street, an icy screech made the air even colder. 'Repent!' A hand bell rang. 'Repent!' Standing on a crate, swathed in black, was a hollow-cheeked preacher. 'You see what disfavour God has shown to this city of sin!' I spat at the ground. Creatures like that seemed always to revel in disaster. A small boy detached from a group of three and crept towards him, before turning and baring his backside. Laughter from his fellows. The old man ignored them, ringing the bell again. 'And this is but the first sign! See you how the terrible judgment alights! Repent, sinners all!'

I continued on my way, making for Cheapside. On London's great commercial road, wooden stalls and booths were already heavy with goods and the smell of cooked meat made my stomach cackle. I purchased a pie and crunched into it, sauce and juices staining my fingers. As I licked them, I saw another long-bearded fellow. No doomsday prophet this, but one of the false magicians who did a more roaring trade than the hell-merchants. In a black skull cap and wearing spectacles on the tip of his nose, which bore, inexplicably, black discs of wood rather than glass, he was holding up a necklace dotted with grey stones of various shapes and sizes. '… carried out of Egypt from the inner walls of the kings of the Egyptians' tombs, blessed by the ancient priests in their wisdom and a sure proof against the dreaded pestilence!' I moved over for a better look. On closer inspection, the stones were soot- rather than sand-stained and appeared to have come from a broken bit of masonry. 'Only a penny per stone, to be kept in the mouth!' Some women were forming a queue, keeping their distance from one another. 'No need to press, sweets. It was a big tomb.'

Church bells clanged, drowning him out. I found myself a barber who was taking custom – once he had measured me up from five yards' distance – and had my hair cut short and beard shaved off. That done, I felt truly a man again, and decided that a man of the city should indeed have a drink. I followed Cheapside east, crunching my way over a matting of herbs – rosemary and hyacinth – which reeked of dung-trodden and unseasonable spring. The smell did not improve, and nor did the bleakness of the air, when the street ran into the Poultry.

The only tavern worth drinking in in the Poultry is, of course, The Three Cranes. Its sign, bearing, unsurprisingly, three cranes, makes for a more pleasant sight than the fluffy dead birds that hang from the stalls of the shops and vendors directly outside, their necks wrung and their feathers grubby. It was on the circuit of the theatricals, and thus a familiar place through my work with the Revels Office. It is a cramped place, and the old jest is that every mug of beer and cup of wine comes with at least one waterlogged feather floating in it – and finding one from the arse-end of a goose is good luck.

I entered, springing lightly on the feather-dotted rushes, and drank deeply of the sour sting of beer-soaked wood and cork. It conjured up memories of a world utterly familiar, safe, and still living.

And yet not. Where's the music-man to annoy those entering? Where's the crowd? Where's the laughter?

I ignored what wasn't there and focused on what was, sniffing like a hungry puppy. My senses satisfied, I smiled as I saw a man I recognised. Thomas Heywood was a playwright – I would not go so far as to say a poet – who had rose to fame after his *The Four Prentices of London* had become a favourite amongst the class of men it depicted.

Suddenly, I was glad I had visited the barber and been freshly tidied. Though Heywood didn't, so far as I knew, share my tastes, I would not want to be caught looking dishevelled and ugly before such a man. You might think me a loose-wit or worse for that, , and probably you would be right. He was handsome and brooding – in his thirties by my reckoning – and, despite being a university man, he was neither boastful nor affected. Unfortunately, like most university men, he wrote dialogue as though he had only witnessed real men and women through a perspective glass at a country mile's distance and guessed at what they might be saying. Their belief, I guessed, was that the figures on a stage should serve as examples, and somehow be better and more glorious in their golden speeches than folk in the true world of men.

He was sitting at a table, a flat cap on a head bent low in conversation with one of the theatrical men of business, Kit Beeston. I raised my hand and crossed to them, pausing only to request a beer from the tapster.

'Good morrow, Savage,' said Beeston. I returned the greeting. 'Revels business?'

'Not today. Unless you have something for me.'

Heywood made a little snort. 'Not we.'

'We're discussing a new theatre,' said Beeston. 'A right good innyard place. None of this nose-in-air cushioned seats for lordly ones.' He was a hefty man, though still young, and he rocked back on his stool, palming his paunch. Well pleased with himself, I thought. 'A new theatre for a new age.' Again, Heywood sniffed.

'Oh? And who do you work for today, Thomas?' I smiled. It was another old jest. Heywood was notorious for fluttering between acting troupes like a bee around a flower garden. He had previously been with the Lord Admiral's Men, Lord Strange's Men, and most recently Lord Worcester's Men. If a nobleman had a company, at some point Heywood would join it.

'Her Majesty Queen Anne,' he said. His accent, like Beeston's, was richly laced with the affected bounce of the theatrical class.

'Working your way up to the king's?' I asked. Beeston bellowed laughter. Heywood only pouted.

'Friend Heywood here is sore. Sore that he ain't been asked to write nothing for the new king's welcome to London. Jonson's been asked.'

'Jonson?!' I pictured the swaggering mountain. 'But he ... surely not.' Ben Jonson, the man who had begun to make Will Shakespeare look out of touch, had been investigated months before for sedition. 'That man has more lives than a cat.'

'Well, he's good, ain't he?' asked Beeston.

'No better than Thomas here,' I said. It felt good to be part of trade talk again. On impulse, I clapped Heywood on the back. We were silent a moment as the tapster set down my beer. In went my fingers.

'Goose?' asked Heywood.

I held up a piece of white, wet fluff between my fingers and squinted. 'Chicken. Is it true that the king is finally come to Whitehall?'

'Ay,' said Beeston, leaning forward on his elbow. 'Now that the dead are finally quieting.'

I considered this, making a show of tasting my beer. Then Lord Cecil would be there too, I knew – hovering like a burnt little hummingbird in his black gown. I belched before speaking. 'So, Thomas, you are sore at the new king neglecting you?' I touched his hands, which were clasped before him on the table. He pulled them away quickly and they disappeared into his lap.

That's you told.

'Perhaps,' I hurried on, 'he wants Jonson's dangerous talk at his coronation revels.'

'Hmph.' Heywood's hands reappeared and he began moving his own mug in circles on the table, staring into its depths as though divining something. 'Then I will write of another coronation. If my verses are not welcome at this ... well, perhaps the people will like to be reminded of better times.' 'And better sovereigns' was left unsaid but invited inference well enough.

Old instincts stirred. Heywood might be planning to write some seditious or questionable matter, as Jonson had done with his *Sejanus*. In former days, I would have silently made a note to tell my secret master, the royal secretary, Robert Cecil, newly minted Baron Essenden. The thought of doing so now gave me twitch. Still, I would have to retain the secretary's patronage. I knew too much about too many of his doings to turn my back on him. If I were to try and do that, I did not doubt that before long I would find a dagger lodged there. Still, I would not betray Heywood. I liked him far more than I liked Ben Jonson. As a rule, I find it far easier to inform on a man if I can find something – anything – to dislike about it.

Well he did just rebuff you…

I would discover later whether Cecil had enquired of me and send him word that I was well and knew nothing of anything.

'The playhouses still closed?' I asked, affecting an air of casual interest. In truth I needed them open if I wished to retain the meagre income I made from ferrying manuscripts back and forward between the Master of the Revels and the acting companies.

'Ay, more's the pity,' said Beeston. 'That's why we need a good innyard. Can get up a petition then to open it even in plague times. Small audiences only, you know? Room for them not to be pressed together like they is in those great enclosed kill-boxes.' He fetched a gusty sigh. 'But I don't fancy fighting the city on it. Months, we've been able to make not a penny from a single bloody man or woman. And yet the king and queen have requested as many plays to be performed for their court as ever the old queen did.'

'Yes,' said Heywood. 'By Shakespeare.'

'Where is he?'

'Back to his stony wife in Stratford.' I laughed. Mr Shakespeare's wife never came to London, as far as I knew, and some of us doubted her existence. 'A fair thing for some to have a place to run when the plague strikes.'

Heywood's mention of the plague brought an uneasy silence to the table and we all slurped to cover it. 'Well,' I said at length. 'When will you have this new play about an old monarch?'

'I cannot say. You shall have it for the office when I do. I will send you a note.'

'Good man.'

'Good man, eh?' barked Beeston. 'If he writes the damned thing, I shall have to find a lad fit to play the title role. When will you learn, Tom? Don't write whatever pleases you. Write for the bloody players we have.'

I raised an eyebrow. A female title role about a coronation. It did not take much wit to understand whom Heywood planned on raising from the dead to strut imperiously again amongst the living. Beeston went on, 'And write something first that the court'll buy, not for a bloody audience that don't got theatres to hear it at. It's the king wants revels, not the folk. Half of them's dead anyway.'

'Yes,' said Heywood, with a grimace. 'The king would be entertained whilst his people die of the plague.'

'God save the king,' I said, picturing King James, whom I had met only once and found to be an unpleasant boor. 'And God give thanks for his kindness to players.' It is remarkable, I thought, how much of the contrary meaning one can pack into the fairest of words.

I finished the dregs of my beer and bid the stage-wrights farewell, before giving the tapster a nod that said they would pay for my beer.

I made my way back the way I had come. As Poultry ran into Cheapside, I caught sight of an old woman squatting in the porch of a plague house. Her skirts were kirtled up to reveal bare, blue-veined legs and her chin rested between her knees. Trying not to look, I started when her keening shriek shot upwards behind me. It fell and became giggling laughter. Some men of the city, I supposed, would move the old crone on – probably to the Bedlam.

24

On Cheapside itself, a man with his lips and nose covered – not unlike the thief at my window – was walking, a red stick held aloft, ahead of a pony-drawn cart with a canvas cloth stretched over its bumpy load.

Are Frere and his wife under there, a tangle of stiffening limbs?

As it creaked along the thoroughfare, people pressed themselves against shopfronts or disappeared inside. Its wheels skidded occasionally in the muck, where the fringe of night-ice had already melted it. With every dip, the load threatened to escape its cloth cover.

How many had died? I wondered. Thousands. Thousands upon thousands. The last I had heard, the plague had spread right out of London and reached its skeletal fingers into the shires.

I wondered if my other family, the one that had long disowned me, had survived.

I slid off my cap, joining those who crept along the flaking walls like blind beggars, pressing my face into the crook of my elbow as the covered wagon of corpses wended its way to wherever the wretches were disposed of. Having had my fill of the mourning city, I was ready to return home. On the way, I slipped into a narrow house on Fleet Street that I knew to be one of Cecil's havens. He had a skilful system, the secretary. He would send messengers out to his secret places with notes, which would remain there until those in his employ visited – and we were supposed to do so far more regularly than I did, even before the quarantine. Thus, we might receive our instructions. In the other direction, we might leave notes containing coded messages for the secretary's eyes, and messengers on the reverse journey would carry them to wherever he might be. Seldom was the same person in charge of the same safehouse twice.

As I entered the place – a nondescript tenement whose whitewash had been thickened with animal blood – I gave my codename: '710' – a jest on Cecil's part because I had apparently borne a great resemblance to the late earl of Essex, or SX, 7-10, in Latin. The gatekeeper of secrets that day was a hoary-haired and watery-eyed fellow. He turned his back to me and disappeared into an inner room. When he reappeared, there was more animation in him. He slid me a note, adding unnecessarily as I read it, 'he wants yer up at the place as soon as can be, matey.'

I nodded, unwilling to thank someone who was sending me back into the maze, whether it was his fault or not. The note had said no more than he had, other than revealing that the summons had been sent two days before. I folded it away with a sigh – I could burn it at home whilst I chewed on some dried mint and picked up a thicker jerkin. The sun had been illusory.

As I picked my way back up Shoe Lane, one final unpleasant sight reached me. It was not the house itself (which is ugly enough, being the butt end of tenement building only enlivened by its dead flowers) but the fact that someone in white was standing at the door, which stood open, Faith framed in it. I drew closer. Again, the thought struck me: something was not right.

A monk? Friar? Confessor?

I had never seen a real monastic – only stage ones, like the blundering friar who had helped bring the hot-blooded young lovers to their doom. Yet the flowing white gown, tied at the waist with a cord, was familiar enough. Only this creature was not shaven-headed and tonsured. It – she, I realised – had a mane of luxurious blonde hair. I quickened my pace, putting out my chest so that the interloper would see my livery.

'Is all well, Faith?' I called out.

The young woman turned. Her eyes were glassy, as though she was on some kind of physick, and a strange, almost mindless smile split what I could readily admit were lovely features. 'You are the father?' London accent, I thought. Local.

'Fath– am I hell the father of anyone!'

Her smile did not falter, and those eyes continued to stare. 'You were touched by the pestilence?'

'What? No. What are you, from the city or something? We are all in perfect health. Our quarantine is over. Is this woman troubling you, Faith?'

'No,' she said from the doorway. 'Her name is … what was it?'

'Angela,' said the woman.

What sort of a name is that?

'She came to see if we were all well.'

'Well we are.' I stepped around her, blocking her view of Faith and the house. 'We came through unharmed.'

'Yet you suffered the plague.'

'I told her,' Faith said, pushing me aside. 'Only my brother had it. And he recovered.'

The woman's smile deepened, becoming almost angelic. 'Praise be. Then one of you is indeed truly blessed. Amongst the Enlightened. You must give him to us. He is especially blessed.'

My heart sank. Another one. 'Oh, for Christ's own sake.'

'My brother isn't going anywhere, mistress,' said Faith. 'But thank you for enquiring.'

'Don't thank her,' I said, putting my hand on the doorframe. Something boiled up within me. I suppose it had started when I saw the prophet-creature and increased with the huckster, the madwoman, the cartload of corpses – and the note. 'Christ, I have had enough of these crack-brained evangelicals. What, mistress, would you have us give up our boy to go and pray to … to whichever God takes your fancy?' Raggedy laughter tore from my throat. 'What is it you represent? A holy cow that shall shower us in boiling milk if we don't take heed of you and repent?' My eyes wandered over her strange habit. 'Oh … bugger off and go and read Master Luther! Else I'll get the watch on to you for a papist.'

With that, I slammed the door in her face and turned, the words, 'mad bitch' already forming in my gizzard.

Faith stood glaring. And David, I noticed, was up too. He had been watching the whole scene with wide, surprised eyes. I closed my mouth, a schoolboy caught by two bizarrely young and censorious masters.

To my shame, I thought only on what the lad must think of me, speaking so roughly to a harmless young wench.

3

The wherry rocked its way upstream, past rag-wrapped parcels of bone which foraged for scraps in the mud of the Thames' banks: the muckrakers who survived by picking through the silt for items to sell. I had almost lost my river legs during my time at home and my stomach jigged and tumbled; as a consequence, I had to sit, and I let my fingers drift in the water, making a wake, because I was alive and I was outside and I could. They numbed quickly. The river itself was wide and dark, its winter coat edged with lacework of ice, and fewer boats than usual carried any well-wrapped cargoes.

I paid the waterman and debarked at the Westminster Stairs. As my boots pounded upwards, there rose into view a murder of black-clad lawyers, heads bowed in a communal cackle near the halls of justice. They'd be getting rich enough, I thought, from all the property disputes that would arise from people leaving unclear wills. Ignoring them, I made my way to the left, through the first of the great colourful gates that led into the palace complex.

Whitehall has always impressed me. Not with its beauty, you understand, for that is as scattered and uneven as a handsome man with badly dressed hair, wearing a good doublet and ruined breeches, and with a beautiful jewel earring on one side and a missing ear on the other. It is rather the size of the place which impresses. It is the palatial equivalent of a gaily dressed elephant, or a huge crowd of drunken theatricals run amok in their splendour.

On the westerly wind drifted the smell of wet grass and effluence. That way lay the tiltyards and sporting places, the hunting grounds beyond. To my left reared up the uneven roofs of the royal administration buildings in a jumble of red tiles. Competing with those roofs, on King Street itself, were a number of tall coaches, the foremost of which was disgorging a gorgeously apparelled man and his dome-dressed lady. Their thickly pleated ruffs made little shell-nestled pearls of their heads. The fellows' chests and sleeves were stuffed hugely with bombast, though their waists were pinched narrow, and there seemed to be a new fashion in men's hair – shoulder-length, tong-turned curls. The women's skirts seemed like tents, protecting the soldiers of their legs who presumably protected the greater prize of their aristocratic maidenhoods. Jealousy surged at the sight of the rich silks and furs. The presence of women made it a different affair from the court I had seen the king keep in Scotland – but it was different too in that the fashions had changed already. Breeches were wider than ever. Hats were taller. The women's dresses were all as frilled and jewelled as the old queen's had been. I had imitation court weeds of my own at home – ones I would never have let burn – but already they were out of date. I felt cheap in my livery, inferior. And yet in it I was wonderfully invisible. It was a conundrum, to be sure, this strange conflict I had long felt within myself: to be seen and unseen, noticed and unnoticed, admired and ignored, remembered and forgotten.

I hung back a few minutes; as the rich folks descended, a throng of petitioners surrounded them and were beaten back by the guards. When the tumult had subsided – at least until the coach could be removed and the next in line moved ahead – I slid past the undiscouraged common folk and made for the taller gatehouse on the far side.

Immediately, my way was barred as two liveried guards stepped into my path. 'What is your business, in the queen's name?' asked the one on my left.

'*King's*!' snapped the second.

'Ah, ay, king's.' The first man hissed, out the side of his mouth, 'been sayin' the other more'n twenty years, b'gar!'

I shot the fellow an understanding look, before opening the front of my coat. 'Revels Office.'

They both relaxed. The first, I noticed, was looking over my shoulder already, frowning at the sight of so many people. 'Who are you looking for?' asked the other, apparently sharper, one.

I bit my lip before speaking.

To hell with it.

'The lord secretary Baron Essenden.'

Both men stiffened. 'Cor, wha' does the secretary want with Revels?' asked what I suddenly realised was the stupider man. His more intelligent colleague made a coughing sound in his throat, and the first fellow began stuttering. 'Mr Secker-tary – ay – yes – yer know where to go?'

'I have been sent to him in the time of the late queen.'

'Then,' said the second guard, 'you *don't* know where to go, my friend. The king grace's moved the secretary.'

That was news indeed. I might otherwise have stumbled about like a fool, advertising my presence in Whitehall still further. More important people than a pair of nobodies might well have questioned why a servant of the Revels Office would have an interview with the queen's secretary – *king's* secretary, rather. The error must have been as infectious as the plague. 'Where can I find him?'

The first guard began, 'well, mate, you've to go back that way. Turn left – I think left – and then … left again, or right? Is it right? Ask someone, mate. It's a big place.'

Thankfully, the second guard was more helpful, providing directions which would take me into the heart of the palace. I thanked him, gave a stiff little bow and a look that I hoped said, 'work, work, bloody work', and went on my way.

The palace itself was busy. Set into the walls were window casements, and, as I stepped as lightly as I could on carpeted and tiled floors, I tried to avoid looking at the richly dressed couples who sat posing in them. I crossed into a network of wood-panelled chambers, the inhabitants of which became progressively less decorative and more useful. Pink, blue, and orange silks gave way to sober and sedate blacks. Here, I thought, was the turning engine of the place – the paper world that supported the gossamer one of the court.

Eventually, I reached my destination – a tall oak door on ground floor level. I knocked three times before a voice that wasn't Cecil's bid me enter.

Inside, my head immediately tilted. Cecil's new chamber occupied two storeys, the ceiling far above carved in a criss-cross of wooden beams, between which hung armorial banners in deep blue and gold. Mother-of-pearl daylight streamed in from coloured glass windows on what would have been the second floor. 'Ned,' shouted the secretary, who was seated at a large desk in the centre of the room. 'You might leave us, Mr Munck.' The colourless fellow bowed and walked past me, rolls of paper tucked under his arm. 'Come, man, sit.'

I padded across the carpet, between the heaving bookshelves on either side of the chamber. Between them were patches of panelled wall, on which hung two portraits that, from either side of the room, faced one another. One was the late Lord Burghley, Cecil's father, in his robes of state. On the other was a study of King James, a pair of gloves in one hand and the other resting on his sword hilt. The secretary had gone up in the world, I thought. And why not? Before he had played the role of the humble servant of a queen who had known England since long before his time. Now he was king indeed, ruling the nation on behalf of a sovereign who had known it less than a year.

I sat on the middle of three stools lined up before the desk. Cecil regarded me from his throne-like chair, shifting so that his one higher shoulder stood bunched even more visibly above the other. A tall marble fireplace made an inverted 'u' behind him. From my seated position, it made him appear quite devilish in the dancing leaps and twirls of the flames.

Roberto Diablo.

He is not an ugly man, the former Sir Robert Cecil, but he had grown as suspicious looking and weary as he had noble. His eyes were gleaming slits, almost black and intensely penetrating. His beard, like his ruff, was a mere decorative frill, as though he were thrifty about both. A vein I had never noticed before seemed to have swollen up on the left of his prominent forehead. Stray hairs, which I had once taken to be blonde wheatsheaves interloping in a fallow field, were now frosty white and more numerous. At length, he said, 'I am pleased that you answered my summons, Ned. Though you came some days after I sent it.'

I swallowed before speaking, breaking his gaze and regarding my hands. 'I apologise, sir.' The words almost hurt. 'There was sickness in my house. I could not stir.'

'I know.'

Of course you do.

'And so I am sorry I have not attended your lordship.'

He waved this away with a drifting white hand. 'But you are all well now? You and your … friends?'

'We are, my lord.' I did not bother fawning over his rise in rank. To his credit, I knew he had no time for the fashionable untruths about unworthiness and humility that gild some servants' speeches. 'Quite well.'

'Capital. You look well, Ned, well indeed. You should keep your hair short and be always beardless.' He stroked at his own neatly dressed chin. 'Let the ghost of the late earl remain buried and forgotten, yes? I was grieved to hear that your household met the infection. This has been a most grievous time for all.' Perhaps I made some sign, because he added, 'believe me or not, as you will, but I have wept tears for this city and all England.'

Yes, I thought, he probably had – whilst lying in his bed at Theobalds, safe in the country and surrounded by physicians and a good store of fresh wormwood, valerian, and snake root. Not that I could decry him for it. Had I the means, I would have packed up Faith, David, and my store of stolen and legitimate treasures and taken the first ship for the Bermudas.

And I trusted Cecil in one thing. He made a prize of order and was guided, I knew beyond doubt, by a commitment to seeing that the people of England might be assured of their security, of their goods and chattels. As long as a safe and happy England locked hands with a secure lord secretary Baron Essenden, he might well shed tears for matters decreed by God and out of his control.

'And tell me,' he said, 'what is the news out of the city? What is being said in Faringdon Without?'

'Naught but death.' I shrugged. 'Some complaints about the plague being brought by the rich but poor given its suffering.'

'Serious?'

'Just talk.'

He seemed to consider questioning me further. And I burned to question him, too, on how many had died. Yet it wasn't my place. 'Oh,' I added. 'And there are more mad ones than ever abroad. Religious types. Crying upon God's vengeance. Coney-catchers selling trash to gull folk that are in fear. Women going from door to door preaching about God and the plague.'

A little dismissive gesture was his first response, followed by, 'such foolery will fade as the dying times die themselves.' Then, a little more sharply, 'no papistry in these Godly types?'

Truthfully, I had to say, 'no, save in their simple dress.'

'No crime, that, with cloth so hard to come by.'

'No, my lord. There is …' My mouth dried. 'There is much crime, though. An attempt was made to break in upon my home. A pair of men, looking to steal. Thought to rob the dead, I think.'

'You and yours were unharmed?'

'Yes. I protected my family. Chased them away. Yet I saw no men of the city I might report the matter to.' I would not have done so even if I had; it was my firm belief that men in London should take care of their own affairs, avoiding constables and other idiots in office wherever possible. Besides, if it became known that I trafficked with the watch against those who danced about the underworld, I could expect more than just a pair of pathetic thieves to turn up on my doorstep.

'Yes, well, I understand that over half of the city watch is dead. Until new men can be trained up, the scum of London will make merry, I fear.'

I bowed my head before looking up at him, my features relaxing into what I intended to be a kind of expectant, waiting mask. He ignored it, and instead began riffling through papers on his desk, his jaw moving silently. I knew his style. Always he would get the unimportant business of the day – the tittle-tattle, the rumours, the flummery – out of the way before coming to what was his primary business. He cleared his throat before announcing it. 'Tell me, do you know of Dr Leonard Gurney? A physician as well as a learned doctor of theology.'

Puzzlement. I tried to think but, put on the spot, I could not recognise the name. Even in David's sickness, there had been no thought of physicians. Even if I had known one, he would never have come – and it was well known enough that physicians would only advise on how the plague might – *might* – be prevented, not what to do when it descended. 'I don't think so. No.'

'A brilliant man. He was in service to the late queen and retained by King James.' I had nothing to say to this. 'A man of great learning in all matters of religion and the arts medicinal. And a friend.' For some reason I thought of Faustus. 'He has been stolen.'

'What?'

'Stolen,' said Cecil, without expression. 'Gone. Vanished. Disappeared.'

'Dead?' I ventured. 'I don't understand.'

Cecil sighed. 'Some months ago, the fellow told me that certain patients of his had been troubling him.' My expression must have clouded, for he added, 'he did not say how. I regret I did not provide aid. I supposed that all men of learning must be suffering likewise – importunities – when the deaths were rising.' He shrugged his mismatched shoulders before settling them. 'He did not follow the court save when it came to Hampton Court at Christmas. He was greatly dedicated to his wife and his practice in the city.

'When the court came to Whitehall a week since, I sent for him to attend upon the king and my– to attend upon the court. He did not respond. My people reported that his house was shut up with the marks of infection upon the door.' He gave a harsh little laugh. 'His wife cried from the window for aid. Shouted that her husband had been taken and she left alone.'

'Has she been asked further questions?' I knew that wives were not averse to killing their husbands, and vice versa, and supposed that there would be no easier time to get rid of an unwanted spouse than when the city had its hands over its eyes.

'She cannot stir abroad. Not without her white stick, at any rate, and then none will go near her. I would not have messengers shout questions and receive shouted answers in the hearing of the world. Not until I know more of this affair.'

I struggled to keep up. 'So, then … if she is telling the truth … if the man has been taken and those who took him painted the mark upon the door to … to keep the world ignorant of his disappearance … they haven't then requested any ransom?'

He smiled, a ghastly, wolfish display of sharp white teeth. 'Is that what you would do, Ned?' Cecil knew of my criminal past. He had recruited me, in the wake of the Essex rebellion, and turned a blind eye to my penchant for taking things that I felt ought to belong to me, whether I could afford them or not. 'No, indeed. It seems he is not a hostage, wherever he is.'

The dreaded questioned formed in my mind and I gave it voice. 'What would you have me do?'

'I need a trusted man to look into the matter. Go to the house.'

He's sending me into a plague house, the bastard.

'Speak to the wife within her walls and discover what she knows. It might be that there is some matter pertaining to the man's disappearance in his chambers. He saw patients at his home.'

'Yes,' I said, knowing that I had no choice.

Cecil sighed. 'I gain no pleasure in this, Ned. This man … he is needed for his wisdom. You know that the king's coronation revels, his welcome to the city, were delayed by the plague? He was most unhappy. King James understands that, until the people see him, he is king only to those few of the state who bore witness to the miracle of his crowning. And in preparing for this great holiday I would consult Dr Gurney on matters of the symbols, the speeches, and so on.' He stopped and, to my surprise, looked down at his white hands and began working them. 'And this man, too, is a friend who asked of me a favour which I did not grant. And I would remedy that.'

The bastard has a heart.

'Yes, my lord.' And then another thought struck me, and I paled with it. If the king wanted this man found ahead of the coronation revels, he would no doubt reward Cecil with even more than a grand chamber for discovering him. It would be an easy thing for the secretary to organise the man's capture only to engineer his discovery through another agent.

It is said that when trust departs from between a husband and wife, a storm of sighs and a sea of tears follow. How much worse it might be when trust departs from between a servant and his master, and what might follow, I didn't care to imagine. But I didn't trust Cecil. I looked him full in those black, twinkling eyes. To my surprise, he laughed, and his white palms flew up. It seemed to pain him, for the laughter was silenced by a wince.

'I assure you, Ned, that I had no hand in this matter. You can believe me or not, as you will. Yet it is true – I am as ignorant of Dr Gurney's fate as you are. Be secure in that knowledge. Go to his house in Foster Lane and speak with Mrs Gurney. I scarcely know the woman. She might or might not be trusted. And discover what you will in his chambers. Perhaps he left something behind that might tell us who was troubling him. Come to me again on the morrow with your knowledge. After dinner, about one of the clock. Wait in the Pebble Court until I come to you.'

'Yes, my lord.'

'I need not, I trust, impress upon you the importance of this matter, Ned. To take a royal servant is to strike at the king's breast. Dr Gurney knows much about King James – the movements of his body. The quality of his humours.' And yours too, I thought. His voice descended to a whisper with his next words and the vein on his forehead pulsed. 'To have a king's physician in thrall is a means of bringing great harm to that king. And in this procession, he and his queen will be in the eyes of every man in the city who cares to look. They will be touched. Gawped upon. Those who have who have evil knowledge of his Majesty might be easily hidden in such a crowd.'

I nodded, already picturing the things a learned man could do if forced. Magic, perhaps. Poison, to be sure. A poisoned arrow would be an easy thing to build. 'When is this procession?'

'March. In a very few weeks.' I considered this. Plenty of time, I thought. His next words seemed to reproach me. 'Very little time indeed to plan such an occasion of state. There is a great deal to be done and I would not have the care and worry of Dr Gurney's disappearance trouble the preparation. You understand me, Ned? Find him. With haste. And discover why he was taken.'

'Foster Lane,' I said, with an air of finality. I rapped my fingers on the edge of the desk in a little show of business and made to rise. 'I will do this, my lord.' I kept my face impassive.

'You need not,' said Cecil, 'feign a distaste for such labour. Shall I tell you what I think, Ned?' It was not a question. 'I think you greatly enjoy my service. No, not the rewards. Well, not only those. The pleasure of it all.'

I wet my lips, trying to frame an answer. There was none. He was quite right, as loath as I was to admit it. The thought of embarking on another piece of state service, even though it was for two men I did not particularly like, was unfathomably delicious. It was certainly preferable to an afternoon lengthened and weighted by boredom. Cecil smiled, watching my mind work through eyes grown even narrower. Suddenly they widened. Darted away from me. He cleared his throat. Still I was half-risen. 'I am pleased we are perfect friends again. Oh. Yes. Ah, there is but one last thing.' I sat back down.

Here comes the sting in the tail.

'I do not know,' he said, making a spire of his fingers, deciding against it, and then inspecting his nails, 'whether you are friend or not to the family which bore you in the north.' Fragments of ice began to needle their way through my veins. 'Nor if you receive news out of that county. Yet ... I hear the news of the gentry, landowners, in Derbyshire.' His eyes flicked up again, hooded in their pouches. 'Adam Norton, the master of Norfield – your natural father – is dead.'

4

I kicked my way up Foster Lane, which lay in Cheap ward, in the City itself, running north from Cheapside. It was not hard to find the house, as it was the only one of the several large townhouses which was shuttered and whose door was painted with the warning mark. Something about the ugly red cross froze me and I let my eyes travel upwards. A fair, broad-fronted place.

As Norfield once was.

The old house I had known was gone. And now the fellow who had been its master had followed it. And what did it matter to me anyway? As I had said to Cecil before leaving, I had no connection with my former family. The old man had been dead to me for years. He had been dead, too, to my brother and sister-in-law, long before his time. When I had seen him the previous year, he had been scattered in his wits – a loose-threaded hand puppet jerked about by a madman. I wondered if men who lost their minds were reunited with them after death, as he might have been reunited with the mother who had disavowed me. Flies seemed to buzz around inside my head.

Perhaps madness passes downwards, like water from a fountainhead.

The problem with words is that they cannot be unheard. Things that one would rather forget, and quickly, become branded on the mind. As much as we wish them not to matter, we are cruel enough in ourselves that we inwardly insist that they do.

Why did Cecil have to tell me? I had known the old man was dying. And yet somehow the not knowing of it as absolute fact had allowed me to ignore that knowledge. The words – 'your father is dead' – forced me to confront it.

And what frightened me more than anything, as I again looked at the plague cross, was that I truly did not grieve for him. In truth I felt nothing other than the gnawing, tearing feeling that to not care was itself a symptom of an unnatural constitution. Some other sign, perhaps, of the corruption within me that sparked unnatural lusts. A man owed allegiance and duty to his parents, no matter what they did. Otherwise they were destined for an unhappy life and a worse fate in the hereafter.

The best method I have discovered for banishing unwanted thoughts is to force more welcome ones to run in their channels. I began battering on the door, more forcefully than I needed to. Some people in the street gathered and stood to watch from a safe distance. My rude greeting was answered quickly, but it was I who jumped back when I saw what stood in the doorway.

'You're not Leonard.'

'Er … I … no.'

Mrs Gurney, as I assumed she was, was a bizarre creature. Fleshy and old, her face was plastered so thickly with paint that it appeared whitewashed, save for the careless smear of red on her lips. Her eyes were round and bulging and appeared lash-less, and her brows had been either shaved or plucked bare. In their place were drawn two perfectly straight black lines. A staying-in cap had been hastily tied over a garish red wig, holding it – somewhat – in place. You will think me a monster, but when the surprise ebbed, my first instinct was to point and laugh at her.

No wonder the good doctor disappeared!

If she was aware of my stare, she did not acknowledge it. Yet, out of shame, I looked past her as I gathered my wits. 'Have you found him?'

'Might we speak inside, mistress?'

'Who are you?' Her solid frame blocked the doorway. Not a stupid woman then, I thought.

'I work for the quee- for the king's secretary. Lord Robert Cecil, Baron Essenden. A friend of your husband's.'

Still she did not move. Usually Cecil's name purchased entry anywhere. 'That livery isn't a secretary's. Yeoman of the Wardrobe, looks like.' Her voice was gentle, though still unyielding.

'Revels,' I volunteered. 'Yet I work a little for the secretary. I understand your husband has gone missing. I am charged with helping find him. Might we speak inside?'

This moved her, and she stepped backwards into the house. As I passed the door, closing it behind me, she said, 'there's no plague here, nor ever was. Whoever took him, they did that. And no one would come near me, nor listen.'

Inside lay a narrow hall, doors on either side. 'When did this happen?'

She had turned and begun walking heavily towards the door on the right, speaking as she did so. 'A week gone. He was taken from his chambers, the rooms he sees patients in. Over there, to your left.'

I stopped following her, considering. 'Might I see those rooms?'

'But – may I not tell you what happened?'

'After, yes.' I did not wish her tale to interfere with my search. If necessary, I could search again after for anything her story pointed me to which I might have missed the first time. 'Please, be settled in your own rooms, mistress.'

'I'll wait. I haven't touched anything in there. I just saw that he was gone and … I haven't touched anything. Do what you must. I'll … I'll fetch some beer. There's only a little left. I haven't gone out. The servants wouldn't come when they saw the door.' I watched as she shuffled into the door on the right, wondering if it was the lack of a maid that accounted for her hideous makeup or if that was simply the look she favoured. Boy players danced through my mind, their faces so thick with paint that even those in the outer reaches of the pit could not forget that they were supposed to be women.

She did not close the door behind her, and so I simply exited the hall through the left-hand door. A fair-sized waiting chamber lay beyond it, the hard bench against the far wood-panelled wall relieved by stout velvet cushions. A carpet sat in lush waves on the floor, rumpled slightly at one side. On the right stood another door, leading deeper into the house. It was open.

Dr Gurney's inner chamber was, like many practising physicians', a library. Good oak shelves were nailed into every wall, all of them warped slightly towards the middle with the weight of books.

It took only a glance to see that no robbery had taken place. The difference between the consulting chamber and the Frere house was startling and immediate. Although some of the books were scattered about the floor and the small desk, they were still there. A thief would have made off with as many as possible, for books, whether medical, religious, or simply for pleasure, fetched a good price. Further, there had been no great struggle, no wanton destruction as the good doctor fought off those who would snatch him away.

He went willingly?

I walked around the room, not sure what I was looking for. I took down a book from the shelf and eased it open to the title page. Dozens of men glared back at me from what looked like a Roman amphitheatre. The woodcut's title read, *Andreae Vesalii Bruxellensis, scholae medicorum Patauinae professoris, de Humani corporis fabrica Libri septem*. I put it back next to the others. On another shelf, I found things called the *Cato censorious* and the *De vera excommunicatione et Christiano presbyterio*. I knew enough to know that I was looking at a shelf devoted to religious debate and theology, about which I cared not at all. One book, however, stood out as recognisable. It was an edition of the *Bishops' Bible*, and it sat on the top of the pile.

Recently used?

I took it down. Its cover was richly ornamented, though the thing was bulky rather than heavy. It declared itself 'The holi bible' and, above the words, a painted image of Elizabeth in her coronation robes sat on a throne, allegorical figures I didn't recognise crowning her. Sure enough, wafer-thin leaves of paper were tucked into it at odd pages. I began teasing them out at random, opening the pages they marked and reading.

Thy dead men shall liue, euen as my body shall they rise againe: Awake and sing ye that dwell in dust, for thy deawe is euen as the deawe of hearbes, and the earth shall cast out them that be vnder her.

I shivered. Beside the thick print that read 'Thy dead men shall liue' was inked a question mark.

Next, came:

And the seuen angels whiche had the seuen trumpettes, prepared them selues to blowe.

The first angell blewe, & there was made hayle & fire, mingled with blood, and they were cast into the earth, and the thirde part of trees was burnt, and all greene grasse was burnt.

Scrawled beside this was 'the vij trumpets? Is this what they speak of?' I turned to an earlier marker:

In a moment, in the twynklyng of an eye, at the last trumpe. For the trumpe shall blowe, and the dead shall ryse incorruptible, and we shalbe chaunged.

The good doctor, I thought, moving to the desk and placing the bible on it, had an interest in the fate of the dead.

Or someone did. Is this what they *speak of?*

It was only when I went behind the desk that I saw the signs of disorder. The stool at which I assumed Gurney would have sat was on the floor, its cushioned top half-sunk in carpet strands. I crouched, and ran my hand under the desk itself.

A-ha!

My fingertips brushed another book. I drew it up. No well-bound religious or medical tome this, but a slim volume similar to those that Faith used at home to keep accounts. It was, I realised, looking at its blank, cheap cover, a commonplace book – the type of thing used by some to note down their thoughts, or favourite prayers and meditations. I opened it at random to find some well-drawn plants and herbs, Latin names and properties inscribed next to them. The next page had densely packed entries in almost indecipherable handwriting. I took the book into the fading light allowed by the small, high window and, to my surprise, realised that it was in English. The metallic properties – sulphurs and salts and mercuries – associated with the colours of urine of various unnamed patients, it seemed, accounted for much of the writing. After a reminder to purchase 'quicksilver, lily water and alum, for the painting of Maud who has no need of it', it read:

I did goe and hear read the play of the Midsummer faerie folk and the young lovers and therein did I laugh most heartily at the goodfellow Puck and so doe wonder at the causes and effects thereof and then in my chamber I did dream of a great feast and awoke with an hunger at my belly though I were not in want before I did sleep and therein I doe wonder at the power of the dreaming to work wonders in our humours.

I knew the play – the thing by Shakespeare that had been read at Hampton Court at Christmas. Entries after it stopped, and so I read backwards. The thoughts were jumbled, and I assumed intended only to make sense to the writer.

'Vita in morte sumus' – what do they mean by this? And still I am sore troubled and yet dare not again vex Mr Secretary on the matter and yet they doe not cease to question me nor spare me their meditations and their questions on the nature of this great pestilence *viz* its coming and why it visits upon some and not others and the causes therein which doe cause some to live after it and some to die most piteously. I doe not know why the pestilence follows upon the death of the late queene and the coming of the new king and yet this they woulde know. I feare me they will never leave me alone until they have drunk dry of my mind and know all that they might know of the pestilence and also of matters of mystery and these visions and of that I know nothing. Yet I cannot turn away from people who were once patients and good, no matter the disbalance suddenly oncoming of their minds and humours.

I was lost. I bit at my lips, trying to make sense of things. It seemed that doctor had, as Cecil had said, been harassed by patients – the mysterious 'they' – who had begun to demand more than simple medical advice. 'Vita in morte sumus' … we shall live through death. It seemed to ring a bell, though I could not say why. It smelt of religion, and that connected it to the biblical verses. So too, I thought, did the stuff in the notebook concerning these people's interests in surviving the plague. My brain felt weighted down. I had done too much, after being too long idle; and still I had to get the painted wife's tale. I decided to focus entirely on keeping things simple.

Dr Gurney had been taken, I decided, by patients who had gone mad, or perhaps had wanted him for his expertise in medicine or theology or both. That meant he was likely being kept alive, a captive somewhere. I decided to take the bible and the commonplace book with me, the thinner tucked into my belt and the thicker under my armpit.

I left the inner chamber, returned through the outer one, and found Mrs Gurney in a large, comfortable parlour, the walls of which were painted in red and gold and lined with stout oak cupboards displaying crystal and plate. I had the briefest impression of myself as I wobbled in a reflection. Again, I thought: if robbers had been at work, it would have been an easy thing to slay a fat old woman and strip the place bare.

I turned my attention to that woman. She was crying softly. A tear rolled over the white glaze of her cheek. She straightened in her chair as she saw me and put a flesh coloured hand to her face. It came away with a chalky smudge. 'Do you know what happened to my husband?'

'We will discover that.'

'Please, sit.'

I did, as she rose and went to a sideboard. From it, she lifted a pewter mug, which she handed it to me. 'The cake was gone hard,' she explained, 'since no fresh ones have come. Leonard – Dr Gurney – he orders the things.' I took the mug and nodded thanks. 'I dropped in the last of the cake to soften it for you. It's just old ale.'

I swirled the mug, and it released a sweet, honeyed smell. Lumps of cake rose from its depths, bobbing as they dissolved. As she regained her own seat, I said, 'to aid us, mistress, would you tell me exactly what happened in this house.'

'He was taken.'

'From the beginning. I understand Dr Gurney had some trouble with his patients. Do you know perhaps of a list of those he tended?'

Pride swelled her coach of a bosom. 'He kept that in his head, sir. He didn't like to discuss his patients with me. He worried it would upset me to know about sicknesses. I only knew that he was sore vexed with a few who came these past months. Since the plague times started.'

I took a swallow of her old ale. It was sweet, heavy. 'Please,' I repeated, 'from the beginning.'

She blew out a sigh. 'Dr Gurney and I married many years ago.'

Not that bloody far.

'1572. The year of the massacre of St Bartholomew. He had been studying then in Paris and it brought him back to London. Well, he had never taken a wife, his head so full of studies. We met in Cheapside and took a liking to one another. I was a widow already, then. It was a good match. Made for love as much as the other.' I nodded. She was indeed an old woman, I thought, hopelessly enamoured of the past. 'I was … a little older than him. Yet he was never troubled by it. As he became perfect in his trade, I kept house for him. We are very happy.' She looked up at this, her startled-looking eyes seeming to dare challenge. I only nodded. 'Are you a married man, mister…?'

'Savage. No.'

A smile. 'Well, you're young yet. There's time. You should have an older wife, one that'll take good care of you and your house.'

I coughed, hoping to push the conversation elsewhere. She took the hint. 'Anyway, yes, he rose in the late queen's favour. Was appointed amongst her physicians in ordinary. A great honour. He always says he could get on because he knew he had a good wife tending to his home.

'And when the queen died, he wished to be only a private citizen. But the secretary – your master – he wished Leonard to continue in service to the new king. I didn't say anything. And with the queen's death … well, the plague. Patients, I know, became wild and crazed with all the fear of it. That happens whenever there's a great outbreak of anything – people who have the money want the best, and that's Leonard.'

'These patients who troubled him…'

'I only know he mentioned a man and woman. He had seen them for a long time. He mentioned to me that the plague was bringing sickness of the mind as well as body, and these people were pressing him on matters of … uh … the stars and heavens and God … as well as the cause of the sickness. Before Christmas, he cursed – he never curses – and said it was either the Bedlam or the archbishop they needed, not him.'

I considered this, gnawing at my lower lip. 'Do you know, mistress, if your husband tended to Catholics?'

'Yes,' she said, quite cheerfully, I thought. I frowned. 'Catholics, Protestants, the hotter Puritans … Jews, even. We're not prejudiced people, sir. Leonard always says that a sick man is a sick man, no matter what he believes. I agree with that.' Her chest burst forth again. I found myself warming to the strange old bird.

'What do you recall of his disappearance?'

She bowed her head and a red curl snaked down the side. She brushed it back. 'He was seeing patients, as is his custom. I never intermeddled with his business. I just made sure that his supper was ready for him if he wished to see them until late – and in these times, he always did.' A little sniff. 'I made the supper, as usual, and I think … yes, I know I heard the door of the house close and supposed a patient must have left and he might be hungry. But he didn't come for it. So I went to his rooms and knocked. He didn't answer. I went in. And he was gone. Well, I thought to myself, it was a strange thing that he would go out in the evening. He always comes through here and tells me if he's going out, if he's visiting with a patient at their home, and he gives me a kiss on the head, and I help him into his coat. But not that time. So I came back through here and waited. All night, I waited. And I grew worried. I didn't sleep that night. Just sat in here, in this chair, waiting.

'And in the morning, he still didn't return. I confess I went into his rooms, but I didn't touch anything. I knew then that he must have been taken away. In all our years together, he has never gone off without telling me. I didn't press,' she added, 'I didn't shrew at him. He's a good man. He thinks of me. And so I made to go outside. In the morning, usually the servants come. Leonard has given them all leave during the infection to remain with their families and bring us only what we might need in the mornings. But they didn't come. Haven't come since.'

Probably dead, I thought.

'And did you go out?' I asked. 'Did you seek news of him?'

'I tried, sir. I went to the door hoping to do just that. But then I saw the mark on the door. I cried out. He would never have done that, not without telling me – and I had no sickness, and nor did he. I shouted

out into the street, but people ignored me or ran away. They …
laughed at me and shouted things. Since then, I've only cried out from
the windows for news. But none will talk to me. I was glad when I saw
you, sir. I've tried every day to keep the house clean and tidy for his
coming back.'

I reached out, on impulse, and patted her hand. The thought of her,
finding her husband gone and her house declared sick, sitting in an
empty house, painting herself up and trying to carry on saddened me.
'We will find him,' I said. I put the mug down at my feet and stood,
moving towards a sideboard, my chin in the air as though lost in
thought. 'He saw both men and women patients?'

'Yes.' Something struck her. 'I think it was a woman who gave the
greatest trouble. He mentioned a "she" when he spoke of troubled
minds.'

'But you don't know the name?'

'No, sir. I'm sorry.' She looked downwards, so that I had only a
view of frizzed red curls and white linen. I made a show of easing the
bible from one armpit, where it had begun an ache, to another. As I
did so, I picked up a small gilded mirror that had caught my eye and
closed my fingers around it. 'Nor even the quality. Leonard would see
folks of any class and ask only what they could afford. I liked that.
Sickness doesn't just visit the rich.'

I coughed a little and returned the mirror. The unwanted books
would have to satisfy my strange lust for possession. Clearing my
throat, I returned to stand beside my seat and asked, 'did your husband
have any friends out of London?'

'Oh yes, many. In France, in Italy. He loved to receive news out of
those places.' I thought, it was unlikely he could have been spirited
out of the country without Cecil knowing of it. 'And in England?'

'Hm. Yes, there was Dr Dee. They sent letters back and forth. Old
friends.'

I nodded. I thought I knew the name. 'I thank you, mistress. I will
look into these matters.'

'With your leave, sir, I think he has been taken by mad folk.'

'Why is that?' I asked, too sharply.

'He said something strange, a few weeks since. He said that the
plague was causing people to corrupt the bible.'

I shivered. 'What did he say?'

She twisted her hands in her lap and the red confusion of her lips
began moving. 'He said, "This shall be the plague wherewith the Lord
will smite … Their flesh shall consume away where they stand, and

their eyes shall corrupt in their holes … and … and there shall be a great sedition among them." And then he said that he thought it would be lunatics who caused sedition rather than the Lord.'

I digested this and made to leave. Mrs Gurney saw me to the door and, as we reached it, she began fussing over whether I would be too cold out in the dying light. I assured her I would not and told her she might wash the paint from the door and return to her life. 'That I cannot do until the other half of my life is returned,' she said. 'I trust you, Mr Savage. You seem a good man. And you have a good face.'

For my previous, shameful urge to laugh at the old wench, I stepped out into the darkening city a smaller man than when I'd arrived.

And a more troubled one.

5

The Pebble Court at Whitehall is a cobbled – and therefore especially cold – patch of ground overshadowed by the council chambers and the great banqueting hall. I had arrived shortly before one o'clock and walked in circles, my coat tightly around my shoulders, as I waited on Cecil. From what I had seen of the to-ing and fro-ing about the palace as I made my way from Westminster, a hunt was being got up. The clatter of hooves and the merry jingle of harnesses drifted from somewhere beyond the courtyard – from the direction of the privy garden, which I understood led into the hunting park at St James's.

I had turned over much in my head during the previous evening and had landed upon the idea that certain patients of the missing doctor, one of them a woman, had decided to take him in order, perhaps, to force him to cure either some case of the plague or else of brain-sickness. Medicine and religion and astrology were all spheres which crossed and circled and made sense in the heads of men like Dr Gurney, who made a study of them. It was not my job to understand why they had taken him but where.

And I confess that, in some way, thoughts of Derbyshire and the old master it had also lost plagued me. Memories of childhood crowded and had to be pushed out. A dead old man had to be forced from my mind by a missing one. My rebel-mind and its mocking voice – my own voice, in my own head – could only be partly mastered.

He used to pick you up on his shoulders when you were very small.

Thus I had been distracted in the morning, smoking much and refusing conversation. My old family, again, seemed intent on causing divisions in my new one. I had left a frosty Faith distributing tasks to David, who had woken without fever. Left to himself, he would simply have sat upon the bed all day staring at the wall. She seemed to understand that the lad needed to be told when to rise, what to do on rising, when to eat, and everything else. I ignored them, my mind full. Besides, I reasoned that it was a woman's job to train a lad, even if he should by rights have been able to think for himself. His years in the queen's chapel choir had unmanned him, making him a slave. That would have to be undone when I had time.

Eventually, and something late, my master appeared, walking stiffly through the archway that led to the courtyard. He looked drawn, but he came directly to me and my hat was off in a wink. Standing, he was over a head shorter – and I am not an especially tall man. 'Good morrow to you, Ned. I regret it took me a little longer to see the king off to his sport after dinner than I had thought it might.' As if in agreement, the halloos of the hunters rose up in the air above a tattoo of hoofbeats, getting farther away. 'His Majesty does love to taste the blood of London's deer.'

And Whitehall's wine cellars.

It was strange to think of the hard-drinking Scot I had met now parading through the halls and rooms through which English Elizabeth had danced, the famous bloody Mary had felt her way blindly, the young Edward VI had strutted haughtily, and the bluff Henry had stumped on his bad leg, issuing commands like a crazed army general. Somehow, Whitehall seemed to me a place of the past rather than the present. 'What news?'

I produced the two books and told him everything that I found in Dr Gurney's house, offering no opinions of my own. Only when I reached the part in my tale about sitting down to talk with the missing fellow's wife did I pause a little. 'Mrs Gurney I found … she is …'

Cecil gave a tight smile, his eyes still on the books he held in a gloved hand. He snorted through his nostrils, dragon-like. 'She was a surprise to you?' I let my silence answer. 'Yes, I have seen the woman. I understand that, some years since, she heard some fool rumour – foolish and false – about the late queen painting herself as white as a sheet to trick men's eyes and appear ever young. And Mrs Gurney became a lover of the art of paint herself. Poor old soul. Yet I know her husband to be devoted to her most admirably. And she to him. Still, I recall on seeing her that she looked to have been surprised at being caught eating a carpenter's store of whitewash and a butcher's bucket of blood. Well, if Dr Gurney finds her a cheerful bedfellow, who am I to judge? What did she say?'

I sighed relief. In truth, I had concocted in bed the previous night an elaborate conspiracy in which the real Mrs Gurney had been replaced by a man in woman's weeds. I was glad not to have shared something so foolish with anyone, nor spoken cruelly of a kindly old woman who had no idea how to make the best of herself. I had seen too many plays, I supposed. I began to tell Cecil of her account, when a pair of black-gowned under-secretaries stepped into the courtyard, looking around until they spotted us. I closed my mouth.

'My lord secretary, I bring you the accounts to be checked for the carpenter's bills.'

'And I three bills of fare for the feasting, my lord. For your approval of which will best suit his Majesty.'

Cecil frowned, handing me back the books as he took the papers. I backed against the wall, sliding across the icy cobbles and watching as he snapped orders, questioned things, jabbed a finger at items on the various papers. Before he had finished, a third man interrupted, begging knowledge of what was to be done about carriages and how many yards of carpet would be required for the route through Cheapside. Eventually, the tumult subsided, the men were satisfied and sent away, and Cecil put a hand against the wall of the banqueting house, wincing and clutching his side.

'Sir?' Alarm rose in my throat. 'Shall I fetch you a physician?'

The plague!?

Cecil breathed heavily. 'Ha. I would have you find me only one physician, Ned Savage.' He collected himself, straightening. 'This business of the coronation. Would that I had allowed the king to have it in July, as he wished. Then it would be nothing now but a memory. Instead, all must be in perfect readiness. For the fifteenth of March. A task that would cripple a warhorse. It must be grander than anything given the late queen, it must be richer, it must have more money spent on it and more men employed.' Baron Essenden, I realised, was not enjoying the burden of power he had fought so long to heap upon himself.

Good!

Something like pity stirred in me as he sat down on the edge of a large stone urn from which sprung a winter-blasted tree. I remained standing and passed him the books again. 'These bible quotations,' he said. 'What do they mean to you?'

'Nothing,' I said. I was not about to be drawn into religious debate. I was not qualified for that and my intestines were lodged happily inside my body.

'Hm. Nor me. I am no divine – I know nothing of determining the true meaning of scripture. Here Dr Leonard himself has inked a question mark and I am not the man to answer to it. And this phrase the doctor noted, this "vita in morte sumus". You speak Latin.'

'In death we live? Through death we live?'

'Media vita in morte sumus. In the midst of death we are in life.' I bowed my head in acknowledgement of his superior knowledge. 'It comes from an old monkish chant. Papist. Yet it has been cut short. If this is connected with the capture of the doctor, it would seem that those who took him were of a religious bent. Possibly papists. And those who serve the tyrant of Rome are not yet happy. Later this month the king will issue a proclamation against the Jesuits, seminaries, and popish priests. It was drawn up before he was crowned and yet I counselled him to wait. Perhaps they have come to know of it, the wretches. But why take Dr Gurney? He notes that they asked of him why the plague came on the death of the old queen and the coming of the new king.' He laid emphasis on the final clause. 'What did the wife say?'

I recounted everything I could recall of Mrs Gurney's account. Cecil stopped me when I mentioned her and her husband's tolerance. He seemed to speak to himself, his voice drifting in white curls. 'Leonard, a papist-lover? No. No.'

I coughed. 'I think, my lord, that if he saw people of all faiths, he loved none above the other.' I hurried on, finishing my tale.

'A blasted shame the woman has no list of the patients he has seen. A woman. A woman troubled in the mind.'

Something came to me, making my heart flutter. 'A crazed woman.'
'What is that?'

'A woman. She said a woman had visited him.'
'Yes?'

'Sir, a woman troubled my house yesterday. In the morning. A woman asking about the pestilence there, the infection.'

'London is full of women, Ned,' he said, a little testily.

'But this one was strange, smiling and strange. And her name. My girl, my friend, she said the woman's name was Angela.

'What did this wench say, exactly?'

I scratched behind my ear. 'I cannot ... I used rough words to be rid of her ... She ... I think she wished to know who had survived the plague. Only my boy. And she wanted to take him with her.'

'Take him? Why should she wish to take a child?' Cecil's brow wrinkled in confusion, mine in disgust. And then his tongue appeared, darting out over his lips. His fingers worked again as he drew up Gurney's commonplace book. 'See you here. This: I feare me they will never leave me alone until they have drunk dry of my mind and know all that they might know of the pestilence and also of matters of mystery and these visions and of that I know nothing. Visions.' He tilted back his head. 'Angela.'

'I do not know the name. It is strange to me. Sounds Italian.'

'I know there was an Angela. Of Foligno. An Italian woman, yes, who claimed mystical revelations. I understand she claimed to see St Francis of Assisi. No doubt she was a madwoman or a false prophetess. As far as I know, even the papists do not venerate her. What do you know of visions?'

'Only that they are trouble.'

He smiled. 'Ay. More troublesome because one cannot sort the wheat from the chaff. We each have visions nightly in our dreams, and what is to separate them from visions sent by the evangel? Or who … Dee,' said Cecil, stroking his chin.

The name was familiar enough. I had recalled, on mulling it after hearing it from Mrs Gurney's lips, that he had been a famous man in times past. 'Dee … I confess I had thought him dead until Mrs Gurney mentioned him.'

'Dead – no. He suffered a fate worse than death. He went to live in Manchester. A town as far from royal justice and favour as one might get.' He stood, taking a book under each arm, and began walking. I followed a step behind and together we clattered over the cobbles, my boots and his shoes making a rhythmic chorus. Women's laughter burbled from a window somewhere above us before it banged shut.

'Yes, old Dr John Dee,' said Cecil. 'Alive. He was a noted man in my father's time. The late queen showed him some favour. My father, too, put some stock in his ventures, though I never knew him to produce anything of note. His mind turned on the mathematical arts, on how numbers might be used to unlock the mysteries of the universe. And he trafficked with angels. He claimed to have means of opening the door to their world and inviting them to cross into ours. I dined with him myself, during the matter of … the late Lord Strange.' His voice followed his eyes in drifting upwards, into the windy places of memory. 'Ten years ago, by God. He pressed for preferment, as every man does.' He looked back towards me. 'Yet he is a great scholar – or was. I believe my father had cause to visit his library on occasion, though I think it was broken up in the late queen's time. If he had any means of achieving alchemy, as my father hoped, they were lost then. Alchemy … angels … the ancient mysteries … you are a young man yet, Ned, what do you think?'

'In truth, my lord, I understand none of it. Mathematics least of all.' The very term threatened witchcraft to me. Simple accounts were reasonable enough, but certain numbers in certain orders were infamously dangerous and dark. I considered, for example, that it was a risk to step outside the day after I had seen a clock strike dead-on midnight. Indeed, I considered myself rather blessed that I could barely calculate – a wicked enough word in itself, like 'conjure' – anything greater than the sum of money owed me in return if I handed a boatman a half-groat. A man with my tastes couldn't afford to meddle with the magic art of numbers. Plenty thought buggery a short step away from witchcraft – and though I always attempted to be discreet in my affairs, one never knew who was watching and might twist things.

In summa: one plus one, both being the same, makes for an unnatural coupling. One plus nothing equals nothing but good.

My master would not save a man accused of witchcraft and buggery.

'Yes,' said Cecil. 'I am largely of your mind. If such things were to be discovered, such realms of knowledge, then they would have been by our time. Before our time, I should think. In the writings of the ancients. Well, it was such arguments as yours and mine that saw an end to Dee. He came back to England after studying abroad and found that the young were little interested in his promises of putting magic in the harness of the state. Yet, for the love she bore him and the service he had done her, the queen appointed him to a post at Christ's College. At Manchester, not Cambridge.' We had reached the archway through which Cecil had come, having completed a full tour of the Pebble Court. 'Between you and I, I think her Majesty was a little shamefaced at her patronage of him and would have had him out of the way. He is now up north. At any rate, I shall have to set this whole matter before the king.'

My eyebrow arched, in spite of myself. I had expected him to settle the thing in secrecy. 'I will always consult with men who are expert in a field, whether they serve me or I them,' said Cecil, tightening his grip on the books. 'His Majesty, if you will believe it, is the foremost scholar on matters of mysticism and the history of the secrets of the occult. And I mean this as no courtly flattery. He has made a study of such practitioners and their doings. As their enemy, of course, as he is an enemy to all filthy superstitions and those who practise them. In our time, in this age of light, we must root out all devilish ceremonies and those that act in them. Dr Dee might be studied to see if he is merely a good scholar, like Dr Gurney, and therefore if he knows what these wickeder mystic creatures do.'

I considered this. A man of mysticism – too close to wizardry – but possessed of a great store of learning and knowledge. And the missing Dr Gurney was his friend. I supposed that men with similar interests would become friends and would know still others. I blew into my hands, making them tingle. 'This Dee might then have been approached by these folk? By letter, perhaps?'

Cecil gave a shrug of his uneven shoulders. 'I cannot say. Yet if they took Dr Gurney for his knowledge … well, that was knowledge I have no doubt he shared with Dee. That is what these scholarly fellows do, is it not? Write and think, and think and write, and trade in ideas and thoughts and matter they have read?'

I did not like the drift of the conversation. 'You might then write to this Dr Dee and ask him if his friend told him about these troublesome people and their interest in visions,' I ventured.

My stomach knotted at his next words. 'Write? Why should I trouble an old man's eyes with letters when I might instead send him a friendly face to work his ears and his tongue? There is some great matter here. I know it well enough by its scent, as the king knows the scent of a buck. Some matter concerning a group who seek divine knowledge – and why else but to use it for evil purposes? At the king's coming.' He sniffed deeply of the air, which was scented still with the smell of roasting meats from the brightly painted banqueting house. 'You left your enclosed quarantine a little early, I think. No, no, I do not condemn you. I am glad of it. I will see that word reaches the Master of the Revels that you remain abed at home. You will not be missed, you see? Go home, Ned. Pack you a bag and see about a stout horse. You have business in the north with a man who has a head full of divine knowledge.'

6

She is beautiful, even in the moment of death. The boy wishes he could stretch up and touch the side of her cheek or reach out and grasp the open palm which seems to reach back out of the canvas to him. Her brother looks to her, ignorant of death approaching from his right side. Both look angelic. Neither suffers pain, or fear, or regret.

Although he is only a boy, the image paints itself into his soul. Later, the girl, Flavia, of the Martyrdom of Four Saints *will visit him and he will tell no one. She will whisper secrets from the great beyond and tell him to do things and he will stop his ears at first and close his eyes. And then he will learn to listen.*

Reason tells him that she lives in the San Giovanni Evangelista. Reason tells him that she does not live at all. And yet, over time, she will become a friend and a mentor. And she will wear many faces.

Does he determine to conquer the fear of death then – when he first looks upon her? Does the birth of the desire to know what the dead and dying feel when they know they are departing the world begin then?

Or does that come later, when, on the same long and sun-dappled journey through Italy, he stands in another church, this time not in Parma but in the city of canals, and looks on Tintoretto's painting and sees St Roch healing the plague victims?

He understands then what the plague does to bodies. It is a sign of the end coming. It is the onrush of darkness and can be fought only by the glow which surrounds the administering saint. He vows then that he will not just conquer pain but death itself. Sinewy flesh is weak and tender, apt to suffer whatever lives in dark airs and vile miasmas. Light is its enemy. To his young brain it seems clear. Yet, even in Tintoretto's image, the faces register no suffering or agony. Art denies the truth, but the truth will not be denied.

He stumbles when leaving the Chiesa di San Rocco, and lands hard on his right knee. Daggers of pain stab upwards and downwards and outwards. It feels as though the kneecap has shattered, fallen out of place somehow. Tears burst from his eyes and a racking sob from his chest. The leader of their little party of Englanders turns and frowns, stamping past the rest of the train and back towards him. Fear compounds the pain. Might he dare hope that the great man will be kindly? No, because he is a great man and they are all short on temper and long on angry speeches.

He is jerked to his feet and ordered to be a little man. Not to bring shame upon the party before the educated and civilised people of Venezia. They continue on their way, walking on tiles and cobbles, over gaily painted bridges spanning murky blue depths where it is said people often fall and drown, unable to scream without hastening the end. He has heard itself that the city itself is slowly dying, the number of its people falling. And yet it remains a treasure full of treasures, a beauty full of beauties, biting its thumb at death.

As he thinks this, the tears stop.

But why had they started?

He is not dead, nor dying, but has merely suffered a little hurt. Wherefore tears? Wherefore the sudden contortion of his face?

It is a conundrum that will continue to plague him all over Italy.

It will, in fact, become a seed planted in fertile Italian-tinctured soil that will grow, and warp, and bend every which way. But then, marching on a sore knee in a train of wealthy Englishmen, page himself to a great lord, he thinks only on death and pain, and pain and plague, and Flavia who seemed to welcome death with a beautiful expression of peace.

***

The knocking at the door sent his visitors fleeing and he let them go. Nathaniel Hope then rose, straightening himself up – the twine belt around his white robe had come loose – and taking the few steps towards the door. The cabin was unpleasant – more like a cell – and it brought back foul memories of that other place. But it was safe. There were no servants here, no warder or keeper.

He opened the door and stepped back. 'Angela.' He smiled, as he always did when he looked upon the crystalline complexion of his favourite. 'Please, come.' He frowned a little on realising she was not alone but accompanied by Amos, his egg-bald head colourless in the poor light. 'Vita in morte sumus, my friends.' They repeated the phrase, their heads bowed. Smiling, Hope retreated to his bunk. No – his berth. Suddenly there came to him the memory of the roll and pitch of a ship at sea and the sewer smell of Venice and the freshening winds of France. And they were real, they were there, swimming up his nostrils, only to be killed by the sudden assault of burning coals from his brazier. He thought he caught a movement in the shadowed corner of the cabin and jerked.

55

No, he thought – he must gather his thoughts and let no distractions trouble him. 'Have you discovered any more of the Enlightened?'

'Yes,' said Angela. 'A new man has come. Amos discovered him. He has renounced his papistry utterly. Surrendered his baubles.'

'Then he is doubly blessed.' Warmth bloomed in Hope's stomach and washed outwards, to the tips of his fingertips and toes. It numbed them, almost. It was the opposite of pain.

Angela hung her head. 'But there are others that will not come. I found one myself, a boy. But he had a cruel master who would not give him up. '

Hope shook his head, anger bubbling like overheated black oil. Somewhere, someone shouted in a childish voice. 'Masters of boys can be most wicked and cruel. The boy must be saved.'

'Yes,' she said. 'There are others too who walk in darkness. That will not listen. Not by any gentle persuasions. Puritans and those who listen to the archbishops and their ilk. They cannot see, Nathaniel. They cannot see that they have been spared for a reason.' Angry, she became more beautiful, a blush creeping into her cheeks. Her hair might have been spun from cloth of gold. She was the stuff of the Italian painters made flesh.

'Then they have no reason.' Hope bowed his head. It was another great mystery, how men and women could see the horrors that surrounded them, be given a clear sign of their salvation in being spared it, and yet wish only to forget all. And to Hope it seemed that every soul he failed to make realise was a soul lost. Sadness threatened. Those who were given the chance and yet refused to join the Enlightened would suffer worse than death.

When the end came, they would not go smiling into the beyond, as the painted martyr Flavia had done, but screaming.

'How many souls have we saved?'

'Twenty-nine,' said the man Hope had christened Amos. He thought he heard condemnation in the words. Thankfully, Angela echoed them more gently.

'What is the significance of twenty-nine?' asked Hope. 'We must ask the doctor. How is the doctor?'

'He is not of the Enlightened,' said Amos.

'He is well,' said Angela, giving her fellow's surliness short shrift.

'He is our guest. Though damnation awaits him. Has he given you news of the coronation?'

'It will be on the fifteenth of March. It is spoken of in the city. Sung by those who sing the news.'

'Fiftee – have you looked?'

She smiled again. 'The doctor looked. 15:3 in the book of Numbers. And will make an offering by fire unto the Lord, namely a burnt offering, or a sacrifice to fulfil a vow, or a free offering, or in your principal feasts, to make a sweet savour unto the Lord, of the herd, or of the flock.'

Hope considered this. Could the means of bringing about their salvation be through fire? Through burning his flock? It seemed monstrous. Extreme. He would have to think further on the matter, to discuss it with the doctor and with the others – the ones who knew everything in this life and the next. 'I will speak to the doctor now.'

Soon, if the world was just, his brothers and sisters would share his gift. They too would be free to speak with the dead as freely as he did, and would learn why they had been saved and what they must do with that knowledge.

Hope followed Angela and Amos out of the cabin. The floor beneath them was steady, but the whole place stank of ancient wood. Seawater seemed to leach up from beneath and sweat from the walls. It felt like being inside Jonah's whale.

'Come back here,' snapped an irate voice.

Hope ignored it, as did Angela and Amos. Together, the trio walked down a dark hall, feeling their way. Eventually, they came to the stern of the vessel: a room that might in better times have been used to store the stuff necessary to put out to sea. Hope slid past his acolytes to take the lead and gently knocked on the door. It was a courtesy. Angela had the key. She passed it to him, and an agonised shriek announced the turning of the rusty lock.

***

Madness, as Dr Leonard Gurney understood it, was the absence of reason. Worse, he was beginning to realise, it was the refutation of reason. He had known a fellow student in Paris who had turned madman, falling down and fitting. Too much study by candlelight, perhaps. Gurney had found it as frightening to see as his fellows had found it worthy of laughter.

But madness was not a matter for laughter. It was a danger to the whole world of men as much as to the body of the man it infected.

The crying lock signalled its return, and he flattened himself against the bulkhead, the light which poured in from the high, open window falling in a shower over and in front of him.

How long had he been here now? It had been over a week since his patient, the woman now calling herself Angela, had come, in the company of another, the bald man who said he had been rechristened as Amos. Gurney knew the names to be religious and had said nothing. He had known and admitted both, sighing as he did so. He had judged it best not to antagonise them. If they wished to take new names upon themselves, that was their right. It was brain fever, he knew, that they suffered from, and there was no sure remedy for it. Maddening them, or even questioning them too harshly, could lead to violence.

For months they had grown worse – since the outbreak of the plague, in fact. He might have gone to the authorities and had them locked up, but that he could never have brought himself to do – not until he had some sure sign that they were a danger to themselves or to others. Besides, troublesome patients, he had always thought, were the lot of physicians, as petitioners were to political men. A courtier visited him every week with imagined symptoms of the clap. A merchant's wife came more regularly, having constantly heard of some new illness at the market and discovered the signs of it in herself.

Yet, as a rule, bothersome patients always came singularly.

Until the day they had come to take him, the former Puritan and the former goodwife had also always visited by themselves. As a pair, they had ceased to be a nuisance and become a threat.

In his private chamber, they had asked him, as they always did, whether life could spring through death and whether those in this world might communicate with those who departed it. And again he had sighed. 'You must turn your minds to some other occupation.' Both had been dressed as they had always done when they had visited in better times – in good city clothes: he in a shirt, doublet and hose with a short ruff and she in the skirts, kirtle, and tall hat of a city goodwife. 'Amos' had been, once, a serious man and 'Angela' a simple young housewife of no strong religion, as far as he had known.

That last time, though, they had been more forceful in their entreaties to know why the plague began and whether, by asking the dead, they might discover why they had been spared. What caused some to suffer it and live and some to die? In truth, he did not know. About one in every five who showed the symptoms recovered, the other four going the usual, agonising route to death. 'Some constitution of the humours … age … perhaps it is God's will. You cannot ask the dead for they cannot speak with us. There is no way.' Just as the causes of the pestilence were debated between favourers of the noisome miasma theory and the theory of divine planning, so too were the reasons behind its strange rate of mortality. His latter answer, though, had brought animation to their faces. Angela had risen from the stool, joining Amos. Their questions were, Gurney had thought, not unreasonable; it was the means by which they thought answers might be found that troubled him. Both had been his patients for years, and both had survived the plague during two of its previous, briefer visitations. How they had become friends he did not know.

'You will come with us,' Amos had growled.

She had restrained him with a delicate gesture of her hand. 'Please, Dr Gurney. We have joined in friendship with a man. Formerly a servant to a great one of the realm. He would speak with you.'

'Is he sick?'

'No–'

'Grievous sick,' Amos had said, cutting her off.

'If you would speak with him … then we shall have no more need to visit you.'

Gurney had assessed the situation as best he could. The thought of being quit of them was tempting. It had not occurred to him – and now he cursed himself for it – that he might be being led into a trap. Only when he had risen to go and tell his wife that he would be leaving for a short while, and found Amos's dagger pressed against his back, did he realise that there had never been any question of his going with them. 'If your wife knows nothing, she is safe.'

'Then let us go,' he had snapped.

And so the three of them had left his chambers and his house. To his surprise, a wooden bucket had been left standing just outside the door, and, smiling, Angela pulled a brush from it and painted a red cross. He had realised then that they planned on keeping him for forty days at least. Through the City had gone hostage and captors, a fairly short distance to Queenhithe.

Why had he not cried out? Fought against them? There had been the dagger, certainly, but so too had there been curiosity. Who was this man? What was this party of folk?

At the docks, he had felt certain he was going to be spirited abroad. And yet instead he had been taken to a small jetty which stood apart from the others, and to a shallow-drafted pinnace with bare masts, which lay amongst those apparently waiting to be towed away to the mud-dock scrapyard at Rotherhithe. It was a sick ship, Gurney had thought, sitting amidst its fellows in a hospital. Had it been a man, he would have advised it to set its affairs in order. At night it even groaned and whined, complaining of its age and cares. It was going nowhere.

He had been shown into the chamber in which he now awaited his guests, and there he had remained since, with white-robed attendants only coming with food and ale and to remove and replace his slop bucket. On the second day of his captivity, he had met with the supposed patient: a man calling himself Hope. He had brought with him books: works by Mercator and Frisius, Galenic texts, which he'd long since abandoned, and an older edition of the bible than the one he kept at home – the Geneva rather than the more modern but still faulty *Bishops' Bible*. It was though as though a student with only the faintest idea of the names of great works had compiled a library in a hurry.

That had been his only meeting with the man thus far, and he had asked many of the same questions as his followers, particularly about why they had been chosen to meet the plague and live. His goal, Gurney had realised, was to gain an understanding of immortality by discovering how to communicate with the dead. It was an impossibility of course – a common enough fantasy of brainsickness, often brought about by grief or even heresy. Yet Hope was insistent that some channel between the dead and living existed and could be mastered through study.

Gurney had considered the matter when Angela and Amos had plagued him about it. He had even written his friend Dr Dee on the subject. And he had concluded that Mr Hope and his followers were dangerously sick in the mind.

As though recalling his first visitation had summoned him, Hope appeared in the doorway as the chamber door opened. He stepped into the room, smiling – a handsome, wilting figure only a little younger than the doctor himself. Gurney did not smile back. Instead he swallowed.

'Good morrow to you, my friend.' Again, Gurney said nothing. 'I hope you are being well treated. I know it is no pleasant thing to be confined. I understand that well enough, in truth.' The man seemed to shiver as he spoke. Flanked by Angela and Amos, Hope looked up at the window and frowned. 'And the *Crown Elizabeth* is an old vessel.' His smile disappeared. 'No!' he snapped.

Gurney had not spoken, and nor had his friends. Mad, thought, Gurney. Peace again descended on the man's face as he asked, 'I would have you answer a question, doctor. What is the significance of the number twenty-nine?'

The physician's mouth fell open and he resisted the urge to shake his head in befuddlement. 'It is one short of thirty,' he said.

The sarcasm was lost. 'And the significance of thirty?'

Gurney put a hand to his forehead. There was nothing else for it but to humour the creatures. To agree with them. To disagree, to provoke – that was always a great risk with the mad. 'The bible tells us … hm …' He picked up the old copy from atop the chest which served, at night, as his bed. 'Numbers. 4:3. From thirty years old and above, even until fifty years old, all that enter into the assembly to do the work of the tabernacle of the congregation.' Amos took a few steps across the chamber, his shoes making a hollow, tumbling sound, and snatched the book, passing it to Hope.

'What does it mean?' asked the leader.

'Only that the priests of Leviticus joined their ministry at the age of thirty.'

'Why?'

'I cannot say. A good age at which to understand and to lead others.'

'I am past forty,' said Hope, tilting his head back. 'And what else does thirty mean?'

'John the Baptist began to preach at thirty. And … of course, Jesus Christ began his ministry at that age too. It is a holy number.'

Angela and Amos turned wide and hopeful eyes to Hope. The strange vacant smiles Gurney knew to be the parishioners of this mad sect's customary expressions were printed on their faces. 'We must make up our number to thirty. Angela, you will do us a great honour by finding that boy.' Her smile became a grin and tears shone in her eyes. 'Go to, both of you. I would speak to our guest privily.'

Gurney cursed himself for a fool, realising he had likely drawn some other poor creature into this mad world.

When the others had gone, Hope beckoned for Gurney to sit. He did so, moving the books on to the deck. The leader knelt beside him. 'I am sorry, doctor, that you cannot become the thirtieth of our number. I am sorry I cannot welcome you into the company of the Enlightened. Truly.' Gurney inclined his head. He could kick the man in the face and run, but it would do little good. There were, after all, twenty-eight of his brethren aboard the *Crown Elizabeth* – and he was an older man. He would have to find some other means of disabling them or talk his way out. 'Tell me, have you discovered anything in those books?'

The works of Mercator he had been given were interesting enough – writings on geography and the celestial spheres. Frisius's works on the globe and astronomy were likewise of academic interest. Yet there was nothing present in either man's writings on what Hope had requested. It was clear that he and his followers had amassed a number of what they, in their limited understanding, thought to be critical ingredients, but were in fact likely to result in a hodgepodge.

Gurney evidently spent too long trying to frame an answer, for Hope asked, 'do these writings, taken together, tell us how we might call up the voices of the dead at our will and command? Will they allow us to control how we might return the dead to us?'

'No,' said the doctor flatly.

'Yet these are the books my lord spoke well of. I heard him myself, and often.'

'I have discovered nothing that will allow you to raise the dead nor speak with them wherever they dwell. It cannot be done. We must accept the dead are gone until the day of judgment, when all ends.' He added, he hoped gently, 'then we will be reunited with those we lose in this transitory life.'

Hope's cheeks tensed, the jawbones standing out. 'And yet I tell you I do speak with them and they with me. And always have. And I would control it!'

An idea struck Gurney. 'Mr Hope, I will write you a list of things. Things that might be found at an apothecary. They might control these … visitations.'

'Physick?'

'Yes.'

'I trust you.' The simple look on the man's face softened Gurney a little and he cursed himself for a fool. Was this madman not his gaoler? 'Write the list. One of my friends will go into the city.'

'Good.'

Hope got to his feet and moved towards the door. Suddenly he paused, clasping his hands behind his head, and bent forward. A string of oaths burst from his lips and he began cursing at something in the corner of the chamber. He finished up with, 'I cannot, I cannot. I will!' Again, Gurney got up and put his back to the wall, feeling like a man dropped into a pit with a lion. 'You deceive us, doctor. You deceive us. The dead do come back. And they cry out to be listened to. They cry out for death to be conquered. And we will conquer it. It will be so. We will invite death onto this very ship, yes, yes, to claim a victim, and we will confront him and bid him go and we will bring the dead man back. And you will help us. Prepare yourself, doctor, for the doing of a miracle.'

With that, he threw the door wide and left.

And the key screamed again in the lock.

CORONATION

7

Picture an ancient gentleman of scholarly bent and you will not be far wrong. Dr John Dee was almost certainly close to what you imagine. Though he was seated, the pulled-up bunch of his legs and his long arms spoke of a tall and slim frame. His long black robes gave him a raven-like look, compounded by his long nose, and his beard was white and sharp, falling neatly over a thick but short ruff. Despite his age, his skin was good and full-blooded, with only the thinnest caul of age draped over it. Only his eyes, I thought, suggested weariness and suspicion, and these hidden beneath a smile and gentle manner as he stared at me over a low desk laden on either side with twin columns of books.

It had taken me days of hard riding through increasing blizzards to reach Manchester. Initially, I had worried about finding lodgings on the road. I needn't have. For innkeepers, it was risk dying of the plague caught from a stranger or risk starving for want of what he kept in his purse. Thus, I was able to ride and rest freely throughout battered England, following the old Watling Street to St Albans, into Leicestershire and Staffordshire, towards the Welsh border, and northwards to the frozen wastes of Chester and Manchester. I was, though unknowingly until Dr Dee smilingly informed me, following the ancient paths of Roman roads. Less smilingly, I informed him that the ruinous roads were bested by the rotting fields and half-empty hamlets I had ridden through. It seemed to me that the countryside, England's patchy quilt of fields and woodlands, had less attentive authorities than London. More than once I had seen bodies lying face down out in snowy fields, wind- and rain-flattened hay bales surrounding them. What the bales signified I could only guess at – crude attempts, I supposed, to close the poor souls off from their fellows. The nation, I realised, would take some time to get back on its feet. And it would take longer to forget the disease.

On reaching Manchester, I had come immediately to the college: an assembly of old monkish buildings standing around a green quilted with white. Dr Dee's lodgings, as warden, were not far from the ancient cathedral whose square brown tower with its four jagged points stabbed at the heart of a bleak sky. The warden's house, as a chaplain I found in the grounds had informed me, was a more pleasant place fit for a man of great learning such as their own Dr Dee. I could tell from the fellow's manner, as he insisted on leading me to the large, red-brick house, looking like a blood spot on a cuff, that the warden was well liked.

That had eased me a little. In truth, I had dreaded coming. Rather like cheesemakers and French vintners, I appreciated the fact that clever divines existed and produced things – but I didn't much want to spend my time in discussion of the production of knowledge any more than I wished to learn about curds or the growing of grapes. I was simply in the city to discover what Dee knew of Dr Gurney's late activities, and what Dr Gurney had been writing to him. Thus, as the chaplain had led me into the building, I haughtily presumed upon my note of introduction from Cecil and insisted on being lodged for the night in a good chamber. It would be a fine thing, I had thought, to sleep in such an old place. Learning and the past; antiquity and knowledge – always these things seemed paired. One could not think of new discoveries without considering the dusty knowledge of the dead. This I had thought as I'd followed the chaplain, until he had knocked on a great oak door upstairs in the big house, before scurrying off to see to my lodgings. Thus I had been left to my interview with Dr John Dee alone.

After he had risen to greet me and we had exchanged introductions and pleasantries, Dee sat again at his desk, gesturing for me to sit opposite him. I did, keeping my hat firmly on my head – though I had done him the honour of touching it – to show him my hurry and my importance.

So this is the great mystic – the late queen's conjuror – I thought. Magic and mysticism were branches of science I knew only from the stage and by repute. I began speaking, not meeting his unflinching gaze. 'I have come on urgent business from London.'

Interest sharpened in his cloudy eyes and he leaned forward. Immediately, one of the towers of books threatened to crash down on him. We each eyed it warily. 'Come,' he said, rising. 'Let us not be so formal.' He stood, his sparse white hair almost brushing the rafters, and moved across the room towards a cushioned casement. As I made to follow, I stole a glimpse around the chamber. More books stood against walls. Several windows admitted good light. A cupboard on the left-hand side displayed instruments and objects I did not recognise. A portrait of the queen as a young woman hung on the wall – one in the old style, looking less than human. And there was another door – one he was very much leading me away from – on the right. Down one side of it were a series of heavy locks. 'Mr Savage?'

I turned back to him and smiled, taking shallow breaths. The chamber smelled, I thought, a little cruelly, of the sour mustiness of old age. Still, I folded myself beside him, close, in the casement. In the wintry light that streamed in, he looked older than he had in the centre of the chamber. More tired, too. My father's face loomed up in my mind and I regarded my hands, turning them over. 'I come on urgent business,' I repeated, hoping that that would work its usual tonic in replacing unhappier thoughts. 'From the king's secretary. I understand you know him. Baron Cecil of Essenden.'

'Know him?' Dee smiled, and then grinned, and then laughed. His great age blurred. 'Ho! Ha! Ho! I know him as I knew the father. Do you imagine an old man like me reaches this great age without knowing the men of state? The faces change but not the wiles. Do you know, when I was born, Cardinal Wolsey was the chief servant of England? Wolsey, the infamous papist! Ho! So many turns of the wheel in one lifetime!'

I liked him. I cannot say why. I fancy I have an instinct with people and, though it is generally safest to assume that every man is a beast or a fool, I trust that when I like someone on meeting them, it is usually for some good reason. 'You must have seen much,' I agreed.

'And not all good, mark you. Now, lad,' Dee asked in a voice creaking with age, 'what does young Cecil want?'

I smiled at that. Informality, I thought, was the order of the day here. 'He and the new king are greatly worried.'

'You know the new king?'

'I have met him, doctor.'

'A Scot.'

'So I gather.' He was mastering me, I felt. A kindly man, but not used to conversation which he did not dominate.

'Is …' A pale tongue swept over his thin lips. His teeth, I saw, were all there, but they were uneven, some backwards and some forwards. 'Does he seek my knowledge of the empire? The great empire of Britain? I can return with you to court if he–'

'I know nothing of that.' I tried to sound as kindly as possible. Cecil, after all, had told me that the old man had been all but banished, an embarrassment to the state. It seemed he had squatted up in the north, hoping not to be forgotten – that he might again be accepted. I wondered if he had a family, or if he dwelt up here amongst strangers. 'The king is only newly come to London. He has not had time to order his court, I should think.'

Dee seemed to accept this. He clasped his hands in his black-clad lap. Thick strings of blue veins criss-crossed the backs of them. I let my eyes wander the room, stopping at the books. 'You keep your ears and eyes on the news out of London? On the sciences and … such?'

'Oh … oh, ho ho! Oh, yes. I might be old, son, but my mind is yet sharp.' As if to prove it, he unclasped his hand and jabbed a finger at his white head, smiling again. The smile faded. 'I fancy I still have some small learning to offer the world. And the realm.'

To hell with it!

'I understand you are a friend to one of the king's physicians. Dr Leonard Gurney.'

'Oh, yes. Gurney. A fine mind. Enquiring.'

'Yet you are not a physician as he is.'

'No, a mere looker on of matters divine. All branches of learning,' he said, motioning towards his desk, 'are connected. Everything is connected.'

'Dr Gurney has disappeared.'

'What?'

'We suspect he has been captured. Perhaps by patients of his who work wicked designs. His wife–'

'Maud! A sweet lady. Is Maud taken too?'

'No, sir. Yet she told me that Dr Gurney recently wrote to you. I suspected you might know something that should help us find him. He might be in very great danger. The kingdom might be,' I added, putting a hand on the breast of my good riding coat. 'Your wit and knowledge might help us find him and deliver us from danger. The king would be pleased.'

Dee smiled. 'No need to flatter me, my boy. Leonard is a friend. I should help you without the airy promises of courtly favour. Tell me what the secretary has discovered.'

I did. As I spoke, Dee stood and began pacing the room, stroking his beard and tutting. Eventually he began lifting books and sorting through papers. I faltered in my tale and he said, 'pay me no heed, lad, I can think and listen and look at once. Go to and speak.' I continued, trying to ignore his muttering. When I was finished, he sat down again at his desk and barked a triumphant 'ha!'.

'Sir?' I asked, rising, and crossing back to the seat before the desk. His perambulations had robbed the columns of heavy books of their threat; he had taken some down, moved others, and set some reverently on the floor.

'Dr Gurney's letters,' he announced, tapping some papers on the desk. I reached out a hand for them and, as quick as a flash, he snapped a stick produced from beneath the desk across my knuckles.

'Jesus! What the fuck!?' The words had burst forth before my mind could harness them.

'Mind your tongue, lad. It is the sign of a weak mind when a man speaks before thinking.' I pulled back my hand, out of range and away from the letters. I could feel my anger blossoming, a thorny rose opening its petals in the sun.

You old bastard!

He spoke again. 'You would read a man's private letters? Ho! You might represent the great high and illustrious Baron Essenden, but I think in England a man has the liberty of privacy.'

You think wrong then, you old goat.

'I must know if these will help us find him.' I kneaded my hand with the other.

'And I said I would give you help. But let us not be as beasts, as pigs, scrabbling in the dirt of other men's secrets. I will tell you what might be of use. Once I have sifted the contents and framed thought to speech, as a man should.'

I sat with my mouth shut, robbed even of the satisfaction of a sullen, frosty silence by the sound of Dee's quiet reading, punctuated as it was by ums and ahs and occasional tuts. 'Here,' he said at last. 'Listen. Item. On the ethical study of patients. My dear Dee, I have again been troubled by the ethical matter of the study of patients viz whether it is right to admit them to my presence or whether it is right that I do go to some higher authority and thereby break as it were the seal of the confessional which binds this my trade.

'It seems that Dr Gurney was troubled in the mind by a patient whom he deemed to be troubled in the mind. Ho!'

'The fellow is missing, sir,' I said, pouting.

'Quite, quite.' He did not look at all abashed. 'Each day now I see two patients whom I think might suffer delusions born of the plague times and they do ask questions of a similar nature though they know each other not, and therefore I do wonder whether madness be a thing of the external which infects as do some other illnesses.'

'Two patients,' I said. 'Two madmen.'

'I must correct you. One mad woman. Another letter,' he said, sifting the papers, 'speaks of a woman.'

'Of course. Yes.'

'He does not name her. The principle of ethics forbids it.'

'What does it signify, the company of a woman?'

Dee appeared to consider this. His eyes widened. Grew evasive. 'I have no idea.'

Cecil said that the famous Italian Angela saw visions. He's thinking of his own history of visions.

I did not press. 'He says nothing of who these people are? Where they live?'

'Certainly not. It would be a terrible crime for a physician to write to a friend, even a learned friend, of the private lives of his patients. He speaks only, as it were, in the abstract. Yet ... he says that both survived the plague and since the fresh pestilence ... hm ... do plague him also about the causes for survival and the causes of the disease itself and – this is a matter of note – whether the dead can be spoken with. Necromancy, it is sometimes called. It risks inviting devils to take the form of the dead and impart false secrets. This, it seems, was their true goal – discovering whether there might be some means of communicating truly with the dead.' He did not meet my eyes, staring down at the paper. Turning it over, he said, 'Foolishness. There is no way, not with the dead themselves. Yet the other matter – surviving the plague. I confess, that is a matter he wrote me about more than once. I share his interest, as all men of learning do. Why does the plague come? Why does it go? Why does it commit so many to the soil and spare others?' He shifted his gaze towards the ceiling as he spoke.

'Why, then?'

'Ho! Do you imagine I sit up here on a golden mound of true knowledge? Mark me in this: when you visit a true scholar, he will have more questions than answers. When you visit a coney-catcher, he will serve you answers enough to feast on and every one sweet and false. I can use reason, lad, to think of reasons. No more than that.'

'And where does reason lead you, doctor?'

'Ah.' He settled back in his chair, crossing his arms over his thin chest. 'Many places.'

Hitherto, Dee had been open with me, I felt – friendly, despite the rap on the knuckles. Suspicion again came into his eyes. Wariness. I smiled, hoping I looked encouraging rather than mad. 'His lordship spoke highly of you,' I lied. 'Of your knowledge and understanding. We must be open in all matters. If we wish to save Dr Gurney.'

'Tell me, son. How far have you come?'

'What?' He repeated his question. 'From London? I ... I don't know. A long way. Two hundred miles.'

'And how many days and how many nights?' I told him. 'Ho! And how much do you have in your purse?' I shrugged and gave him a false number. 'And how much does that weigh?'

'I don't know,' I said, fighting to keep the irritation out of my voice. *Madness is catching.*

'What is the point in these questions?'

'Five. Five questions. One a compound, I own. And you answered in numbers.' I said nothing, and the levity drained from his face. 'What do you know of my studies?'

'Nothing. Not much.'

He shrugged. 'I make no secret of them. I have no doubt the lord secretary learnt of them at the knees of his father, the late lord secretary. I believe, my boy, that there is a universal design. To all matters.' I had no response to that, for I did not understand it. 'And, further, that we might discover that design if we can find the language it has been written in.'

'A book, sir? A lost book?'

'A book not yet written. A book that is coded in the language of the angels. Revealed to us in their celestial speech. And when they show it to us, the language of the world will be revealed. And the design which created it.' He delivered this so calmly I did not even wonder at his wits. 'You know of Adam?'

My mouth ran dry. Adam was the name I had been christened with. The name I had rejected. 'Yes,' I managed.

'Adam in the time before history must have spoken, yes? Well, we are not so proud in England that we think he spoke in our tongue. Nor in any tongue invented by the races of man. Yet speak he must have, else how did he communicate? Eve, too. I once … I once hoped to learn the entirety of that language by scientific means. Now … now I suspect that the nature of it is informed by numbers.'

'Numbers?'

'Quite. You see, just now, how you spoke in numbers? And in doing so, you admit that all is divisible. They hold together our little world. London is so far from this city in a number of miles. The way to the New World, the globe itself, is reckoned in numbers. Our whole world can be divided. In doing so, we find order. The earth is divided into nations and each nation has a language and each language an alphabet. And each alphabet a fixed number of letters. And what is our world but a shadow of God's? So, there must be a fixed number in the language of the angels.'

'Is this what you and Dr Gurney discussed?'

'Amongst other things, yes. You see, he remarked that one in five men suffer the plague and die. He wondered why. I believe that, amongst the many mysteries of the cosmos, the answer lies in the book that is not yet written. And the key lies in our understanding of the study of numbers and how they hold together everything. Everything. All matter. The size and weight of the world. The distance to the celestial spheres. The story *before* history.' He sat back, his nose in the air, well pleased with himself.

'I know nothing of this.' If I did not detest numbers before, I certainly did now. 'I wish only to know what Dr Gurney and his patients sought.'

Dee sniffed. 'Dr Gurney was like me. A follower of Ficino and Paracelsus.'

'Who are they? Are they in England?'

'Indeed.'

A letter from Cecil would get me to them, I thought. 'Then I will speak to them, sir. Where in England?'

'Peace, lad. Their teachings are in England, in France, in Italy, and everywhere as long as men of learning correspond. Yet if you wish to speak to them you will need secret knowledge beyond my ken.'

'What? Where are they?'

'Ho! You are an ignorant. Both scholars are long dead. The body of their genius lives yet. Through us.'

I resisted the urge to swear and began to rise from my seat. Dr John Dee, I decided, was a crack-brain. The trip had been useless. 'Sit, sit, boy. I apologise for my rudeness. It is a long time since I have had a chance to speak freely. My chaplains, the fellows here – they don't care about anything other than training their voices in song. But wait awhile. If we wish to discover who took Dr Gurney, you must seek to think as he thought. Then you will know what his captors want from him.'

I sat down, but my lips remained firmly downturned and my cheeks taut. 'Well?'

'Ficino, the great Ficino, wrote of the immortality of the soul. Life and existence beyond death.'

'Heaven?' I asked. 'Hell?'

Dee shrugged. His eyes drifted towards the locked door. He seemed to weigh something up, before gripping the edges of his desk and standing. 'Come.' I followed him as he moved towards it, fishing out a string of keys from a hidden pocket in his sleeve as he went. He turned each of the locks before pushing the door wide. No light stirred beyond it and he made no move to enter. 'Go on,' he prodded.

I hesitated.

Don't go in there.
And then I stepped over the threshold and into darkness.

***

The door banged behind me. Total darkness pressed in from every side. A dry rattle told me that Dee had not locked me in alone but joined me. I did not move but tensed, ready to punch, to cry out.

'We are all as little children, lost in the dark. We seek not only light, but the means to give us light.'

I started at the sound of his voice. I thought it might have lost a little of its grandfatherly warmth – but told myself that that was merely my sudden fear. It was not making me hear things but stopping me from hearing them.

What is this place?

A spark. Another. The birth of a flame.

Dee had produced a tinderbox and lit a candle. It illuminated only his chin and lower face, sending wavering shadows around his eyes. He turned from me and began lighting others. Gradually, the chamber came to life.

Of a sort.

It was not a large space and it had evidently been designed for secrecy. Its single window was covered tightly with cloth. On shelves were more scientific instruments, which looked like they might be based on ancient designs. Ornamented staffs carved with strange designs stood against the walls. And on top of a closed cupboard rested the top portion of a human skull.

Dee moved towards that cupboard and opened it. As he did so, I moved away, towards the walls. They were decorated in maps – things I had only the faintest familiarity with. What they depicted I couldn't say. Other things were nailed up too – sheets of paper with bizarre symbols drawn up on them. It was like being inside the mind of a madman. Or a genius.

'All volumes,' said Dee, standing back to show the contents of his cupboard, 'of the *Theologia Platonica de immortalitate animae*. And each of the *De vita libri tres*. The three books of life.'

'Books of life?' My voice came out a distant echo, despite the small room.

'The first on health. The second on stretching the life. The third on the influence of the celestial spheres. Ficino understood that our actions each have consequences. He and Paracelsus spoke of the

72

macrocosm – that is the world – and the microcosm – that is you. And me. And each man and woman. Paracelsus saw farther than the ancients, than Galen and his four humours. I have here his *Astronomia Magna* and his *de Peste*. I lack Ficino's *On the Immortality of the Soul*, alas.' I could smell Dee's breath as he moved towards me. It was faintly sweet, like almonds. 'I had many more. They were lost to me when my library at Mortlake was sacked by ignorant vagabonds whilst I travelled abroad – saw witchcraft in science, the fools.

'You wish to know what Dr Gurney and I discussed, young Mr Savage? I shall tell you. We discussed the harmony of mankind with the greater world. The unity of the microcosm and macrocosm. The perfect state of this world. And what happens when that harmony is disrupted. Dr Gurney believed, as I do, in three humours of the body. Disease comes when one falls out of balance with the other two. The parts of our bodies, the organs, function as an alchemist functions, separating purities from impurities. We each have certain minerals in our bodies – special stuffs – which must be balanced. But what causes imbalance? And how do we fix it?'

Dee turned back into the room and went to his cupboard and for a moment I had only the impression of his tall, black back. Then he swivelled and began shuffling towards me again. 'I have something for you, my boy.'

Breathing heavily, I held out my hand, palm upwards.

A flash, the candles wavering.

And pain seared through my palm.

'Ow! Stop it!'

'Ho! Ho!' Dee chuckled, before returning to put back the thin rod he had caned me with. 'Such mewling. There is a word for such soft men as you.'

'I'm sure there are many. And worse than you're thinking.'

He laughed again. 'Were you never given correction as a lad, and harder than that?'

'Just fucking stop hitting me!'

'Ho!' He shook his head. 'Merely a demonstration. You are hurt?'

I rubbed my hand where, for the second time, the bastard had struck me. 'If you do that again, I will strike you back, sir. That I promise.'

'You would hit an old man?' He put his hand to his heart. 'Let me see.' I folded my hand into my armpit and gave my chin to him in defiance. 'The pain will go. Yet it is there, I think, now. You see, I am an outside agent. Do you understand? The plague acts as I did. It comes from outside. Whether from God outside the spheres that make up our universe or the foul airs that send the little universes of our bodies out of balance. My striking you is a small matter. The plague striking us is a bigger matter. The world grows unbalanced. Whether by the death of the late queen or ... I cannot say.'

'This is what you and Dr Gurney discussed?'

'Many things. We cannot say what causes the plague. Yet we can speak of the minerals one might use to cure it. To send the organs and the three humours back into perfect balance. Dr Gurney is interested in the properties of alchemical substances. Whether they might cure or cause illnesses of the mind and body.'

I considered this. And, in doing so, one word came into my head. *Poison.*

I did not give voice to it, but I wondered what the missing doctor might be up to with his captors. Instead, I said, 'And these substances – they effect cures?' I paused for a moment. 'So that a man, if he has a plague, or an ague, or an unnatural lust, he might take them as physick? That manner of thing?'

Dee gave me a long, measuring look. 'That is the theory.'

I hurried on. 'Illnesses of the mind. Dr Gurney spoke of visions. He said, "of these visions I know nothing".'

'Yes. Yes, he mentioned in his writing to me that the woman patient pleaded with him for knowledge of visions. Their causes. I own I have a special interest in such matters. In disproving the false ones, you understand.'

'And ... how do you know which are false?'

'Why,' said Dee, looking over my shoulder at the door, 'by inviting true ones to reveal the deceit of those who would trick us. Visions, you see, are claimed by four people. The mad, for one. Those who practice deceit and falsity. And those blessed with the gift of that special sight.' Silence fell between us.

'And the fourth?'

He blew out a long, dusty breath, and for a moment he appeared a very aged man in the guttering candlelight. 'The fourth. The man who devotes much study and the application of needful items to inviting such mysteries. To the art of scrying. Though I prefer to think of it as the science optical.' He went again to the cupboard, but this time he closed the door on the books and lifted the skull. From the hollow brain-chamber, he lifted something before replacing the eyeless bone and returning to me. The thing winked blue and purple. A crystal or glass orb set in silver and hanging on a silver chain.

'What do you know of death, Mr Savage?

'I ... I know that I will die.' I put a hand on my hip. 'And probably it will hurt like a bastard.'

'You counterfeit bravado. You know nothing of the beyond. And none know the true nature of the soul. Does it live beyond death or die with the body? Does it transform? Does it seek its celestial home?' His hand, holding the end of the chain, became a lumpen fist.

'What is it?'

'It is a little world in itself. This sphere is a microcosm. You understand the composition of our universe?' I let my silence declare myself a novice, having received only the most basic sense of the earth as a globe within a world of heavenly bodies. 'Imagine the great burning sun. Now imagine it sitting at the centre of a sphere. On the circumference that sphere, and moving in circles on it, is Mercury. And it sits within an even larger sphere, on which moves Venus. And it within a sphere larger still, on the circumference of which our planet moves. And so on, balls within balls, ever larger, always turning and revolving but fixed in their movements. There are eight of these spheres. Numbers, you see? And beyond the spheres...?'

'Heaven?'

'The endless void, in which God moves, and the stars rise infinitely up. The great sphere of spheres sits in this expanse of Godly nothing, as it were floating in a vast and black sea. As this little ball,' he added, jerking the silver chain, 'floats in this dark room, moved and watched by such as we, containing its own worlds in itself.'

I looked at it, imagining myself a bird, flying up and out of the room, into the sky, breaching our sphere, and the next, and the rest, until I flew up into the endless void and found ... what? God – an old man holding what I had emerged from on the end of a string, twirling it endlessly through the darkness? I felt pinpricks, this time along my arms.

Forbidden knowledge, like your wicked and lustful knowledge of man.

Dee held the thing up between us, letting in swing slowly. 'I speak now,' he said slowly and clearly, 'to those who dwell in the outer spheres. Do you hear me?'

Nothing.

'Is there any angel inscribed in this stone?'

Silence.

'Anael – do you hear me?'

I looked into the crystal, squinting hard. In truth, I saw nothing but the minor imperfections deep within the stone. 'I see nothing,' I whispered.

Dee did not answer me. 'Ah. Ahh. Ahhh. You speak of Angela.'

The hairs on the nape of my neck tickled up beneath my ruff. Chilly fingers danced their way down my spine. 'Angela,' I echoed, still barely above a breath.

'Fire and water. A final dissolution. Another wonderful, horrible alteration of the world.'

'Stop,' I said. 'I see nothing. There is nothing.'

Dee froze. His eyes, I saw, had rolled back in his head and they returned. Blinked. He shook his head. 'Angela,' he said, raising a bushy eyebrow. 'Who is Angela?'

'I don't know.' I turned on my heel and fled the room, scrabbling at the door and emerging back into the warmth of sunlight. The crown of my hat smacked into the lintel; it lifted up from my brow and nearly fell off. Behind me, I heard Dee fussing about, presumably replacing his mystical orb back in its equally orbital hiding place.

When he came back to me, I was standing by his desk, straightening my coat. 'Did you,' he asked, 'understand anything in that? The woman's name … an Italian name … fire and a horrible alteration. Water.'

'Nothing whatsoever.'

He came to me, closing the door behind him but not locking it, and put a bony hand on my shoulder. 'Still … if it gains in significance … you will tell the secretary of my aid? Of the wonders that might still be achieved in understanding the order of the universe?'

'Yes,' I said, smiling and fixing my hat properly back on my head. 'If you will allow me to leave this place without beating me once more.'

'Ho! I assure you of that. You are welcome to stay the night. We might divine more.'

'No.' I was suddenly eager to be gone. I patted his hand and looked into his grey eyes. I thought again of my father. 'I thank you, sir, but with your leave … do your maps show the fastest route to Derbyshire?'

'You need no maps for that, my boy.' He told me the road to take out of Manchester, gesturing with his finger as though a map hovered in the air before us.

'Then I thank you again.' I gave him a formal bow and began walking towards the door out of the outer chamber.

'Wait.' I froze, turning slowly. 'You might look into the men who trade in the arts scientific in London. It might be that Dr Gurney was not the only fellow these strange patients troubled. In fact, I should say assuredly not. Look for those who claim such rare knowledge of how to speak with the dead. They may know where these people dwell … seek out the secretive men of London. Not the divines, not the physicians, but those who sell their knowledge like painted whores. Or practice deceit, rather. Find this Angela and those she and her fellow traveller have meddled with and you will find my friend. And do give my best to his wife. God go with you, Adam.'

'What?!'

'I said God go with you, Edward Savage.'

I nearly tripped in my haste to be out of his presence, brushing off the quivering chaplain who awaited me in the hall.

It was only when I was well away from the warden's house, walking my horse from the green and hidden in the shadow of the great cathedral itself, that I slipped off my hat, tipped it upside down, and removed the letters I had stolen from Dee's desk and hidden inside the crown. I read quickly through clouds of smoke that blossomed from the pipe I'd stuck in my mouth.

And there it was, in the same tiny script that had appeared in Gurney's commonplace book.

'The woman now calls herself Angela and I connect such a fancy with the famed prophetess of Foligno. Does the changing of a name signify madness *viz* is the desire to change the outer a mark of a shift of the inward mind?'

The old fraud, I thought. So much for Gurney hiding behind ethics to protect the identity of his patient. Dee had tried to cozen me, hiding his knowledge of the woman only to reveal it through his conjuring trick. One last attempt to get me to intercede with Cecil on his behalf. I had, I felt, borne witness to something like an old – a very old – player recounting as many lines from as many plays as he could remember to try and convince an acting company to welcome him back aboard.

And yet … and yet … there was nothing in the letters about fire, water, or an attempt to bring about a horrible change. And had he really said my old name or had I somehow misheard. And if he had…

Guesswork?

I decided that, if anything of the rest of the strange prophecy, loose as it was, proved true, I would commend Dr Dee. After all, despite his penchant for beating me, I still rather liked the old goat. God knew I was not a man to judge a little deceit. His guidance in seeking out the seers of London – the scum of London, as far as I was concerned, having lived and learned with tricksters and gypsies when I had first arrived – might also be useful. It was something to chase, anyway, upon my return. I knew where they lodged and raved because I took care to avoid them. I did not discount cunning men and women entirely but neither did I tangle myself up with them, reasoning that if any one of them should have the magic eye, they might see things in me that they might use against me. Yet, because he was a theatregoer, I knew exactly the man who enjoyed fame as the city's finest seer in the arts of astrology.

Leading my horse to a low wall from which I could mount, I prepared to follow the old man's directions towards Derbyshire.

8

I have a broad mouth. Not physically, course – it's a very fair size and well-proportioned in fact – but in its propensity for speaking hot words. So it was that I had last left my natural brother and his wife on the worst of terms, vowing to myself that I was finally free of the pack of them.

And yet here you are.

I stared at the plain marble tomb – a sarcophagus, really, built into the west end of the north aisle. It read, with some of the carved letters fresher than their fellows:

Here lyeth the bodies of Adam Norton, sometime of this parish, gentleman and Jane his wife: which said Adam left the land and inheritance of NORFIELD to his only begotten son, Thomas. Also he hath given to the village of NORFIELD ten pounds to put poor children to prentice: which said Adam departed this life in the year of our Lord God, 1604.

Their only begotten son, I thought. My brother, Thomas. I had been disowned and worse: erased from the history of the family for my refusal to wed Ann, the childhood friend who had gone on to marry my dutiful younger brother. I had not seen my mother since my flight to London several years before. She had died some time before my father, whom I had last seen ranting and raving in the madness of his age shortly before the queen's death. Then he had repeated his opinion of me: that I was a disgusting and perverted creature, given to twisted lusts and vices.

And he was hardly wrong.

In truth, I had lost any sense of time, and I cannot say how long I stood beside the tomb. I had no clear idea of why I had come. My plan had been to offer my sympathies to Ann – and perhaps, I suppose, to make amends. With the old man gone, I saw no reason why I might not repair relations with the people I had once loved, even if they need play no role in my life.

And … and … I wished Thomas to know that I was not a simple criminal working in the dark and filthy world of the London stage-writes. I wished him instead to realise that, regardless of how superior he might feel, I was a man who had met with a king and who was admitted into the secrets and mysteries of the state. A man of credit in the great city. I had even dressed for the occasion – out of the black weeds I had worn in Manchester, I was in my best suit of colourful, bombast-filled sleeves and breeches, a good falling band, and a doublet with a silk flower. It was out of fashion, to be sure, but none in the country would know that. It was a petty thing, I admit freely.

I put my hand out and touched the frigid marble, but I said nothing. I had long held that whatever I was, the pair in the tomb must somehow have made me. If I was disbalanced – and whether my body was composed of three humours or four – then it was an imbalance that had troubled me since before I was old enough to know better.

I turned away, my boots clopping on the dirty stone floor. Odd, I thought. I had always known the place to be kept up. The tiny parish church, more familiar than my own hand (for it had not been beaten by an old man), was innocent of its master and even its wardens had not challenged me on my approach. Nor had anyone rung the bells, from what I had heard. It was cold, too. As I left, I wondered how long the tomb would last in such a church. Would men in a hundred years speak of my mother and father and make them live again in others' ears, as Dee had spoken of Cardinal Wolsey and the elder Cecil and thereby conjured them into the room between us?

Stepping outside, my breath misted. Above me a stained woollen sky issued oddly aimless specks of snow. An inquisitive wind jabbed at my silks as I returned to the horse I had tethered at the gate of the church and began leading it deeper into the little town. My goal was to strike off on the path which led to my old family's home, and yet something made me drag my feet.

A warming of courage.

I took the horse to the ostler at the local tavern, paid him to watch her, crossed the barren yard and stepped inside. Low rafters hung over a broad, empty square hall, its floor stinking with old, soiled rushes.

The Three Cranes looks like a fine palace of a place now.

A bench lay against one wall, a couple of men lounging on it with outstretched legs as the tapster, across the room, worked at opening a barrel. On seeing me, the three heads turned, and I felt the chill of suspicion. No one recognised me, of course – and nor did I recognise them. Each wore the surly expression shared by every countryman I had seen in every place outside London. It said, 'you are an outlander and you are here to rob us and seduce our women.'

I ignored the men on the bench, ignored the scoffing sound the older one made as I strode by, and made for the tapster. I ordered a mug of small beer and he grunted his assent, holding out his hand for the money before dipping a mug in the barrel and thrusting it at me. He warranted no thanks, and so I took the mug without giving it. 'Give it back when yer done,' he said.

Turning my back on him, I sipped. 'So, he'll get it tonight fer sure?' asked one of the men on the bench – the younger of the pair, I noticed. His fellow elbowed him. 'What d'ye do that fer?' The elder mouthed something at him, his eyes on me. On my clothing, rather. I downed my drink, uninterested in whatever petty scheme occupied the minds of country bumpkins. Poaching, probably. To them, I must appear a courtier down from London – a king's man, perhaps, who bore them no good will. It only struck me then that there ought to have been more people in the tavern – in the church – around the loose string of thatched cottages and shops which made up the village.

I wondered if the Bills of Mortality took any notice of those who had died in the country.

With that thought, I set my empty mug on the floor and left, retrieving my horse and striking out through the woods. The old house I had known from childhood was gone but the woods had remained unchanged. I am no great lover of forests and yet I confess to a secret love of the wooded lands around Norfield. The path runs between clumps of old trees whose branches make of it a tunnel, and on sunny days the setting sun lies at the far end, towards the estate, shining over a low rise so that it feels like you're walking into light.

But not today. Today, the bare branches made a skeletal welcoming canopy, the path was churned in varying states of brown, and the undergrowth was choking. I followed the path over the rise and round its bends and turns, eventually passing the scarred land where the old house had stood. Its replacement grew ahead of me: a double-winged home with a recessed front porch, of the type beloved of the gentry. Ostentatious, I thought – lacking in class.

Activity in the stables beyond paused me, and a mounted rider emerged, passing the front of the house and coming towards me. I pulled my own horse in to the side as a man in clerical black rode by, touching his hat to me as he went.

That solves the mystery of the missing parson. Secretive fellow.

I went to the stables myself and found no groom – and I certainly lacked the confidence to begin shouting for one. It is a strange thing – being in a place connected with childhood, even if it has been changed beyond recognition, can make a child of one. Norfield Manor was not the old Norfield Hall, and yet Norfield was Norfield and I was an empty-headed brat whenever I was here, scrambling about in the woods, playing at pirates and burying treasures, taking beatings from my tutors, and listening to my mother's voice.

I tethered the horse in a stall myself, let her nuzzle my hand a while, enjoying the steam of her breath, and then forced myself back out. I crunched over gravel and went to the door of the house. Raised my hand. Let it fall in hesitation. Knocked.

Nothing.

There's something not right here.

I turned and made to leave, hesitating again. So it was that when the front door opened, I was caught out in a stuttering half-step, my back to the door. 'Adam?' said a voice I recognised as my brother. I turned to find a face I did not.

My brother, Thomas, is a long-faced, chinless fellow, lacking in vigour. Or, at least, that was how I had, in my resentment through the years, imagined him. He seemed now to have grown into the creature of my imagination. He had lost weight, loose skin hanging jowly from his neck. His eyes were red-rimmed. If I didn't know better, I would have thought him a drunk. 'Thomas?'

'Why are you here?' His voice was husky. 'Come to claim the place through Chancery?'

I frowned, crossing my arms. 'I've told you before, I will have none of this place.'

'Then why are you here again?'

My chest rose. 'I wished to see Ann. I heard about the old man. From my friends at court.'

He sniffed, his eyes roving over me. 'Ann is unwell.'

I had begun moving towards him and the words stopped me. The last time I had seen her, she had been pregnant. The child must by now have been born. If she was unwell … I looked again at him.

Plague. Run.

I skittered over the gravel towards him, pushing past and stepping into the shadows of the porch. He made no effort to stop me. 'Ann,' I cried as I flew into the entrance hall. 'Ann?' Receiving no response, I turned back to the front door. Thomas lurched through it, closing it behind him. 'Where is she? Where is everyone?'

He opened his mouth to speak, but a sobbing sound shut it. It came from upstairs, and I immediately began climbing the staircase. 'Stop,' said Thomas, some strength coming into his voice at last. 'This is no house of yours.'

'Ann?' I shouted again. I followed the sobbing down a tapestried hall and opened a door, turning my head around to find the source.

And there she was, sitting on a settle, very unpregnant and almost lost in the depths of her black velvets. A small ruff seemed to be the only thing holding her head upright. 'Ann,' I said, relief washing into my voice. 'I thought you might have ...'

Oh.

I stopped, halfway across the room to her. Only then did she seem to realise my presence and look at me. 'The baby,' I said, the words mere breath. Suddenly it made sense. The parson, the quietness of the house. Norfield Manor was a place of mourning, but not for my father.

Another sob erupted from her.

'You've upset her.' Thomas's voice, behind me, made me jump. 'I'll be rid of him soon, Mrs Norton.' He gave her a formal little bow, as though he were a stranger. 'Go away, Adam. If you've come here to see what you might inherit with no heir living to us ... do it through the courts.'

'His name isn't Adam anymore,' said Ann. She groaned as she rose from the settle. 'It's ... what is it?'

'Edward,' I said. 'Ned. Ned Savage.' She gave me a wan smile. Thomas, on the other side, snorted. I felt caught between them – and caught between reaching out to pat at Anne with one hand and slapping my quondam brother across the face with the other.

'Ned Savage Norton, then,' she said.

'What?' barked Thomas. 'Have you forgotten what he said the last time he was here, woman? What he said when the child was in the womb? His wicked words? A curse indeed, it was – witchcraft!'

I had not forgotten them. I had told them that the name Norton was cursed and foul and I was well shot of it. Further, I had said that whatever foul affliction blighted me, swaying me towards strange lusts, it was a taint in the blood as like to be inherited by the child in her belly. And I could never, ever make them unheard. I said nothing, longing only to run.

'Be silent,' she said. She was a small woman but fierce in her rich black.

'But I – he comes here, again, to cause us trouble, dressed like a court strumpet in his French shirt and padded breech–'

'Holland,' I snapped, raising a hand to the lacy white falling band which was easier to ride in and richer looking than a ruff.

'Be silent, husband. He is your brother.' I smiled in triumph, looking at Thomas. 'And you too, Ad- Ned.' She drew a handkerchief from the lace at her cuff and dabbed her eyes. 'You are children, both of you. There has been grief enough in this house without you two making more. Ned, you will observe we lost our boy. It is the fate of little children to be ... to not always be long in this world. At their starting.' The words caught in a hiccup in her throat. 'As the parson says, it is God's will and we must let the word of the Lord be our comfort and light.'

Parsons, I thought. Fucking useless.

Humbled, Thomas and I stood in silence whilst Ann moved towards us. She took her husband by the arm. 'We have a guest. Ned, the servants have ... some of the servants have been lost to us. The pestilence has been hard.'

'Hmph. Dead or fled. The scum of the county,' growled Thomas.

'Yet you might stay.' Thomas bristled and she went on, raising her voice. 'It must be late. Grey becomes greyer here. Your father's old room is not used. The bed remains there. Perhaps you would like to rest and ... we might then all speak in the morning.' She gave Thomas's arm a little shake. 'Your brother comes from London. He has friends there. Perhaps ... perhaps he can help us.'

'Stay...' Muttered Thomas. 'In this house.'

'Yes,' clipped Ann.

'Help?' I asked.

'In the morning. Yes, husband?'

'Hmph. Our troubles are not his troubles.'

Troubles? What has the new master of the house got himself into?

'Ay. Maybe. Help us in London.'

She led him out of the room, and I followed, feeling small, and allowed myself to be shown to the small chamber in which, apparently, my father had been confined when his mind had started to wander. Ann beckoned me inside, bid me sleep well, and closed me in. A solid bedframe with a good mattress stood in the room, though its hangings were gone. The frame itself, I noticed, had claw marks on it. Leather restraints trailed like dead eels from the middle and bottom. A slight smell of urine soured the air, despite the spicy dead herbs which had deposited flecks of black from a bowl to the shelf on which it stood. Traces of his presence, I thought. They lingered despite his death, ghostly and unpleasant. I wished my father's ghost, if such things as ghosts existed, to see that I had won.

When our souls go to the void beyond the spheres, do we leave such traces? Can we be brought back?

I cursed John Dee, and Leonard Gurney, and the people who had taken the doctor. I forced the bizarre and heretical thoughts they had driven into my head back out as I stripped down to my shirt and lay on the bed. When man died, he went to God and was judged and that was that. Knowing or asking any more was dangerous. It risked accusations of witchcraft or heresy and it might drive you mad with cares.

Instead, I tried to enjoy my triumph, such as it was. As the light faded through the barred window, I considered that my father was dead and gone – just gone – and yet I imagined what he, and my mother too, would think if they could see me now, in the grand new house they had built.

They had scolded me. Been disgusted by me. In truth, I think they had come to hate me and wished to erase my existence from the world. And yet, here I was, in my father's old bed. In the most pathetic of senses, I had won. Victory, I supposed, should be tonic enough to help me into the little void of sleep.

And I was partway there, my mouth sticky and drool beginning on my chin, when a rending crash yanked me back into the world. 'Wha'?' I asked no one.

The door to my chamber opened and I drew my knees up primly. 'Ned,' said Ann. A candle lit her face, and, in its pool, I could see Thomas, his eyes wide. 'Please help us. We are being attacked. I think they mean to kill us all.'

I leapt from the bed and began digging through my pack until I found the dagger I carried on the road. Skirting husband and wife, I went out into the hall and listened. Voices drifted up from downstairs. Cursing. Some laughter. I felt along the wall until my hand met a sconce and I removed the torch from it, returning to Ann to get a light from her candle.

With it in hand, I descended the stairs two at a time.

Movement.

I crept along, the voices growing louder, until black shapes resolved into the outlines of men. There was no sense in trying to hide; my torch gave me away. ''ere comes one of 'em,' bellowed the larger of the shapes.

'What is this?' I asked. 'Who are you? What do you mean by this?'

My answer came swiftly. In the form of a meaty fist slamming into my chin. As I fell, the torch flared and died.

9

The journey home from Italy is long and full of terrors. Sea spray stings his skin as he stands at the low railing on the deck. Sailors' voices rise in song above the waves.

But the air turns sour.

Their song changes in pitch, rising, becoming shouts of alarm. He crosses the deck and looks out over the water. A smaller craft is cutting a path towards them, French dolphins dancing and tumbling in its wake.

He tries to hide as the new craft assails them. The word 'pirates' reaches him. It is not good. There is nowhere to hide on a ship. The pirates know this and search, discovering each Englishman. In rough, Flemish voices, they demand to know whose ship they have seized. Only the fame of his master's name and title preserves him and the others. As the plunderers claim the ship, as they strip him and his fellow Englishmen – even the great earl, his master – down to their shirtsleeves – he hears the voice of Flavia and sees her, her beautiful face leaning from the bulkheads and staring from the sails. She reaches out, as she had done from the painting in which he had first seen her. She gives him strength with encouraging words, and she threatens him with horrors. Like the others who appear to him, she is never stable in her speech, but mixes fair words with foul. He does not know if the voices and faces which only he can see are friends or unfriends.

He is kicked, and beaten, and mocked, and even the earl joins in in condemning him as a fond fool for listening to and answering Flavia, whom they will not see. When they make it back to England he flees and falls into darkness. In the secret places of London, he is used and sold, and his airy visitors come often. But only to mock and to warn him that conspiracies against him lurk, and that he must trust no one and that perhaps he should kill himself. The days are dark and long, and he does not wish to look upon them. Through the mercy of Christ, he is found and returned to his master's service. He goes willingly, with a burden of shame on his back to match the earl's shame at meddling with one of the queen's ladies.

But no matter. He is at home in service, a page turned gentleman. And it is indeed an England of rising power. In London's dunghills the green stage poets are just beginning to sprout, their honey sweet perfume still rude. Marriage is the talk of the day – how the queen is to marry a frog, who comes hopping across the Channel to puff life into her sunken cheeks. And, as he is a man now, his mind turns on marriage too.

Her name is Margery and she serves the earl's lady – the countess whom the earl himself detests most wickedly. But that does not matter to the boy – the man. His name is Hope and it is a good name for a marriage. Although the queen does not wed, and though her frog hops away to the Netherlands, the young couple does, and there are double Hopes. Life blooms in Margery's face and in her belly. She does not mind his strange speaking, which he tries hard to control, nor his constant fears. A married man, he thinks, should not speak with unseen forces but only with his true wedded wife. At the earl's insistence, he takes physick to control the stuttering waves of visitation.

For a while, the people who are not people – the angels, he has begun to see them as – still. He works for the earl again and it seems that all might be well. Margery is with child once, twice. And the babes are born whole and healthy and it seems they will live, with God's grace.

Until the plague visits.

Then, he feels the burning. The sickness. The rising swell of buboes. And then Margery has it.

And then the two boys have it.

They are all shut away then, in a single room in Aldgate paid for by his master, and left to die. The earl does not wish to retain servants who carry the infection, of course, and certainly he does not wish them spoiling the good country airs at Wivenhoe. The husband and father hopes that death will be quick in snuffing out the burning, twisting pains; the man who once spoke with angels and had breathed the sweet airs of Italy and married a woman for love is ready for it.

Yet, when death comes, he takes only Margery and the children. Hope is left alone again, his buboes bursting painfully but not killing him. The fever subsides. When he opens the door and cries into the street that he is not dead, by God, the people stay distant. He turns, expecting to see Margery and the dead boys restored, as he had been, but they will not waken.

Instead, the angels return, crying on him that his whore wife and bastards are dead and that he is chosen to live. Sometimes they say she was an angel herself, Margery, and gone to join them. He accepts this.

But, sometimes, he thinks things that the angels cannot hear. And he thinks, 'I will discover the meaning of this. One day I shall get them back from the place of the angels and devils.'

***

Nathaniel Hope bit into the stale bread which he had purchased from the vendor near St Paul's and munched as he moved into Paternoster Row, where a number of booksellers kept their stalls. It felt good to be out in the world after the confines of the *Crown Elizabeth*. Being shut away too long brought back unpleasant memories of the dark place with its beatings and taunts.

He turned on the spot, inhaling deeply of the outside air. Perhaps, he thought, he had not given the doctor enough for the fellow to understand how to ford the great river that separated life from death. The books he had procured for him were those he could recall the earl owning, but that had been many years before. No doubt the world of progress had marched on apace.

A pamphlet caught his eye and he swallowed, throwing the remainder of the bread back into the street for urchins or rats to scramble for.

'A penny,' said the seller, a man with yellow teeth and a great beard stained with tobacco. 'Very new, very good, very cheap.' Hope cocked his head. The title read of the slim volume was *The Passage Of Our Most Drad Soveraigne Lady Quene Elyzabeth Through The Citie Of London Westminster The Daye Before Her Coronacion.*

Elizabeth?

'The queen is dead,' said Hope.

The seller looked at him through narrowed eyes. 'I know that, mate. But folks want to read about her coming to t'crown,' he wiped a streaming nose with his sleeve, 'afore the new king and queen do t'same. The coronation, mate. Ain't that why yer in London? Now the plague's abatin', the town'll fill up again and you'll be glad you bought now.'

'I …'

'Come on, mate – a penny. And the great Elizabeth'll live again for ye.'

At those words, Hope began scrabbling at the purse at his belt. 'Give it to me!'

He moved away from the seller, and from Paternoster Row, with his new find. The square of St Paul's, paved with stones from the chapels and chantries which Henry VIII had set to be destroyed, was populated by groups of people. The groups seemed to be keeping well apart as they hurried about their business.

A voice at his sleeve spoke. 'Nathaniel.' He swivelled and saw nothing.

And then, there she was.

Queen Elizabeth restored to life.

She was not near him, as she had sounded, but moving amongst the people. They took no notice of her. She was a woman of middle age, with a long face, wearing a shimmering gown of cloth-of-gold. She looked, in fact, as she had when Hope had last seen her at court, after the earl's friend Raleigh had ensured that the fallen favourite had been forgiven his seduction of a lady-in-waiting and was once again able to be received there with his train. All that was strange was that the pearls in her hair and the gold on her dress did not glisten in the light; instead they looked flat, as though she remained truly on the celestial plane.

Hope fell to one knee in the gutter.

People laughed. Something hit him in the shoulder. He ignored it.

'Your Majesty.'

'Off your knees.' Her voice was harsh, edged with steel and dancing with malice.

He rose and looked upon her. 'I thought your Majesty dead.'

'Dead, ha!' She looked right back at him, staring down her high-bridged nose. 'I live. We have lost our earthly crown and thereby gained a heavenly one. You are being watched, Nathaniel Hope, always watched. You must trust no one but your faithful friends.' Hope looked up, into the queen's face. There was something wrong in it, as there always was in the faces of the angels. It was as though snakes writhed behind the skin. 'You must conquer death, man.'

'Yes, your Majesty. I do try.'

'Try harder! You are sworn to kill one of your own. You must do it. And we will return them to you if your faith is strong. You must kill as many as we will you to, to light the path forward. Let your loved ones be as torches showing the way to salvation. Life eternal comes through death.'

'Vita in morte sumus,' he said. He had heard instructions that he kill his followers before. When? Yes, when the doctor had told him he could not speak to the dead. And yet here was a dead woman, a queen, speaking with him.

Elizabeth repeated it. 'I am but a shadow until this is done. What is this pamphlet?' Her black-eyed gaze had dropped to his hand. He held it up. 'Ha! It is an old thing printed anew. You know this. You have seen this before. The coronation. It is a ceremony of life-giving, of baptism into the higher world of divinity. We are wetted and blessed and come to live forever. I regret that a coronation must mean death in order to bring new life. You see that pamphlet? I live. I go on. And life comes through death.'

Hope thought he understood. 'The coronation is key. But ... the king is crowned.'

'Crowned but not yet crowned. Only a part of the great ceremony has passed. The rest is still to come, as the bookseller told you. When Scotch James comes through this city, this city of the dead, you must be ready. You must by then understand the sacrifice which must be made to bring perfect knowledge of the angels. Go to, Nathaniel Hope. Study and use your doctor. Slay your brethren and we shall return them. If,' she said again, 'you love us, and your faith is true.'

'I will, your Majesty.' Hope bowed again, and when he raised his head, Elizabeth had gone.

Excitement pulsed in his veins and he began turning again, looking around. People had stopped, their backs to the grey stone buildings, and were gawping at him. The queen was right – he must be always alert to the prying eyes of the wicked and unenlightened. A fat woman in the striped petticoats of a prostitute hitched them up to her knees and cackled, 'I'll be yer Majesty for ye, mister. For a price.' He scowled and turned his head. 'Mad bastard,' she shrieked, as he scurried away and through the tunnel-like streets southwards for Queenhithe.

As shadows swallowed him, the golden chain links between the deaths of sovereigns and eternal life shone in his mind, the light reflecting off them making them indistinct.

The heaviness of wet mud and dead fish rose up from the water as he picked his way amongst rotting ropes, making for the ship graveyard with its monuments of broken masts and spiderweb rigging. The *Crown Elizabeth* stood as it always did, dark and dying. She would never see the open sea again, he thought. Or would she? Would she return to life too?

Before he could climb the warped planking that led to her upper deck from the jetty, he heard his name called again. Turning, he did not see the queen's angel, but Angela. Like him, she was dressed in out-going clothes – for her the plain grey and white gown of a serving woman. He had decided that they must preserve their simple robes for the ship, on realising that they might attract accusations of popery.

One of her arms was raised in benedictive salute.

'I have them,' she said. Her face was flushed, her golden hair a joyful tumble. Love swelled in his heart – not the sensual lusts he had once felt for his wife or even for the occasional beauty who crossed his path, but a pure, flaring love. And, he felt, her amber eyes returned it in full measure. 'The things the doctor requested, the herbs and physick-stuffs.'

'I love you,' he said. He had not meant to speak.

'I love you too,' she replied. 'I ... have the things, Nathaniel.'

He shook his head to clear it and thoughts tumbled around like passengers in a falling carriage. 'You had no trouble?'

'No. The doctor's note was enough. Though I think the apothecary took me for a brainsick zany. He knew me of old. Such a goose look he gave me.'

Hope knew the look. He smiled, taking her hand. 'Our new boy,' he said, remembering. 'The cruel-mastered boy who lived after the plague. He is not with you?'

'No.' A frown threatened her, and he wished he had said nothing. 'I went to their house. In Shoe Lane. His sister and a young man stood before it. I ... I must find him alone.'

'Yes. Yes, there is time enough.' She beamed again, and their footsteps made rhythmic, hollow *thrick, thrick, thrick* sounds on the bare and buckling boards as they climbed aboard the derelict. Taking a short ladder, they descended through the great hatch opening and into the largest part of the ship – a space which had once held all the guns and whose interior wooden walls had also long since been stripped away. There, on the main deck which ran from port to starboard, slept, ate, and prayed the Enlightened. At the sight of Hope they rose as one and smiled, waiting. One of them, an old woman whom Angela had brought from the City, where she had apparently been running to madness, cackling in the doorway of her dead family, had to be helped. She giggled as she was raised to her feet, and Hope wondered at the wisdom of bringing such a creature. He stifled the wicked thought. The old woman was a survivor of the plague – she had been touched by it and lived – she was chosen, as he was, and Angela, and Amos, and the rest.

Love swelled again, like water set to boil in a cauldron.

He bit back the words, and said instead, 'I must have one of you. It is commanded. I have been visited by an angel. The spirit of the late queen who promises life immortal for one brave enough to taste it.' He remembered the pamphlet, still tucked under his arm, and he let it fall to the deck. 'We have all been spared once. The plague could not touch us. Now we will defy death again.'

Amos stepped forward, leading a stout man by the hand. 'This fellow I found,' he said. 'He was once a follower of the Roman religion. Now he sees the light.'

Hope set his head on one side and regarded the man as he stepped into a circle of light admitted by a porthole. Doubt threatened. Was he putting too hard a construction on the queen-angel's words?

No. It thundered in his head, in her voice. Another, more querulous voice chimed in with 'kill yourself,' but he ignored it.

'Brother,' he said. 'Will you take this journey with us?'

'I ... I will.' He cast a nervous glance at Amos, who nodded, and then he repeated the chant of the Enlightened.

'You,' he said, addressing himself with Amos and battling the dislike that tainted his soul, 'have done well.' His brother only nodded.

'He is only here because he is fucking Angela', screeched a voice from nowhere. He closed his mind to it, determined to drown it out.

'Have you discovered any more of the cunning man in the city?' he asked. Amos's task for the day had been to enquire of the famed London magus whether he had any knowledge of the dead and, more importantly, whether he would join them as a fellow survivor and potential Enlightened one.

'Hmph. He speaks only by appointment, as though he were a true physician. And prefers women.' He spat. 'Angela would be welcomed.'

Hope considered this. 'Perhaps.' Then he turned to his newly Enlightened brother. 'What is your name?'

'I don't got a new one yet. Please, give me one. If it'll help me to ... to understand why I lived when my wife and daughter died.'

'Your name is Isaac.' A ripple of approval ran through the room. 'You do this for us all,' said Hope. 'Angela, Amos, you might come and bear witness. Dr Gurney will see also. He will see this fellow baptised into life everlasting. Anointed. Wetted and blessed to live forever, even in the grip of death.'

The four of them left, moving through the murky passageways of the *Crown Elizabeth* until they reached the doctor's cargo hold. Hope unlocked it and went in. As before, Gurney flattened himself against the far bulkhead.

Anger rose. Hope fought it back. The fool could not – would not – see. He thought the whole company mad, and him by repute a learned man, respected by the late queen and the earl. He swore, unaware of what he was saying.

When the fit of fury had gone, as quickly as it had arrived, he whispered to Amos to fetch a pail of water. His follower grinned, showing his missing teeth, and went to do as he'd been bid. 'Remember, Isaac, I love you. We all love you. The angel has told me of your reward: you are to be returned to us. As you were returned before from the brink. As we all were.' He turned his attention to Gurney, who had a pudgy hand up to his throat. 'You, doctor of divinity and learning. You will now kill this man.'

***

Gurney's mouth dropped open. 'I … what?'

'It is well,' said the man, Isaac. 'I'm blessed. Can't be touched.'

'Is this a jest?' Hope's face remained impassive. 'I have sworn an oath, sir, to harm no man or woman unless it should be to cure them.'

'And you will cure him, doctor. You will cure him of death. The miracle of all cures. Is this not the natural, the final, reward of the study of the medical arts? He will be brought back. He will suffer no pain but will look on death with smiling countenance.' Apparently unable to control himself, Hope grasped Isaac by the shoulders and embraced him. The human sacrifice, if that was what was intended, was wearing white monkish robes; the others, Gurney noticed, were dressed in forgettable street garments. It was as though, when hidden on the ship, they aped the communal dress of true faiths, and when they went abroad, they hid now as city folk. Curious. Strange. Frightening. It seemed a new form of madness. The madness of unquestioning belief. It was not faith, not worthy of the name – but an attachment to fancy and invention.

'I am held here against my will, sir. You told me to study and seek means of calling up the voices of the dead and receiving answers of them. I have told you, and I trust satisfied you, that it is impossible.' He stopped short of condemning them for seeking necromancy.

'That is not why you are here, it is not, it is not, it is *not*!'

Gurney shut his mouth. That had most certainly been the supposed reason for his captivity. Yet the prize of mad people, he knew, was amorphous and ill-defined – a moving target. Hope had instructed him to study hard and, with nothing else to pass the time, he had done just that. He had thought to thereby announce his lack of discovery, followed by his departure, and to see if the crazed creatures let him debark. And now this latest demand, born of their scattered wits.

Was this what Hope had planned all along? To have him kill rather than to have him read? Were the mad even capable of rational planning – or were their minds as autumn leaves, dropping thoughts at random into a messy pile of sludge?

'Did you get me my things?' he asked, hoping to turn the conversation away from its turn towards lunacy. 'I am here, as I understood, an enforced guest, to help you in certain matters of study. I should like to complete them and return to my wife.' At the word enforced, he noticed, the woman's lip curled, and he fixed his gaze on the unknown Isaac. The fellow wore the same slightly dazed look as the others.

'Here are your things,' said Angela. She crossed the cabin and set a twine-wrapped paper package atop his pile of old books. As she moved back to her fellows, the cabin door banged again and Amos reappeared, a sloshing bucket sending rivulets streaming down its sides and onto the bare deck. He set it down.

Hope pushed the stout man forward. 'Kill him, doctor. Do your worst.'

'No. I will not. No.'

'He defies us,' snapped Amos. 'I know this man of old. A court follower, a man of arrogance and pride. He has no faith.'

'Peace, Amos. Why do you deny us, Dr Gurney?'

The doctor did not reply. It was plain to him that reason and argument would mean nothing. 'I'll do it,' said Amos. 'I believe. I have faith. He'll see.'

Gurney shook his head. He had never liked his former patient, even before the madness of this new sect had infected him. Before, he had been as violent in his zeal for the Puritan cause. 'Yes,' said Hope. He then, Gurney noticed, seemed to hear some whispering in his ear and he threw up his hands as though pain gripped it. 'Fucking kill him now!' he screamed. 'They're watching us!'

All in the room started at the sudden show of fury. Gurney had not seen the leader of the sect angry before. It came upon him like a vice, tightening quickly and retreating. He chanced a look at the package of physick. And he wondered.

Movement tore his gaze back to the others. Amos had taken Isaac's arm and pushed him forward. With his other hand, he punched the man in the back, and he went to his knees, his white robes bunching and making a pool on the cargo hold's floor. The poor fellow did not resist. Instead, he put his arms out to either side, his fingers waggling. Like a man about to be tended by the headsman, thought Gurney. 'I am ready,' cried the condemned. 'Receive and return me. I am–'

His words were cut off by a darting motion as Amos forced his face into the water. The liquid rose, spilling over the side in a dark burlesque of Archimedes. 'Pray for him in your hearts!' cried Hope.

Burbling and gasping. *Garruuup! Glawp!*

Isaac's head broke the surface and he sucked volubly at the air.

Grunting, Amos forced him back under, crawling onto the back of his legs and putting his weight on the man's back. The pail itself bucked and wobbled.

'Stop this!' cried Gurney, stepping forward. He addressed himself to the man calling himself Amos. 'Harry, recover your senses, man!' Pain seared in his cheek as Angela slapped him. As he turned to her in surprise, Hope stepped around the pair on the deck – around the murder taking place on it – and pushed him against the wall. 'You said – you said you had to be a certain number! If this man dies you will be short!'

'He will be returned. If you are a true master of the world's mysteries, he will be returned. You will see.'

'This is madness! Me? What have I to do – stop this!'

The struggle on the deck began to quieten. Isaac's arms no longer flailed like landed fish. Still, Amos, his wolf-grin plastered across his narrow face, held the man's head down. He was breathing heavily, Gurney noticed – in apparent excitement. 'It is done,' he wheezed.

Released from Hope's grip, the doctor tripped his way over and kicked the bucket away. Bloody water washed across the wooden boards, seeking escape between the cracks and joins. Isaac's face slammed into the deck. 'Jesus. In the name of Jesus Christ,' Gurney whispered. 'What have you done?'

'Return him,' said Hope. He repeated it, more forcefully. 'Bring him back!' Unsure if he was being addressed, Gurney rolled Isaac over anyway.

The man was dead. He had bitten into his tongue and gnawed some on his lips. Bruising was already evident around his eyes and the rim of the bucket had given him a red-welt necklace. Still, the doctor beat on the man's chest and, forcing the mouth wide, thrust his fingers into the bloody hole and tickled the throat. It was useless, and he knew it.

'What is this?' asked Hope.

'He is dead, you – you twisted *mooncalf* – dead. Your brute slave here killed him.'

'He … he looks to be in pain. Why is he in pain, doctor? He went most willingly to meet death and would return to speak of the secrets he learnt whilst across the blackness.' Gurney did not respond. Instead, he looked up from his bended knees and gave Hope a look of what he trusted was disgust. It did not seem to register. The man looked amazed. Tears were starting up in his eyes. 'You are supposed to understand these matters of the body. Why the pain? He was blessed. He went willingly. Why did you let him die, doctor? You have failed. We must try again by some other means. We must get this right and satisfy the angels before the king's party progresses through the city. The coronation.' He looked up into the shadowed wood above. 'It must be then, indeed. It must be then that all who are not of the Enlightened will die the death.' His milky eyes returned to Gurney. 'And you must be truer in your heart. Your lack of faith killed my true brother. It will not rob us of our time to ascend.'

10

I reeled backwards, the spent torch falling, and my dagger flying in a thrust both outwards and upwards. Even through the sunburst that blossomed from the blow to my chin, a grunt told me that I had managed a glancing blow. A scream would have been better. An answering cry came from another shape.

Two of them.

I blinked, trying to bring vigour to my eyes. I slid backwards, away from the noisy men. Country louts, I thought. Unskilled and brutish, lacking the skilled criminality of London's ruffians. To fight a bull, you do as the Spanish do and lead it. I hissed for silence as I heard Thomas's voice behind me, his footfalls beating a tattoo on the stairs. When I met him, I gripped him by the arm and drew him into the blackness beside the staircase, the dagger hilt nestling in my palm, its blade another finger.

'Draw them,' I breathed.

Thomas made a sound of understanding.

Still, the two fellows were coming. Alarmingly, a blundering crash issued from beyond them, towards the front of the house. A window coming inwards, perhaps, from yet more of the creatures hidden outside. Excited barking rose from the distant kennels.

They could not see us, I realised, and thought we had gone to hide upstairs. 'Don't think it ain't right to be meddling with no woman's lost her babe.'

'Bit late fer them nice thoughts now, lad,' growled an older one.

It took me a few seconds to connect them with the pair I had noticed slouching in the tavern, discussing who was going to be getting it at night. Well, I had my answer to that question. Another rose to replace it: why?

'You go on back and let them others know we're in and've run 'em to ground, lad.'

The younger voice squeaked agreement and I could see his outline retreat. As I heard the first heavy *thunk* of the older one's boot on the first step – upwards and towards Ann – I slid away from Thomas.

A dim kind of light drifted weakly from upstairs, and I supposed she must have lit other torches up there. It drew a dark line about the house-breaker's body, giving me a clear view of a broad, black back. In a wink, I slithered around the newel post and, emerging behind him, snaked my arm around his neck, my blade to his throat. 'Make no sound,' I said, my voice low.

'Eyaaah!'

Balls!

The fool's cry of alarm brought running footsteps from the front of the house. Suddenly, I heard Thomas shout, 'for the defence of my house!', and I had the brief impression of him bursting from below the staircase, the long, thick shape of our father's old broadsword high in the air. He was far from a good swordsman – certainly he had been nothing as good as me as a child – but he knew how to use it and he had the advantage of country bumpkins.

I could not see the melee and decided to ignore it. My own captive had stilled, and I could feel his big body quivering below my arm. 'Why are you here?' I asked. 'This is no thievery.'

'Nothing, no thievery, nothing.' Though he was scared, he sounded calm.

'Tell me the truth or I'll gut you.'

A high-pitched scream cut through the air behind us. 'My boy,' he said, 'has he killed my boy? Let me go ter 'im.'

'If he's killed him you'll go to him soon enough if you don't tell me. Why?'

He swallowed. 'It's them enclosures what the master 'ere's been about. 'e means ter break us. Leave us starving. This is our land. We won't let no new master force us off.'

More scuffling, whimpers and cries sounded. I heard Thomas's triumphant, 'ha! Be gone in the name of the queen.' He did not correct himself. Crunches over broken glass began to grow louder, turning to the gentler pad of slipper on carpet.

'Get the hell out of here,' I whispered. 'Go. Through the back.' In truth, I had no knowledge of the back parts of the house and assumed – hoped – that there was an exit there. My captive made a liquid sound in his throat, as though deciding whether to thank me. Apparently, I did not deserve it. He fled into darkness, his footsteps punctuated by the exclamation mark of wood on wood as something – a club perhaps – fell from his grasp.

'Did you slay him, Adam?' Excitement made a rousing chorus of Thomas's voice.

'No. Did you slay his – the other?'

'I think not.' He hesitated a little, as Ann began to descend, a torch in one hand and a long knitting needle in the other.

'Are you hurt? Either of you?'

We answered in the negative as she began to light the house. As she lit the hall's sconces, I noticed that the portrait of my mother looking austere and imperious had been slit. From the middle of her forehead down to her chin, a broad flap of her face hung limply, her painted eyes seeming to cross inwards to survey the damage. I said nothing. I felt nothing.

We followed Ann as she turned left, into the room from which the shattering sound had come. As it sprang to life, the sharpness of her breath being drawn in brought us both to her side. She was staring at the floor, where a severed hand waved from the carpet. 'Ha! I got the bastard,' snorted Thomas. He picked up the thing and threw it out for the foxes and other scavengers to fight over. 'And you, Adam – you allowed the other to walk from this house? He might be gathering his forces.'

'We're not at war,' said Ann softly.

'He's a countryman. Not a general,' I added. 'What the hell is going on here? These were country people attacking us. Farmers and ploughmen, I shouldn't wonder. Our folks. *Your* folks.' Memory stirred. 'You said I might help you. In London. Some trouble here. What is going on?'

Thomas began spluttering something about country scum and the decline of the county, but Ann silenced him with a pained noise, one arm cradling her flat stomach. We fought over who should lead her to a chair and I allowed him the win, satisfying myself with being the one to right it. She sat, smiling her thanks, worry drawing lines on her brow. Eventually, she said, 'I said we're not at war. In truth, we are.'

'I think, wife, I can explain to my brother the nature of affairs here. It's the people. They're wrong-headed and stiff-necked in their obedience. Adam, you might return us thanks for allowing you to rest here by going to the constable in Duckmanton in the morning. He is a friend. He will ensure that the animals around this place are dealt with. They are grown rebellious.'

'They wish to go on using the land as they have,' she said.

'To go on using it wrongly. Can hardly pay us anything. Tenants, indeed – pauper tenants. It's our land and I follow our father in turning it over to sheep. There is profit in sheep.'

'You're forcing the old families off Norfield?' I asked. Thomas pouted. For the first time, I really saw his resemblance to our father. It was less in his features than his carriage and the set of his body.

'We need the money. I intend to purchase a knighthood from the new king. It is said his Majesty is most kind and generous in selling such things.'

I bit my lower lip and moved to another seat, sliding my dagger home before I collapsed in it. A bloody knighthood, I thought. That was what I might be wanted for – I might be welcomed again as a lost sheep if I could prove useful in securing my brother's future as a man of substance and quality. And then I would likely be forgotten once more. I did not grudge him the title, nor think badly of his desire for it. Sir Thomas Norton of Norfield sounded about right, and they had doubtless paid their taxes to the state to fund the Spanish wars. Yet something rankled. 'Enclosing land. It's not well liked.' I had only the faintest understanding of the practice and no strong opinions on it. It barely touched London.

'There is no better time. Half the damned peasants are dead or dying. The sheep at least are spared the pestilence.' I folded my arms. If Thomas was for it, that settled matters. 'And they have done for themselves now, the wretches. Breaking into this house. Intruding upon a father's grief. It is monstrous. It is rebellion is what it is. Rebellion or treason else what is it at all? Did you see their faces? Could you point them out?'

'What,' I asked, 'are you doing if not intruding on their grief, as you put it?'

'What?'

'You said that the folk are dying or dead. And you use this time to take their land?'

'*Our* land!'

'They used it in our grandfather's time.'

Thomas threw up his hands. 'You just prefer to be contrary. We need the money.'

'You have Ann's dowry, do you not?' That much-vaunted dowry had been the reason my parents had insisted I marry her, my refusal to condemn her to a sexless marriage speeding my disgrace and disinheritance.

'It has gone into the making of this house,' she said.

'Speak with him not, wife. He will not help us.'

'Give them the land. Just as it always was. And I will see to your knighthood. Maybe more if I can. I have friends around the king.' It was a promise I had no way of keeping. But they could not know that.

Thomas began to splutter again, to argue, redness breaking out on his forehead as he claimed that it had always been our father's intention to reclaim the so-called common land and put it to good use. It struck me then that whilst the old man might be dead, his problems were still alive.

Rising, Ann cut the discussion short. 'If I might speak freely, husband?' He frowned but did not silence her. She began moving towards the window, looking out into blackness and tapping the knitting needle on the side of her nightgown. 'It seems to me this way: if we continue as we are, forcing the common people away, we might face further dangers. This was a weak and ill-considered attack. Now they will both hate and fear us. We can gird ourselves against that with the constable and justices, but ...' I sensed that she had no clear plan and was simply thinking aloud. 'You have hurt one of them. Badly.'

'Good!' barked Thomas.

'You might make purchase again of their thanks and obedience by returning the land to them.'

'What?'

'Hear me, husband.'

'You grow fond, woman.'

Her face and tone betrayed no fondness. 'I will be mistress of nothing and no one, otherwise. We might trust Ned here to procure you your knightly weeds. You will thereby become Sir Thomas, as you wish. And those tenants who are now probably out there, in the dark, weeping and fearing the noose, might have their land. And so, you and they will have what you wish. Is this not a fair thing?'

Thomas and I both remained silent, both thinking. Certainly, her plan was what I hoped for – Thomas doing what I proposed and not getting the land he wanted even if he did get the title. It was no solution against their old age, to be sure – if he hoped to make the place fat and rich on sheep, he would find himself instead a still-poor knight. But a knight nonetheless – if I could manage it. As for the problem of money, he would just have to manage the estate better and hope that new men came to replace those who had died of the plague.

'I will think on it,' he said. 'I will sleep here tonight, in case there is further trouble.'

'As will I. For your better protection, Mrs Norton.'

She gave a faint smile, offered her cheek to us both, and retired upstairs, an ascending cloud in her linen.

When she had gone, my brother and I settled in for a night of watchful dislike, in a parlour room full of broken glass and icy air. 'I hear there is terrible snow in the north,' he said at length.

'There is.'

'It is usual enough. Hard winters. Up there.'

'Ay.'

It was my policy that one should speak as little as possible to one's natural family. To do so risks inviting them to speak back. Silence made itself heard, inviting coughs and inhibiting loud breathing. I thought I heard some snot whistling in Thomas's nostril and wished I might slap it back into his throat. Then he asked, abruptly, 'Why do you call yourself Savage? For its ferocity? Are you a tax collector in London?'

'Settle yourself, Ben Jonson,' I smirked. The jest was lost on him, bumpkin as he was himself. 'Why? Because I like it.'

He muttered in his throat. 'As you like going to London. That city is why you ceased speaking with your natural family.'

'No. That was *how*. The wherefore and why are lying in their tomb.' I rose and left the room, finding the kitchens and liberating some biscuit bread from the otherwise empty larder. Taking it back, I broke it between us.

'Tell me,' he said, through a mouthful, 'do you truly know the king.'

'Yes.' It was true enough. Meeting a fellow once counted as knowing him. I could feel the royal touch on my face still – his knobbly, grasping hand. 'Yet my business is with the Master of the Revels and … the secretary. Lord Robert Cecil, Baron Essenden.' In response, Thomas let out a low whistle before cuffing away the peppering of crumbs on his scraggly beard.

'I will speak with the secretary. He is generous to those who do him good service.'

'Ay.' He seemed to chew not on bread but on potential words of thanks. 'I … Adam … Edward … I wish you to know … I never hated you. I do not hate you. Yet I do not understand you, I own, nor the things you … your … what made you leave this place.' I felt prickly heat rise in my neck. I did not intend for a close discussion. 'As my natural brother I … in truth I spoke up for you to father. Mother too. You left so suddenly – I was still so young and little in understanding. You never said farewell to me, from what I recall. And yet I spoke up for you, it is true.'

And so what?

I stood and moved over to the broken window, looking out into nothing as Ann had done. What did he expect, I wondered – my own grovelling thanks? In truth, his claims to have spoken up for me annoyed me. I would not have had him or anyone taking my part against parents who disclaimed me. To them, Adam Norton was as good as dead.

And yet here I was, alive and in their house, with a new name.

You can be sure of two things – your past and your death.

I shivered, and said, 'I should not go to the constable. Pay some of our people here to repair this wreckage. Pay a barber-surgeon to tend the lad's lost hand.'

'Pay?! For … defending–'

'Just see to it. Repair your relations with these people, if you can, and be a good master. Or you will have many such nights as this. I daresay the beasts might discover fire next time and put it to good use as revenge for a young man's working hand.'

'They will have many hangings! Revenge – it is we who are warranted revenge. Working hand … it is their necks they need have a care for. If they think by threats that they can win what they desire, we shall be always in thrall to the common hordes. They seek what they think is theirs now – think on what it will be that they seek after they discover they can frighten us into giving! I think you have been too long amongst the wolves and ravening beasts of the city.'

I shook my head. I thought that he spoke more from bluster and anger. When I had gone, I felt certain he would do as I suggested – he simply could not let me see that he would do it. My silence seemed infectious and his ranting ceased. After a time, though, he asked, in a queer voice, 'do … have you … do you ever wonder whether … had you married Ann, as they wished you to … whether you might then have lost your … the taste for …'

I did not need the light to know that he was reddening with embarrassment. 'No,' I said, and honestly. The thought had truly never occurred to me and now seemed obscener than what he called my tastes. 'We are a strange company. A strange family. I might … when I secure for you your knighthood and you come to London, you might visit me there. I have good rooms. And … perhaps I might come here again. Once you are Sir Thomas. And instruct you on how to dress as a knight of the realm.'

'You might … do as you wish. I have never known you to do anything otherwise.'

We sat, eating biscuit bread, and I smoked my pipe a while, until the darkness lifted its shroud and shafts of sunlight speared their way through the broken glass. Ann came down and found us some butter for our bread and we all three ate together, saying little. I suppose it might have looked an oddly sweet family scene – if you didn't know us, that is. I determined to be off as soon as I had eaten. Staying any longer risked the tedium of warm words before Ann – and I felt a faint nausea at the thought. The notion of a loving family basking in the glow of firelight sickens me with its falsity.

Still, I left Norfield in a different state from the hot, pathetic, tear-splattered fury of my previous visit, and for that I was grateful. As I clattered over the rutted path to the deserted village, and so on the road to London, I had a resolve to put to bed the matter of the missing physician and thereby get my brother his bloody knighthood.

I had then the arrogance – the stupidity – to think that it would be a simple matter.

11

Entering London invariably causes a rush of strange feelings to soar within me. There is the warmth of homecoming – and with it the glow of safety and familiarity. There is the feeling of life after death – the city seems to blossom in the midst of flat, bleak countryside. And there is the joy of welcoming sights, especially after days of picking a horse across frozen rivers and streams and sleeping in draughty, cheerless inns. For large chunks of the journey I had given up renting beasts entirely, saving some of the money Cecil had given me by begging rides on carts. But for the last, weary leg, I was again mounted, my joints aching.

One is first greeted, of course, by the welcoming and unwelcoming conflict of Bonehill: the first signpost announcing the city on the road from the north. With its whirling windmill, the hill presents a joyous sight, more friendly and cheerful than the aggressive cluster of piercing church spires and the innumerable columns of smoke which otherwise make up the city skyline.

The last time I had returned to the city following a trip north, the sight of Bonehill had chilled me, for its unwelcoming truth is that the hillock is an artificial construct covering a vast mound of skeletons that had overtaken London's many churchyards and which had to be disinterred and moved to make room for the fresh dead. As my horse clopped past it, I thought about the horrible nature of life on and within the earth after death. Yet Bonehill carefully hid its cache of corpses, its jumble of intermingled dead – even though it hid them in the plain sight of its name. Dee's skull leered at me, and I wondered whose flesh had once encased it. Artists, I knew, loved to remind us of our own mortality. In paintings and woodcuts, skeletons and skulls grinned and beckoned and hovered. Yet there was no need for artist's impressions. The real world offered quite enough reminders of death and, besides, once we died, our skeletons were the toys of other people – people like the prince of Denmark, whom I could recall in the Lord Chamberlain's Men's tragedy of *Hamlet* speaking to the skull of the fool. It did not answer back.

Because dead man can't speak. Their bones are just bones. The rest, the essence, the soul, cannot be brought back to earth.

Perhaps I understood the artists a little better. They were not reminding us that we would die, of which we hardly needed reminding, but that we must live and speak and laugh whilst we could, for in death we would be silenced, un-tongued and sightless.

But the people who had taken Dr Gurney did not accept it.

This confused and, I own, entirely grotesque pot of thoughts roiled and boiled as I passed between the marshy mists of Finsbury fields, which seemed bowed under the weight of cold air, and on to Moorgate. Even in this pathetic little postern – I always thought of it as the naughty back door in and out of the City – that led directly onto the goodwives' laundry ground of Moorfield, security was apparent. I was obliged to dismount by the waving arms of an official in City of London livery.

'From where've you come, stranger?'

'I am no stranger,' I said, sliding to the soggy ground. I told him, producing the letters Cecil had provided me with, and was hurried on. Still, I noticed, his piggy eyes roved over my face, my armpits, and he kept well back, occasionally sniffing at a rag full, I assumed from the sheen on his puffy fingers, of protective herbs and butter. Once I was passing under the archway of the gate and the moor's overgrown grasses waved before me, I turned, threw my head back, and essayed a sneeze. His scurry into the protection of the gatehouse was reward enough.

I rid myself of my mount at the first trader I found in Lothbury – and was pleased to do so, as the poor creature was immediately spooked by the interminable clanging din of the candlestick makers, casters, founders, and other Vulcans who called the district their Olympus. Thereafter, I walked south to the Poultry, on into a far busier Cheapside than the one I had last seen. There, at its eastern end, at the Great Conduit opposite the Mercers' Chapel, women were even lined up drawing water, some with their faces masked and keeping well apart, others almost toe-to-heel. Life was returning.

As though in proof of it, I saw three men I knew from my working life standing in the porch of a tavern, hard by the wall-pissers. One was Ben Jonson, a notorious blabber-spout, as puffed up in belly as he was with pride at having eclipsed William Shakespeare as London's finest playmaker. He was wheezing out his wit to the others: his fellow poet Dekker and one of my colleagues from Revels, the latter yawning. I pulled my hat brim down until it almost touched my nose, put a hand over my face as though fearful, and kept my eyes on the herb-sodden ground as I paced on. I was losing the conveyance fee for whatever Jonson and Dekker were handing my fellow but was mindful that the Master of the Revels must think me still ill. I did not wish the office to know I was on my feet and had been for over a week; a servant who feigned illness was one who served two masters, and a man who served two masters was not to be trusted.

And so I continued westwards towards what I had claimed to my brother was my good set of rooms in Shoe Lane. I was just, in fact, rehearsing some lines of wit in my head to announce myself to Faith and David ('home is the hero' seemed rather weak, but might do, I reckoned) when I turned off of Fleet Street and saw them.

Why does my house seem to be more popular than ever?

The door was open, Faith standing in it, but she was not being assailed by a madwoman in white. Instead, she was blushing and speaking with a young man of her own age who hung back a step from the door. Wearing, I noticed, the good, plain suit and woollen cap of an apprentice. Every now and then she would reach up and straighten a hair and seemed to be speaking with a hand hovering over her mouth as though worried about her teeth or her breath.

'Good morrow,' I said.

Both of the young people started, as though their strings had been pulled. 'Ned!' cried Faith. She gave a look I didn't like to the lad, who turned a bland face towards me. His skin was clear, I noticed with envy – it had the unlined appearance of a man not yet twenty.

'Good morrow, Mr Savage,' he said, his back poker straight. 'Mistress Faith Is My Salvation has spoken well of you.'

'Is that so? She has said nothing of you. Who are you?'

Faith, I noticed, was looking from one of us to the other, her face red. Ignoring her, the boy said, 'Nicholas Hopgood, sir, apprentice weaver, with your leave. I … er … I called upon Mistress Faith with … hoping … I should like to step outside with her for a turn on the morrow, with your leave.'

I sniffed, inhaling the general smell of burning hair that hung around London like a smog as I regarded him. He was not the type of fellow I should have liked at her age. Far too much like a reed. And besides, prentices were in the charge of their masters for a seven-year term and free to do nothing but trifle with girls. 'Mistress Faith and I are well enough for woollens and weaving, young Hopgood. So you can do us a good turn and hop off.' I pushed past him and took Faith by the shoulder, steering her into the house and closing the door. I knew she had had trouble with prentice lads and their importunities before and turned my face for her to bask in the thanks and welcome.

'Why did you do that?' Her hands were on her hips and her face had gone a shade beyond red.

'Do what?'

'Nicholas is a friend.'

'Nicholas?' A jealousy I could not account for stirred in me. I did not want her having friends, I realised, though I could not say why, and I did not like the reflection it cast upon me.

'I haven't been able to go out at all, Ned. Not on my own. With you away and …' She crossed the room to the cot, where David was sitting, a playbook quarto in his lap but his attention on us. 'I would have gone out with Nicholas and taken a turn.'

'Would you, now?' Shame welled in me. I had left the two alone when I went off on my business, telling them only it was of great importance. And she had not forgiven my part in causing the little one to fall ill, I thought. Though I had tried to suppress it, to replace the memory of it with business, still it burned, a column of flame between us. David was her blood, not mine. I was just the fool who had given them a home.

And caused the boy to sicken in his first months in it. Because you are a proud and greedy fool.

But, damn it all, the boy had come through – there he was, hale and hearty. If I had erred, then there had been no harm done.

'Go out with him, then. Have your little friend,' I said, throwing back my head and drawing in my cheeks. 'Go and tell him now. You will catch him.'

Faith stood, hands still on her hips, but her face relaxed. 'No. No, I … I have to watch David. I don't like to leave him alone.'

'Pah!' I flopped down on the bed next to him and ruffled his red hair. He looked down at his lap. 'We'll be well enough, won't we?'

'Yes.'

'Yes, *Ned*,' I said.

'Yes, Ned.'

'Ah, *Cynthia's Revels*?' I asked, eyeing the quarto. By bloody Ben Jonson. 'You like this one?'

David looked up at me. 'Yes, Ned.' This with more animation. Perhaps, I thought, there was something there I could push. On the heels of the thought came the waspish memory of how I had caused his illness, and I batted it away. 'It has the gods. And … when I read it, I think Asotus is you. That's what I see in my mind.' I frowned, thinking, and then barked laughter. Asotus was a foolish courtier, a spendthrift who drank from the pool of Narcissus and fell in love with himself. 'I have never loved any other quite so much, I confess.' I looked back at Faith, my eyebrows up. 'Well?' I fluttered a hand in the direction of the door. 'Go to, then. Nicholas doesn't look like a lad who runs. Perhaps he's looking up at the window upstairs, imagining it's yours.' I made kissing sounds and David sniggered.

'I ... I will, then.' She turned on her heel in a swish of grey and left, the door banging behind her. I gave David a little hug and got to my feet.

Damn, I thought. I would have to go and visit the magus the next day – and make contact at the safe house with Cecil. And I could not now recall Faith and tell her that her walk about town with the mealy-mouthed weaver's lad was off – not without us both losing face.

I yawned, and aches shivered through my thighs and buttocks.

The lad was recovered. He would be well enough on his own for a short while, I supposed – and it was time he learnt to be a little man.

12

Bribery or fear? Money or threats? I turned the two possibilities over in my mind as I stepped from the wherry which had taken me from Whitefriars Stairs to Lambeth upstream over a river thick with floating chunks of ice. When you have no appointment with a man – when a man in fact might not wish to see you – the only means of forcing him are coins or threats.

I had risen late, tired after my journey into London the previous day, and allowed breakfast and dinner to become one big meal. With an air of indifference – why was I still troubled? – I saw Faith off, dressed, I thought, with more than her usual care. Nicholas what's-his-name was waiting, also buffed, and combed, and red-faced. It was their youth, I decided, that bothered me. Petty envy. Afterwards, I muffled myself against the winter chill and set out, leaving word at the Fleet Street safe house that I had returned. I had half-hoped but not at all truly expected to find a note there for me, declaring that Dr Gurney had been found or returned and my task concluded. No such luck.

David, I had told to do as his sister might usually do about the house – tidy things, sweeten the rushes with water, wash the walls, and stay out of my room. As I had left, already he was going about the business with all the animation of a mechanical, his face its usual colourless, freckled pallor and his red hair a dancing fire of tufts.

I knew where my quarry lived, if not the actual house. Decamped from north of the river – or run out, as I thought likely – Simon Forman had married and retreated to a family home in Lambeth. He was the type of fellow who cultivates a reputation as a farmer grows and tends crops – a little like Ben Jonson with his carefully styled fame as a master of letters.

Forman's reputation, however, was even less respectable. He was, as half London knew and the other half feared, a hedge physician (the jest being that he found his license from Cambridge under one), a man of medicine, a seer, a conjuror, and almost certainly some kind of alchemist or wizard. I knew him by repute and had seen him often enough at the theatre, where he went to be seen as much as to see the plays. Always dressed in expensive black, he would frown and throw his hard-faced head back, and tug his beard, and in general pull as many expressions as the actors. He must, I supposed, have had literary pretensions too – as a man worthy of impressing.

I ignored the creamy-stoned waterside palace with its flying pennants and gilded cupolas and thrust out into the warren of streets with their crowded buildings, overhanging eaves, and would-be wooden balconies. I did not know the exact house and asked my way with what I hoped was an air of business. To my surprise, the man who gave me directions added, 'and I hope you find the witch.' It seemed redundant, and I wondered whether he meant Forman or not.

It was not difficult to find the right house. It stood alone, with a white-plastered front and good timber cross-boards, nothing special about it save the deep garden which stretched out before it and ran all the way around, skeletal trees dotting it. A crowd was gathered outside, crowding the rain- and sleet-flattened grass. Women, I noticed, in black-brimmed hats and with good skirts and kirtles. Some of them were weeping.

He's dead.

I hurried towards them and asked for the news. 'It's sweet Simon,' said one, a handkerchief to her streaming nose, 'he's been struck down.'

'Plague?' I asked. I shook my head before she answered. She and the rest would hardly be here if there had been plague about. 'Is he wounded?'

'Wounded grievous. I don't know how bad. Sweet Simon.'

I pushed through the tearful crowd and entered the house without knocking. It opened into a reception hall, in which stood a smiling woman, her back to me as she gently tapped a hanging painted cloth, expelling the dust from it. She turned at my greeting and I was surprised at how young she was, and pretty, despite the dark smudges under her eyes. 'Yes?' Her gaze took in my clothing. I had worn a plain dark suit.

'I am seeking Simon Forman.'

'My husband.'

'I heard he is … wounded.'

'Oh yes,' she said, quite brightly. 'He cannot see patients. He is with a man of the watch.'

Thinking quickly, I said, 'I too am of the watch and would speak with him.'

'Oh. Upstairs. In his rooms.' She resumed her cheerful humming and continued what appeared to be a rather lackadaisical attempt at housewifery.

I continued through the house and up a steep flight of wooden stairs. Plain walls hung with cloths gave way to more elaborate imported tapestries. In between them, astrological symbols had been painted directly onto the walls, seemingly beckoning Forman's guests into his private world of the mystical. They were not badly done.

At the far end of a narrow, dim hall, voices spilled from an open door. I paused, listening to the rise and fall.

'So, to be clear and for the avoidance as it were of any doubt, you say that, number one, a woman processed, so it seemed, by many devils, attacked you?'

'Possessed.'

I recognised the questioner as Duguid, one of the city watchmen who normally worked north of the river. We all knew him as Dogwood. The man was a notorious lack-wit. The other, I assumed, was Forman himself, his ratchety voice booming and trembling with exasperation. I rolled my eyes as I listened, wondering whether the watchman was a genuine fool or whether he acted the part so as to avoid being given any more serious duties.

'Two: she spoke sharp words and did strike you and did knock your pet. A dog, was it?'

'My pate. See, here?'

'Mm. Just so. Three: it was a woman who did this.'

I decided to relieve Forman of his talk with the imbecile and thrust myself into the room. Two pairs of eyes turned to me. I slid off my hat and essayed a little bow, studying the men. Dogwood was of no interest. Forman, though, looked at me with suspicion. He was an ugly man in his fifties, his brow enormous and lined, but he was well dressed in a scholar's gown. His beard was a tangled, bristly fan, which stood to attention over his falling band. Any attempt at a sombre, flinty air was enlivened by a skull earring through one ear and a string of charms hanging on a taffeta ribbon around his neck like a woman's beads. What was most apparent, however, was a bruise over his left eyes and the distinct red lines of scratch marks raked down his cheek. He was seated on a string-framed cot which lay in the centre of the surprisingly tall, round chamber, around which stood cabinets of curios, books, and even drawings of naked anatomies. Stars were painted on the carved wooden ceiling, dotted around a central image of the sun. A fireplace, I noticed, stood broken, its shattered stones spilling onto the carpet. Memory stirred.

'Was this the man who robbed you?'

'It was a woman and she did not rob me,' boomed Forman. 'I was like to have been killed!'

'Kindly take no tone with me, sir.'

'Doctor!'

'Just so. You called upon the watch, crying assault.'

'And now,' said Forman, 'I dis-call you. Go, Dogwood.'

'Duguid.'

'Go your ways. I'll have no more of this.'

'Hmph. It is a fine thing when the law is left to pester,' muttered Dogwood. 'To conclude, this is little better than false report. I shall alert you if we find the man.' He gathered his things and manoeuvred his bulky body past me, giving me a searching look, a shrug, and then leaving.

When we were alone, Forman muttered, 'that man is fit to be mocked. A waste of time.'

'I'm amazed that you didn't foresee that,' I said, affecting a wintry smile.

'Who are you?' His little blue eyes, surprisingly delicate under the heavy brow, regarded me. 'I know you from somewhere.' As though not to be outwitted he added, 'here for a remedy against limpness of the member?'

'I live in the town,' I shrugged. He waited, crossing his arms, and making no attempt to rise. I took a deep breath, inhaling the scent of herbs I didn't recognise. 'I understand you were attacked by a woman.' I knew his reputation as a womaniser – though, looking at him up close, I could scarcely credit it – and had not allowed my hopes to rise. 'I seek also information on a woman and her friends who have been … vexing and sore troubling the people of this city.'

'Oh? Who do you work for?'

Shrewd. To hell with it.

'Lord Robert Cecil, Baron Essenden.'

This got his attention and he tilted his lumpy head backwards. 'Is that so? What is the bitch, some kind of a plotter?'

I shrugged. 'A woman attacked you. It might be that she is the woman the secretary seeks. What did she look like?'

'Hmph. Ay, attacked me. I did nothing, save give her an audience. She has importuned me for days now, and some man before her.' I repeated my question. 'Fair enough a woman to look upon – yellow hair. Blue eyes. Tits like turtledoves in a sack.'

'Her name?'

'Angela. She gave no other. An Italian, likely. Bloody poisoners and witches, the pack of them. Spoke English well enough, though, and sounded it.'

I fought to keep my voice measured and my expression blank. It was possible that the woman had approached Forman because she had received no good answers from the missing Dr Gurney … and that meant that the doctor might well have been got rid of. 'And you say she has troubled you before?'

'Oh, for some days now she has attempted this house. Begging an audience to discuss my being … uh … specially blessed because I survived the plague.'

'You had the plague?'

He nodded. 'Ay, back in '92. Merely the red pest.' A dismissive hand cut the air. 'Lanced the pustules myself and lived.'

'This woman – she wanted you to join her?'

'So I thought. And she had some enquiries, as I understand, about calling up the voices of the dead and speaking with them on matters of the great plague. I refused her audience until … she came yesterday, and I saw her through the window. And said that I might, in fact, be free in the night. It is better to discuss such matters in the night. The stars are more visible.' He gestured vaguely around the room. 'She came last night, and sore vexed me with crazed questions, like a woman possessed, about the end of days. Crossing the water between our world and theirs, and other such trumpery. A special calling by providence. I sent her packing. She did not take it well. Struck me, scratched me like a cat, and knocked me to the floor there.'

'I see.' It did not take much imagination to imagine what had actually passed between the infamous bawd and the madwoman. I thought quickly. 'We think this woman has friends who each share in some desire to understand the mysteries and call those who lived after the plague to them. They have approached other learned men, but I think received no answers. And so they come to you, thinking you might become one of their own.'

'Well,' said Forman, finally standing and arching his back, 'answers I have, for them that can pay and do not importune.'

'Yes. I saw your legion of partisans outside.'

He smirked, his face darkening. 'Ay, a pretty little lot.'

'What do you give them?'

He shrugged. Then he gave me a harder look. 'I am a physician. A man of learning.'

'A man who reads the stars, so I've heard.'

'They're up there. Someone has to make sense of them.'

'Why do you think this Angela came to you? What might she do with knowledge?'

'I cannot say. What does anyone do with knowledge? Use it.'

'You mentioned plotters. It might be that if this woman is a plotter, you will find these chambers searched. Your secrets uncovered.'

'Let me see your papers,' he said, wariness creeping into his voice. Duly, I produced the letters with Cecil's seal which I had carried north. 'What is this? What is the matter here?'

'We seek only this woman and any friends, Dr Forman. She has been making a nuisance of herself. It is best you are therefore truthful. Is this woman seeking knowledge that will cause some alteration in the state? Some plot?'

'No! She had nothing from me. I simply sat beside her and ... and she struck me. I sent her away. She is a witch, a devil. I have no interest in such heresies – I merely – I cast horoscopes.'

'Lord Essenden opposes all such things,' I said. I had no idea if that was true, but I was keen to keep him talking. Men in fear will pour forth more than they mean to. I stepped over to the fireplace and bent down, picking up a piece of broken stone. I had remembered where I had seen similar pieces before – sold on the streets by a false medical man, presumably some hireling. 'From the tomb of an Egyptian king, yes? Such deceits are not well-looked upon by my master, no matter whom you pass them on to to sell for you. I shall have to tell the secretary that you have met with this ... witch, did you call her?' I made to leave.

'No, wait. I swear before God, I sent her away. She is ... I don't ... look here, sir, I ... it is my business to tell people what they wish. I never touch anything that touches conspiracy or treason. It is no crime to tell housewives when their husbands will regain their potency, when best they might try for a child. Whether buried treasure lies in their garden. Or whether a son at sea will sink or swim. That sort of thing. What sign their child will be born under or their enemies *were* born under. I did not like the look the woman had. It was mad. A fond smile, eyes that looked staring and witless.' Inspiration seemed to strike him. 'I called up the watch. Would someone in league with witches and plotters do that?'

'No,' I said, pretending to scratch a non-existent itch on my chin. 'I suppose not.'

'There, then. I am not to be tainted by any wild folk who happen to ... to misunderstand what I do here.'

'Hm.' I measured my words, deciding how much sauce I might reasonably spice them with. 'You are therefore a mere quacksalver?'

Forman bristled. 'I give people answers.' There was more dignity in his words than heat. 'There are mysteries that man has not penetrated.

I think, now, they cannot be penetrated, no matter the reading and learning a man does. I have tried, sir, and discovered more than any man of great learning, I think. Because I realise the futility of seeking heavenly knowledge and they continue asking questions of it. Yet people demand answers. They sleep ill unless they can *have* answers. About tomorrow, and the next day, and the next. I say, if a fellow or his wife cannot accept that some things cannot be known about tomorrow, it is no harm to make them feel a little better today.'

I crossed my arms. He was right. I didn't judge him. 'Do you know anything that might lead me to this woman and her people?'

He sat again, quite primly, and folded his hands in his lap. 'No. She gave me no place of lodging. I never ask such things of those who visit unless they mean to beg credit. She would not tell me even when and where she was born so that I might read the signs. People come here to ask questions, not be given them. I can only tell you what I divined by listening to her as a man with eyes and ears planted in this earthly realm.'

'Yes?'

'That she has fellows. That they think there is an end time coming. Some sects, they think this.' He shrugged. 'They think it from the stars. I say the stars tell us what we want to see.'

'And so ... there is no end time?'

'Hmph. Not that anyone could ever know until it happens.'

'I ... if there is some plot in train...' I struggled. 'A plot must have an end. Some wicked deed, as the killing of an enemy or the taking of power.'

'I know nothing of that. Only ... you and your secretary, I should think, are men of logic, yes?' My raised chin gave answer. 'Yes. Then you are at a disadvantage. There is no logic in the mystic and the magical. Oh, some very clever men will be fool enough to think they have the wit to find it. But it is not there, or at least not within our little ways of knowing. Nor will it ever be, I suspect. God would hardly give us the means to truly know His mysteries.

'So, if these people are plotters, I would tell the good lord secretary not to seek any plans seeded with logic. Instead, seek the wildness of madness. The absence of logic. Crazed plans, dissolute.'

Lost, I asked, 'But – if they seek answers about the dead, the plague, the end of days–'

'The great reckoning. The end of time when the wicked will be damned and the good saved.'

'Then they will be disappointed. Like you say, it's not something people can know.'

'No ... not unless ...' I nodded for him to go on. 'I observe people, sir. It is my business. I look at this one and think "she wishes to hear that her husband will die". Or that one: "she wishes to be free of a mother-in-law". Then it is an easy matter to soothe them. Tell them that the stars promise what they will. And so I looked at that bitch, that yellow-haired cat, and I thought "what does this one seek?"' He paused for, I assumed, the drama of the theatre I knew he loved. 'She sought death indeed, and knowledge of it. End times. This is what she wanted to hear – that the dead can be spoken with and will tell us all how to conquer death through the great apocalypse. When the saved will be sent to heaven and the rest damned. And I would not promise her that such a thing was written in the stars now or any time. I should say that such mad creatures will seek to bring about what they will not be given. I called her a witch and a plotter, sir, and for good reason. You might carry that back to Cecil. A man who is mocked for his little learning – ay, and as a mountebank too – can see a dangerous creature well enough. And with no need of celestial spheres or imaginings.' Something of confidence seemed to return to him. 'And then let him do as he will with me. I have friends enough amongst the great who will speak up for me. I wish you good morrow.'

I bit on my bottom lip and then thanked him, before whipping the stone across the room. It flew over his shoulder and he turned around on the cot, leaning down and fishing for it. His distraction gave me just enough time to take one of the crystals on his curio cabinet from its place and slide it up my sleeve. It was not as pretty as the thing Dee had owned, but it had at least the grace not to be frightening.

I made my escape quickly, out of his rooms and past his fluttering wife, away through the crowd and back northwards.

Could it be, I wondered, that this woman was part of a sect – part of some mob which thought themselves saved and sought to bring about the apocalypse? And by what means would they attempt it, if even a mountebank like Forman would not encourage their crazed thinking? Would Dr Gurney help them or – almost as bad – would he have discouraged them and been silenced?

The word 'witchcraft' sounded in my mind like an evil incantation.

Answers.

They began to form in my mind, the product of a several things adding up like

everything is connected

numbers. What the woman had said on our doorstep about 'us'; what

John Dee had said she and her fellow had sought from Gurney; what she had sought from Forman. There was a plan afoot, alright, a plot, a conspiracy, call it what you will. I did not understand it, but it was there, and it smelt bad, like...

rotten corpses in a dead city.

It was still sounding when I'd crossed the river and made my way up the crumbling Whitefriars Stairs towards home. As I entered Fleet Street, I saw Faith and her prentice milling in the doorway, and I forced a false smile and an air of brightness, bounding up to greet them. I was barely within spitting distance when I realised something was wrong.

'Ned!' she shrieked. Her cap was askew and her eyes wild. Nicholas Hopgood was waving ineffectual arms, trying to calm her. 'Where the fuck have you been?' My mouth fell open. She rarely cursed, and I made to scold her. The words died on my lips. 'Jetting about the town! You left him! You left David! He's been taken!'

13

Faith's voice rose to such a cacophony of panic and anger that it fell to the hapless Hopgood to explain what had happened, stepping into my house ahead of me. When we were all inside, where the hearth was still sizzling with excitement, he began, 'Mistress Faith and I were taking a walk, Mr Savage, only as far as the Guildhall at Basinghall Street.' A posy of flowers, limp at her side, said what they had been doing there. 'We were gone only a short time. A few hours. To see the works my masters are preparing for the king's coronation procession. We came back just now, not far ahead of you. And we found you both gone. We were just told by the fellow down the lane that the little lad went off with a woman, a woman with–'

'A woman with blonde hair,' I said. My voice sounded flat in my ears.

'That bitch,' hissed Faith, turning on the spot. It appeared she was looking for something to throw, for she picked up the playbook David had been reading and hurled it against the wall. Then, as though she were bred to do it, she picked it up and replaced it on the cot. She then wheeled on me, her green eyes unblinking. 'Where were you? You were to watch him – you said – you promised! Where were you?'

'I had business. Work. I was only gone–'

'Work! Work!' Her hands were balling, and she shook off Hopgood's. 'Leave off! Your work again, is it? It was your work that gave him the plague! It was your work that damn nearly bloody well killed him! You think about no one, Ned Savage, never, not no one but yourself!'

There, I thought. Finally, she had said it. I hoped it made her feel better.

And it's true, isn't it?

I swallowed. The memory I had so long pushed out came rushing in, a river-tide of shame. Almost mechanically, I began fumbling for my pipe. The truth was that, when the plague was burning its way through the city, I had refused to heed the warnings to remain at home and avoid those places where it was hottest. I had heard them, of course, the London news being full of instructions, but I had not listened. Not when I heard, as I was buying tobacco (a ward against the bad airs which carry the pest, some said), that the new king wanted plays for the Yuletide festivities at Hampton Court. Then I had laced up my points, slid on my Revels Office livery, taken David, and went to work ferrying manuscripts between the playwrights, whose theatres had been closed, and the office in Clerkenwell. 'You see, without me the king should have no entertainment,' I had said. 'And nothing to take his mind off the sorrow of the plague. I met him once, you know...'

Showing off.

Why? To make a little money, yes. But in truth it was indeed to show my new acquisition, young David, what his patron could do.

Edward Savage, royal servant. Edward Savage, a valued fellow. Edward Savage, a man who knows those who are worth knowing.

Pathetic.

Yet there had been method in it too, I'd thought. I had sought, I told myself, merely to let the boy see the world and look to find himself in it. He was far too biddable, far too content to stay seated when told to sit, to eat when told to eat, to piss when told to piss. He needed his eyes opened to the world of work and toil and power and entertainments – to the world of 'out there'.

And as the price of breaking the general behind-doors rule so that I could reread and approve the plays for the king – old stuff in the company's stock: *A Midsummer Night's Dream*, *Julius Caesar*, *The Fair Maid of Bristow*, all of which they could perform at a turn, creeping in at the window and working from memory – my boy must have been exposed to the infection. Between the solemn, cheerless Christmas of ravaged London and the equally cheerless New Year, he had begun to sicken. To sweat. To complain of pains in his armpits and throat. And I had known, and Faith had known, and we had cried together and barred the door. She had not blamed me then, but I knew that it had been festering.

And it had all been my fault. Had I stayed at home or even just kept him there, he would never have taken the bad airs that were prowling the streets, delighting in the easy prey of little boys.

And now here it was, out in the open. I had cursed the boy to the plague and now to these lunatics with their strange beliefs about survival.

He is amongst the Enlightened. You must give him to us. He is especially blessed.

I wished to be calm, to project an air of mastery. I could not. I stuttered, stammered, and eventually said, in a timid voice, 'it was not my – I didn't mean to ... David is ... I think he is safe. She's ... collecting people who survived the plague. Seeking knowledge of why.' I did not add 'from the dead.' As the words flowed out, I forced myself to believe them. I kept telling myself that I knew the woman's face, I knew she was part of a group, which meant a lair, and I even knew something of their plans (at least enough to know that they would be mad and involved bringing about the end of days).

They won't kill him. He is part of their plan, whatever abominable shape it might take.

Who is Angela? Where is Angela?

Cecil, I thought. The secretary knew everything that passed in London, had eyes and ears everywhere.

'I have to do something,' said Faith. 'Now. Find him. They can't have got far. Why are we standing here?' She hopped about from foot to foot.

'We shall,' said Hopgood, raising his chin and putting a hand on his hip.

'Yes, *we* shall,' I said, fighting an unfair surge of dislike. 'I shall go to the king's secretary, to the king himself if I must. You two, you might … go out after them, down Fleet Street. See if anyone has news of where they went, the direction. Go now.'

I left, my plan unformed. It was getting darker and colder, the smell of fires already thick in the street as I stepped into Shoe Lane. Faith and Nicholas Hopgood were at my back, but I didn't wish to speak further. In truth, I felt I could not speak freely to her before her new

interloper

friend.

My first visit was to the safehouse in Fleet Street, where the agent, a thin, unsmiling woman whom I did not recognise informed me that my note of the morning had gone off and no reply had yet come. That made sense. I should likely have had to wait until the morning before finding one.

But I could not wait.

It was an unwritten rule that no one in Cecil's employ should approach the secretary directly without invitation. As much business as possible was to be transacted through various agents. Even when important intelligence was discovered, one was supposed to take it to a safehouse and have a messenger conduct it to him, waiting there for the reply. Yet I found I could not sit in a grubby little parlour in Fleet Street, a stranger ignoring me, until word came back from Whitehall. Not with David missing so newly.

Instead, I returned to Shoe Lane and quickly threw on my livery – the risks of being seen be damned – and took off through the dark streets for the river, over-paying to be taken upstream to Westminster. I had to resist the urge to run through King Street – running makes a man look like a criminal and nothing can attract attention more quickly – until I came to the gatehouse into Whitehall.

'Your business?' asked one of the sentries.

'Revels,' I said, feigning a bored look. Inspiration hit. 'New writings for the coronation. Ben Jonson wrote them. Sent over from Clerkenwell to get 'em checked. Bloody writers. Couldn't have waited till tomorrow so I could get home to the wife, eh?' I stamped my feet in irritation, blowing into my hands for good measure.

Don't overdo it.

The sentry gave me a smile of sympathy and waved me into the palace precincts. I followed the path as best I could remember it, through carpeted corridors with offshoots and branching hallways. I must have taken a wrong turn, getting too close to the royal apartments; the sound of distant, raucous music began to dance through the air, alongside gales of rambunctious squawking. I was not stopped, but I came upon a richly dressed man in a sky-blue suit locked in an embrace with a blowsy woman whose voluminous pink skirts were hitched up to her knees like a country maiden plucking weeds. They were making no effort to hide themselves, but reeling drunkenly together through the corridor, the thick carpet folding up under their stuttering gait. She was giggling, hiccups punctuating the mirth. He was mumbling words in Scots. 'Ma wee angel, eh? Gie it up, gang.' His hands were all over her lower legs, as though he had dropped something and hoped to find it there.

I froze. Turned. Expected a barrage of abuse. Instead, more laughter followed, and I fled the music and lust. It was a different court, I thought, from the old queen's day. Once, intrigue and ambition had filled the corridors of power. Now, it seemed that merriment and excess had taken their place – or at least concealed them.

Eventually, I found my way to the hallway of administration offices. I was not fool enough to burst in on Cecil, if he were in his new chamber, but instead sought out the secretary's secretary, Mr Munck. He was at his desk, whey-faced and sharp-eyed as he bent over a scatter of papers, a glass held between him and the page. Breathlessly, I said, 'I must speak with the lord secretary. It is a matter of urgency.'

Munck set down the glass and stood, studying me without words. Apparently recognising, even without the aid of the glass, he said, 'The lord secretary is not here.' My heart sank. 'He is with the king. Is this a matter of the papists?'

'No, I … it is for the lord secretary's ears alone, I regret.'

'I understand. I will fetch him. I think he will come as quickly as he might.' Relief flooded me, increased in its flow by Munck's understanding, his refusal to take offence at the bluntness of privy matters. I thought that something of a smirk passed the man's face. Perhaps Cecil did not enjoy King James's company. If so, Munck would no doubt be thought well of for rescuing his master from it. 'Wait here.' He carefully took up his paper and locked it in a compartment of the desk before leaving.

I stood waiting, not daring to sit. My thoughts tumbled: firstly repeating that David must be safe, at least from physical harm; secondly, that Faith and Hopgood might turn up something; thirdly, that if we might find Angela, we should have the key to the whole mess; fourthly, that David must, must, must be safe.

I did not know how much time had passed by the time Cecil appeared, Munck towering over him. The king's secretary looked distracted, and he did not greet me as he walked to his office, removing a key and unlocking the door. He stepped into the threshold and turned, his white fingers hooking the air as he beckoned me to follow. I did, almost colliding with Munck, whom I had expected would remain outside. Instead, the man went to the fire and lit it, before moving around the room, inspecting it as though he had turned chamber-groom. I stood, a little awkwardly, as Cecil watched him. The two men eventually nodded to one another and the secretary's secretary left us.

'What?' asked Cecil bluntly. 'You are aware, Ned, that this is not the manner of things in my service. I trust you have received some intelligence of Dr Dee? That you have found the whereabouts of Dr Gurney?'

Quickly, I ran through everything that had passed, between my visit to Dr Dee and my encounter with the wounded Simon Forman, omitting only my uninvited trip to Norfield. When I had concluded that portion, he hissed in irritation. Softly, he said, 'the king now more than ever would have his physician to hand. His Majesty takes it as a great affront that the man should be stolen away, and he forced to rely on Atkins. An assault on his estate, says the king's grace.' He returned his attention to me. 'I have made a study of the books you brought me from Dr Gurney's house and the letters. He does not give the names of his wicked patients but mentions that they are two and they have taken on new ones – false confections he means to study. I suspect that this Angela is one. Where there are two there are more. You might take the damned things and see if you can find anything further, but I doubt you will. Is there anything else?'

I finished with the news of David. At this, one of his lopsided shoulders sank a little and he spoke softly and, I thought, quickly. 'If the boy is taken you must find him, of course. Speed is the very essence in such matters. These people, if they are plotters, must be discovered. I wonder at you coming here and not wearing out the soles of your boots in the chase. They have now stolen from you as well as the king.'

My face fell. 'But … sir …' I went for it, despising the despair. 'You know everything that passes in this city. You are its master.'

A smile tugged at his lips, replaced almost immediately by a warning frown. His eyes, I noticed, went over my shoulder, towards the door. 'I am not.' He sighed. 'Your faith in me is a warming thing, Ned. Yet, I fear, misplaced. I confess I hear a great many things and take note of them. Do you know how?'

'I …'

'It is by employing such men as you. If I know of matters that pass in the city, it is because my friends, men in my service, discover them and tell me. I should know very little if every man spent his time here asking me news rather than out there finding it.' Perhaps I looked sufficiently abashed, or pathetic, or both, for he went on, 'my news out of the city has been somewhat weaker, I regret, of late. Many of my men are dead, and those who live are occupied in … other matters. We have a week only until the great revels. All must be seen to be in perfect order or else the common folk will think the new reign a cause rather than a remedy to all the sickness and troubles.' His small head wilted a little over his ruff. 'Queen Anne is minded to hold a great inspection. A looking-in on the preparations for the great day, some time this week. Her Majesty would have it done publicly with the king. His Majesty would have it done privily with only the queen – and the common people well apart. I – I must find some middling way.' He let forth something like a snort through his nostrils and then regarded his nails. 'The queen finds much delight and unrestraint in her foreignness; the king denies his utterly. When Elizabeth was king, she had no queen to trouble her. So, Ned, you see there are matters of security that engage those men I have left. And those who are willing to go into the dark places of the city where the plague struck hardest are few. Yet … I have heard some reports.' He cleared his throat. 'This woman, this Angela, and several like her have visited divers' houses which bore the sign of infection, seeking people who suffered the pestilence and lived. I that these creatures are all of her band.'

'Suffered and ... like David! They're making a band of plotters!'

He pursed his lips and I closed my mouth. 'Further, various households ... twelve, perhaps ... have reported missing people to the city watch. Fathers gone missing, wives, sons.'

'Gone to join this band?'

'I cannot say.' He shrugged and again his eyes darted past me. 'In these days it is hard to know which to credit. Some will have crept off to die, others might have taken themselves into the Thames when they saw the marks of infection.'

'Yet some might have gone to join this band.'

Witches!

'Witches!' They were as real, I knew, as Catholics, even if I found them likely to be less dangerous to the state. I had even seen one once, being tested at Tyburn. Her long grey locks had destroyed the scissors the magistrate had ordered used to cut them and had then caused sparks of fire to fly into the air when the hair was ordered to be burnt. Well, I had not actually *seen* it – but I had heard about it and the image was so powerful I felt that I had. Witches were real enough and crazed enough to think their doings had power. 'Witches and heretics and crazed people, that's what they are, stealing others to enchant them. Divine knowledge, that's what they want, for wickedness, evil.' I was rambling and I realised it, closing my mouth.

Cecil, I saw, had stopped listening. Instead, he leapt from his chair and tore his jewelled velvet cap from his head. 'What?' I asked stupidly. I turned to follow his gaze, nearly tripping on the carpet.

The door behind me had opened without a sound.

I gawped, fishlike, for a few seconds, before dropping to one knee and scrabbling for my own woollen bonnet.

In the doorway, light casting him in an ethereal glow, stood the choleric king himself.

14

He stands, now, a widower, in the company of three-hundred others. He is there as part of a smaller party, on the command of his master, the earl, who had helped invite death into this great hall. Every man in the room is there on the order of some great one or other, so that he can have an honest report of the death, its circumstances, its pageantry.

It is quiet, save for the occasional echoey cough; even whispers are stilled. The business of the day is too important to England and the world for its witnesses to be laughing and speaking freely.

And so they wait, pressed in silence and gloom and the wood-dust of a newly-built scaffold, its tiny motes hanging in the still, cold air like specks of eternity. Even the fetid puff of six-hundred lungs does nothing to battle the chill.

Does Death, he wonders, prefer the cold?

There is some disruption in the entranceway to the great hall, though he cannot see it. Voices rise and fall in a score composed in musical French and Scots. Sobs and sniffles leaden the air. Inside, Hope scuffs his feet on the bare stone, and the movement ripples, like a stone on a millpond, as others begin to murmur. The fracas of the lady's entrance breaks the spell of silence that had held them in thrall.

He looks up, over the hills and dales of heads and shoulders that make up the bleak landscape in front of him, a dozen torches their suns. They do not obscure his view of the queen. She is a tall lady, all in black. Her head bobs with her steps, visible above the men who are come to see her die. Though she is a black shape in her satin and velvet, a snowfall of white cascades from the peak of her headdress, running down the curved stoop of her back. She moves slowly, like a dancer who has given up the art but not lost the memory, towards the centre of the room. She does not move like a fearful woman. Hope cannot see the scaffold for the forest of bodies, but the queen rises still taller as she approaches death on its heights.

Some of the soldiers surrounding the scaffold bristle, the plumes in their helmets twitching. The former gaolers shift in their seats, as though seeking a clearer view. Hope rises on his tiptoes. There is some muttering, which sounds odd and whispering in the great hall. It is soon drowned by the reading of the commission, for which the spectators fall silent. It sounds like authority and lends an air of good, clean order to the death.

Another figure appears on the scaffold, and his airy voice pecks at the air.

'Mr Dean,' says the queen, her own broken English rebuking him, 'I am settled in the ancient Catholic Roman religion and mind to spend my blood in defence of it.'

Mind to spend my blood, thinks Hope.

She embraces death like one of the many lovers infame claims for her.

Two other voices sound, indistinct, the speakers masked by the crowd. More talking, more muttering. The muted bangs and thuds of feet on velvet-padded wood. The dean again, barking out prayers like a yapping dog. The queen, speaking over him in the purer music of Latin. Someone else scolds her, and she argues back. Hope, like the others in the hall, strains to hear what is said; he, however, is not close enough. All that reaches him clearly is the calm and measured lilt of her voice as it bats away the insistent drumbeat of theirs. It is a matter of the viol against the tambour. One final competition of the musicians, and then the hall falls silent once more. More badly lighted figures writhe about on the scaffold, swarming the queen, and Hope thinks of spirit-angels and demons fighting over a soul.

Not now, he hopes. It would be a grievous thing if the voices and spirits visited him now.

But it is only the queen's ladies, undressing her for the end.

Under her black gown, her kirtle is rusty in the torchlight – the colour of age and rot and saintliness and old blood. The women slide red sleeves onto her arms too, and she says something. He cannot hear it, but it causes sob-laughter from someone up there.

Her lips, he can see, split her face in a smile. There is no sign of terror or horror or fright. He wonders what she is thinking. She has lived in the shadow of the scaffold for so long. Perhaps she welcomes it now as an old friend who had promised to visit often but never came. As the sobs of her friends win out, graduating to tears and throat-choked moans, she turns to the spirit-ladies and says something to them, reaching out her rusty arms and offering them her hands. They clasp at them. 'Pray for me,' he hears her say, and it seems an invitation to all the world. 'Even unto the last hour.'

Her women release her hands and for a moment the queen's head disappears below the heads of the other spectators and out of his view. It appears again, but robbed of its sight by a white handkerchief, a similarly white coif over her thick russet hair. She sinks again and

127

does not rise; but her voice does. Over the heads it comes, ghostly now that she has gone: 'In manus tuas, Domine, confide spiritum meum.'

Something silver and glinting rises above the crowd, the man wielding it unseen. It hovers in the air a moment and then drops. A wet crunch announces its passages.

Cries pierce the air, anguished and beyond sobbing.

It is drowned out by the mutters of the men near the front.

The silvery axeblade rises again, higher in its second appearance, and comes down harder.

This time, the men's voices are quite distinct in their disgust. 'Ugh.' 'Oh.' 'Uff.' Their breathy chorus is accompanied by movement of the heads: those directly in front of him all rise as the spectators seek to see what is happening; those at the front appear in profile, looking away and grunting out their displeasure.

Despite the queen's graceful welcome, Death has not, it seems, come easily. Further wet sounds rise from the scaffold – the sound of a butcher at work.

Finally, a voice cries, 'God save the queen.'

A flash of white appears as the headsman lifts the severed head aloft.

Another joins in with, 'so perish all the queen's enem–'

Thud.

The flash of white is gone – if it had ever been there. More groans and squawks of disgust from those in the first rank of witnesses. 'So perish all the queen's enemies!' finishes the fellow up on the scaffold.

Later, he overhears others in courtyard hastily comparing their version of the event. His own is quite clear in his mind, and so he listens.

'They say the papist whore took a motto.'

'Eh? Ay, and what's that?'

'In my end is my beginning.'

***

Hope was meditating in his cabin. It was the closest he now came to praying. It helped keep the now almost constant bombardment of ideas and thoughts in his head. Silence led the way to purity of thought. He tried to sort through what he knew.

The king's coronation marked the end of days – if he knew how to bring it about.

He and his would be judged and found faithful and pure – they had survived the plague.

Only he was granted visions of the dead still, but the others would too once the doctor managed to dry out and mix the physick he claimed would help them to share the gift.

Because the doctor was a liar and Angela was swiving Amos and he should kill himself and the wicked new English government was watching him and in my end is my beginning and Queen Elizabeth and immortality!

He thrust his head hard against the bulkhead and the resulting jolt of pain drowned away the jumble of singing thoughts. Suddenly, tinkling laughter filled his head and he turned, squinting into the shadows of the cabin. A bulky black figure stood in the corner. A white lawn veil covered its face. 'Who are you?' he asked.

But he knew.

'En ma fin est mon commencement.'

'Vita in morte sumus,' he replied. 'Why are you here?'

'Behold,' she said. Her voice seemed to be that of a Frenchwoman he had once known during his travels with the earl. 'I will tell you a mystery. We shall not all sleep, but we shall all be changed, in a moment, in the twinkling of an eye, at the last trumpet. For the trumpet will sound, and the dead will be raised imperishable, and we shall be changed. For this perishable body must put on the imperishable, and this mortal body must put on immortality.' He recognised the verses – from the bible; he had shown them to his acolytes before.

'What must I do?'

The tall, broad figure of the dead Queen Mary limped towards him, her head bobbing as it had on the day he watched her die. 'You are doing nothing. You know that you are watched, always. You have only days. You must prepare for Death's approach.'

'How?' He closed his mouth as she drew back her veil to reveal a broad, double-chinned face and tilted eyes. Her features seemed a little blurred. He wondered at the celestial power that had reattached her head.

'In my end was my beginning. I died and yet I live. As others who have died as I did live in the mouths and hearts and minds of many.'

'As others,' he echoed. 'Do you know why I was spared to live? And my friends? Why?'

'Why? You learnt nothing at my death. My murder showed you the way. The deaths of princes bring about great changes. My death made me eternal. You see, I go on. You must learn of it.'

And then, suddenly, the queen became a charging cannon ball of black velvet, flying towards him, her fingers hooked into claws. He yelped and fell to the deck as she scratched and clawed at his face, hovering over him. Perhaps he screamed, because the door flew open and Angela tumbled in.

'Nathaniel! Are you … oh, no – you are bleeding.'

She was at him in three steps. The Scottish queen had vanished, and his beloved Angela, his faithful love, was helping him to his feet. She frowned at his hands, which he noticed with detachment, were bloody – the nails especially. Fire tore jagged strips of pain down his face. Why were his own hands bloody? It had been the devilish queen who had torn at him. He allowed Angela to fetch a pail of water and wash him. The stinging pain and the refreshing blessing of the river water seemed to banish the confusion and he smiled at her. Of all the company he had saved, she remained the closest to his heart. She was well free of her evil husband.

'I have done the like,' she said, dabbing the hem of her robe on his cheek, 'to the false doctor in the town.'

'Who?'

'The man Forman. He is known as a man of answers. Yet when he took me into his house, he tried to touch and kiss me. Claimed he had merely the red plague and not the black, whatever that means.'

Hope felt his spine stiffen and he began to rise from the cot. 'Wicked creature!' There was the proof, he thought, that the Scottish queen's spirit was telling the truth. Those in the world outside were indeed monsters, out to hurt them. 'He was never one of us. He meant only to trap us and … and …'

'Don't fret. I clawed him. I would have bitten him.'

'And so we have no means of …' He collapsed again, shaking his head. He wanted more than anything for his friends to be able to see the visions of the dead as he did, to share with him the purity of angelic knowledge before the end came. His whole family must come together or … or he might not be reunited with his old family in the after-times. 'The things the doctor had you fetch from the apothecary – have they given you anything?'

'No.' She frowned and the urge to kiss her bobbed up. 'I have not yet taken them. He says he is working on the right and perfect concoction. The dose makes the cure.'

'Cure? We are not sick.'

She shrugged. 'He says he needs a little more time.'

'Time. Time is what we lack. The coronation, the revels, they are coming … I have been visited. The death of the prince will bring about the great reckoning. I know it. And then we will be saved again. The Enlightened will suffer nothing.'

'The death of the prince?' Angela smiled.

'It has been revealed to me. We need only to have the means.'

'Yes. I believe you.' Even more brightly, she added, 'And I have brought us the boy.' She explained again who she meant. 'Another to be saved.'

As she did, fear gripped him. The Scottish queen's voice drifted out of the corner, where she must have been lurking invisibly. 'His master is a spy with the evil eye. My son's wicked and corrupt government is watching you.'

'They are stealing our knowledge,' said Hope.

'What?' asked Angela.

There seemed no way of explaining the idea, so Hope stood and took her hand. Together, they left the cabin and creaked their way out and down to the main deck below, where their people lay. The chamber, as always, was a sea of white bundles, smelling of sour food and farts and herbs. As they crossed it, clarity descended on him. He found Amos guarding a red-headed boy of about twelve, who sat cross-legged on the floor, wearing a fearful look.

'You are welcome to our family, child.' Big eyes turned upwards.

'I'd like to go home now.'

'You are home. You like it here, don't you?'

'Yes.'

He lies. Kill him.

'You are safe here. You have taken the great plague into your body and expelled it. That makes you one of us. Enlightened. You are specially chosen.' The boy gave a pained looking smile. 'Soon it will be time for us all to go to Heaven. The dead speak with me. It might be that they speak with you too soon. They will share the path with you then. This world will end, and the rest will die the death. Can you say "vita in morte sumus"?'

The boy did and in a high, clear voice. Hope felt his heart sing. 'I love you, son.'

He turned to Angela. 'I have borne witness to another great vision. Fetch the doctor. Another miracle will soon become apparent.' And then to Amos, he said, 'this boy's master is a wicked creature. He spies on us with many eyes. I would have him destroyed for the safety of us all.' Amos nodded, grinning. 'But first, my dear brother … find me an axe.'

15

'Your Majesty,' said Cecil, moving to stand before me and bow.

The air in the room seemed to shift, becoming pregnant with nervousness, both mine and Cecil's. The king's presence seemed to overwhelm the office. It had become a presence chamber.

James ignored his secretary and shuffled across the carpet towards me. 'Up, man, up, up.' I rose stiffly, keeping my eyes fixed on the gold points which laced the hose plastered over his ungainly legs. 'And you, Beagle, I telt you I would come. I give you leave, laddie,' he said, his voice darting at me. 'Set a peep upon your king.'

I looked up.

I had last seen King James in his palace at Holyrood. Then, he had been soaked in the gall of frustration as he awaited news of his succession. He had it now – he had, in fact, everything he had ever wanted, for he had England, and Scotland, and Ireland, and the ancient pretence of France.

If you might imagine the cat who got into the cream, you will still be a country mile from the king who got the kingdoms. His puffy face was florid with wine-cheer, and spillage stood out in dark blotches down the front of a pearled, gold-threaded cream doublet. There was something impressive in just how unimpressive he was. I had never been alone in a room with the old queen, but in my imagination she would have dominated it in quite another fashion – more in the vein of her famous father, whom I had always heard made every man quake with fear. James had the look of a country schoolmaster dressed in a stage costume. Any fear he engendered was more born of the restless, nervous energy that seemed to quiver from him. He took me by the elbow and jerked me to my feet. The smell of heavy musk and alcohol washed over me. 'Come, laddie, and know your king.'

'This is Edward Savage, your Majesty.'

'Aye, so it is. I recall the man. 710. Back in the days when I was master only of that kingdom.' He stood in front of me – a tall, spare man almost lost in the bombast-padded clothing. He waggled a finger, grinning and showing white but uneven teeth. 'And he left two dead men in my city in the north. That was a fine mess. Where is the lang ane?' He referred to the man I had travelled with on my trip to Edinburgh and I looked to the carpet. Cecil gave a discreet cough. 'Och … aye, I see well enough. No harm done, heh? And we must apologise, aye, for the rude reception you must have had in that place. We regret our northern subjects are not so well civilised as we find in this town. But they will be brought to perfect civility.' Not so well inclined to perfect, grovelling obedience to him, I thought, wondering how they might be brought to anything by a king lodged four-hundred miles away and in another country. 'We find the southern folk's tongues well sounding in wir ears and well enough to look on.' His padded arm jerked wildly at the office. 'Our secretaries in the north of our island would be lost in such a place. You are well settled in this chamber, Beagle? You find it a fitting kennel to sniff out secrets?'

'It is a fine place, your Majesty.'

'Fine, fine, aye. Then do not stand there frowning and gurning like auld Granda Twackle.' He turned to me. 'Well, when my man told me he had an old friend waiting and what the matter of his coming was, I thought I might reacquaint you with wir former friendship.'

James began moving around the room, whilst Cecil and I stood rooted, watching as he picked things from the desk, cast an eye over them, put them back, and continued his loping stride. He moved, I thought, as though his strings were operated by two drunken puppet-masters who hated one another. 'Our very good lord secretary here has telt us that you, Savage, are charged with discovering my physician.' He looked at me, his eyes bulging.

'Yes, your Majesty.'

'But you've not found him.' I said nothing, and James tutted. He had managed an almost complete circle of the room and reversed his route. 'I am come to perceive that it is some band of plotters who have lifted him. Their design, man, what is their design?' Cecil began speaking and James cut him off. 'Let the lad speak. Beauty comes before age, heh?' The secretary and I had a brief eye conference before I cleared my throat and began.

'Witches, your Majesty. I think they are a sect of witches.'

'Hm. Aye. Do you believe in such things?'

'Yes.'

'Good, good. There are wicked and ignorant fellows who deny them, who would hold that we should ignore the rotting pustules who spring up across the land. Fools. I am right glad a bonny looking lad like you has a fit mind. You are right. A monstrous assembly of witches does spread out in our land – and there are more in our time than in times past, and each seeking the end days. The toppling of kings and the end of civil law, aye, and Christ's too. But also you are wrong, laddie, and I shall tell wherefore.' He stopped moving and folded his arms across his puffed chest. Something like a smile quivered on his fleshy lips – amusement, I thought, at the confusion I could feel distorting my own features. One long finger shot up. 'If what the Beagle here tells me is true, they are not witches but necromancers. There is a difference. Open your ears a wee thing.' He coughed, and when he spoke again his voice had assumed the tone of a lecturing divine. 'Witches are mere slaves to the devil, tempted by greed or jealousy. They cast spells and other suchlike wicked things to cause harm. Those who practice the black art of necromancy – why, they are in type two: the learned and the unlearned, and both to be rooted out by any Christian king.' I kept my eyes on the carpet, silently vowing not to recommend Dr Dee – who might not find a welcome in this Christian king's court. 'From what my wee secretary here has told me, we have magicians at work in the form of unlearned necromancers seeking purer knowledge of their wicked and foul art. It seems to us that they are at present imperfect in their works and hope to construct a better understanding. On the doctor's knowledge of physick and astronomy, which they will subvert to the false study of astrology and the preaching of stars. They do not understand that the days of prophecies are past. Any visions or imaginings now are plain evil. Is that not right, Beagle?'

Cecil inclined his head. He looked, I thought, mighty uncomfortable. Always I had seen him as a master of his people, and it was a strange thing to see him mastered. Something in it pleased me.

'They have taken my boy,' I said, not looking directly at the king.

'Boy? You have a son? It was my kenning that ...'

'He is my ... adopted child.'

'Is he now?' I looked up to see a sly grin cross James's face. 'You naughty fellow. Your lad and my physician. Is the bairn baptised in the faith?'

'Yes.'

'Hmph. Then he is safe enough. The papists claim that the devil's creatures take – on his evil command, mind – unbaptised bairns. Then they cook them in a cauldron until the whole flesh comes off the bones to make a soup they might drink.' He made a wet, slurping sound. 'Papists. No, your boy is safe enough if he is baptised and these are not true witches. Yet why, then? Why have this child and my physician been taken?'

'I ...' I blinked away the Catholics' image. 'I think they seek knowledge of the end days. They gather an assembly of those who had the pestilence on their bodies and lived.'

'Aye. There is pride and curiosity in their hearts. They think themselves blessed to have survived the plague. And the devil sees their damned curiosity and has tempted them into seeking further knowledge through him. They run to him like little children.'

'They are mad, then?' I asked, hoping to please.

'No.' James thudded a fist into his other palm. 'This is not madness. It is the temptation of the devil. A madman is imbalanced and raves. A wicked man has invited Satan and his minions into his heart, thinking to master them. But he is deceived. It is he who is mastered.'

'Or she,' said Cecil. 'A woman–'

'A woman is a slave to her master-man,' snapped James. 'I have looked upon the doctor's book as you have. It mentions troublous patients in the plural, a man with a false name as well as the cot-quean. A man must have rule of this daft wench.' He moved over to the secretary's desk again and began turning over books and papers, muttering to himself. Cecil's colour fled.

'Is there anything I can find your Majesty?'

'Aye! My book, man, where is my book? I gave it you.'

Cecil joined the king and ducked underneath the desk, bobbing back up with a slim book bound in black. He passed it to James, who sat down in the large, carved chair, and set the thing before him. He remained a while, adopting the post of a great thinker, his elbows on the desk and his chin on his balled, knobbly fists, whilst his lips moved silently. Then, abruptly, he shot up again, picking up the text and moving in my direction.

'This is my study of the black arts. Did my man here not tell you your new sovereign was by turns a tedious old scholar?' He held the book aloft and tapped its cover. 'By title *Daemonologie: in Forme of a Dialogue, Divided into three Books*. A learned thing, I fancy, though I am but a green prentice in the scholarly arts. How do you like that, secretary's dug – a scholar for a king and emperor, heh?' He came close to me again and thrust the book at my chest. I took it, muttering thanks. 'You will find Gurney and your boy too if you study it.'

My mouth fell open.

Find them by reading?

The king seemed to read my thoughts and he gave an unpleasant smile. Again, his finger jabbed at the air. 'This is a fine big city, as I perceive it. These creatures haunt it. They must have some hole within it. You shall be keeking out a wee hidey-hole where they shall have their marks. Circles and symbols and other suchlike mad gew-gaws. That book will tell you what you are after. Not only people, not only a woman and man who speak wildly, but their dark abode – the place they creep back to after they stalk the city. You must hunt them'

'Do you have any notion, your Majesty, of where these creatures might gather? What they do with those they take?'

James began roving again, over towards the fire, where he stopped and held up his hands. 'A fine questing mind you have there, boy. Aye, and good questions born of it.' For a spell, the only sounds were his whistling breath and the soft crackle of flames. 'As to where they gather, I should seek dark places. Out of the sight of honest Christians. These necromancers come to despise all that is good. As to what they do with those they take … my good Gurney, I think, they will mine until they have what they can of him. Your boy … I can see only a wish to corrupt him in their wicked ways. To give him to the devil as they have given their-selves.'

Fear prickled up my back. I had thought only of witches – crazed fools using spells and potions to deceive or harm their enemies. My fingers whitened on the book the king had given me. I did not want to read it – did not want to know what the scholarly sovereign had to say about these creatures.

'You understand their ends, of course?' James wheeled. His eyes first went to Cecil, who bowed his head, before landing on me. 'You understand what these foul devil-lovers seek?' I said nothing. 'Their black design is to subvert God's world and commune with the devil. It is God's will that we rule this island in perfect unity, wir subjects one race and people. The beast of discord and his minions oppose God's will and thus are at squares with this unity. This he will tell them as he skirls a dolorous jig before them.

'Oh aye, the devil might take many forms in the discussions – the form of false angels or the shapes of the dead. But it is always the devil who sends these apparitions and the devil ever seeks wir destruction. These necromancers have taken our well-beloved physician because their end is our destruction and ruination.' He spat on the carpet in disgust. 'And as we are the state and the state is us, they strike at destroying this wir realm.'

'We shall search,' said Cecil. 'As we search out papist plots.'

'Aye. And right you are to do it. These necromancers ape God's services. As we publicly meet to worship Him, these creatures will meet in their numbers to praise their wicked master. Forbye, they counterfeit and scorn God.'

James trundled towards me again and I stood firm as his hand reached up to my face. 'We would have you seek them. And reward you for the discovery.' His hand fell and his nose twitched. 'You have been taking tobacco. A foul practice. Makes a filthy furnace of a man's insides. I intend on making a study of it in a scholarly way.' Abruptly he shucked my chin and then stepped back from me; but he continued speaking. 'Search London for these damned necromancers before wir entry into the city. And,' he winked, 'see you that you stay out of the wicked dens of vice where whoredom reigns and we hear there are foul practices of sodomy practiced. Abominable, heh?' His finger wagged again in my face. 'Detestable!'

What has Cecil told him?

I tried to keep my face unmoving but could not help blinking. Given what I had heard about King James when he ruled in Scotland, it felt rather like being lectured on the evils of adultery by Henry VIII.

Double-tongued indeed.

As though to give the lie to his warnings – and I knew from my own experiences that some of the men who speak out most vehemently against sexual congress with other men are most likely to be found seeking it in Southwark – a soft knock came at the door. 'Come,' barked James. A young man – a very young man, about Faith's age – in a pale green suit with blood-red silk spilling from slashed sleeves entered. His face was flushed.

'Yer wantit at the tumbling, yer Majesty.'

James held up his hands. 'Ach, it is not a king's place to dance.'

'Dae ye not wish tae watch?' The young man's eyebrows rose, his lips following in a smirk. James lumbered over to him and touched his face, as he had touched mine, in a lover's caress.

'Hawd your wheesh, naughty one. Peep at you as you have a tumble? Aye. Aye, there is a sight to see.' He leaned in and seemed to sniff the over-dressed boy's hair. He was, I realised, whispering something to him. The lad giggled, before pressing a finger to his lips. The king swivelled his head to us. 'We must away. We turn to beauty. Is my friend here not beautiful, Savage? Is he not?'

'I …' I was at a loss, in honesty. I eyed the lad. Too young for my tastes and as peacocking as any old theatrical could lust after.

'Aye, yet such rare birds you shall not find in the grubby parts of this sinful world. You, laddie, must turn to the uglier parts of this city and thrust your fingers deep into them, heh?'

I realised something then about King James. Like some desperate older men whom I had known – and had learnt to avoid – he was a great lover of beauty. Ageing, not beautiful and never having been so, he sought to surround himself with beautiful people. It was sad, I thought. Perhaps he found that purchasing the transitory love of more attractive people would reflect some of it on himself.

His croaking voice broke in on my thoughts. 'Get you gone into those dark places, Savage. Find the assembly of necromancers before they can work their wicked designs and you will find your laddie and my beloved servant. Read my wee book. It shall be a help to you. Remember always that a true hunter need not chase down his prey in ignorance. A true hunter is already awaiting it, unseen and ever ready. Gang, now.'

With his friend, he made to leave.

'Your Majesty,' called Cecil.

'Whit?!'

'I ... the matter of the queen's great inspection.'

'The queen!' spat James. 'Our loving wife. Are you married, Savage?'

'No, sir.'

'Hmph. Daft wee dug. A man should have a quim waiting at home. Only it is a shame and a pity that they have other lips, aye, and tongues that never still.'

'The inspection,' prompted Cecil. 'Of the route of the procession. We must discuss it.'

James fetched a theatrical sigh, leaning on the boy. 'You ken how a king must tend to all, eh? What is needing done, eh – telling the most illustrious Guild of Worshipful Old Bastards which cheeks of the royal arses they maun bend and kiss?' He smacked his lips. 'We have days yet, my Beagle. We shall discuss it on the morrow, before hunting, aye? I fear my lady will have her wee way, and no harm done. On the morrow. Take you to bed, man. You look like you have been ridden hard yourself. Eh, eh, Savage?' He laughed, turning away from us, and his minion giggled too.

Cecil bowed and I followed suit.

King James lurched out of the room, his arm around his young page's waist and his hand working at hunting something in those pale green breeches.

When they had gone, I licked my lips and turned to Cecil, the king's book still in my hand. Something James had said had given me an idea, and, for it to work, I should most certainly need permission.

A hunter need not chase down his prey...

No, I thought; a hunter might draw it out.

16

'It's simply just numbers,' said Faith. 'That's all there is to it.'

She, Hopgood and I were standing in my front room. I had decided not to share my plan with her. Her words of the previous afternoon had stung. They were right, but no less hurtful for it. I knew well enough my role in David's illness.

His being taken, however, I had decided was in no way my fault. Even if the necromancers had seized him because he had survived the plague, my part in causing him to get it in the first place was not at fault. If Faith thought so, she kept it quiet, and I decided not to point out that wicked people doing mad things was only ever their fault.

She and Hopgood had spent the previous night walking their pattens flat, going around the surrounding streets and following the passage of the Angela woman and David. They had, they had told me, only given up when the watch sent them home. They had lost the trail somewhere near Little Trinity. My guess was that she had taken him on a wherry downriver – which meant that they could be anywhere. It might take days to find the right boatman and bribe him, and even then it would be a guess whether he told the truth or not. I would not risk being led down blind alleys.

Over a breakfast of stuffed eggs, bread and dried apples, Faith outlined her plan. A lover of mathematics, she had divided the surrounding area into three sections, each containing an equal number of streets. Each of us was to take a section and work through it, knocking on every door and asking every member of every household whether they had seen anything of Angela or any of her ilk, either yesterday or ever. It gave her something to do, and I realised that she was in need of that. More – it gave her something to talk about: a thick mound of words to cover over the hard ones she had thrown at me the previous day.

I have said enough, in my time, to know that words cannot be taken back. What is worse is that one cannot make good on causing someone pain with those words. Until the witches of the world, or the men of natural science, find a way to reverse time, we will always hurt one another, say our little sorries, forgive and forget. But, at the first, in the moment of the hot words or cruel actions, the hurt caused can never be undone. It can never unhappen. So, I realised, it would be that Faith had wounded me then and, even if she were to apologise and I to laugh about it once we had rescued David – as I knew we would – it would always be true that I had anguished a little in my soul at her words. It was much like how sometimes I recalled making Thomas cry when he was only four by smashing some toy of his; though we were grown men now, somewhere, frozen in time, a little boy was crying from hurt.

And so I listened, saying nothing, affecting no air of hurt or pleasure or approval or demurral. It was, I thought, a good plan – if we had a dozen more people and all the time in the world.

About a week, Cecil had said, until the coronation procession. And fewer days than that until the inspection tour of the king and queen. I felt certain that the creatures would attempt something then; though I could not conceive of the madness of necromancers' plans, I knew well enough that such creatures put stock in certain days, as much as they did in symbols and words of enchantment. I had, in fact, flicked through King James's book during the night, a candle at my side. It was not the type of thing conducive to a good sleep.

The book was divided into three parts which, in summation, explained the prevalence of witchcraft, witches, and necromancers, the difference between astrology and astronomy, and the presence of the devil in our world. It told dark tales of their penchant for poisoning; of the symbols they used to conjure Satan; of the stones they used (I fished out Forman's and locked it in a box, knowing I would have need of it); of the images of people they made and burnt; of the storms and tempests they raised. One particular passage I read and reread, so closely did it give me twitch. On the subject of how devils can enter into houses, the answer given was:

They will choose the passage for their entresse, according to the forme that they are in at that time. For if they have assumed a dead bodie, whereinto they lodge themselves, they can easily enough open without dinne anie doore or window and enter in thereat.

I had, on reading all about the devil troubling dead bodies by carrying them 'out of the ground to serve his turn for a space' and having them climb through windows, sprung up from the chest on which I slept and stuffed bits of clothing into every gap in my shutters. On reading of a demon which takes people sleeping in their beds, I had closed the book altogether and cast it aside. Then I had got up and covered it over with a spare canvas doublet, just for good measure. If night terrors, I thought, were the wages of scholarship – a fear of things that had never before troubled the mind – then the dusty clerics and scholars and physicians – and kings apparently – could keep it.

But if what King James had written were true, and his book was impressive in its references to the greats and its histories of the dark arts, then there was no life after death for the body. Separated from the soul, a corpse was an empty thing that could be raised only by devils with evil intentions.

Those whistling sounds at the window – are they the winter wind or are they father's corpse, raised and shambling?

In the deepest gutter of the night, I would have sworn I could hear them. Still unable to sleep, another thing the king had said had played upon my mind. The woman, Angela, must have some master. Not the devil, perhaps, but another. Her fellow patient, with whom she had harassed Dr Gurney? It seemed a reasonable guess.

Or are the two of them mere foot-soldiers, acting on the orders of some general, as pickpockets and whores will answer to an upright man who remains hidden in the shadows?

It was small wonder that I was little in the mood for conversation in the morning. None of what I read I shared with Faith over breakfast, nor with Hopgood when he arrived, looking as though he hadn't spent the previous evening jetting about London.

'So are we settled in this?' she asked. Her face was eager as she looked at us. 'A search by numbers. It is the only way. If this bitch is able to come and go about London so often, she must live within a certain distance of us.'

But London is a maze: a huge, sprawling network of dead ends and crumbling homes.

I looked at Nicholas Hopgood. To his credit, he had not run away but in fact had come back. What I noticed also, with a flare of annoyance, was that he seemed perfectly willing to enter into her plan and again take foot.

Bloody young people.

It was, I supposed, a good thing. Any other prentice would have run a mile at finding himself caught up in such madness as a missing brother. Moreover, he did not seem to be at all cowed by Faith's shameless flaunting of her ability to count and plan. In fact, I thought, looking at his moonstruck eyes, he seemed fairly bowled over by her. 'Yes, Mistress Faith – Faith.' He blushed. 'We'll find him today.'

I murmured my assent. She did not press me. Perhaps, I thought, she felt a little embarrassed about her outburst too, and we should let the thing be buried by time, cooled tempers, and other action.

I watched them leave and disappear down Shoe Lane, where he briefly touched her hand and they parted. I was heartened to see that neither attempted to steal a kiss from the other. Though I too frequently tumbled into bed or down alleys with strangers a sight handsomer than Nicholas Hopgood, I held my girl to a higher standard.

Once assured that they were well on their way, I waited a while, before heading down to the Whitefriars Stairs and carefully picking my way down the slippery, ice-crusted steps. Securing a wherry, I ordered it to cut across and up the river.

I had not expected to find myself strolling through Lambeth again. As I picked my way towards Forman's house, my mind mocked me with the stupidity of my plan. I should have been searching London, kicking down doors and questioning those I knew in the underworld who made it their business to watch out for the antics of zanies and other dangerous creatures. Yet the self-doubt did not win. I kept my pace, up the steps and past the palace, through the tangle of streets until I came to the garden. None of his female admirers were present, I noticed. I knocked on the door and the fragrant Mrs Forman answered.

'I told you whores to get to f– oh!'

'Oh.'

'I thought...'

'I have come to enquire of the doctor again, Mrs Forman. Some news of his attacker.'

'That creature,' she said. I did not know if he meant her husband or Angela. 'Yes, he is here. He is in the garden at the rear.'

'Thank you.'

'God go with you, sir.' She closed the door on me.

I skirted the building, my boots sinking into the marshy ground, and went to the back of the place. To my surprise, the vista was of open ground and marshland rather than the backs of other houses. Cold, misty air swirled. And hunched over, pulling weeds with gentle motions and casting them aside, was Simon Forman.

'Good morrow, Dr Forman,' I cried. 'What news?'

The older man straightened, turning and frowning. The scratch marks on his face, I noticed, had been smeared with a thick, greyish ointment, flecks of dried herb still visible in it. He had no scholarly robes on, but a plain black doublet, its buttons undone, and the linen shirt beneath was unlaced to reveal a thatch of greying hair. Realisation dawned in his eyes, swiftly replaced by a sardonic look.

'The lord secretary's man.'

'Quite. A good memory you have.'

'It lasts a day, I confess, even in my old age.'

'My garden,' he gestured. 'A perk of my lease here. I hope to put up a fence against the common. Stop the local folks taking my fruit and herbs in season.'

'I think that can be arranged most easily,' I said, looking out over the green-brown wasteland.

'Yet you have not come to discuss gardens, I think.'

'No.'

He crossed his arms, wincing a little. 'I own I am amazed to see you. I thought you conceived a hearty dislike for me.'

He's going to be difficult.

I smiled. 'Do not flatter yourself, doctor. I harbour a hearty dislike for most people.'

His granite face split in a grin. 'Why are you come? Have you found the mad bitch who had at me?'

I produced the stone I had taken from his chamber. I no longer wanted the damned thing anyway – though I collected pretty objects, I would no longer give something tainted with mysticism houseroom.

To some the devil gives such stones or poulders as will helpe to cure or cast on diseases.

I held the thing out, its cool, carved surface cold against my fingertips. 'We are satisfied that you bear her no company and have told us all you know and truthfully. I come to return your property.' He squinted at it, and his smile disappeared. The heavy lines of his big, flat brow deepened still farther. 'I regret that it had to be tested by the king's physicians,' I lied. I could think of no other way of being rid of the thing and having him not think me a thief at the same time – if he had even noticed the loss.

'That.' He took it and put it in the pocket at his belt. 'A thing of no great value. Or so I thought. It seems you found it a loud-voiced thing with much to say.'

'No. Nor no great mystical properties in it either. Yet I have come for more than the return of your property.' I considered adding 'my friend' and decided that would be too unctuous. 'What I hope … what the lord secretary wills … is that you might be of further help to the king.'

'The king?' he asked, his bushy eyebrow rising. A light rain began, cold and needling. 'Come into the house.'

We entered through a backdoor into a large kitchen, where a pot boiled over a good fire. A cook stood at a table, chopping root vegetables. He touched his cap at our entrance, and we passed through the steamy warmth and into a parlour. His wife opened her mouth to speak, saw me, and scurried away.

'You married, Savage?' he asked when the door was closed.

'No.'

'Shame. Fine thing, a wife. Even if that one is become worse than my ancient mother, and she a harridan whom Death fears to come for.' He beckoned for me to sit.

Once we were settled in the parlour – a room devoid of any signs of mystical sorcery and instead furnished like any city gentleman's of good repute – he hunched forward on the narrow chair he had taken and said, 'how might a simple doctor like me serve a king who mistrusts all … ah … of the esoteric arts?'

I cleared my throat. 'You are known by many about this city, doctor, as a man well versed in these arts.' His expression betrayed nothing. 'When you give out word of strange or mystic matters, people listen. They come to you for the news.'

He sat back. 'I have a little fame, it is true. In such matters.'

'And you have friends – servants, I might say – in your employ in these matters.' I was thinking of the mountebank in the dark-lensed glasses who had been selling bits of Forman's fireplace as magic stones from Egypt sovereign against the plague. Forman only shrugged. 'My lord secretary wishes you to put one of these men in yoke. On the morrow.'

'In yoke? To what purpose?'

I told him and he listened carefully, by turns confused and amused.

'… And in conclusion of the matter, you might put about word of this miracle today. Amongst the city, the town. I am sure that word from you on so wonderful and amazing a matter will draw a crowd of people.'

'I am sure it might,' allowed Forman. He leant forward again, his elbows on his knees and his chin in his hands. In his loose black suit, he looked himself like a devil. 'Yet crowds are not allowed.'

'They are when the lord secretary wills them. And with the playhouses closed, people will hunger for some entertainment. A little light herb pottage to spice their stomachs before the rich meats of the coronation.'

Forman seemed to consider this as he stood, stretched, groaned, and made his way to a fine, unbroken fireplace. With his back to me, he began speaking. 'Mr Savage … I understand you have formed a

145

certain impression of me. And I would have you know something.' I essayed a polite smile, though he did not turn. 'At every turn of the path, I have met with scorn. And the sneers of superior men of physick. I tried, for many years, I tried to attend to matters their way. And they would have none of an honest, good man from the country. And now, you see, the great and the good flock to me because I give them what they desire to hear.' He exhaled through his sharp nose. 'I have recalled where I know your face from. You're the man who used to look like Essex. You work for the playhouses. You've seen the players and stage-wrights, haven't you?' I murmured in the affirmative. 'What a fair little circle they make. Barring all others, scorning them as unlettered. Well, the college of physicians makes that company of he-cats look like a great welcoming family. And I note that you and the good lord secretary come to me and not them in your troubles.'

I swallowed, and said, 'you have skills and friends, doctor, that they lack.'

'This is true. Yet this scheme of yours ... I think it the maddest thing I have ever heard. And I have heard much. I assume it is some plot to draw out the wretched woman who attacked me, yes?' I said nothing. 'Hm. As I say, a mad thing.'

My heart sank. 'Then you will not do it?'

'Not help the secretary with a mad and venturous enterprise?' Finally, he turned his attention from the fireplace and looked at me, raising his hands. 'Of course I will do it.'

17

If ever England will see a year of wonder, it is surely this year. All talk is of the designs of the evil King Philip and the City of London – all greater London itself – is on guard. Soldiers have gone to Tilbury and Hope with them. The earl, after all, has been outfitting ships against the Spanish threat since the death of the Scotch queen.

He is no soldier, of course, but every man is expected to do his part. Why is he here?

Perhaps he hopes to see how men behave when Death wields a mighty, flaming sword of battle. He arrives amid the smoke of rumour and blazing imagery. English ships, it seems were lit aflame and sent fiery amongst the Spanish. The sight of fireships had frightened them and driven them off – no one knew where. The ships themselves would have plunged, dead, to the ocean floor.

He is sorry he did not see the sight of fire on water.

Perhaps it will happen again.

As he stands amongst the others for inspection, his armour provided by the earl and better than most of the homemade stuff of his fellows, he watches, and he waits for the great Elizabeth to appear.

Eventually, the men fall silent and, over the heads of the assembled company, he has the brief impression of the torch-flame of an orange-red wig as she rides alongside a bobbing feather – her friend and reputed lover, the earl of Leicester. Every now and then wig and feather stop as the couple pause to speak with some soldier or other.

When they have gone, it washes through the soldiers and so to Hope that the queen is giving a great speech from wherever she now is. In fragments, it reaches him, no doubt mangled and altered by the succession of tongues it has passed over.

'Let tyrants fear!'

'I will lay down my honour and my blood!'

'You have deserved rewards and crowns!'

'My faithful and loving people!'

The soldiers cheer unevenly, and Hope's voice is amongst them, his fist raised in aggressive joy.

But there is no battle, at least not on England's soil. The Spaniards do not try again but flee and are scattered by the winds. Days pass, and weeks, and months, and the soldiers, like dogs starved of a bone, are released.

Death will not be so easily cheated, though.

The sailors are kept locked in their ships for too long and disease catches fire. The soldiers light up with it and carry it back to London. Hope is spared – again, surely a miracle of salvation – but as he winds his way back to service in the earl's household, he sees the starvation and sickness of those who stood beside him at Tilbury. Most of the sailors are said to be dead in Margate and those soldiers who make it back to London drop dead in the city's streets.

Victory is in every man's mouth – victory against the failed Spanish invasion. Yet a more dangerous and far older enemy has defeated England's mariners and soldiers.

Thinking on the fireships as his feet grow hard with blisters, Hope is assaulted by other images of fire.

St Catherine and the burning of the philosophers.

The wonderful fire spotted in the sky in the old reports of the 40s.

The infamous Bonfire of the Vanities.

Archbishop Cranmer steadfastly thrusting his hand into the flame in the Book of Martyrs.

Three women being burnt alive in the same book, a baby bursting from the womb of one and being tossed back into the fire by the wicked Mary Tudor's executioners.

The string of fires lit across England to celebrate the death of Mary of Scotland.

In my end is my beginning.

Vita in morte sumus.

His head seems to leap and twirl with flames.

***

Hope turned over on his berth and let out another cry of anguish. His eyes stung from the tears; they felt raw and dry. The Scottish queen's promised miracle had no more come to pass than the promise by the spirit of Elizabeth he had seen near St Paul's. And worse, the spirits had stopped appearing to him altogether, leaving him to plot his own path.

It had been a ghastly affair.

With the doctor again present, he had ordered the old woman Amos had found – she had been a cackling creature who would have been taken for a witch if they had not saved her – and named Huldah to have her head struck off.

In her end should have been her beginning.

The water did not work and neither did the axe. He had had killed two of his loving and beloved followers and neither had been returned.

'Come to me!' he cried into the shadows of the cabin. 'Please! Tell me!' Silence. Or did he hear mocking laughter coming distantly, as though through many closed doors? As if in answer to the thought, the door opened.

'Angela,' he said, sitting up, his feet finding the deck. He wiped the tears from his eyes and attempted a smile.

'My love,' she said, and his smile became real. 'We have released Huldah into the water.'

Tears threatened again and his voice caught in his throat. 'We have failed. The spirit was rather a demon, tricking us with false promises. Neither drowning nor … the axe … will light our path.'

Light, he thought, as the word emerged. Fire.

'No. But you will find our way. I have faith.'

'Tell me,' he asked, 'do you think this ship might sail again?'

'I … I don't know. I know nothing of sailing matters.'

Hope put his fist to his chin. 'We might have some of the others speak with the sailors out there. The unemployed ones. Enquire of them. If they can be trusted. Secure us sweep-oars.'

'Brother Joel – he was a sailor. Said his brother and father died at sea. He – he can speak to them out there.'

Hope beamed. 'Yes. A marvel. I would … I would have life everywhere again. The *Crown Elizabeth* returned to life as she had enjoyed it when the earl first fitted her out. A resurrection, truly.' He could see it too, the old sails rigged and unfurled, the anchor raised, the sweeps plying the water as the old girl tasted the open water of the Thames once more. 'And it was you who thought of Brother Joel. A marvel, you are. I love you.' He thought he saw a blush in the half-light of the cabin. 'You are a true angel.'

She clasped her hands in front of her as though in prayer. 'The doctor–'

'Pah.'

'The doctor has concocted his physick. He says it might help us.'

'Help us to what?'

'To share in your visions.'

'Oh? I thought he said that it could not be done.'

Again, she shrugged, but her hands unlocked and went to her belt. She detached a small pouch and stepped closer, opening it up. Hope stood and bent to it. A small collection of crushed and powdered herbs. A foul smell rose from it, like the sweat that gathered and dries in the hair of an armpit. He sniffed and then stepped back, his head already spinning.

'Fire is the way! Fire!'

'What?' Hope asked.

'I didn't say anything,' said Angela.

Hope's eyes grew wide and slid back to the pouch. 'I think this an efficacious physick. Is it eaten?'

'Dr Gurney said I might dissolve it in our water and share it amongst the company.' She slipped her hands down to his belt, returning the key to the doctor's cell.

'Do so now,' said Hope, hardly daring to imagine the useless Gurney might have found means of distributing the miraculous visions. Angela nodded, folding the cloth back over her stinking herbs. As if on impulse, she stood on her tiptoes and kissed him before leaving.

Could it be true? Hope wondered when he was alone again. Were herbal potions the means of sharing his gift with his family? He did not entirely trust the doctor. The fellow had battled him over the baptism of Isaac and positively screamed the ship down until he was restrained over the beheading of Huldah. Yet the angelic voices had returned even from sniffing the crushed herbs.

Yes. It must be true. Everything, he knew, had a pattern. Nothing happened by chance. He had been led into the earl's service and thereby come upon knowledge of Dr Gurney for a reason. The man was not of the Enlightened, but he had the knowledge to help them on their way.

He rinsed his eyes with water from the pail Angela had left with him and made ready to go and eat – and drink – with his people. As he descended to the great deck, he saw Angela standing at a large pot, stirring the herbs into the usual pottage. Already the Enlightened were beginning to queue up.

They know two of their fellows have now been released from this life and yet they remain, he thought, and fought the urge to run and kiss each one. Before he could do so, a voice rang down from the hatch above. He looked up. No angel, but the hard face of Amos was framed in a halo of grey.

'Nathaniel! News out of the town.' The man's head disappeared and was replaced by a flash of dark clothing as he began to swing down to the lower deck. When he landed, breathless and panting, Hope frowned but nodded for him to continue. 'It is in every mouth out there. A great spectacle. The magus Simon Forman–'

'Forman! That foul creature. Seducer of women!'

'He has discovered a man who suffered the pestilence and lived. And now claims holy visions of glory. Of the new king enthroned and crowned in light. He is to display the man at Southwark today, at two of the clock.'

'Southwark?'

'Ay.' Hope's mind reeled. 'We must go – we must have him.'

'I …' Something turned, the sound of key unlocking a door in his head. 'False. Lies.'

'What? I speak the truth.' Amos's face hardened further and a hand went to his hip.

Hope put a hand on his shoulder and felt hard muscle through the sleeve. 'Not you, my brother. This Forman.' A voice rang through his head, blessed and angelic, and he screwed up his face in concentration. When it had ceased, he blinked at Amos. 'It is all lies. I have been told nothing by the spirits of a new man with the gift. This is … this is some wicked plot meant to test us. To break us. A trap. We are being cozened.'

'But … who? The king's men?'

'I do not know. Enemies! We have many enemies. Spies.' He shook his head. 'The boy's master. Where is the boy? Where is Samuel?'

He turned away from Amos, back to the queue of men and women waiting to be served their pottage. The red-headed child, who had said his name was David or Dust, stood at the back. 'Samuel,' barked Hope, his footsteps clattering over the deck as he crossed to him. 'Samuel!' He gripped the boy by the shoulders, ignoring the look of panic that brought colour into his cheeks and made his freckles stand out. 'Your former master, that wicked creature – who is he?'

'Ned,' stuttered the boy. 'I don't know no other name.'

'Ned.' He released the boy, who backed away. He did not re-join the queue but fled into the shadows beyond the light of the portholes. Hope turned to Amos, who had followed him. 'We should have dealt with this creature before. It is he – he who aims to stop us. He is a devil. He will be at this false display. Take him, Amos. Make an end of him.'

Amos smiled and gave one hard nod before making his way back towards the ladder. He would not receive the gift of the herb-infused pottage but no matter. And Hope would not partake of it either – not now his own blessed voices were returning to warn him of spiery without it. Instead, he smiled and watched as Angela held the ladle to the mouths of the others.

151

***

In his cargo cell, Gurney reeled back from the latest bout of vomiting and steeled himself to look into the bloody water and piss of the slop bucket. It had been unnatural. The drowning had been a terrible sight, but the beheading…

Again, his door had been unlocked and the grim farce of the madmen enacted. This time, their victim had been a crack-brained old woman with grey hair, who bent down meekly, giggling and talking to herself, even as the brute Amos had raised an old sailor's axe and begun hacking away at her neck. He missed on the first blow and the dull blade had crushed the back of her skull. That had quietened her and she had gone limp. He had tried again, and again, until eventually the grizzled head, its hair soaked with blood, had fallen away.

And again he endured the tears and cries of the leader, Hope, who had expected a miracle and begun raving about the long-dead queen of Scots and her apparent promises of life after death.

He had decided then to stall no more. He had given them their drugs and decided upon escape.

He threw a cloth over the slop bucket, which was still gory from his attempts to clean the old woman's blood from the deck. It might have been his imagination, but he thought he could still smell the metallic tang of it even over the foul reek of the henbane. He had no aversion to blood, of course, but he very much objected to its being wantonly spent. He looked around the hold. Mercator and Frisius, he did not think, had much to say about unlocking sealed doors from the inside. Nor did God in His wisdom leave teachings or commandments on how to break free from cargo holds on rotting ships.

Rotting.

When a corpse began to rot, it fell apart, the tissues and sinews failing. Why not a ship? He picked up the pestle he had been given and had used to grind the herbs, smashing it against the frame of the door. It did nothing. Brute force was the answer. He was a bulky man who had, in truth, been running to fat. Standing well back, he turned his shoulder to the door and ran at it, bouncing backwards and falling to the deck. His arm caught the trunk with the books on top and they fell. Cursing, he clambered to his feet and tried again.

Nothing.

He regarded the door once more, tracing its frame. The lock, he knew, was in the middle of the left side. He kicked at it, feeling the muscles in his leg tearing and pulling. Still it held fast. Again and again he kicked, sweat begin to pop out on his temples. He could feel it running down the side of his face, mingling with unbidden tears. His vomit-flavoured breath came in ragged gasps. The door remained closed and locked and he fell to battering it with his hands – a futile gesture of frustration rather than any attempt to open it.

And then the lock clicked.

Gurney, sliding to the deck and landing on his backside, began to back away. He had attracted Hope, his gaoler, and keeper of the key. Who knew what mad scheme the lunatic had in mind? Or perhaps he had understood the noisy attempt to escape and had come to put an end to him...

When the door opened, Gurney gasped. Standing in the doorway was a child – a little red-headed boy wearing an over-sized white robe that trailed behind him. The key was protruding from the lock like a skeletal finger pointing the way to escape. 'What – who?'

'Who are you?' asked the boy, his voice low. 'I thought my sister might be here. Or my brother.'

Gurney clawed at the bloodstained deck in his hurry to rise. They had a child, he thought, these mad creatures – probably one of the children of a member of the sect. He would not tolerate the murder of a child, if that was any part of their plan. 'Come, boy, we must away. What's your name?'

'David. But they call me Samuel so maybe it's Samuel now.'

'Come, David.' Gurney bent down. 'I don't know if your mother and father are amongst them, but–'

'I don't got a mother or father. They're dead. They went to Heaven. But I got a sister and a brother.'

'Well, those people out there are not ...' What to say to a child? 'They're not right. In their wits. Do you understand me?'

Before David could answer, a chorus of cries crowded the air behind him, rumbling from amidships. It was an amorphous sound, part joyful, part wild, part frightened, wholly without sense. 'Come, now – we must get onto the docks. You didn't eat anything did you, anything they gave you? Today?'

'No. No, I hid.'

'Good.'

'What's happening to them all? She made me come. Said I had to, so I did.'

Gurney took the boy's hand and led him out into the dark tunnel of the passage beyond. It stank not of blood or herbs, but of damp wood and earthy silt. He was at a loss. He had thought only of escaping the hold – beyond that, he could not recall the structure of the ship other than that it was small, with its narrow passages running into one another like a little forest of arteries.

He set off ahead, one hand in David's and the other feeling its way along flaking bulkheads. The thing, he supposed, was to find light and an incoming rush of good air. Ahead, the passage ended in a T shape, a door directly in front and the hall running left and right. The deck beneath him, he could feel, sloped slightly downwards towards the head of the T.

'Left,' he whispered, 'or right? Where did you come from, David?'

'I came from – there.'

As he said the word, the door ahead flew open and the guttural cries and wails intensified. Standing in the doorway was Hope. 'Doctor,' he cried.

Gurney released the boy's hand and tried to shield him with his body. But Hope did not seem angry or even surprised. 'I … I was … the door was …'

'You have given them the gift,' the man cried.

Shrieking laughter rose over his shoulders. Someone shouted, 'I see! I see fairies!'

Another: 'I see nothing – all is black – I am blinded!'

Still another: 'They rush at me!' Laughter followed. 'I see my son! He lives, but I cannot touch him!'

Hope smiled again and, Gurney thought, for the first time the man looked truly and supremely happy. Tears glistened in his eyes as he said, 'they understand. They see as I do. Dr Gurney, we thank you for this blessing.'

Gurney stood, irresolute, as the man's thanks and his followers' drug-crazed cries washed over him. Henbane caused intense and powerful delusions, forgetfulness, confusion, and oftentimes robbed people of the ability to walk sensibly. In strong doses, it could kill – but there had been enough killing on the ship and he had been very careful in mixing just enough to un-wit the creatures of the Enlightened. He opened his mouth to speak, but Hope's face changed, his eyes growing suspicious. The leader cocked his head to one side as if listening to something. 'How did you get out?'

Gurney's chest rose. 'Mistress Angela left the key in the lock, sir.'

'No. No, she returned it to me.'

'You are mistaken, Mr Hope. Your mind wanders. It is a symptom of your gift, the forgetting of things. Imagining of others.'

Hope frowned, crossing his arms. His neck twisted as he peered behind Gurney. 'Samuel?' Gurney felt his heart flutter and his stomach sink beneath the sudden flapping.

'The boy caught me,' the doctor said smoothly. 'I own I was going to leave this ship. I have given you what you wished. Your people have the visions. I think some will see the dead, as you wished. My work here is done.'

'Leave?' Hope's face hardened and he shook his head. 'No. I cannot allow you to leave. There are spies everywhere, doctor. We are watched by the unenlightened and the wicked. Samuel's former master is one of them – a demon in the form of man. You must remain with us. Samuel, return the good doctor to his chamber, please.' Gurney's shoulders slumped and he began to turn back towards the cargo hold. 'You will be pleased to be hear, doctor, when the end comes. We will now all see the path ahead. I see it already. It is lit in dancing flames, as red as … as Samuel's hair. Boy, you will watch over our guest. I trust you. I love you. We must all have some occupation until the great day, and yours will be to lodge here, outside the door, and keep him good company. Go now.'

18

If you are going to stage some enterprise of dubious legality, do it in Southwark. I had passed the previous afternoon, after my visit to Forman, helping to spread word of the miraculous sight that was to take place the following day: a man who had survived the plague and now saw wonderful visions. It was, further, a case examined and assured by the celebrated Dr Simon Forman of Lambeth, attendant physician to many great and famous persons, etc.

Faith and Hopgood had arrived at Shoe Lane not long after I did and I counted it a success that they had heard the news, though not, of course, from me. It should have reached into every corner of London, including whichever bolt-hole Angela and her fellows – and perhaps her necromantic master – lived. And where they had taken David.

Or so I hoped.

Other than that, the pair had found only a number of households which, as Cecil had said, complained of missing family members who had suffered the plague, lived, and then gone off somewhere. It was not much, and they told me that they planned to attack Hopgood's district of Holborn today, northwest of us and up the hill, away from Fleet Street and the City. As he had made ready to leave, Hopgood lingered, I suspected, for a kiss. Faith merely gave him a harried thank you and squeezed his hand.

I encouraged her over breakfast as she awaited him in the morning, meekly accepting and silently ignoring my orders to go, ironically, to Lambeth and knock on doors there, as they would be doing northwards.

If she is right and you are wrong, David's blood will be on your hands.

I ignored the persistent voice of doubt, dressed in a thick canvas doublet, stout breeches, and a warm frieze coat, and even slid Dr Gurney's book inside, where the thickness of winter clothing would keep it tight – for I intended to ask Forman if he could divine anything from it that Cecil and I might have missed. Thus attired, I waited until Hopgood arrived to pick up Faith. He did, faithfully, like a puppy, at eleven, and together they left. I wished them luck in their search and had it returned.

I did not intend to take a wherry downriver to Southwark – I had caught my wherryman of the previous day by the ear and paid several others to spread the word too – but began my walk through the city. The onslaught of bright spring sunlight made me blink. It was a good thing, though; a dry, sunny day would encourage lookers-on to spend outdoors the time that they might, in better days, have passed in the theatre.

As I left Shoe Lane, already well into the morning, I had the uncanny feeling that I was being followed and spun, expecting to find that Faith and her little playmate had hidden in wait, intending to catch me out. They were not there; no one was there. I relaxed my hand on the dagger hilt at my belt. Nerves, I suspected – or guilt at not doing what I promised to do. Again.

I had not gone far along the great thoroughfare of Fleet Street with its jumble of tumbledown houses, shops, and piemen, when I spotted the vaguely familiar figure of a straight-backed man hobbling alongside a young girl. I bit at my lip, trying to place them, when it hit me: they were the steward and maidservant who had worked for my old landlord, Richard Frere. I raised a hand and stepped towards them. My greetings, which I had intended to follow up with the news of the spectacle, died in my throat. Both were ragged and patches of dust stood out on their frayed clothing. 'Good morrow, man,' I said. 'Are you looking for work still?'

The old man turned to me, his military bearing stooping. The girl took his arm and shook it. 'He's the man wot come into the old house,' she said. 'You looking for help, mister?'

'No, I–'

'Come, Dorrie. We'll find work at St Paul's.' He started to stomp away, and she tugged on his arm.

'I have work for you. A fine mistress, a physician's wife, whose servants have run off or died. If it please you.'

Dorcas smiled, hope shining white in a grimy face. The former steward looked more doubtful as pride battled desperation. 'A physician?' he croaked.

I held up my hands. 'A royal physician. He is not at home at present. You'll find his wife there. Foster Lane. Tell her the man who visited the other day enquiring of the doctor sent you with his good account.'

After some grumbling and to-ing and fro-ing, I won their agreement and they began stumbling down towards the Fleet Bridge. As Dorcas essayed a little curtsey to me and turned away, I mouthed, 'see if you can't do something about the old bird's painted face.' The doctor, when I found him, would owe me something for procuring him new servants, I decided, smiling at her eager nods.

There, I thought: a good turn done for three people, and I might be about my greater business.

Less guilt for the lying bastard that you are.

My mission was to stop at every tavern on the way to Southwark, and I did so, from the grimiest and worst-reputed kens to the stage-wrights' and poets' haunts. I was pleased to see the music-men had returned and, happily, they paid me to tell them the news so that they could charge others to hear it sung. Between Fleet Street and New Fish Street, I attended upon every apple-wife, lawyer, apprentice, Jew, vintner, student, labourer, merchant, whore, and cutler I came across. The words 'marvel', 'wonder', 'miracle', and 'illustrious sight' were seldom off my lips. By the time I came upon the rickety-looking crowd of houses and shops that tottered on their stilts over London Bridge, I fancied I had amassed quite a following of people, all intent on seeing the sight.

It had been months now – the better part of a year in fact – since the theatres had been closed and mass gatherings outlawed. The people of London were starved of entertainment, having grown used to it over the many years of Messrs, Marlowe, Kyd, Shakespeare, Greene, Heywood, Dekker, Marston, Middleton, and yes, even the blowhard Ben Jonson. Eye-delights were in their blood now and they were hungry for the sweet sights of horror, mystery, and magic that Forman and I promised. It was all a nonsense, of course, but so was seeing a boy dance about the stage counterfeiting a pretty lass, with a swarthy bearded man pretending to be her youthful lover. If a little gunpowder could spark and smoke to help conjure Faustus's angels, so too could a learned doctor have a mountebank convince the penny-worths that a man saw visions. And today the show would cost them nothing.

I crossed the span of the bridge, the assembly of people not quite with me but drifting in the same direction, telling others. It was like a snowball rolling downhill. Before too long, there was no need to tell people myself. The sight of a large crowd moving towards the south bank was enough to attract them. Fools with nothing better to do were following simply because they saw others going somewhere and supposed something must be happening. Others, those with things to sell, saw a great, hungry beast made of people and picked up their goods and brought them along, touting them to the crowd. Excited chatter accompanied the musicians who joined us.

'It's the king's wot I 'eard – the new king's gonner appear. 'eard 'e's a drinker.'

'It ain't that. It's a madman. They're gonner 'ang 'im.'

'I 'eard it's a witch.'

'Nah, ain't that, mate – it's a seer, one of them prophets like wot's in the bible.'

I confess, despite the seriousness of what I had to do, my heart swelled at the sight of my adopted city blooming again, and in the new spring season, into its old noisy, ugly, greedy, stupid, sheep-like way of life.

I left the crowd and its carnival atmosphere in Bankside, where it could pulse outwards between the bear pit and the locked and bolted playhouses of the Globe, the Rose, and the Swan. Only the brothels, with their white-painted fronts (which were almost constantly refreshed, plague or not), were open and thriving, disgorging whores of both sexes to entice those in the crowd to delights other than the expectation of a prophet.

Me, I picked my way through the sudden mob of fallen men and women with shining pennies for eyes and walked through the streets with their crooked overhangs until my boots met honest dead grass. Paris Garden spread before me – a park-like space to the west of the bear and dog pits. I ignored their blank wooden stares and quickened my pace until I was deep into the garden and came upon a large, square-fronted mansion with a moat surrounding it.

The Holland Leaguer, as the brothel was known, was the most exclusive brothel in London, and it was popularly said that the nobility of the realm were not unfamiliar visitors. In theglare of the day, it made an odd sight in Bankside. With its cheerful white paint, red-tiled roof, and smoking chimneys, it might have been lifted by a giant hand from a gentleman's estate and placed carefully amongst the crooked wooden playhouses and gaming dens.

Crossing the small drawbridge over the moat, I met an imitation royal guard complete with halberd. Only his much-broken nose gave the game away. 'Good morrow, Hunks,' I said. I knew the fellow of old. He was a hire-hack for whom beating up and throwing out drunken patrons was honest work.

'T'ain't ne'er Ned Savage, yer?' He squinted at me.

'Ay.'

'Didn't fink you wiz one fer the ladies wot give it up up yonder.'

I closed my eyes and inhaled, searching for the words. It had been on Forman's instructions that I met him at the whorehouse. As though he had heard my curse, a window above – made of horn, for discretion's sake – opened, and the doctor hung out of it. He was wearing only a shirt, on his upper parts anyway, and it was again open to reveal the forest of his chest. 'Let him pass, Hunks.'

A woman in a dark wig, her lips as heavily painted as Mrs Gurney's, joined him. 'Yer, Hunks. Let 'im pass.' The big doorkeeper meekly stood aside, a semi-toothed grin on his face.

'Them'll make a man outta you, Ned Savage,' he said as I slipped inside.

The parlour looked more like what one might find in a real knight's house, I thought. At least on first glance. There were tapestries on the walls and chairs and benches set up alongside gaming tables. Curtains covered up entrances into other rooms. On closer inspection, however, the illusion failed. The tapestries all depicted either grotesques or erotic scenes – naked nymphs hiding from impossibly muscled, hairless men. And the furniture was all too new, too polished. In a real mansion, such things were older, inherited from ancient ancestors. Unfortunately, I had no chance to spot anything small that might be slipped into a pocket. As I stood measuring the place up, looking for the staircase, two women appeared, the first pulling aside a curtain.

'Good morrow, pretty sir,' said the first one. She was good-looking, but very young. Her dress was cut low, to reveal the upper part of budding breasts. Her fellow was sturdier and older, her enormous bosoms threatening to burst their stays. Immediately, both were at my side, pawing and cooing.

'Peace, ladies,' I said. 'If ever a wrong mark was shot at, I'm it. Tell me, how do I get to the doctor? He's expecting me.'

I flattered myself they were disappointed, though probably only that I would pay them nothing, and they led me through a curtain to a room with mirrors on every wall. I stopped to admire myself only briefly, before taking the narrow staircase half-hidden behind another tapestry.

Three people were in the room upstairs, standing beside an enormous tester bed with red hangings: Dr Forman, the whore (an older woman, whose sallow complexion was flawless), and a third man I did not recognise. 'You cast a wide net, doctor,' I smirked.

'Be off with you. Ned Savage, this is Bess Holland, the lady proprietor of this house.' I bowed, removing my hat and regarding her. I had heard of her, of course, and if I shaved a few years off her, I thought I might even had seen her in the days before she had been run out of her establishments north of the river. Yet the kind of bawdry she sold was out of my willingness to pay and divorced from my tastes.

'Donna Britannica Hollandia,' she corrected the doctor in an exaggerated accent. In return, he took her bare arm – there were no sleeves attached to her dress, it being all bodice and bustle – and kissing it along its length.

'Oh, ti amo, ti amo,' he breathed wetly. She gave a throaty laugh, her bosom heaving.

Even as he smothered her arm, she tilted her head to one side and looked at me. 'You might do well enough, duckie. Or woulda done ten years back. Ain't no call for a man in 'is twenties, love.'

Why, you pox-quimmed old trull!

''ere, leave it aht, Simon.

'I doubt,' I said, a hand on my hip, 'that any in London could afford me.'

'P'r'aps the new king might fancy it,' she returned.

The image of that great over-padded rooster clucking at me brought a shiver. I coughed and jerked my head towards the other man. 'John, mate,' he said. 'The doctor 'ere reckons you've seen me already.' He turned and bent to a scarlet carpet, pulling forward a sack and letting some of its contents spill. The sooty stones from Forman's fireplace. 'From the tombs of the kings of Egypt, most rare, most sovereign against the plague,' he said in a quite different voice that I recognised.

I smiled. 'You hope to sell a few more today?'

'Might be,' he shrugged. 'A great shame to waste a crowd. Can hear 'em already out there.'

'John here is a skilled player. Better than any I've seen in yonder playhouses, mark you,' said Forman, lacing up his shirt. 'Should have a good number of groundlings.'

I pouted. 'Don't say "groundlings", Forman. Only Will Shakespeare says "groundlings".'

'Ha! And what Mr Shakespeare says, the rest will follow.'

'So he would like to think.' I could picture the balding playwright: a quiet man with an open mind about his works – but fierce in his desire to prove his wit by having others steal it. Forman did not reply immediately, tutting at a difficult lace. As Bess helped him into his doublet, he went on, 'I'll introduce John here. He'll play his part. You watch for that hell-cat creeping out to steal him away, speak to him, whatever the bitch does.'

I nodded. When Forman was dressed and busily running a comb through his hair, Bess attended to John, whitening his face and drawing circles around his eyes 'to give 'im a right 'aunted look abaht him.'

When we were ready, we all three went downstairs, John already murmuring to himself and looking around. I carried his sack of stones and Forman led the way, springing down the staircase like a young man in his prime.

We left The Holland's Leaguer and melted into the crowd – or I did. People made way for Forman and he walked purposefully, his head down and his features twisted in contemplation. All trace of the lustful old man had gone. He had learnt well, I thought, from watching the players at their craft.

As if by magic indeed, the crowd parted in the shadow of the Globe, which seemed to stand watching in irritation as the play unfolded outside its circular walls. I let my two fellows step into the centre of the space made, falling into the opening ring of spectators, a woman selling dried oranges on my left and a man with a tabor on my right. 'Good morrow to you, friends, all,' boomed Forman. His gravelly voice silenced those nearest, and the silence seemed to run through the crowd.

Just like the first speaker in a play.

'You have heard, I think, the news of this wondrous sight, this spectaculum mirabilis. I have made study of–'

'Stop! Stop this!'

The shrill voice cut across Forman's and the doctor paused, shading his eyes and searching the crowd. I followed his gaze. A snarl of muttering and hissing voices rose from the other side of the mob as a man pushed his way through, waving an arm in the air.

I closed my eyes upon recognising Dogwood in his dirty and ill-fitting city watch livery. 'Stop this,' he barked. 'What's this, what's this? Do you have percussion for such an assemblage of people? There has been pestiferous plague in this town. These playhouses are closed. That is to say shut. They are not to be opened. The playing of plays is disinhibited!'

More boos. The woman next to me plucked a dried orange from her basket and hurled it at the watchman, who wheeled on the spot. 'Who threw this grenade? It's a capital offence to abuse and otherwise harass a man of the watch!'

'Bugger off!' she cried. I shrugged and did the same. It became a chorus, joining with similar abuse and another torrent of thrown objects. I considered hurling one of the rocks in the sack at my feet but decided that that would have been excessive if not outrageously dangerous.

Still, Dogwood bowed to the realisation, picked up an orange from the filthy, rush- and herb-strewn ground, and began sucking it as he stomped away. He did not, I notice, leave entirely, but retired into the crowd.

Forman resumed his speech, whipping up the crowd with promise of marvels and wonders. John stood stock-still, his chin on his short ruff and his eyes closed, looking for all the world like a puppet whose strings had been cut. Eventually, the doctor said, 'arise, sir, arise!'

John looked up, squinting above the heads of the crowd, which stood in fascinated silence. He pointed. 'I see,' he said quietly. He repeated it more loudly.

'What do you see?'

'I see a choir of angels. I see the king enthroned. A crown of light. They sing to him. They blow upon many trumpets. Can you not hear the music? And they speak! They speak!'

'What do they say?'

'They say that this king will reign long and goodly. It is a well sounding thing. Can you not see them? Can you not see them bathed in light?' Hundreds of necks craned. 'They say that the coming of this emperor has banished plague and England shall suffer no more. England is saved. See St George! See the dragon, the flames pouring from its horned nostrils, its fangs and claws turned inward. It tears at its heart. He has tamed it. And both St George and the great dragon bow to this our king. I see the old queen smiling fondly. She passes her earthly crown and it joins the crown of light. Joined crowns! Do you not see them?'

He was doing well, I thought. Yet not too well. Some disturbance behind me was intruding on my pleasure in the show – some murmuring and tutting. Tutting myself, I turned around, nearly tripping on the sack.

I was just in time to see a hard-faced bald man in an old, dark suit of clothes, his eyes wide and blood-flecked. A dagger was poised in his humped fist. I had only a second or two to recognise it and reach for my own when it flew out and stabbed me in the gut.

19

I went backwards as the cries of excitement and curiosity erupted around me. 'A fight! Fight! A fight!' My feet found the sack of stones and I landed hard on my backside, my hands scrabbling at my gut. Pain bloomed there, spinning outwards from where the blade's point had struck.

The dagger had not hit home. Canvas, frieze, paper, and linen had blocked its passage. But the force behind it had winded me. Diverted, its edge had skidded across the lines of my ribcage. I sucked at the air, trying to assess matters. My attacker had come at me brazenly, as though he knew no fear. And he thought he had won. His blade was in the air again as he leapt forward. I rolled sideways. Stones scattered about the dusty ground and a soft 'ooh' rose from the crowd. As I moved, I had a brief impression of whirling faces, calves, hose-clad ankles and striped skirts, pattens and shoes. The people were making way for us, hoping for a good, long, bloody scuffle.

The man recovered from falling on rough ground rather than soft flesh. He grunted, his head twisting towards me. I threw my arm towards it, aiming my fist. As I'd rolled away, I had picked up one of the stones – a good, sharp one – and it connected with the side of his head. He howled.

I had the advantage, if only briefly, and sprang from my knees onto his back, grasping at his arm, bending and twisting and forcing it in every direction, hoping for a snap. I did not get one, but the dagger fell. He made the foolish mistake of focussing his attention on its recovery, squirming towards it. I forced my knees into his back, hissing like a cat. He tensed. Stopped moving. Then his elbow shot backwards and into my already bruised stomach. It was my turn to growl.

I relaxed, forced by the sudden bolt of pain across my ribs, and thereby he was able to buck me. As I slid sideways, the howls of the crowd grew wilder, more furious. How quickly they turned, I thought, stars soaring through the inky void of my head, from friends to blood-thirsts.

The man
who is he?
why?
was worming his way across the ground, intent again on his dagger.

I seized the sack of stones and lifted it by the rim, tightening it, raising, swinging, and bringing it down on his legs. My arm muscles cried out. And then he did the same. He stopped moving.

Breathing deeply, I ignored the cheers, jeers, and laughter, and began crawling back on to him. I thought then that I had won – that I had crippled him. As I reached the small of his back, hoping to take him by throat, he rolled suddenly and threw me.

'Oooohhhh!'

'Ahhhh!'

The shrill of someone whistling.

I wobbled and fell, landing on my shoulder. Pain blasted me. And then I was the one on my back, dust rising around me and falling, stinging me. Weight pressed down and with it the unmistakable reek of an undershirt that has been too long friends with a back and too rarely a visitor to the wash pot. Then his face hovered above mine and I looked into a madman's eyes.

'You spy!' He hissed. 'Foul spy!' He was breathing heavily, his spittle landing in my eyes, in my mouth. 'You won't stop us. You are dead, already dead. We are the Enlightened. We will … destroy all and be saved!'

I took advantage of his talking and tried to knee him in the groin. He shifted. 'The boy's ours, spy, ours, one of us.'

David! Alive!

'Where is he, you stinking shit-bag?' As I tried to raise my shoulders, he pushed me back to the ground with a whump.

'You'll see, you filth. Our master will bring your … judgment.' He leant his head back and then jerked it forward, spitting in my face.

And then the pressure on my body was gone.

He had fallen away, fallen off me.

No – he'd been pulled off.

I lay still a for a few seconds, insensible, and then began rolling sideways again, balling my body.

'Mr Windham! Harry Windham!' I did not recognise the voice. I stopped moving, trying to catch my breath. The tumble of the legs and bodies that had been the crowd resolved. Booing and shouting burst from them in a battle cry.

I sat up, my head twisting from side to side.

Someone had my attacker by the elbow and was shouting at him: a man in a good black doublet and breeches, an orange forgotten in his other hand. 'Harry Windham, what is this madness? Cease this at once.'

'Get away from me, you filth,' cried the lunatic. He shook the man loose, but he did not resume his assault. Instead, I thought with a queer kind of detachment, he looked suddenly frightened, a deer caught in the aim of a hunter's bow. 'I am Amos. My name is Amos. Touch me not! You are damned!' He got to unsteady feet and then began looking for me.

Some stones had scattered across the ground and I made a grab, picking it up and hurling it in one movement. It caught him in the arm and his look of fury met mine. I threw another, this one cutting a red line across his brow. Then another, slicing his chin. Blood began to pour, and he screamed.

The crowd, cheated of a fight, began throwing its own things – oranges again, stones, clumps of dirt. He turned on the spot, shouting wildly. I heard cries of 'madman', 'moon-man', 'zany' and some scattered laughter. Amos, as he had called himself, took a step towards me, wiping at his face with one hand and shielding himself from incoming objects with the other. And then he shook his head and ran at the crowd. It parted, no one wanting to actually touch or be touched by a madman.

Slowly, too slowly, I rose to my feet, trying to follow his passage. But the people had closed it, their backs to me. 'Where did he go? Where is he?'

Forman's scratchy voice cut in, close to me, making me jump. 'Who was that? He looks like one of the creatures who kept calling at my home before the blonde came.'

I ignored him and he repeated his question. 'A friend of that woman's, ay. Angela's. I must give chase.' Without turning to the doctor, I stumbled forward, my legs aquiver, and nearly hit the ground.

'Peace, Savage,' Forman said. 'You will give no one chase this day. You are all disbalanced.' The pain in my stomach answered him and it forced a thin stream of vomit from my mouth, where it mingled with dirt, stones, and half-sucked oranges. 'You are not stabbed?' His squat, questing fingers found their way under my clothing, under Gurney's book, and probed. I winced at the coldness and the fresh waves of agony. 'No. Some blows only. They will heal well enough. A sugar poultice will soothe the aches.'

I shook him off and took a few unsteady steps towards the mob, reversing direction in a drunken spin, looking out across the uneven line of black hats and white caps. I considered grabbing at people, asking where the man had gone, in which direction. Yet I knew it was fruitless. The sovereign rule in London – a rule I had observed myself often enough – was that whenever a crazed or excited person begs directions, they should be given a very detailed route to the Bedlam.

The man who had saved me by stopping Amos was standing, his hands on his hips. A grave look was drawn on his face. 'You,' I said. 'You – who are you? You knew that man?'

He regarded me quizzically. 'Who are you, sir?' He had an intelligent face and his voice betrayed someone of learning.

'Forgive me. My name is Edward Savage.'

'And why did Harry Windham attack you?'

'I ...' I looked again towards the people, cursing the fact that I'd let the creature get away. The mob was drifting now, aimless, breaking up into clumps. When I returned my attention to the well-spoken man, he was bending over, retrieving the forgotten dagger from where it was being trampled into the Southwark mud. 'Might I speak with you, sir? Privily?'

'Hm?' He held up the blade as though it were a scientific object. 'Yes. I think we might.'

He would not hear of setting foot in The Holland's Leaguer, and so I parted company with John and Dr Forman, leaving them to make what they could from the thinning but noisier herd. Scattered fights, inspired by my unwarranted scuffle, seemed to be breaking out, women swinging at their maids, masters at their apprentices, labourers at one another.

My new companion walked quickly away with me to the first tavern on London Bridge, where we shook off a musician and ordered two mugs of small ale. The place was quiet, with the great concourse of people still out in the streets, drinking their ale from vendors. I sipped shallowly – breathing too deeply still caused pain from where I had been stabbed at and pressed.

'My name is Ned Savage,' I said. 'I am seeking out the man who attacked me. And his fellows. You called him Windham. Harry. Who is he?'

'I am Matthew Ellis. Lawyer, of Gray's Inn.' He slipped a napkin over his shoulder as though at table in a fine house before he took a drink. 'Henry Windham was my client. Lately a man of Blackfriars.'

'Blackfriars! He lives in Blackfriars?' Images of a bolt hole sprang up in my mind – some grubby house, an upper storey, where they congregated to worship the devil. Where they were holding David and Gurney.

'Lately,' said Ellis, setting down his mug. 'The house has a new lease-holder. I saw to the matter myself.'

The Lord gave and the Lord hath taken away.

'But … where? Where does this Amos or Windham live?'

'I cannot say, Mr Savage. Harry … his family died during the plague. They were a Godly lot, of the Puritan bent. He suffered it too, yet he lived. Only some months back – before the fall of the leaf – he ended his leasehold and sold everything. You will not find him there, alas.

'I presumed he intended to go to Scotland or Geneva or some suchlike place hotter in the reformed religion. He had fallen in with even more religious types after the loss of his family, was my thinking. I assumed they must be Puritans and intending to go abroad. Amos … that is a biblical name. One of the lesser prophets. In truth, he must have gone stark mad.'

'He spoke of the Enlightened. Did he mention that word to you?'

'I cannot recall.' Ellis leaned back on his stool and fixed his gaze at the ballads plastered to the wall – looking, I thought, but not reading. 'Yes, I think he did. I thought it some Puritanical sect or other, some doctrine.' He shook his head lightly. 'You know how people are these days.'

I considered the word, frowning. Enlightened. The woman Angela had said something about it on my doorstep the time I had seen her, though I could not remember what. I did not like the sound of it. She had then been seeking David, and now she had him. They must have decided that those who suffered the plague and lived were part of this 'Enlightened' sect – that much was clear. Something else hit me.

'He spoke of a master to me, Mr Ellis. A master bringing judgment. Do you know who he served?'

'I cannot say. No.'

'Balls,' I hissed. I had a name at least. Three names, in fact: Harry Windham alias Amos, and the Enlightened, his sect of fanatics. That had to be progress of a kind. I slurped moodily, one arm cradling my abdomen.

'I must away,' I said. 'I thank you, sir, for your kindness in buying a wounded man a drink.'

Ellis raised an eyebrow in a smirk and held out his hand. I shook it. 'I say, after one saves a man's life, the least one might do is then water him.'

I hobbled out of the tavern, laying it on a bit thickly, I admit, and set out for home. By the time I arrived back at Shoe Lane, the moon was already playing games with the dying sun behind frayed cloth clouds.

To my surprise, I found Faith in the front room, cutting bacon for

Nicholas Hopgood, who sat on my stool. Her eyes widened. 'Ned, are you hurt?'

'No, no. I'm well enough.' With gritted teeth, I bounced across the room. 'Did you find anything?'

'Yes. We've got seven houses now, seven that said someone who had the plague but didn't die has since left. One house – a woman – in Holborn even said flat that her husband ran off with a yellow-haired whore. That has to be her, doesn't it? That has to be Angela?'

'Yes. It sounds so. You did well. And,' I said, feeling I ought to be generous, 'you too, young Nick.'

He bowed his head. 'Thank you, sir.' His cap was in his hands as he stood. 'And you, did you discover anything?'

I hated him again. 'I ... I found a fellow working with her. Name of Amos, formerly Harry Windham. He attacked me.'

'Attacked?!' Faith was at my side, touching my face, her freckled hands fluttering. 'You were hurt! Oh no. Was it in Lambeth? Have you found where they lodge?'

'Not in Lambeth, no. It was ... I was ... in Southwark.'

Her hand dropped. 'Southwark?' She repeated it and I could almost see the engine of her mind turning. 'Over three miles from Lambeth.

'Is that not where the great spectacle was to take place today? All those people going south of the river...' began Hopgood.

I felt myself trapped, run to ground by a pair of young bloodhounds. 'I ...'

'The spectacle in Southwark,' said Faith. 'Ned ... did you go to Lambeth today?' I tried to think of a lie, a good one that would hold. But I took too long. 'That was you, wasn't it? You were part of all that madness when you said you were looking for David like we were.'

I held up my hands, backing towards the door of my inner chamber. 'Let me tell you. It is – I was – this was a design to entrap these creatures and find David. And I did find one – drew him out.' Something clicked in my mind, though not fully. 'I think he came for me rather than the spectacle. Brazenly, fearless, through a crowd. There is madness here, I –'

'You lied, Ned,' said Faith. There was no great heat in her words. Worse – there was disappointment. She moved, very pointedly, to stand beside Hopgood.

'With reason,' I snapped. And out poured the whole tale, from my meetings with Cecil and King James – that caused Hopgood to gasp at any rate – and the missing doctor, to the likelihood of a sect of necromancers stealing away survivors of the plague and trying to bring about the end days. When I had finished, I collapsed onto the cot. 'So now you know everything, you can see I have had no choice. I have been a servant of the crown in these matters. It is only with the crown's power that we can find David. He will be safe, I know. They are trying to save people they think are as blessed as they are. In their own crooked and mad way.' I sat like a penitent on the edge of the low cot, my hands clasped between my knees.

Neither of the young people spoke to me. Instead, Faith drew Hopgood over towards the fire, which she started to dampen, muttering all the while. I caught his voice, the words, 'can't go against the crown' and her more insistent hissing.

I stood, preparing to go to my own chamber and leave them to it.

'Wait, Ned.' I turned at her voice, my hand already on the handle. 'I think it might be best if … I'm going to go and stop in Holborn a while. Search for David from there. Nicholas's master's wife is looking for someone to clean and that and she's quite willing. It's all arranged. We've talked it through, all right proper.' She did not meet my eyes and focused instead on fixing a red strand that had wandered free of her cap.

Have you now?

Her voice betrayed practice. She had organised this already, before she knew I had lied. And doubtless Hopgood was behind it, distrusting her living with a man – even such a one as me.

I drew in my cheeks, my lip curling downwards. 'Ay, a good thing. A good idea. They know where we live. Reckon I was followed from here to Southwark by that Amos. Watching me to see if I was part of a plot to drawn them out. You'll be safer in Holborn, I'm sure, with sweet Nicholas's master's wife.' I looked at the boy, whose face was crimson and whose hands fiddled with his cap, turning and twisting and nearly dropping it. 'Well, go to then. I'll bar the door when you've gone.'

I thought, the woman is only after a slave. And then, stupidly, I said it.

Then, flouncing into my chamber, I slammed the door.

I could not rest, but began pacing in the tiny space, picking up objects – my gap-toothed ivory comb, my miniature of the late queen … and my little crown-shaped pin cushion which Faith had bought me. Biting at my lip, I squeezed it as I heard the front door of the house bang closed.

And then I slammed it back down. I had been well enough, I thought, before I had taken her into my home, and I would be well enough if she buggered off with her simpering puppet. Moreover, I would find David before she did and then he would hold fast to me and not her.

As I undressed, Gurney's book fell to the floor. Only when I was in my nightshirt with a fur cloak about my shoulders did I stoop to pick it up. Idly, I turned the pages. The drawings of herbs and plants, the descriptions of piss, the notes on makeup and the troublesome patients – the ones with false names now known to be Angela and probably this Amos – seemed to mock me.

I cast the thing down again.

Useless.

All physicians are bloody useless. Only ever say the same things.

And then it struck me. In looking at the physician, in considering what a physician might write about his patients, I was looking in the wrong place. A physician, whilst he occupied the role coveted by the wealthy, was only one part of any treatment. I put my head in my hands, cursing myself for a fool. And then, so that I did not have to think about my empty house, I began planning my attack on the place that would lead me to Angela and her creatures – and their master – on the morrow.

20

Hope sees the great throng of people, hears their excited chatter. The news, whatever it is, has caught fire and the fire rages. He steps out into the street, where the crooked roofs of the buildings cannot fall on and bury him, and asks, 'what news?'

A long-faced man answers, plucking at his beard as he speaks. 'It's the poet Morley. The playwright. One wot wrote Faust. 'e's dead. Killed 'imself.'

'You lies in yer teeth,' cuts in another voice – a hurrying boy in the weeds of a labourer. ''e's been done in. Killed stone dead. Stabbed through the eye.' He mimes it, jerking his head back as though he doesn't quite trust his own pointed finger.

The older man shrugs. 'Saying he's something to do with the queen's secker-trey. Some creeping spy.'

The shadow of Walsingham flutters from under the eaves where it has been hanging, bat-like, invisible to the common rabble. He is everywhere.

Hope thanks the man and continues plodding through the street. He hears it again and again, told in all the colours of the rainbow. One would think the queen had died, such is the excitement in London at the loss of one of its playwrights. He has seen Edward II *played, and both parts of* Tamburlaine: *his master the earl is a great lover of the theatre and has even written some good comedies. He wonders if the dead Marlowe's words will keep him alive. Is that a means of returning from death, or are words merely a pale echo? The notion seems foolishly poetic. A man's words might be twisted to other meanings once he is dead and cannot correct those who would mangle them.*

As he passes, walking aimlessly, he begins to wonder about spies. Voices sound, higher and clearer than those of the gossiping Londoners.

'You are being watched.'

'None trust you.'

'They are trying to kill you.'

'They would have you dead too.'

It is impossible to ignore the onslaught. So powerful is it that he stops dead, letting out an ear-splitting screech, followed by a drawn-out groan. He cries, 'get away from me, you slime, fucking slime, fucking slime!' at no one and everyone. People stop. Some come to him, asking whether he is harmed. He spits at them. These must be the spies, the deceivers. They soon back away, hurling the word 'madman' at him.

Others should about the plague. He hears a woman say, 'fetch the watch. Take the madman up.'

He runs, his boots skidding on rushes dried by bright spring sunlight, until he reaches his home, pounding upstairs and closing the door behind him. It remains the pathetic little room in Aldgate where Margery and the children had died. He slides the bar which locks it and, for safety's sake, pushed the cot against it. And the only other piece of furniture, the barren sideboard, that must go against the single window.

The spirits sing to him as he works at blocking out the wicked, ever-listening world. The government, Walsingham, the spies. They got Marlowe and they will get you. They're watching you now. They're watching you always. Only in darkness, utter, unflinching darkness, can he feel that he is not being watched.

If he is ever to be safe, he realises, he must find somewhere out of the watching city, away, and admit to it only those who will see and hear as he does.

And even then, the spies, the government, will never leave him alone. And anyone might be a government spy.

***

'You failed.'

Amos hung his head, crusty as it was with dried blood, and wore a look of defeat.

'But I love you,' said Hope, and the fellow looked up. He was still ugly, still had a hardness in his face, but he was one of the Enlightened and worthy of affection. He stood in Hope's cabin like a penitent child. 'It is not your fault. These … these spies – everywhere – everywhere they lurk. Always watching. Listening. Fucking spies!' The profanity burst out unbidden and he shook his head.

'Fucking spies,' repeated Amos.

'There is no need for that, brother.'

'Those sailors are spies too, those rough brutes Joel had tend the ship.'

Hope put a hand over his heart. 'They are gone now? Their work is done?' Fear jabbed at him. He had had Joel, the Enlightened's former sailor, bring aboard a small company of unemployed sailors, using the company's pooled money to pay them to make the *Crown Elizabeth* ready at least for operation on the Thames. Perhaps the spirits were telling him that those sailors had been spies, government spies. He shook his head. He had told the Enlightened to remain out of sight whilst the men worked, and had told Joel too to say nothing other than that the old ship would soon be sailed to another dock for its breaking up.

'Ay, they're gone and good riddance. I'll get that bastard Savage next time.'

'No. No, he knows your sweet face. Some other can make an end of him. Stop him before he can try and stop us.'

'But I–'

'This is my will and the will of the angels.'

'Yes.' Sulkiness threatened in Amos's tone and he scuffed his boots on the bare deck.

'I have other work for you. For you and the rest who wish to aid us.' The frown turned into a look of joy and Hope reflected it. 'Where might we find stores of powder?'

'Gunpowder?'

'Just so.'

'Uh … grocers. Ironmongers. It's used by builders and the like, maybe their yards.'

'We must have some. Purchased in small bags. Many small bags.'

'I will. I'll tell the others. Set them to it. And secretly. They must let none discover it. We must all be wary of spies. Watching men.'

'Thank you. Will you see the doctor about those cuts?'

Putting a hand to his face, Amos frowned. 'No. No physician. Don't trust that Gurney, Nathaniel. He's not one of us. I won't trust anyone that isn't with us. That hasn't been chosen as we have.' The words hung in the air between them for a while, dark and full of dangers. Hope had to admit that his brother in faith was right. No one could be trusted. Those who lived outside the ship as it rested, waiting, in Queenhithe were all sullied, all wicked, all out to get them.

Amos departed the cabin, leaving the door swinging. He left just in time. A shadow swooped down in a corner – a long black shape, as though a dyed shroud had materialised in the air. Hope started, thinking of the queen of Scots in her velvet. But this figure was faceless – a dark oblong bearing only the vaguest shape of a human. It resembled, in fact, a giant, hanging bat, its papery wings folded around its body. The cabin itself became a crypt, the shafts of light coming in through portholes that were merely cracks in the ancient stone. Peepholes, where the curious – spies – might look in upon the corruption and rot.

His footsteps echoed on the deck as he crept to the hanging shadow-thing. Suddenly it widened. It was a man indeed – a man who had been hiding within a black cloak and now threw it wide. Within its folds stood the long-dead Sir Francis Walsingham, spymaster to the late queen, his lugubrious features expressionless. 'Trust that man not,' it said. Hope had never heard the man speak in life, and in death he sounded curiously like the earl. 'Trust no one, even in your own house.'

'But ... he is Enlightened.'

'Trust none. You are watched. There are spies. My people got the poet Marlowe. Now they come for you. They have secret writings on you. Ciphers. They know everything that passes within this ship. They peep at keyholes.'

'Spies,' said Hope.

'Trust none. None are real.'

'They are my friends,' Hope said. Fury bloomed. 'It is you who are not real. You are false! False and dead!' He leapt towards the figure and, to his surprise, it did not melt away but fought back. He found Walsingham's throat and began squeezing, choking, crying out again and again, 'the Enlightened are my brothers and sisters. You are the spy. You are not real. You. You. You.'

Walsingham choked. Spluttered. Slapped at his face. His skull cap fell off and blonde hair spilled out. When he spoke, it was in a woman's voice, familiar. 'Nath – Nath – Nath – el – stop!'

Hope's looked at his bunched hands, white and blue-veined and squeezing a pale neck. He gasped, releasing Angela. She bent double, and stumbled away from him, coughing and spluttering. 'Sweet Jesus,' he said, before repeating it more loudly. 'I – I was deceived. My dearest – they deceived me. A wicked spirit – most wicked. I am sorry. My love, I'm sorry!'

Before she could answer, he took her by the hand, whimpering as she cringed from his touch. 'Come, we will see the doctor. He will know how to help.'

He led her through the fetid gloom of the ship, she still choking, and on to the passage that led to the cargo hold. The boy, Samuel, was curled up asleep, a little pool of white topped with red, outside the door. 'Wake, lad, wake!' Hope nudged him with a foot.

'Faith?'

'Yes, I have faith in you, brother. Pray unlock the door. We have need of Dr Gurney.'

***

Gurney stood, his grip tightening on the pestle, determined that he would fight his way out of witnessing another murder. As the door opened and Hope and Angela tumbled in, he relaxed.

'She has been hurt, doctor. Help her.'

'What happened?'

Hope led Angela to the trunk and helped her sit. Gurney eyed the door, in which stood only the little boy, David. 'I was deceived by a spirit. I think rather a devil. She was strangled.'

Gurney frowned, looking away from the door and towards his former patient. He examined her, rubbing her throat and looking down it, before fetching some water from the bowl David had brought him – he refused to drink anything from the bucket that Isaac had been drowned in – and helping her to drink. 'She will be well. Speak only little,' he said, turning to her. 'Until the pains and the swelling ease. Do you understand.' She nodded slowly.

'God be praised,' said Hope. 'She will be well. They have not deceived us as they hoped. Why are devils coming upon me now in the guise of spirits of the dead, doctor? Do they mean to stop us?'

'To stop you from doing what?' asked Gurney. He moved towards the pestle he had set down. He had already decided that he would not be leaving without the lad. Though God had not given him and Maud children – her age was always against it – he would nevertheless save one if he could.

'From our ascension, doctor. The day draws near. I can feel it. That is why these visitations come. The end days are coming now. The coronation of the king, this great festival of sin – it is when we must act.'

'What,' asked Gurney, trying to keep his questioning simple, 'do you mean to do?'

Hope lowered his hands. Slyness crept across his handsome, tired features. 'Questions? You … are you spying, doctor?' He began moving around the hold, feeling the bulkheads. 'Do they peep in at the cracks, your friends in the king's government? Where are they? How do they pass? Do you mean to help them stop the reckoning?'

Gurney did not flinch but put his chest out. 'Stop this at once. I have spoken to none save your people since you brought me here. A captive.'

Hope ceased his harried wandering. 'A guest,' he said. His smooth, smiling expression returned. 'A friend. Until the end. But tell me, doctor, why am I plagued by false visions?'

Gurney put a hand to his chin as though in contemplation. 'Did you eat or drink of the powders I gave you?'

'No. Yet my brothers and sisters did. And they saw. We would have you mix more.'

'I will. And you must take them too. They will … they will sort the angels from the devils.'

'You do promise it?'

'Yes.'

'Yes,' croaked Angela. Gurney turned a warning look to her, pointing at his own throat. She ignored him. 'It is wondrous to see the sights, Nath-an-iel. I saw my baby, shining in gold cloth. They will … help you … too.'

Gurney hung his head. He knew that Angela, under her former name, had lost a child. It was a common enough thing, but she had taken it very badly. He thought of Maud again, denied children but still thinking as kindly of them as he did. What it might mean to a woman to have one child and to watch it die he couldn't know, and thankfully never would. All the prayers and promises of future babies and the will God – the things he had told Angela before she was Angela, and other women besides – were gusty words formed to silence and soothe simple wenches. They meant nothing.

Angela, however, was not alone in having her grief sicken into madness. All of them, it seemed, everyone on the ship, every survivor of the plague, had lost people either to the pestilence itself or by some other means. Women were softly made creatures, ever apt to be swept away by men's words, but grief could make men grow womanish and weak too. And the weak minded of both sexes were easy prey to those would make use of them and subvert their wills. Madness was a corruption of the soul, but it stemmed from something outside the afflicted. Grief seemed to be the external agent at work here – and there was no sure remedy to rid anyone of the melancholia of grief...

Out of the corner of his eye he regarded Hope. The man had clearly enchanted them with promises of salvation, and of seeing their loved ones again. Yet, the doctor suspected, the strange leader himself must have been driven to his madness – or farther into it – by loss.

'Mix me this wondrous physic, doctor. Please. I will take it when … I will take it.'

Gurney gave one hard nod, and watched as Hope, moving like a fussy old woman, helped Angela up and out of the hold. When they had gone, David moved to close the door.

'Wait, son,' said the doctor. 'Stop.' Dutifully, the boy did, his hand on the key in its lock. 'Stay a while and talk with me. Come, share my bread.' He had instructed the boy to eat nothing offered by the sect, and he supposed the lad must be hungry. Gurney settled himself on the still-warm coffer as the boy stepped into the hold. 'You said you have no parents but a brother and sister. Where are they?'

Tears started in the boy's eyes. 'I don't know.'

'How did you come to be here?'

'That lady, she brought me. Said my family was here.'

'You know, don't you, that these folk are not your family?'

He shrugged. 'My family was the boys in the queen's chapel.'

'Is that so? Then I have heard you sing. Did you like it there?'

'No.' The boy sat down on the deck, wiping his eyes on the hem of his robe.

'Don't cry.'

'Not crying. It smells bad in here. Like farts.'

Gurney barked laughter. 'That is the henbane, son. You grow accustomed to it. Why did you leave?'

'My sister and new brother came and got me when the queen died.'

Gurney looked at the open door. The T at its end was lost in darkness. Then he returned his gaze to the boy. 'And you lived with them?'

'Yes. But I got sick. With the plague. After Ned took me to see the players.' Finally, some light came into the boy's eyes. In the dull light, their natural green browned to hazel. On impulse, Gurney reached down and patted his head. He squirmed away. 'I got bad sick. My skin went red. And I got better and the lady came and Ned sent her away and she came back and she said,' he paused to breathe, 'she said cos I had the plague and didn't die of it, I was one of them. En .. en ...'

'Enlightened,' said Gurney.

'Yes. But I didn't feel nothing. I don't. But I ... I'm scared to tell them that.'

Gurney stood, ignoring the creaking in his bones and beneath his feet. 'Your symptoms. What were they?' Bewilderment overcame the lad and Gurney said, 'what signs were on you when you were sick? How did you feel?' David explained, and for a moment Gurney forgot that he was prisoner on a ship, held captive by madmen who appeared to be plotting some evil design, and he was simply a physician again.

When they had finished their consultation, the doctor clapped his hands. 'Aryotitus. Sometimes called the gaol fever. Red skin, pains, aches in the head and joints. Even your great sweat.'

'I wasn't never in gaol for nothing!'

'Bah, a mere name for the common tongue. I'm telling you, young fellow-my-lad, that you never had the blasted plague. Though your brother was quite right to quarantine and tend to you.'

'So ... so I'm not one of them? I'm not En-light-ened?'

'No, indeed, and nor are they. They seek meaning in the medical and spiritual worlds. And they make what they don't find. You say you did not want to go with her, that woman?'

'No.'

'Then why did you?'

'She ... told me to. You do what you're told or you get the whipping.'

Gurney folded his arms. 'Forget what you're told, David. Stop your ears if you must. Think on what you desire, not what you're told to. It is the way of being a man.'

'So I can go home?'

Gurney turned to him and hoisted him to his feet. 'You will go home, lad. We both will. But ... but say nothing of this. Stay close.'

The distant chant of 'vita in morte sumus' rumbled its way down the hall. He did not want to think what the crazed creatures might do with the boy if they suspected he was not one of their demented circle. Consider him a spy, if Hope's wild suspicions were any indication. 'Wait in the hall out there. Lock the door, as always. I ... will think of something to get us both out of this madness. In the meantime, we must keep those people free of all suspicion. I must make up more of their ... ah ... farty infusions.'

As the key shot its bolt home, he began silently praying that he could.

The day draws near, he thought.

21

I rarely visit medical men of any stripe. My guiding principle has ever been that the thought of retaining the coins in my purse, which I would otherwise hand over to a physician or apothecaries, is better for my health than any of their herbs and poultices. If my arm was hanging off, I should probably visit a barber-surgeon, but other than that, physicians were for the rich and apothecaries a balm to those who were weak enough to let running noses and aches in the head lay them low.

Nevertheless, I asked my way calmly to the apothecary nearest to Foster Lane, where Dr Gurney kept his consulting rooms and his over-painted old wife. They were a gentle lot round that way, and none found sport in directing me towards the Bedlam.

My reasoning was simple. Physicians were piss prophets who read books and opined from them. They would then send their charges to the apothecaries with notes instructing those potion-peddlers what to mix up and sell. Angela and Amos had been patients of Gurney even before their apparent descent into madness and their pestering of him, and thus it stood to reason that at some point he had sent them to the medicine man with requests. I did not need their names, nor even Gurney's book. Logic dictated it was so. I had, in fact, been so intent on finding information in the book that I had not stopped to consider that what was not in it – the names and notes of remedies he gave to his patients – was more important than what was. Cecil, I supposed, would never have made the leap. For all my master was a clever man – too clever – he was petted and spoiled and had likely never visited an apothecary's shop in his life, being attended only by physicians in his own homes, who could fetch whatever they prescribed directly from his mansion's herb gardens.

But no such fool was I, at least not now that I had relinquished the idea that the commonplace book held the answers to Angela and Amos. If I hoped to find them, I must know who they were and what they had been doing. There was even, I supposed, an outside chance that the apothecary who served them knew where they lived. But I did not let that hope grow.

Still, it was a pleasant thing to feel cleverer than the mighty secretary, even belatedly.

I found the place from the stuffed reptile which was secured with ropes and dangled from the overhang of thatch. It drifted a little in the cold wind that crept the streets, looking alive as it swung, its teeth still visible despite the tight string holding its jaw closed. Stepping under it, I pushed open the door.

The shop was well lit from the windows on either side of the entrance. Divided in two by a counter, the small room gave little space for its customers. I stood to one side whilst a large woman watched the apothecary, a grizzle-bearded blackamoor in a black cap with lowered side flaps, measure powders onto scales. She seemed not to blink as she watched him work, though she spared me a suspicious glance before resuming her stream of talk.

'And do you know, I didn't see nothing, not up close, but they say there was a fight, a right proper fight. Feller's vision caused it, he saw angels in the sky and somefink came down and set men to fight wiv one another. An' Jesus bless me, I never saw the like of it, fighting and drinking and music right through Bankside, same as if the play-'ouses 'ad come back.'

I smiled to myself, letting my eyes wander. Behind the counter, behind the busy apothecary himself, were rows of shelves running fully from the left wall of the chamber to the door to the man's private room on the right. Large, round bottles stood shoulder to shoulder, with not enough space between them for a sliver of paper. Around each was fixed a label, and names like 'mugwort', 'peony', 'betony', 'borage', 'centery the less', and 'tormentil' stood out in elegant black script. The air was faintly spiced, like a hot herb pottage sweetened with syrup.

The woman went silent as she fished for her purse, unstrung it, and set it on the counter with a muted, leathery *chink*. Her hands flew over it and her lips moved as she counted out coins and exchanged them for a wrapped cloth package. She gave me one last look from head to toes and back again before bustling out of the shop.

I moved to the counter myself, just as the apothecary was sweeping away the lingering dust and herbs with a fine, thickly bristled hand-brush. 'Can I be of service, sir?' he asked without looking up. 'I have Venice treacle, theriaca andromachi, a guard against the plague, brought in from the shores of that distant land.'

'No, thank you.'

He set his brush down and looked at me. A spiderweb of wrinkles deepened around his dark eyes as he smiled. 'Naturally. I make purchase of crates of the stuff. A month ago, everyone wants it. Today?' He shrugged. 'Ach, people would forget that the plague ever existed when it retreats. And that, I think, is why it returns so often. Well, young man, what do you seek?'

'Information only.'

'Oh?' A grey brow rose. It seemed more suspicious than interested, and so I opened my coat to let my livery show. In my experience, few men knew it was only Revels Office; the sight of any royal livery would make them instantly friendly and willing to help.

'I seek information on a patient lately of Dr Leonard Gurney, physician in ordinary to his Majesty King James.'

'Where is Leonard?'

'I ...' had not been expecting that question.

'His house has been released from the quarantine and yet,' he held up bare, gnarled hands, 'poof! Gone! No one sees him.'

'I understand he is following the court at present.'

'And sending me only one note of remedies. In all this time. Is he using the king's herbalists otherwise, and robbing me of business, the naughty fellow?'

'What? One note?' I decided on honesty, of a fashion. 'Sir, Dr Gurney might at present be in trouble. In truth, we have not seen him at court for some time. The king demands his presence. You say he has not written you?'

The old man put a hand up to his throat, his eyes widening. 'In trouble? I ... Leonard had written me nothing for weeks. I sent word up Foster Lane – I thought the pestilence might have taken him – but his wife told my boy that he was indisposed only. And then, a few days ago, he sent a patient with a note. It was signed by him. I know his hand as well as my own.'

'What patient?'

Doubt crossed the apothecary's face and he glanced down at the polished wood of the counter. 'I ... such matters, names. Private matters.'

'Sir,' I again pulled my coat wide, 'this is a greater matter. The doctor's life might be in danger. Others too. Who was this patient?'

He returned his attention to me, his jaw steely. 'She calls herself Angela.'

Got her!

'Yet,' he went on, 'the name is new – only lately taken it upon herself.'

'Do you know her real name, sir, her old one? Where she lives? I must speak with her.'

'Has she done something – something wicked?'

'Yes,' I said flatly.

'Such a sweet lady. Poor creature. Lost a babe and … Dr Gurney would have me give her rose oil and decoction of poppy for the washing of her hair. A guard against the growth of melancholia. Yet I think she found religion more like to soothe her addled mind. She took upon her the name Angela. And she stopped coming here. I assumed she had been put away, sir, in the Bedlam, or else come out of her darkness. Until she came here again, a few days since, with a note from Leonard.'

'What did it say? Do you have it?' Excitement gripped me. Might the doctor have written his location – perhaps some code? Or would these Enlightened brutes have checked for such a thing and the doctor not risked angering them? I fought the urge to reach across the counter and shake the apothecary.

'I burned it, I regret. It was written on a page from an old scholarly book – no room left to make use of it by writing further.' I gripped my head on either side, my fingers digging into my hair, into the hard flesh of my scalp. 'But it was what it requested – what I gave her.' My hands relaxed. 'Henbane. Hyoscyamus niger. A great quantity. And lesser quantities of atropa belladonna and datura stramonium. Deadly nightshade and thorn apple.'

'What are these things?'

'Powerful things. Deadly if a man – or a woman – not expert mixes them. You know what is said – the dose makes the poison.'

I clutched at the word. Could Dr Gurney be planning on killing his captors? If so – why had be not done so and returned home? My heart leapt. If David was amongst their company, he might unwittingly be poisoned too.

'And you gave the bitch – you gave this Angela this stuff?'

The apothecary looked suddenly fearful. 'Dr Gurney gave it her. It was his name signed. I seek no trouble. Leonard and I have an agreement of long standing. He sends me business and I never fail to supply those customers he sends. She was his patient. For a long time. And Dr Gurney, he knows his art. If mixed correctly, these things are not deadly. They were used by the monks of the old religion to – to see things. Fantastical visions and the like.'

I slowed my breathing.

Fantastical visions.

What game was the doctor playing with these people? Why not just kill them?

'This woman's true name. What is it?'

He did not answer immediately, but seemed to be wrestling with something, his eyebrows working wildly. Eventually he said, without further prompting, 'Mary Glover. Wife to George of that name. Birchin Lane.'

Wife, I thought. The woman had worn her hair loose and so I had assumed her unmarried. But no matter. Birchin Lane. I knew it: a good street full of drapers where a man might get good bolts of cloth for new suits of clothes.

'I must away, I must go there. Now. Thank you, sir.'

The apothecary only nodded, his hands clasped at his breast, as I bolted from the shop and made my way hurriedly along Cheapside, skirting the crowd around the Great Conduit and into the Poultry. In my mind's eye I could see it – a townhouse, perhaps, its upper storey now taken over by a group of necromancers, their symbols on the floors, their stones at the centre. The City had never seemed so big, and I made each farthest house or shop in my sight a measure of my progress as I gained it.

The people were thick around me, some wearing vizards, most not, and I cursed them. There must have been nearly as many as had flocked to Southwark the previous day, and all seemed to be heading in the same direction as me. As I followed the tide, I was barged into, wheeled around, cursed at – and I returned that in full measure, believe me – until I reached the quieter Lombard Street, where yet more people seemed to be coming towards me but the thoroughfare was mercifully wider and the ground well gravelled. The Exchange, I thought – the shops of the Royal Exchange must have all reopened and be staging something.

I leapt over an old man with an unlit pipe jutting from between his teeth who sat with his back to a fence and swung left into Birchin Lane. At its far end, where it met Cornhill, I could see the colourful drift of people. Rather than ask a stranger and be lied to, I ducked into a draper's shop, past the brightly hued display cloths hung outside, and was given directions to the Glover house.

It was a modest place – a tenement pressed between the newer townhouses of those drapers who had made money selling their wares to Queen Elizabeth's great peafowl of preening peacocks. The front door was unlocked, and I slipped inside, the street noises – bells, cries, the hammering of the new king's triumphal arches, cheers, curses – instantly dying. I understood well enough that more than one family must have the run of the place and knocked on the first door. No answer. I tried again, and eventually a harassed-looking woman with brown hair opened.

'Glover? Mary Glover?' A child cried from somewhere inside and the woman hissed, jabbing her finger upwards before slamming the door in my face.

I ascended the stairs. At a landing was another door. No amount of hammering brought anyone to it. The stairs went up still one more flight, and I pounded them, my boots slapping on the rough wood. Again, I knocked, pounded, and punched. No one answered. 'Goddammit to hell!' I shouted, turning and retreating to the staircase.

A soft voice. Muttering.

I froze, my ear cocked. Someone was inside.

In an instant, I was again at the door, punctuating my blows with cries of, 'open up, in the name of the king!'

My fist flew through the air where the door had been and I jerked it back. A man stood in the doorway. Handsome, I thought, or he looked like he might once have been. Now his eyes were bloodshot and his skin falling loose, as though dragged down by the unkempt beard.

'The fuck are you to be waking me up?'

'I … is Mary Glover here. You might know her as Angela.'

The man spat a thin gob of phlegm at my boots. 'What, you come here looking for m'wife?'

Wife!

'I seek news of the woman Angela, formerly Mary Glover. You are … you're her husband? Where is she?'

The man turned his back on me but did not attempt to close the door. Instead, he began shuffling back into the rooms. Warily, I stepped over the spittle and followed.

The place was foul – not in its construction or its appointments, but rather in the state into which they'd fallen. As Goodman Glover – George, the apothecary had called him – moved from the hall into the front room, I had to step over buckets of what smelt like piss. It seemed the man had relieved himself as he felt the need, depositing the buckets in the hall to be collected and thrown out by a wife who wasn't there.

So much for magical symbols.

In the main chamber, Glover flopped himself down on a stool, knees spread wide and elbows on them. He jiggled as he sat, wobbling slightly from side to side. Empty bottles, sucked-dry oranges, apple cores, breadcrumbs, and the crusts of pies were scattered in profusion over the bare boards, desolate shells on a beach. He did not invite me to sit anywhere, nor would I have done so. 'The hell you after that whore for? You can see for yourself she's not here. Not to do her duty, tend my house nor feed her husband.'

You could fashion a whole loaf yourself out of the scattered crumbs.

'Where is she? The king's secretary seeks her.'

'Fancies a fuck, does he?'

I folded my arms, frowning. 'Dangerous words, Goodman Glover.' My own seemed to have effect. He sat a little straighter and looked at the floor, one hand scraping back lank hair. 'Your wife is involved with wicked and dangerous people. Traitors. Where is she?'

'She ain't no papist, Mary.'

'I didn't say she was. I asked where she was.'

He laughed – a dry, rustling sound. 'Run off weeks ago. Months. I don't know time so much no more. No one to tend the place, tend me. This house'll be gone soon enough. Bitch's bled me dry, she has.'

'And with whom has Goodwife Glover run off?' I tried to keep my voice and my accent as official as possible, lacing it with authority.

Again, he laughed. 'Some crack-brain. Went mad, she did, after she got our boy killed. Was born and died. Always the woman's fault, that. Bred weakness into him, she did. Sent her to a right good physician – a man of physick and learning. Cost a pretty penny, too. Nothing. Nothing but shite to wash through her hair.'

'And? Goodman Glover, time might mean nothing to you, but it does to the king.'

'And,' he mimicked, 'she caught it. Caught the madness. Went down right bad with it, she did, and I went off to my folks in Hoxton. When the plague come.'

'When was this?'

'I dunno. After the old queen died. Summer last.'

'So you left your wife here, in this house, when the plague was about?'

He bristled, sitting up again. 'She'd already had it once. You don't get it twice, they say. And I didn't want no plague. And I didn't get none neither. She could go out and get food. Them downstairs, they liked her. They'd tend to her in her raving. And when I come back, she'd lived through the sick times. Was proper mad, though.' He tapped his head. 'Cracked. Been talking to some man, the strumpet – some madman who told her she'd been chosen, special-like, to live. Fresh out the Bedlam, I heard. Can you believe that? Mad bitch listening to some prick fresh out the Bedlam as though he was fucking Moses. Started plaguing that physician herself. Calling herself that fool name.'

'Angela,' I said.

He ignored me and went on. 'Told her if she was whoring with some madman, I'd have her in the courts for a bawd. And do you know what she did? She struck me. Me! And I'd never laid no hand on her. Not till then, anyway. Proper laid her out that night, I did. And in the morning, she was gone.'

'Do you know where to? Where this madman out of the Bedlam lived?'

He shook his head. 'Nah. He'll have some place, though. Probably full of stolen wives turned whore. You know how these preacher folk get them wetted up.'

My lip curled. 'Is there anything you can tell me that might lead me to find your wife?'

'Told you it all. She's mad. Go where the mad folk are. Maybe they've picked her up.' I gave him one last look of dislike before turning on my heel, narrowly avoiding a brown apple core cloudy with insects. 'Wait!' I paused, turning back. 'If you find her ... tell her to come back here. Tell her I won't take her through no bawdy courts. I won't hit her again. If she'll come back and fix things up, like.'

I did not answer him and instead skipped out over the litter of filth and left him to rot in it. He had annoyed me more than he knew. I did not want to pity a madwoman. I needed to despise the bitch who had stolen my boy.

Mad.

Where the mad folks are.

Fresh out of the Bedlam.

When I reached the street, I refilled my lungs with the purer – slightly purer – city air, washing away the taste and smell of staleness and desperation that had made a miasma in the Glover house.

There was no choice. I had to go to that dreadful place – the hospital haunted by the mad. Perhaps it had been Amos whom Mary Glover had met in the street, Amos who had turned her into Angela. But I did not think so. A preacher, Glover had said. And King James's book was clear enough that necromancers served a master. He thought that master the devil.

I thought that it was this former Bedlamite.

These thoughts distracted me, but only so much. I could not ignore the real world that was buzzing around me as I stepped up Birchin Lane – for again, it was pressing in on me, nudging me, pushing. I snapped, 'what news – what is this?'

'King and queen up at the Exchange, man.'

The great inspection. When I had met with Cecil and King James, the secretary had been pressing the king on the matter. I stood for a few moments, shoulders buffeting me, thinking. The route northwards from Birchin Street to the Bedlam would pass Cornhill and the Royal Exchange. I decided to follow the crowd, more out of curiosity about the queen than a desire to see whether King James could behave graciously in public or not. As I entered onto Cornhill, I had reminder enough of the coronation festivities. A huge, canvas-covered and partly-painted archway, fifty feet high, made a crude rainbow of colour over the people – one of the new king's triumphal arches. Parts of its wooden ribs were still visible where the canvas had not yet been fixed.

I shook my head in wonderment. The things were going up everywhere, it seemed.

The Exchange, built by Sir Thomas Gresham, was visible to me above the thatched roofs of houses as I turned left out of Birchin Lane and marched along Cornhill. Several stories high and rectangular, the tower at its front wing was surmounted by a golden grasshopper, for reasons I had never bothered to learn. And on top of that, as always, a seagull had landed and was regarding us little humans milling beneath.

The building itself looked like what I imagined one might find in Italy – a wide palazzo with red-slate, sloping roofs. Light reflected from dozens of mullioned windows along the front, and on the ground floor, open doors and windows displayed the goods for sale. If much of London looked and smelled like the past, I had always thought that the Royal Exchange appeared to have been conjured out of the future.

The place itself was a great centre of shopping and, outside of the plague times, always thronged. I was given little alternative than to go to it – the crowd had become irresistible, sweeping me up and dragging me along.

The Exchange grew larger, looming up over me, and I was carried into its central courtyard, which was devoid of its usual stalls and instead packed with people. At the centre of activity now, the great rush of feet stopped, and men and women spread everywhere, passing around drinks, calling out to neighbours, some pointing excitedly at the upper storeys. Discordant music rose from various parts of the place.

I pushed my way around, aimless, wondering at the stupidity of being swept in, when I spotted a banner that made my lips purse. Held up on either side by poles and wavering over the good hats, white coifs, Monmouth caps, and even the bare heads of children hoisted upon shoulders, it had painted on it two wyverns rampant supporting a shield with three leopards' faces.

Weavers.

I turned away, cursing the boy Nicholas Hopgood. Then I completed my revolution, my feet irritated at my mind, my mind at my body, and began edging my way through the confusion of people.

'Mr Savage, sir,' shouted the boy. As I'd expected, he must have finished his toils in Holborn and been forced to actually do some work – the dogsbody work of any prentice. His white hands were curled around one of the poles which held the banner aloft.

No wonder it wavers so.

Faith was not there. 'Good morrow, young Hopgood. Making yourself useful to your master, I see.'

'Yes, sir. We,' he shifted his grip as I drew out my pipe and made a fuss of lighting it, 'we have to be seen. Ahead of the big day. Master didn't want us to miss this chance. The shops here will be doing a good trade, sir. I've even seen some people we know. All are here.'

I mumbled wordlessly, trying to think of something to say to him. To warn him that Faith was not of a coming-on disposition and ask what his intentions were, I supposed. Or even just if she had found good service with his master's wife. In truth I had no idea. I had no experience and no authority over the girl, being neither true father nor brother nor any other kin. It was too public a place, I thought, to say anything of the like – and nor would I be heard. I was saved from saying anything by a sudden cry that seemed to erupt as one from the crowd. A hundred – perhaps a thousand – heads twisted in one direction. Mine followed.

In an open, railed gallery above, two figures appeared. One of them was King James, who stood white faced and glaring. It was difficult to tell, but he seemed to be frowning. Beside him stood, I assumed, our new queen, Danish Anne. She was wearing an enormous silver and white dress with a stiff wheel-drum at her waist and a pale pink open ruff at her neck. The ruff ended at the corners of a jewelled bodice. Adding more colour was a huge blood-red rose at the centre of her bosom, a cascade of pearls seeming to pour from it.

A pure and swelling heart spilling love.

Her hair was in the fashionable style of the impossibly stiff beehive, golden brown and also bearing a number of jewels. James, on the other hand, was wearing a silver suit not much different to the one I had seen him in a few nights previously.

'Why ain't the king speaking?' I heard someone rasp.

He did not receive an answer, but one formed easily enough in my mind. The Londoners would not like or well understand his accent. They would not love him as they had loved Elizabeth, because he could not speak their language as she did. As if in proof, King James stepped back from the railing, his arms folded, whilst his wife leant over it, an arm raised in an almost soldierly salute.

She knows how to work a crowd, at least.

I appreciate movement in people. The roll of the hips, straightness of the back, the spreading of the hand and fingers in gesture. Queen Elizabeth had understood it, and Queen Anne appeared to understand it too. She was shouting something, and occasionally threw her head back and laughed. Her deep, husky voice was lost, though, in the chorus of cheers that went up for her. I kept my mouth shut and my hands down, straining to see where the king had gone.

The cries of the people changed in pitch, turning to confused moans as the queen was jerked back on her feet. I had a brief impression of the king, flanked by two soldiers in morion helmets, pulling her away, and her resisting, trying to turn again. Her hand flapped in one last wave and then she stomped away. There was something manly in her carriage, in her bearing and the direct way she had sought to woo us. And then the royal party was gone, apparently ordered to end the unwanted festivity on the orders of King James.

Jealous.

I continued watching, as did the rest of the crowd, to see if the queen would reappear. Not a beautiful woman, but I found a certain charm in her. I was reminded, in fact, of the old days of Queen Elizabeth, before those final years when she had rarely appeared – and then as a shrunken old creature lost in her clothing. I almost smiled at the thought. Queen Elizabeth. The Elizabeth part was dead; the queen part was not. Instead, the hook-nosed Danish woman in the gallery above us all had taken on her weeds. It seemed a shame that the lumbering and lecherous Scotch schoolmaster had taken on her crown.

A halting cry broke out behind me – some squawking woman.

'Mr Savage, sir. Mr Savage, sir!'

I turned away from the gallery and back to Nicholas Hopgood. His face was white, and I saw that a sallow, gaunt woman was standing at his side, pointing and almost hopping. Grey hair began to tumble from her coif. 'What?' I asked, moving closer to them.

'Mr Savage, she says that's her husband – one of the men taken like David – that's him, there! Get him, sir!'

22

The weavers' banner collapsed on Hopgood's side as he let the pole slide through his hands. The woman at his side was shrieking in fury, 'Anthony! Anthony!'

I turned to where the boy was pointing and saw, looking back at the woman through wide eyes, a thin man in faded, threadbare grey, his breeches sagging and his sleeves and doublet unpadded. He seemed frozen in place as he stared at the woman.

Looking back into the past.

I began towards him, tutting as other heads and bodies moved between us, fools moving around, discussing the appearance of the king and queen in a frenzy of giggling, excited chatter. My pipe was knocked from my hand and I dared not even stoop to retrieve it for fear of losing him.

But the fellow – Anthony – simply stood, staring in the direction of his abandoned wife.

Shouting burst into the air behind me, shrill and persistent. I turned briefly, to see Hopgood restraining the woman from giving chase.

Good man.

And then I returned to it. As I drew close, he seemed to see me. I recognised something in his face. Madness, I thought. It was about those wide, staring eyes. His lips were moving soundlessly, as though he were arguing with himself. When I was within touching distance, I reached out and plucked at his arm. He yelped as though scalded. 'Touch me not!' he cried, his voice rising over the general hubbub. Some others stopped to stare. 'Spy! Spy!'

He wheeled, almost diving into the crowd. I cursed. Leapt after him. People began to part, hands everywhere flying to protect their purses. Around and about I heard the cry go up: 'thieves!'

'Stop him!' I yelled, pointing. I could see Anthony's hoary head bouncing ahead, as though through a forest of other people. 'Anthony, stop – Anthony!'

The sound of his name halted him and put his hands over his ears. He did not turn to me but disappeared. He had, I realised, hunched forward. I took the opportunity to run, pushing and shoving my way. My alarm seemed to spread, and people moved away from him.

'Not Anthony, not Anthony, not Anthony! I am Jonah!'

A few steps away, I sprang from my heels, landing hard on his bent back. He fell forward, muttering. 'Call the guard!' I cried. Then, for good measure, 'treason! Treason!'

Beneath me, Anthony began rolling and keening. I fell to the side, the cobbles sending shivers of pain through my shoulder. My quarry, I realised with horror, was reaching for something and instinctively I scrabbled for the dagger I kept in my boot.

Don't kill him! Keep him alive!

As my fingers groped, leaden and panicked, I saw his fly up and I braced myself for the blow. I was not wearing my good, thick canvas and frieze, but my thinner livery and coat. I abandoned the dig for my dagger and threw a hand over my chest.

But Anthony had no dagger. From somewhere he had produced a bag of something, and he was mumbling again. He shouted, 'take it, angels! Back to the family!'

His hand flew upwards and outwards and I jerked my upper body back – just in time to see the brown bag

a purse of coin?

fly up and over the heads of the crowd. I looked between its passage and its thrower, biting my lip. What was it? Should I go for it?

No.

I had him.

I threw myself again on the man, who was now grinning as he lay in the dirt and dust of the cobbles and I held him fast, pinning his arms to the ground. He did not resist. When I had him, I looked again over the crowd, which had made way for us and was watching and shouting.

What did he throw?

It was useless to ask. Whatever it was, it would be the property of someone else now, scooped up and retrieved by a member of the crowd or one of the pickpockets who was surely creeping around the tangle of legs and skirts that stood around me. Answers could be beaten out of the creature.

Pushing through the crowd came his wife, Hopgood at her elbow. 'Anthony, you rotten knave!' shouted the woman. 'You abandoned me! Where have you been? Whoring?' Laughter and catcalls bounced between the high walls of the Exchange. 'Get off my husband, you brute. Give him back.'

I remained on top of the unmoving Anthony. 'I am Jonah,' he hissed. And then, 'vita in morte sumus. We are the Enlightened.' And then his laughter joined that of the onlookers.

'He's run mad,' said his wife, drawing back. 'He ran mad with the plague.'

Whether the word 'plague' or 'mad' did it, the crowd began pushing back. Into the clearing, finally, stepped a guardsman in royal livery, his morion helmet making a high peak above the crowd.

'What's this about treason?'

'A traitor! This man is a traitor.'

The guard surveyed us, hands on his hips. He looked, I thought, unsure. Seeing him, Anthony began hissing and cackling. 'You will all see when the judgment comes, you will not be amongst the chosen.'

'See,' shouted his wife. 'Mad. Abandoned me out of plain madness.'

This seemed a popular assessment, and I could hear folk in the crowd repeating variations on accusations of madness. I gave in, forgetting all about treason. 'I am mistaken,' I said. 'There is no treason. This is a simple zany. Scattered wits. He must go to the Bedlam forthwith.' I kept my weight pressed down on his hips but swivelled my upper body to reveal to the guard my livery. 'King's business,' I said quietly, adding a layer of confidentiality to my tone. 'We must convey this man to the Bedlam.'

The guard stood staring again for a few seconds. And then he nodded, the light glinting on his helmet.

I smiled. Perfect, I thought. The Bedlam was closer than the Tower or any other place where the fool might be questioned privily, and the guard would not linger there, would not interfere.

Sliding off of Anthony, I dragged him to his feet. He came, unprotesting, and stood between me and the guardsman. His wife began to put up a fight, arguing, clearly regretting her recourse to claims of madness. My new friend, scowling, turned his helmeted head in her direction and growled, 'you wish to accompany him, wench, to the madhouse?' She closed her mouth.

With the captive between us, we walked through the path cleared by the crowd, out of the courtyard and to the left. Under his breath, the madman brabbled and chattered and giggled, smiling and repeating his strange chant. The guard ignored him, and I attempted to do the same, listening only to see if he revealed anything of note. As far as I could tell, he did not. Along Cornhill eastwards, we turned left again onto Bishopsgate Street – a thoroughfare which was home to at least one building – a house – I would rather forget. On we went, decent people making way and less reputable ones shouting what they assumed to be wit at the prisoner. Some younger lads turned and bared their arses at us. We passed the cool stone of Gresham College and the tall, thatched box of the Bull Inn – a playing place lay in its yard, I knew – until we reached the wall. At Bishopsgate, the guard made short work of gaining us passage and suddenly we were outside the bounds of the old City.

And there, on our left, stood the forbidding, squatting hulk of the Bedlam.

***

We all live, I suppose, cheek by jowl with ugly, ill-natured buildings of wicked repute. The house on the street where a man slew his wife. The inn in which known criminals congregate and plot murders. And we learn to ignore them – to keep our heads averted as we pass by; to simply pretend the dark spots do not exist.

The place itself was, like the Exchange, a quadrangular building surrounding a central courtyard. There the similarity ended. Occupying only one storey, the old grey stones were higgledy-piggledy and there were only a few small windows visible. But it was the smell that cried out for attention – a sour, choking sewage reek that combined foul linen, shit, piss, and bad food.

'Smells like an ass's fart,' I said. I received no response from the mumbling captive or the guard as we turned towards the tall, stained wooden doors, one of which stood open. Suddenly, Anthony seemed to realise what we were doing with him and he dug his heels into the rutted ground, swearing and wailing. Together we lifted him off his feet, dodging his kicks, as he began yelling, 'not the place! Not the place!'

We manhandled him inside, not without difficulty, and found ourselves in a front hall with a counter partly screening a door to the courtyard. No one stood at it, and so the guard, still gripping Anthony by the arm, began beating it.

Eventually a warder slouched in from the yard, his clothing a worn buff. The smell of tobacco about him revealed what he had been up to, and I silently cursed the loss of my own pipe, dropped and undoubtedly stolen in the press of people in the Exchange.

Like Anthony's pouch.

'What's this?' the warder asked.

'A gift for your keeper,' said the guard. 'A madman who surprised the king and queen.'

The warder whistled, looking Anthony up and down. 'Brain fever, is it? A frantic? Or a touch of the melancholy?'

Anthony began bucking between us and we held him tighter.

'Release me, you filth. Filthy spies. I am of the Enlightened. You cannot keep me.'

'Religious,' I said. 'I would have answers from him on certain matters.'

'Who's paying for his keep?'

'What?' I frowned.

'We don't board no men here for nothing. This ain't a gaol. It's an 'orse-spittle. Fifteen pence a week. His parish or his master – who's paying?'

'The king's secretary. Baron Essenden.' Warder and guard both gawped at me, whilst Anthony quailed.

'Heh. You sure you ain't itching for a room here, mate?' I didn't answer. 'Might have to see the keeper about that. He's gone to see the king. I ...' The warder looked at me and then at the guard before addressing himself to me. 'We'll take him. Ay, we've a spare chamber in the Abraham ward. Stick him in there.' I was unsure if the fellow truly believed me, only wished to believe me, or was simply unwilling to risk disbelieving. Turning his attention to the guard, he said, 'you can question him all you like there, mate.'

'I have no questions for the filth,' said the guard, his chin rising and the helmet tilting back. 'I shall return to my post. You, hold him.'

The warder stepped around the counter and took Anthony's arm instead, leaving the guard to give me a curt nod. He hurried from the Bedlam, not looking in either direction, a hand held up to his face. 'Good morrow, friend. My name is Toby.' He spoke as though to a child. 'You come and we'll find you a good room and you can have a sweet little lie down, eh?' Then, to me, the singsong gone, 'Abraham wing, mate. Follow me.'

We went out into the courtyard, skirting a sad-looking chapel in the centre, and crossed some dead grass to one of the side wings. A door led into a dingy corridor, and the opposite wall was punctuated by thicker wooden doors, each bearing smaller grates that could be opened.

Just like prison cells.

'Just down to the end, mate,' said Toby as we dragged Anthony between us. 'Wasn't expecting no one today. We've been busy of late too.'

'Many madmen?' I asked, hope rising.

'No, mate, no. Looky-loos. Since the plays've been off, them as want ... ah ... entertainments ... they've been coming here. Peep at a puddle-wit for a penny, that's the game. Course,' he added, tipping me a wink as we passed a door, 'have to be careful, like. Lad in there, he does nothing but yank his own yard-shaft raw day and night. Dunno how he still has one. Had a woman peep in once, she damn near fainted. And me, I says, "gracious mercy, madam, I didn't mean no offence". And, says she,' his voice rose and his nostrils flared, '"it ain't that, warder. It's just me 'usband's ain't near 'alf that size".'

I laughed in spite of myself. It faded as we passed another door, behind which someone seemed to be raving. Crying came from the next, and nothing in the one beyond. Toby stopped at it, throwing the door wide. 'Now then, old boy … what's his name?'

'Anthony, his wife said–'

'Jonah! I am Jonah. And you will die the death. You, all of you, die the death when the great day comes.'

'Keep that up,' said Toby, 'and you'll be dying the death.'

'Ha! I fear no death. We have conquered death. The dead have spoken to me. Vita in morte sumus.'

A shiver tickled its way through me. I needed to be alone with the man. 'What's that mean?' Toby asked me. 'That some kinda Spanish?' I shrugged. 'Now, old boy, you just settle yourself all good. Look what a pretty room we 'ave for you.'

There is painting the lily and then there is gilding an unrefined turd.

I thought instantly of the so-called master's side wards in one of the London gaols. The cell's walls were of plain, undressed stone. Dampness had darkened them to an almost greenish, slimy brown. Its single window was high up in one of them, barred and unglazed. A single cot was attached to the far wall, its sheets filthy and straw bleeding from its mattress. Semi-circular bands of rusty iron were dotted around, leather restraints hanging from them. Like the ones, I thought, my brother Thomas had attached to my father's bed when he went mad. I knew why. I feared madmen more than the wiliest criminal – because a criminal could always be understood, his motives discovered, his goals. More, he could be bribed or frightened into giving up his secrets. The desires and schemes of madmen lacked all reason, and a total lack of fear was the deadliest of weapons.

As we released Anthony into his new home, Toby asked if he ought to be restrained. 'Not yet,' I said. 'Leave me alone with him a while. I'll cry out if I need you.' The warder shrugged and left us, closing the door gently.

Now, Anthony.' He looked away at the mention of his real name. 'Where do you live?'

'Vita in morte sumus. I am not alive. Not yet. None of us are.'

'Where is us? Where are your fellows not alive?'

He said nothing, spitting on the floor instead. I stepped closer.

'Where is my boy, David? Your woman took him, Angela.' He froze at the name and turned to me.

'You spy! He was right – he sees all – the angels tell him.' His hands flew up to his mouth, making me start.

'Who?'

Nothing.

'Where is David? Where is Dr Gurney? Tell me, you fucking lunatic!'

He turned his back to me, and I slammed my first into the back of his head. He went down on one knee, grunting. 'What was in the bag you had? Where is my boy?' I kicked him. If threats and bribes wouldn't work, by God I would beat answers out of him. To my surprise, he began a hacking laugh. It drifted up from his prone position on the floor, frightening in its oddness.

In its lack of reason.

'You will be dead in days. All will be dead. Only we will be born again. Us. The Enlightened. Death cannot touch us.'

'What does that mean?' I kicked out again, my heart thudding in my chest. 'Where are they? Where have you hidden him?'

The door opened and Toby stepped in. 'Jesus, man. Stop. I'd heard the lord secretary's men were a hard lot. Jesus.' He fumbled at his doublet, reaching under the plain buff coat. A pipe appeared in his hand. 'Come and have a smoke with me. It's good for you. It'll blow away that fury.'

My heart began to slow. 'Ay,' I said. 'Maybe.'

We left, Toby locking the cell, and went out into the courtyard, which was bleak under the grey sky. He set the pipe going and we passed it between us. 'Something big afoot? Papist, is he? Priest?'

'No.' I breathed in the smoke, coughing and shaking my head – something I had not done in a while. And then I remembered something – the reason I had been coming to the Bedlam before Hopgood had discovered one of the Enlightened lot. 'Here – would you know of any man released from here in the recent times.' I tried to remember what Glover had said, but didn't think he'd mentioned exactly when the mysterious leader had escaped or been released from the place.

'I daresay. Been here five years. Some of this lot been in longer than that. Strange thing – don't reckon they want out. Get used to getting their arses wiped, maybe.'

'This would be another religious one. Like him. A man who had the plague once – maybe a long time ago – and ended up in here. And got released and started preaching.'

'You mean Hope?'

'Who?'

'Ay, sounds like the man Hope. Must be over forty. Melancholic. Talked endless on death – on why he survived and others died of the pest.'

I nearly choked again, and then almost dropped the pipe. 'Hope – what's his first name? Who is he?'

'I … it'd all be in the keeper's records.'

'Where are they?' I stepped towards him.

'Hold, mate. You don't need no records. And wouldn't be allowed to see 'em, neither.' I advanced again and he held up his hands, sliding the pipe from my grip. 'Steady, there, secretary's man. I'll tell you. Nathaniel Hope. Put in here by his neighbours in Aldgate parish. They reckoned he'd turned sour in the head.' Toby held the stem of the pipe up to the side of his head and gave it a few revolutions. 'So they paid for him to be put in here.'

'And? How did he get out? What did he say?' I closed my mouth, shaking my head. 'I'm sorry. It is a matter of – of security of the state. This man might have turned dangerous.'

Toby inhaled and blew smoke up into the cloudy, darkening sky. Other warders were beginning to set light to torches, as though doing so might add cheer. 'Hope … his wife had died. Couple of little lads too. In the plague, but in the eighties. But he was cracked before that, I reckon. It just set him off – gave a kind of reason to the madness maybe. He saw things. Some of them do – see visions. Talk back to them. You must've seen the like. People just laugh.'

I had, and I had done the same in the past. But the problem now was that some people – like the wretch Anthony – had listened.

'Apparently he started preaching out that he was saved. Visited by spirits. He was a strange one. Could be right charming when he wasn't having one of his fits. Spoke right well, all them good and gentle manners. His Godly fits, we called them. Bothered his neighbours claiming he'd discover how to share his gifts. So they got him locked up in here. And he got worse. One minute charming and all gentle words, the next cursing like a sailor and shouting about spirits.' He shrugged. 'You get used to that kind of thing in this place. Learn not to trust the gentle words. Ever.'

'How did he get out?'

'Parish stopped paying for him. Said his master had stopped paying his lease so he wasn't their problem no more.'

'Aldgate, you said? Who was the master?'

'Ah. Now that's a ticklish thing. We don't know. I mean, we know who he said, but he was a madman. Might as well have said it was the old queen herself that he served.'

'Who?'

Toby drew in some more smoke and watched his colleagues working. 'An earl. The earl of Essex, I reckon it was.' I closed my eyes. Essex had been dead for years. A dead end. 'No wait.' I looked at him again. 'Here, wait.' He handed me the pipe and stepped out into the courtyard, hollering a salute. 'Daniel! Dan! You remember old Hope – the one with the Godly fits we flung out last summer? Who was it he used to rave about, say was his master? Earl of Essex, wasn't it?'

'Oxford,' returned the other man, shaking out a torch. 'Earl of Oxford.'

'Thanks, Dan.' Toby returned to me. 'That was it. Claimed up and down that he served the Earl of Oxford and the big man would look out for him. You hear that kind of shite a lot too. But the strange thing – a note arrived from a servant of an earl. Liveried, like – offering him work on his getting out of here. So maybe it wasn't plain madness – that part anyway.'

I grinned, snatching the pipe off him and taking some smoke. I knew Oxford – by reputation if nothing else. He had had a company of child actors a few years ago and had even written some comedies that ended up passing through the Revels Office. They hadn't been bad – but better suited to his touring company of boys than to any serious players on the London stages.

Best of all, though, Oxford was still, as far as I knew, alive and lived somewhere in London.

I poured out thanks, slipping the pipe into my belt, and was waved away by Toby, who seemed pleased to have helped out a secretary's man. I left him hurrying back in to see to Anthony, deciding that I should have nothing from the man that I couldn't find from a loftier, saner figure.

I was right.

I had only got as far as the entrance hall and was on the point of crossing the gap in the battered counter when a breathless Toby arrived behind me, wheezing, gasping, and coughing up phlegm. I cursed, preparing an apology for mistaking his pipe for mine. Before

I could frame it, he said, 'Anth – Anth – your man!'

'What?'

'He's dead, mate. 'anged 'imself from the window bars with his sheets.'

23

There has been starvation in England, years of it. People have begun to eat grass and acorns. Country folk flood into the great city and die in the streets, the city authorities unable to keep up, so that it is not unusual to find human bones on the side of the roads. And then there is death in the world of the great, after the other earl, Essex, rides abroad and cries out for it to be delivered to the queen's secretary.

Hope goes along to Smithfield some time after the earl's wild ride. There is mischief afoot. A wicked man, a libeller, has been caught: a lawyer's clerk named Waterhouse. He stands on a cart, stripped to his shirt, as the noose – wits call it the collar – is fixed around his neck.

The cart is pulled away.

As the knot tightens, his face bulges, his tongue protruding, eyes popping. He swivels in circles, legs bucking. There is something courtly about it, something prim – and yet grotesquery and suggestiveness dance in the thrust of his hips. Is he dancing with Death? Making love to it like a husband at last reunited with a wife from whom he has been too long apart?

The spectacle ends. He stills. And yet he is left to hang there, his swelling head lowered, a black fringe of hair curtaining his face as if to tell Hope and the other onlookers that the play is done, the actor-engine of his mind gone.

Gone where?

The visions come frequently now, and he is never too long out of the house in Aldgate. He goes out only for food, drink, and death. And to warn the neighbours of his ways. They watch him constantly, whisper about him certainly, and must be themselves suspected always.

He returns home and writes to the earl – one of many letters he has sent and never yet received a reply. The great man stood in judgment of some of those involved in the late rebellion – that much he has heard, but he will not write to an ageing servant who has lost his youth and charm. And who has gained some little fame in the district as a loose-wit. It is a marvel how much he can write. Endless pages, writing over writing, between writing, around the sides of writing. He writes so much that he thinks his hand will drop off from it.

And yet only to a man who never listens – who might not even receive his letters.

He needs someone who understands – many who understand. The angels sing to him that there are others – others who have bit their thumbs at death as proof of their divinity. He will find them, he decides, if he has to begin preaching more openly in the streets.

***

Hope stood on the deck. The smell of it now was terrible – it was a wonder any man could stand to be a sailor. Every day their waste went into the water, following the poor bodies of Isaac and Huldah – but still the stench of sweat and piss and shit was heavy.

It reminded him, in fact, of that other place.

He took one deep breath, trying to ignore it, and refocused his eyes on Amos. 'Where is he?'

'We don't know. He went to buy powder with the rest. Only he failed to return.'

'Poor Jonah,' said Hope, feeling the tears – surely they were more frequent now? – threaten. He blinked them away as an angel sang through his mouth. 'Fucking traitor! He's deserted us. Find him and kill him!' Then, as though he had said nothing, he said, 'poor Jonah. He must have been taken up. I pray they discovered no powder, the spies.'

Amos's hand went to the string around his robe, which was weighted now with several bags of the stuff. He cupped one. 'I told him, Nathaniel, told them all. Don't get caught. And if you do…'

'Yes?'

'If you do, fool them with a false death.'

Hope nodded. 'Good. Put as much of it as you can below. In the old beer store. In the magazine. Pack it well, with care. And just one small bag for each of us.' Amos went on chattering, but he ignored him, looking out to the far bulkhead. An enormous crucifix was nailed to it – a hideous popish thing with its gory carving of Christ. The saviour's head was hanging, as the man Waterhouse's had hung at Smithfield. Yet he could hear Jesus speaking, his voice drowning out Amos.

'Do you see how I suffered? Do you see my passion?'

'Yes,' he mouthed. He had to compete with the distant hum of Amos's voice. But that dull sound could not compare with the glory of Christ's message.

'And you must suffer so on this fallen earth. Through the great fire, as you know. I am the resurrection and the light. And the false king in his stolen earthly crown must feel the fire as a crown of thorns.'

'When?'

'In a moment, in the twinkling of an eye.'

Hope recognised the words but did not understand. He mouthed his confusion. In reply, the carved, painted eyelids of the crucified Christ popped open, revealing solid white eyeballs. Tears of blood began to course down the painted wooden cheeks. Hope started, horrified and entranced.

'The sails rigged and the sweeps – what?' Amos broke off his speech.

'Fire!' said Hope. Jesus had gone. Never had he had so divine a visitation. He felt swollen with it, ready to burst. He gripped Amos by the shoulders. 'Fire is the answer.'

'Ay.' The fellow looked doubtful. Confused. Stupid. 'The powder. For the king.'

'For us all, brother! But first we must give a burnt offering. The most perfect of all the sacrifices that might be offered. Jonah might have been taken from us – lost to us perhaps – and so we will offer a sacrifice by fire. Where is the boy, where is our beloved Samuel? He is our purest soul, the best of the Enlightened. We must give him the gift of fire. He must be given up to the flames.'

***

Gurney passed a piece of bread to David and the boy was chewing intently when the door opened. Hope eyed them both suspiciously, before breaking into smile. The doctor stood and moved before the child when he spotted the murderer Amos. The fellow was wearing an excited, expectant air.

'Samuel, it is your time.'

'His time for what?' asked Gurney.

Hope pushed him aside and he slid against the bulkhead. 'You are of the Enlightened, young brother, and the spirits have chosen you as their offering. You must embrace the fire and go to them. To eternal life, to the life immortal.'

'What?' the boy asked.

In response, Amos thundered in, grasping the back of the boy's head and pulling him off the coffer.

'Peace,' said Hope, 'he will go willingly.'

'He will not.' Gurney, his breath returning, put his hands on the deck and rose. 'You will do nothing of the sort.'

'Stay out of this,' snapped Amos. 'Or you'll join him.'

'Now, now, we are not murderers,' said Hope. 'No threats. You will come happily into the dancing flames, Samuel. Death has no terror. You have had the plague and lived. You are blessed against the darkness.'

'I haven't,' said David, quite coolly, Gurney thought. He then pushed Amos away. 'I had the aryotitus. Sometimes called the gaol fever. Red skin, pains, aches in the head and joints.' Gurney's mouth fell open, as much at the boy's extraordinary memory as at the dangers he had just presented.

'What is this?' Hope frowned, looking down. 'What?' Then he turned to Gurney and repeated the question.

'It is true,' said the doctor. 'He described to me his symptoms, his suffering, and it is clear to me that this child did not survive the plague, as you creatures did. He has never had it. He is not one of you. And therefore you will not touch him.'

Hope's eyes became round white O's. 'Deceivers,' he said. 'Spies. You, brat, have been sent to spy. On behalf of your wicked spy master. Deceiver!' Amos began to speak and Hope lurched backwards, as though propelled. His lips began moving in grunts, his eyes closing. And then he spun, springing towards the door. 'Fucking liars! Everywhere – you'll die, both of you, in this ship. I am the resurrection, and the light is fire. You'll burn and you won't come back, and the fishes will feast – and let the waters teem with the dead and the great fish who swallowed Jonah and Jonah was in the stomach...'

Hope's voice continued, ceaseless, rising and falling, rambling curses and bible verses all the way down the passageway. Amos, left in his wake, grinned and said, 'you'd best get to work on our physick, doctor. You haven't got long left.'

And then he followed, closing the door and locking Gurney and David inside.

Gurney thought, I've conveyed the boy out of the frying pan...

24

I waited in an anteroom in King's Place, the London residence of the Earl of Oxford, in Hackney. Light streamed in through mullioned windows which looked out over a walled Italianate garden. I had not told Cecil of my coming. I had sorted through my knowledge of Oxford after leaving the Bedlam and recalled that the old boy had at one time been married to the secretary's sister. Whether the men were friends or enemies I knew not and nor did I care to have anything of a personal nature interfere with my mission of finding David and the doctor.

Soft music quivered through the air, muffled by the door ahead of me. I had been questioned hard on arriving and eventually gained passage by admitting that I was a servant of the Revels Office and had need of the earl's knowledge of verse for the great coronation procession to take place the following day. I knew just enough to be sure that this would get me in, as Oxford was well enough known as a lover of music. Thereafter, I had been shown into the antechamber and told to wait, as the earl, in his age, did not rise before eleven. And so I did.

And I waited.

And waited.

As I did so, I wandered the room, enjoying the feel of the thick carpets beneath my stockinged feet (my boots having been ordered off at the door). I wiggled my toes and looked around the walls. Portraits stood, floor to ceiling – I had noticed them on my arrival but not really looked. I stepped over now and saw, to my surprise, that they all depicted the same man. They each showed, in fact, the Earl of Oxford, Edward de Vere himself, in various costumes and at various ages.

What kind of a man is so in love with himself that he filled one of his chambers with pictures of himself? I wondered.

Jealous?

Although I had never met the earl in person, I knew the type well enough. Spoiled, petted, cossetted, expecting servitude and deference, and so happily and proudly noble that his turds probably arrived tapestried.

The music – a virginal, by the sound of it – ended, as bells outside rang out midday. The door opened and I fell to one knee, my cap in my hands. I knew the game well enough. But it was not Oxford who stepped out – rather, a handsome, smooth-faced lad with soft brown hair falling to his waist. I hid my frown but I wondered – was Oxford known for a love of boys? I thought not, having always connected him with a string of noble whores. Perhaps, like King James, he loved beauty – and unlike King James, he could have it about him without needing to touch and kiss it.

'My lord will see you now, and it please you.'

I rose and whispered across the carpet, slipping inside as the boy stepped out and closed the door. My eyes darted around the room until I saw the earl, and again I made a leg. 'Come,' he rumbled. I got up again, and moved across to where Oxford lay, supine, on a sagging settle. And then I made my bow again, theatrically turning my cap inwards and holding it before me so that I could regard him without appearing to.

In my time, I have seen many portraits – big ones and little ones, copies and miniatures, engraving and woodcuts – of the great and terrible Henry VIII. For a moment, I blinked stupidly, as I felt myself looking at one of them come suddenly to life.

The Earl of Oxford was a bloated wreck of a man. Like the old king, age seemed to have swollen the earl around the middle. Oxford's eyes had grown piggy within his big, round, reddened face, and his mouth was a stubborn, childish moue. A jewelled nightcap sat demurely on his head and his body was swathed in yards and yards of tawny velvet that had been fashioned into a dressing gown. He lay there, impressive in his bulk, lacking only the beard and moustaches to complete the picture of the old tyrant.

'My lord,' I said, regaining my composure.

'Mm. You are come from the Revels Office.' He made a harrumphing sound, shifting himself on the settle. He had not asked me to stand and my knee remained sunken in another carpet. 'What are you, one of the caterpillars of the court come to burrow into mine poor flesh?'

There's enough of it.

I bowed my head and let his querulous voice drift over me. 'You heard, I think, my composition?'

'I … did, my lord.'

'A trifle.' His pink hand fluttered in the air before falling across his forehead. 'I am not well. I fear my end draws near and a lifetime weighs heavily upon me. I think I will no more come to court and thus will end my poor posterity.'

I could feel his gaze dart towards me, begging me to demur. 'Your lordship would be much missed. I understand the court is starved of entertainments, having only playwrights to charm it.' I thought of Jonson and Dekker, writing their pageants for the morrow – and Shakespeare's old plays given out at Christmas and New Year.

'Pah. Stage-wrights. Mere apes of the art of music and verse.' He sighed.

'Did your lordship not pen comedies? Very good comedies.'

'Mere playthings,' he snapped, 'for my little boys to delight with. I did so love to see them caper. And now even they have fled me.'

I had remembered what had become of Oxford's Boys, his company of child actors – starved of material, they had ceased their touring of the provinces and joined with Worcester's Men. 'Still, my lord ....'

'Still! I tell you still that the sweet music of song and poesy shine brighter than the dull and gross stuff of the common stage. Do you defy me, man?' His hand shot out and took the curved top of a cane. 'Have at you, sirrah.' He jabbed it at my chest as though his stick were a rapier and then began wheezing laughter. 'I jest, man. I jest.'

I smiled.

'Now, let us end this. Who are you? Why have you come here? It is not to ask an old man to write verse and music for that Scotch urchin.' My mouth fell open at the treasonous talk. He smiled again, showing several missing teeth. 'Look at me, sirrah. I will be dead soon enough. Think you that I fear being carried by stout men from here to the Tower? Out with it. For whom are you spying in this house?'

'Sir, I–'

'My *lord*, boy.'

'My lord, I am seeking a former servant of yours.' I looked up and saw curiosity pass his features. I supposed him to be beyond wariness and so did not bother with veiled threats of the new king's interest. 'A man called Nathaniel Hope. Formerly a resident of the Bedlam. He is now at large and dangerous. He has ... he has stolen away my boy and another man. Several people, in fact.'

'Stolen? I did not think Hope to be a sodomite.' I kept my face neutral and said nothing to that. 'I regret I cannot help you. I have not had word of Hope these many months. For years I paid for the creature to ward in Aldgate. I had forgotten I was still paying for the scamp's leasehold until I was sent word that he had been taken up in the Bedlam.'

'Who is he?'

Oxford made a dismissive gesture, with his great, tawny arm. 'A page of mine in my youth. He was of my party in Italy. Ah, Italy,' he sighed, 'I shall never again smile upon your pretty places. You, I think, will never have been to Italy.'

'Not outside the playhouse.'

'Pah. No journeyman stage-wright's words could conjure that land.' He sniffed. 'I do not like that common labourers and trulls might walk the streets of this town thinking themselves to have been in the great states of Italy. And just from the hearing of some poxed stage-wright's honeyed words, spoken by fools.'

'But Hope, my lord–'

'An orphaned son of a gentleman. I gave him office as a page and thereafter he acted as my agent in various matters. Looking on at things I could not. As you do for someone, I imagine.' His great head rolled towards me. He grunted, as though in pain, and began coughing.

'Can I get you something?'

'Wine,' he spluttered. I found the jug, of pure silver, by the look of it, alongside a number of musical instruments on an old sideboard and took it to him, holding it for him to drink. He did not thank me but grunted again when he had finished. Then he smacked his lips wetly. Closer to, I realised that his resemblance to another man was only superficial. Henry VIII was said to have been tall as well as broad, unlike the earl. Further, Oxford's hair was blonde rather than red and he lacked the long Tudor nose. I stepped back as he cleared his throat and began speaking again. 'Oh, yes. Hope, if I recall, was amongst my witnesses at the death of this new king's mother. He went mad, of course, and began writing me many letters. I burnt them. Nonsense. I read nothing from mad slaves. My servants tell me he raved on death and stars and the world hereafter. If I see it before him, and I trust I will, I shall send him word, what?'

'You knew he was in the Bedlam, you said, my lord?'

'Indeed.' He lay back and seemed to enjoy the aftertaste of his wine. 'And I would not pay to keep him there. Nor his parish. Yet I fancy I did my duty towards him, as a noble man of honour must.'

'Yes, my lord,' I said, feeling disappointment threaten to overwhelm me. Another golden promise delivering nothing. Another dead end. 'You paid for him to live in Aldgate.'

'Oh, that. No, I did not speak of that.' I looked up again, barely hoping. He seemed to sense my expectation and sat a little more upright, milking his moment. 'I mean that other. My final gift delivered to him. Something he might have and sell and thereby get himself some lodging. In the Bedlam or otherwise.'

'Gift?' I asked dumbly. I was hoping for a lodging house.

'A ship!' Oxford grasped at his cane again and swept it into the air. 'The *Crown Elizabeth*. What do you think of that?' I could not resist a little head shake of disappointment. 'Well?' he persisted. 'Was that not kindly done of me?'

'Yes, my lord,' I said without expression. This Hope and his sect were hardly sailing around the world.

His laughter rumbled again, and I wrestled the desire to roll him off his settle and take the cane to him. 'Only it was not. The ship was dead. An old pinnace I outfitted for the '88. Fear not. He did not sail to France nor Italy either.'

'Was he a sailor, Hope?'

'A sailor? No, no. Interested in the battles of '88, for a spell, only. As he loved to know of all forms of death and dying.'

'Then why, my lord? Why a ship?'

'A pinnace. Because I could get no money for it and could not convince my debtors that it was indeed worthless. I gave the thing into Hope's hands, that he might sell it and buy himself some lodging, as I said. That was ... ah, summer last. Perhaps my last summer. Before the new king was given his crown in Westminster. By now I suppose he has sold the old girl for scrap and bought himself – I cannot say. Leasehold for a year on a modest house in a fair borough if he made a good sale. Yet I think any merchant with wiles would have seen a madman for what he is and taken him for a pretty price, what?'

'Yes, my lord.' My hope had again dwindled and I saw nothing ahead but a long, fruitless search for the sellers' deeds at the ports, which might again lead to a dead end – for he would hardly have had to tell the scrap merchants which lodging house he intended to buy with the money they gave him. Hopeless and Hopeless. 'Which port was this ship–'

'Pinnace. The *Crown Elizabeth*.'

'Where was it–'

'She.'

'Docked? My lord.'

'You got one, you ignorant doddle-head. Good man. Oh, Queenhithe I believe, or Rotherhithe.' His hand wobbled through the air again. 'High and dry on a hithe now, at any rate.'

I rose, pain shooting through my stiff knee, and bowed. 'Thank you, my lord. I will find him and recover my boy. And the others.'

He shrugged, already bored. Then the piggy eyes sharpened. 'Do tell my brother Cecil I wish him all the very best in tomorrow's revels and festivities.'

I inclined my head, replaced my hat, and backed from the room, the door instantly opened by the pretty young man who had evidently been spying. Out in the antechamber, I put my head in my hands and began fumbling for my new pipe as I stepped through the gallery devoted to the earl's self-love, wondering vaguely at what kind of madness it was that made a fat old man flatter and taunt his current self with his past. Out of irritation at not being thanked for feeding him his wine, I lifted one of the miniatures and palmed it even as I began stuffing tobacco into my bowl.

***

I did not take a wherry to Rotherhithe and nor did I go to Queenhithe on my long walk back to the City from Hackney. It was full dark by the time I returned. Further, the coronation pageants would take place the next day. There was no time to run around the town anymore chasing down people who knew these Enlightened lunatics.

As I walked through Cheapside, I found the freshly swept street almost deserted. Already, wooden railings had been set up on either side and already people were obeying them and keeping to the covered shop fronts. Some men were fussing at the Great Conduit, apparently testing its outflow. The great archway at the western end, another fifty-foot-tall wonder, straddled the street like a colossus and I passed under it, eager to be out the other side lest the thing, its bright colours hard to read in the dark, collapse on me. I had already passed through one of the things at the eastern end.

Cutting down to Watling Street, I took my usual way home, round St Paul's via Carter Lane and up Ludgate Hill to the Fleet Bridge. Everywhere seemed suffused with the same quiet, jittery excitement. As a child, at Norfield, Thomas and I had had the same feeling the day before New Year, as we were always given gifts. Likewise, on Christmas Eve and on the eleventh day of Christmas, everything would be swept and kept clean and our parents, the servants, and we would all have the same silent, excited, waiting air, observing the rule of keeping off the newly-swept floors and fresh-beaten carpets.

And the Christmas Day dinner was always dull and the New Year's gifts a disappointment.

I could not face going home immediately to my empty, Faithless and Davidless rooms. Instead, when I got to Fleet Street, I looked out towards another of the monstrous arches, shivered, pulled my coat about me, and ducked into the Mitre.

Nothing like a beer to chase away the worthlessness and failure.

The tavern crowd was thin – I suspected because few wanted to be too belly-sick to miss the grander drinking the following day, when the fountains of the city would run with what the London officials boasted was wine. In truth, it would be as it always was – water soured and reddened with just enough of the cheapest French piss to flavour it and offer the poor folk lightened heads (one never saw wealthy merchants or lawyers or gentlemen crowding the wine-flowing conduits on festival days).

I surveyed the room through the lazy drift of tobacco smoke. A tapster stood near the bar, his elbow down on it. Some of the more hardened drinkers were hunched at tables, not speaking to one another. And then I saw a small group I knew, at the far side, on a raised wooden part of the tavern that bore a railing and looked like a shallow stage or scaffold. At the long table there, a table made for supper parties, were sat some of the Lord Chamberlain's Men – or the King's Men, as I knew they had become. I wound my way through tables and stools, most unoccupied, and hopped up to the group, taking them in.

A gaunt Augustine Philips, the players, Will Sly, Richard Cowley, and the fat-nosed Richard Burbage, and the player-playwright and still-bright star of the stage, Will Shakespeare. They must, of course, all have been in town for the coronation revels – as a company chartered in the king's name, they would have had little choice.

'Good evening, friends,' I said, sliding onto a free stool opposite them and walking my fingers over the table to a piece of cheat bread.

'Mr Savage,' said Philips. His voice was weak, I thought, and jagged around the edges. A little fear trembled – if he was ill, I did not want to share in it. 'I see the revels on the morrow bring out the parasites of the court.'

I shrugged. 'I'd find little blood to suck from you, Mr Philips, by the look of you.'

'I am not well,' he said, shaking his head.

'Have you all a part to play tomorrow?'

'Part?' boomed Burbage. 'Part? We have no part beyond baubles. Swathed in red, we must run like blood after the king.'

'We have been given yards of red cloth,' grinned Sly. 'And made,' he coughed, 'grooms of the chamber.'

'A fine thing that.' I thought of grooming James in his chamber and shuddered.

'A marvel,' said Cowley, an old hand in the company who had hooded eyes and specialised in playing second-fiddle parts.

211

'Players are happiest playing,' said Burbage.

'And writing,' said Philips, giving a pained smile and touching Shakespeare's falling band. The playwright gave a sardonic smile. I knew his plays well enough, and knew that his writing, although starting to look old fashioned, was a greater joy to him than playing. I had often enough tried in vain to find sedition in his plays as my colleagues and I pored over them in the office, and yet there always seemed to be something to contradict even the hint of dangerous words.

The playwright seemed to read my thoughts and his soft brown eyes met mine. He cleared his throat. 'I rather would be known for poesy than for playing.' His gentle country accent rounded his words. He drew his mug up, raised it slightly, and sipped, those eyes dancing.

'Yet all the writing for these revels has been done by Dekker and Jonson,' frowned Philips. Some good-natured hissing went around the table. 'Dekker boasts and brags and struts about the town that the king will hear his verses first – when he enters at Bishopsgate. I hear old Jonson has threatened in public to stab him.'

Sounds like Jonson.

'And we, the king's own men, to play nothing. An outrage,' snapped Burbage. 'Dishonour through the passing of honour – a fine thing.' Shakespeare nodded slowly. I said nothing, disliking speaking in front of playwrights. One never knew if your words would be stolen straight from your lips and put in the mouth of some fool.

Just as I was thinking it, the players looked up as one, over my shoulder. I turned to see another of their company, the ugly little fool Robert Armin, bouncing across the tavern. He threw himself down on a stool beside me and made to deliver a slobbery kiss on my cheek. I threw myself sideways as the whole group laughed. As it subsided, the little man said, 'none to be had nowhere, lads. Barely enough to light a torch. Booze and salt it'll be.'

'What's this?' I asked.

Armin ignored me. 'Nor swevels nor firecrackers. We were too late.'

I repeated my question.

'Mr Armin,' croaked Philips, 'has been hunting for powder.'

'Boom!' announced the fool, rocking back on his stool and throwing his arms wide. The table shook and everyone began tutting.

'If we cannot play,' said Burbage, 'we hoped to delight the king with fireworks. Great dancing flames.' I considered this. I had seen their antics in the Globe – rigs called swevels: wires fixed from floor to ceiling along which firecrackers shot, counterfeiting lightning; powder thrown into candle flames to create flashes; flames produced from strange salts and alcohol. It was impressive stuff, seen from the pit.

'No luck,' said Armin, putting his head in his hands. 'We are undone. London has been sucked dry of powder. All bought up, from every grocer and ironworker in town.' Groans rose, and Armin's head shot up. 'Not counting this!' He opened his palm to reveal a little brown pouch. 'Enough for a bang and a flash and a merry show for the king! Ha!'

As the surprise and the mutters rippled, the company cheering its little imp for his success and cursing his attempts to deceive them, my eyes remained fixed on the pouch of powder which lay, like a dead rat, on the table.

I jumped up from my stool and began stumbling down from the raised gallery, barrelling through the other tables. Behind me, Armin cried, 'did we light it under you, Mr Savage?'

I ignored him.

In my mind, I was seeing a pouch very much like Armin's sailing into the crowd at the Royal Exchange.

25

He is in the evil place now. In a cell and spoken to like a child by men with faces far younger than his. Life it seems is a succession of dark and light places, forever competing with one another. Just as it is a constant battle between the dark and light spirits – the former telling him to do wicked things, to kill himself and others. the latter promising his salvation, that he will be freed from this place, that he will find people who will listen and understand.

In the cell, his hands are sometimes manacled. Often, he is strapped to the bed like an animal – and is it any wonder he cries and raves to the spirits to come upon him? They never touch the stuff of this world, but they are there watching and speaking endlessly and on.

It is an earthlier angel who frees him.

The great Earl of Oxford's note comes just as he is told he can leave the evil place. With it is promise of his reward for service – a pinnace to be sold at his pleasure and its worth in coin to see him into his old age. It is no coincidence that this gift comes just as he is freed. There are no coincidences. Everything in life has a pattern to it – there is always a design. Nothing simply happens.

And so, freed, the summer sun a stranger, he goes to see his gift and knows that he cannot sell it. He does not yet know the great design, but it is clear that the Crown Elizabeth *is part of it, even though the news abroad is that the queen is dead and her successor, a Scot, travelling through England. The son, in fact, of that queen that Hope watched lose her head at Fotheringhay. It is said also, by those few who are about, that the plague has returned in fire and death and horror.*

That same plague that had taken everything from him now rages again on his release.

It is a sign.

He knows nothing of ships, but there is promise and beauty in the pinnace. He decides that it will become his home, and the home of those he knows he must find. And it is on that same day, as he wanders the half-empty city, intending to begin begging or preaching or both, that he sees a vision of loveliness, marred only by the fact that she is crying as she wanders aimlessly through Blackfriars.

He stops her and she looks at him, her face wet.

'I love you,' he says. It has occurred to him that one of the world's

great ills is how few people ever know that they are loved. She does not run but looks at him curiously. 'You have suffered,' he says. 'But it will end soon. All suffering. What is your name?'

'Mary.'

'A lovely name. But I shall call you Angela. You will see, like the Italian Angela, beyond this sad world. And then you will cry no more.'

They walk together, he talking and she listening, and then the other way about. When he discovers that, like him, she has survived the great plague, though she lost a child, he understands the reason behind their salvation. And the Enlightened are born out of the misery of a dead queen and a dying city.

***

Despair forced Hope's head into his hands. 'But the procession must cross it. London Bridge is part of the royal entry. I have read of the old queen – Queen Mary Tudor – she passed over London Bridge in her triumph, her entry.'

It had all been so clear in his mind. The hideous thread of houses and shops that was London Bridge, erupting in flame as a beacon to the end of days. The *Crown Elizabeth* the taper that lit it. And the cleansing fire racing to the City on one side and the sinful Southwark on the other. The new king would be crowned with fire, as the angels had said, as he rode across it.

Only … he wouldn't ride across it.

'You are deceived. Angela is lying to you. She's a gutter whore you raised from the streets. What kind of whore goes off with a stranger, abandoning her husband?'

'Shut up!' shouted Hope.

'What?'

He looked up. Angela was staring at him, innocence shining in her eyes. She was no liar, whatever the devil-voice who roared in his head said. He took her face in his hands, and she winced a little, as though worried he might mistakenly choke her again. The little shiver reverberated through his hands, up his arms, hurting. In the dim confines of his cabin, so much like the cell in the evil place, her hair provided his light.

'How do you know this? How do you know the Scot will not be on the bridge?'

'It's said in the town.'

'Spies. Liars. Deceivers. They mean to stop us.'

'I have seen the arches, Nathaniel, monstrous things. Built across the street. They show his route. He will come from the Tower and go through the City. Towards Fleet Street, the last of them, and to Whitehall. He won't cross the river. He'll follow those arches and they say he'll stop at each and listen to interludes.'

'How many are these arches?'

'Seven.'

The word was left to hang in the air between them.

Seven.

Hope's eyes rose to the shadowy ceiling, sloping and warped as it was. And then he jumped to his feet, making Angela jump too. 'Come!' He took her hand. They left his cabin and moved through the ship, his feet feeling as though they were skipping through clouds rather than over grubby, scuffed deck.

At the stern's cargo hold, he unlocked the door and went in to Dr Gurney and the liar, David, who no longer deserved an Enlightened name. The pair were speaking in low tones, plotting, no doubt, in the darkness of the evening. Without preamble, he said, 'Doctor, what is the importance of the number seven?'

Gurney, looking exhausted, said, 'the number of days of the week. The number of completion and perfection. The number of deadly sins and goodly virtues. The number of years it took Solomon to build his temple. And Revelations speaks of seven churches, seven angels, seven seals, seven trumpets and seven stars.'

'Trumpets!' said Hope. The word seemed to blast a note in his soul. 'Where is your bible, doctor?'

Sighing, moving too slowly, as though the excitement and wonder did not touch him, the physician turned, bent, and retrieved the book, which had been lying forgotten on the deck. 'Mr Hope,' he said, 'Mistress Angela there troubled me with queries about these verses in the past. When you sought to speak with the dead. I tell you, they mean nothing to me.'

Hope snatched the bible from him – it was unthinkable a man of learning should be so blind – and passed it to Angela. 'You remember the passage, my love?'

Smiling, she took it and turned the pages, many of which seemed stuck together with dampness. 'Here,' she said. 'Foretold in the book of Corinthians. In a moment, in the twinkling of an eye, at the last trumpet: for the trumpet shall blow, and the dead shall be raised up incorruptible, and we shall be changed.'

'Yes,' shouted Hope, triumphant joy thundering in his chest. 'And in Revelations we hear of the trumpets. At the end. You see?' he looked again at the doctor, challenging him. 'You have missed this, learned man. At the end of times the dead shall rise. At the seventh.'

Gurney said nothing.

'The seventh arch?' asked Angela, putting a hand on Hope's sleeve.

'Yes. Oh, my love.' He hugged her to him. 'This is my great task. I shall be there at the seventh and shall see the king crowned there with fire. I will spend my blood and my life in it and be raised up, incorruptible. And you, you shall be with me.' He kissed her forehead. 'So you were with me at the first, you will be with me at the last. And you,' he said, turning to the doctor, 'you shall prepare us our physick one last time. And then you will remain on the ship when it heralds the end. You and the deceiver will sail into the flames with the others, but you will not be raised up as they shall be.'

'But …'

'Peace, my love,' he said, taking Angela's face again. The decision had been irrevocable. Both bridges and boats must be burnt behind the Enlightened. 'Our design will go ahead as planned, though only we two will visit it upon the false king. The *Crown Elizabeth* will be reborn in the flames and take the others into the resurrection with her. And she shall still see London burn and light the path to the end. And the temple of God will be opened in heaven, and there will follow lightnings and voices and thundering and earthquakes. All will fear our divine flame and we will be born again under Pisces and the feet will kick at the head.'

He took Angela by the arm and together they turned to leave.

'Wait!' snapped Gurney.

'What?'

'I need some stuff. For the final preparation of your physick.'

'You have all. There is no time to visit an apothecary before tomorrow.'

'Not the herbs – I have those. Something to make a fire. A tinderbox, perhaps. And a brazier. And some fresh water.'

'Braziers?' You needed no fire before. Suspicion bobbed like a cork.

'It's for me,' said the little spy, David. He stepped around the doctor, who put out a hand, which he brushed away. 'I'm feeling a fever. If it please you, Mr Hope, a little heat would help me. Dr Gurney says he can't work right if he's worried about me and needs to tend me.'

You'll have heat enough on the morrow, spy, thought Hope. But he smiled. 'You shall have it, then, in the morning. If the doctor is an honest man and provides us what we will have. My people would go to their reward with the visions singing to them.'

He turned on his heel and left, Angela following, pausing only to close the door on the blank, stupid faces of Gurney and David.

***

Left alone, Gurney began kicking at the door. 'Do they mean to blow up London. To kill the king? Or is this more raving fantasy?' Another kick and pain raced up to his knee. 'You did well, lad – a fine player.'

David smiled and stepped over the deck to him, a brown pouch in his hand. The boy had stolen it from Amos's belt when the man had been on the verge of killing him – it had been one of many, and Gurney could guess what the rest were intended for.

The king crowned with fire.

London burning.

He kicked again.

But they would get nowhere.

'Will they bring it? Brazier – fire?'

'I hope so, son. If I make them this physick – enough to scatter their wits. Perhaps … perhaps the drugs will dull them. And when that man and his wench are off to attempt something on the king … then, if we have a flame, we will have this door off its hinges.'

'Then what?'

Gurney sighed, turning away from the door and moving towards the coffer in which he'd stored the smelly henbane, deadly nightshade, and thorn apple. 'Then we have only the rest of these madmen standing between us and the streets. And perhaps between us and the saving of this city.'

26

'And the last of the interludes will be at Fleet Street, making seven in total,' said Cecil.

I had never seen my master looking so harried. Nor had I seen him in a state of undress. He was wearing a long nightshirt, around which he had fastened a thick, black fur cloak. He paced the room as he finished his description of the procession route.

We were in a study in his house in the Strand, which I had come to despite the late hour after having realised the gunpowder might – must – play a role in something the Enlightened were planning.

'What can we do?'

Cecil gave a wintry smile. 'I am pleased there is again a "we", Ned.' The smile faded. 'There are to be fireworks on the water. Yet the king will not be near those, save if he wishes to view them from the gallery at Whitehall. If it is these creatures who have been buying up gunpowder … so much is for no mere pistol.' He paused, looked at his nails, and then resumed his pacing. The study was small and bore none of the affectations of his grand chamber at Whitehall, though it shared the sharp hazy perfume of vinegary ink. Here were no portraits of the king or of his father, no tapestries, even – instead, every wall was lined floor-to-ceiling with dockets for papers, scrolls, and books. There was no imposing desk, either, but simply a small, portable thing, such as one might find in a schoolroom – perfect, I supposed, for the diminutive secretary to work at ease at home.

'We might alter the place of entry, lest some evil deed is planned there. The king is due to enter the City at Bishopsgate and there hear Mr Dekker's pageant. I suppose his Majesty might instead be persuaded to come up Mark Lane and enter at Fenchurch Street.' He began nodding slowly to himself. 'Yes, and there he might be welcomed by that loose-tongue Jonson's pageant instead, meeting the Genius of the City, as the interlude runs.'

I pursed my lips, looking towards the corner of a bookcase. Jonson would be happy – and trust him to write an interlude featuring a welcome by the mythical Genius of London.

'And then along Gracechurch and through the City to Fleet Street. Yes. That might upset any plans they have for the king.' Cecil stopped walking and sat down at his desk, leaving me standing on the carpet.

'But tonight…'

'It is late, Ned. And I have yet much to occupy me before tomorrow.'

'Will you be there, my lord?'

'No.' He stifled a yawn with his hand. 'I will be at Whitehall, waiting to welcome the king there. Yet ... powder ...'

'Could it have been placed in the arches? Around them? At lodgings nearby? They must be planning something for tomorrow or else why buy powder?'

'I will call up the city watch and what men I have left. There are some, I know, who will work through the night for a little money.' I nodded, picturing the type of enforcers Cecil employed – hard-faced men who seemed to operate beyond the law. 'The arches will be searched before the morning.'

'And I, my lord?'

'You can go home. Sleep. I would have you continue to search for whoever bought this ship given away by that fat fool Oxford tomorrow. Matters of security are ... I shall deal with those. Your task remains to find the doctor and this Hope who has taken him.'

'And my boy.'

'Yes. Go home and sleep. I trust all will go well tomorrow. If this Hope shows his face, we shall have him. If not, then you must keep hunting.' He waved me away again, his own face contorting with another abortive yawn.

***

Unsurprisingly, when I was locked securely in my house, I could not sleep. As I had walked through the dark, silent town, I was not surprised to see several fellows overtake me. Dressed in black, I had no doubt that they were Cecil's men, and by the time I reached Fleet Street, they were already at work opening flaps in the great triumphal arch there, presumably to climb about, monkey-like, through its skeleton, feeling for concealed stores of powder.

For lack of anything else to do, I decided to read. I could not bring myself to touch King James's *Daemonologie*, so instead turned to Dr Gurney's useless commonplace book. Idly, I turned the pages, squinting in the half-light afforded by my stinking tallow candle.

When I reached a passage I had read before, Cecil's voice rang through my head.

And the last of the interludes will be at Fleet Street, making seven in total.

I stared down at the page, and the words:

And the seuen angels whiche had the seuen trumpettes, prepared them selues to blowe.

The first angell blewe, & there was made hayle & fire, mingled with blood, and they were cast into the earth, and the thirde part of trees was burnt, and all greene grasse was burnt.

Flicking back, I saw again:

In a moment, in the twynklyng of an eye, at the last trumpe. For the trumpe shall blowe, and the dead shall ryse incorruptible, and we shalbe chaunged.

I blinked. Coincidence? It was not Cecil's voice which answered me, but John Dee's.

And the key lies in our understanding of the study of numbers and how they hold together everything.

Dee was an old fraud, but Dr Gurney had trusted him, and these men had taken Dr Gurney. I rolled onto my side on my coffer, gnawing on my lips. If there were any plan to blow up the seventh arch, then Cecil's men would find it.

But what if this Nathaniel Hope – this lunatic necromancer – intended to appear personally to blow his trumpet and thereby make the dead rise?

27

I rose early on what promised to be a cool, dry, sometimes sunny spring day, and dug into my remaining stock of clothes for something black. It was my intent to counterfeit the clothing I had seen often enough on Cecil's band of hard-men, and ultimately I found a faded black doublet with grey threading and wooden buttons, grey breeches, and a blue coat so dark it was almost black. I complete the look with a black cap and set out.

Shoe Lane was deserted, but as I stepped into Fleet Street, I met the beginnings of a crowd, the people pressing against the wooden railings which had been set up. On the street itself, lengths of red cloth had been laid, making a carpet for the king to ride along. Every fifty feet or so, soldiers in their morions were posted, their faces to the crowd. I watched as a young man in a carnival mask turned sideways and put a leg over the railing. As he prepared to bring its fellow over and onto the carpet, one of the soldiers broke free from his position and clattered over, slapping the man back onto the public's walkway.

It had occurred to me in the night that I should go to Cecil at Whitehall and tell him of my suspicions about the seventh arch, but I knew he would have had it searched fully during the night. I began moving through the crowd – still thin, as I supposed most people would have gone eastwards to the see the beginning of the parade and its great shows, or to drink the rotten free wine – towards the archway. As I had thought, men dressed not unlike me were lounging in the shadows underneath either side of the behemoth's canvas-draped feet. There was no need to repeat to the secretary to do what his men were already doing.

You should go to him, though.

No, there is no point.

Still the battle raged.

To drown out the agony of indecision, I began walking, clinging to the sides of buildings as I went. Rag ends of conversation reached me.

'The queen coming, is she?.'

'Ay, and Prince 'enry.'

''eard the prince ain't nothing like the father.'

'What's 'e look like? You seen 'im?'

'Christ, this wines a fine thing. Ain't never 'ad wine before in me life!'

As the morning passed into day, I purchased a pie from a vendor and, as I ate, I watched the crowd thicken. I felt like a city watchman myself, albeit, I hoped, a less useless one. It was obvious when the royal entry had started, for music began playing, seemingly from everywhere, and from where I had come to, near Fenchurch Street, I could see the crowd clotted. Cheers rose, and I assumed the king had arrived, though I could see nothing over the sea of heads in front of me, some of them again bearing children, who were themselves waving lit torches that smoked and dropped curls of ash. I pushed my way through, towards the railings, and had an impression of three men in armour practising thrusts on the carpet, whilst someone disguised as an old man – complete with trailing white beard and wig held in place with a wreath – was waving a goblet and a bundle of twigs. Cecil had told me about this one – St Andrew and St George would have a very careful and much-practised swordfight, only for the old, peaceful hermit to subdue and unite them. It was not hard to suppose what that was meant to represent. At present, however, they were warming up, and entertaining the drunken crowd with their thrusts and parries.

I moved back through the knot of people, someone immediately taking my place, just the early part of the procession – the judges and state officials – arrived on the carpet to muted cheers and flat trumpet blasts.

Stopping in at a tavern, I treated myself to a few drinks, enjoying the chance of being able to do so without being bothered by anyone. For once, the air inside was less smoky than that outside, free as it was of the drift from torches and bonfires. The tapster seemed grateful for the custom, presumably not expecting to sell anything until the fountains outside ran dry.

Cecil, of course, had said that I should continue my search for David and Gurney, but there was no hope of finding people to question on such a day. The evening, perhaps, when tongues were loosened – then I might find threads to pick at. As I slurped, sitting at a battered table in the empty room, tracing the scars on it with my finger, I heard the rise of cheers and cries outside and knew that the king had come. I had no interest in seeing him. Instead, I finished my drink and, when I left, he had apparently ridden on to the next pageant. The street before the tavern was now empty, the railings toppled as men, women, and children poured over it in a great tide to tear apart the carpet for souvenirs.

I began making my way back the way I had come, sticking to my side of the street. It was slow going, but every time I met a crowd too

223

thick to pass, it seemed I had just missed the king, who must have been rattling his way through the interludes. I wondered if such things would bore a man who thought himself of a scholarly and serious disposition. Thus it was that I could move with ease – especially since I took the empty and uncarpeted Lombard Street whilst the procession, I knew, had gone north up Gracechurch.

I found myself, then, ahead of the king, as I'd hoped, and on the southern side of Cheapside, where the railing still stood. I went purposefully, stepping around people, smiling one of the same vacant smiles they wore.

And then I paused.

For a moment, I thought I had seen something familiar on the other side of the street, behind the northerly railing.

Blonde hair over a familiar face.

Nothing. There are blonde-haired women aplenty in the City.

I forced my way to the front of the crowd, pushing this time and jabbing with my elbow, ignoring the angry punches and slaps that came my way. When I reached it, I saw her, across the red carpet, her face appearing and disappearing as state officials and knights passed by in procession.

Angela.

She was standing beside a spare, attractive older man with sandy brown hair and the saddest eyes I had ever seen. His clothes were old and worn, the sleeves and breeches flaccid. Both were hanging over the front, looking to my right – in the direction from which the king would be coming. She looked up and our eyes locked. Confusion wrinkled her brow. And then, I thought, recognition. Anger wiped it away and she put a hand on the man's arm, tugging at it. He looked at me too and then whispered something to her. And then his hand went to his belt and he produced something.

'Look out!' I screamed. 'Get down, everyone – treason!'

My shouts were lost but still I hunched over the barrier, throwing my hands behind my head. When I looked up, I saw that they had produced no powder. Instead, they appeared to be sharing something from a little bottle.

Is it really her? You're mistaken. Husband and wife drinking, only.

Their next move gave that the lie. They turned their backs on me and were swallowed up by the crowd, new faces replacing theirs. I shouted over the carpet again, 'Hope! Angela!' And then, stupidly, I began to climb over the railing. A guard appeared, of course, and swiped me across the side of the head with his steel-sheathed forearm.

'Back, you dog!'

'I'm with the secretary!' I shouted. 'Robert Cecil, lord of Essenden! Let me pass!'

'Aye, and I'm Queen Anne. Fuck off.'

I shook my head, my cheeks taut,and again tried to find Angela and the man I assumed was Hope. It was useless. And then, to confuse me further, deafening cheers stabbed at my ears as the king began his ride through Cheapside to a chorus of trumpets.

The seventh arch.

It was the only idea I had, and the only thing I could do. I jerked my way back through the press until I was under the wooden awnings of the shop fronts and began creeping my way along the procession route, at the back of the crowd, all the way along Paternoster Row, falling behind the spire-less, squat St Paul's on the opposite side of the Stationer's Hall, and so up Ludgate Hill and over the bridge towards Fleet Street. Every time I felt I was making progress, the frenzied screams of the crowd mocked me, as the king seemed to be keeping pace, preceded by the bevy of his court.

I was trapped, trapped on the other side of the procession route from that which Angela and Hope were on. But when they had fled, had they been planning to move in my direction, towards the seventh and final arch on the other side of the red carpet?

Yes, because that must be their design.

No, because they have already laid their trap and that wasn't even them anyway and you are an idiot.

I reached Fleet Street panting, war raging within me, and bent double, sucking at the air. When I rose, I could see the great arch soaring ahead, and I limped towards it, my calves and thighs aflame. As I staggered onwards, the ever-present cheering rose in pitch yet again, and, with a grunt, I pushed a child off of an upturned crate and stood, looking out over the rows of people before me, to see the king.

James was dressed, I had to admit as I sucked at the air, very finely. His suit was cloth of gold and silver, his ruff yellowish gold, and there was an array of rings on his fingers. Each one glinted in the sunlight, his hands held aloft around the reins of an enormous white horse. More gold shone around the jewels which girded the band of his tall black hat, and an ermine trimmed cloak even managed to add an air of true majesty.

His face belied it. Rather than smiling graciously and waving at his people, the king – the emperor, as he called himself – kept his gaze fixed ahead. His unsmiling face spoke of boredom and, as he rode slowly past where I stood, it seemed that the heavy lids over his eyes were weighted with it. He drew the horse to a halt near where I stood, which was about thirty feet away from the Fleet Street arch. Ahead of him the boy prince had already disappeared under the archway with a number of great lords, and behind him glittered a mule-drawn carriage presumably containing the queen and her ladies. For a moment James was alone and exposed, the attendants, on smaller mounts on either side of him, busy holding up the poles which supported the canopy over his head.

Some men in city livery stepped out from under the arch, accompanied by a child dressed as an angel. Before they could begin to make their oration, however, the king half-turned his horse, putting a hand over his breast in a seeming gesture of offence or surprise.

Or fear.

The railing on the other side had been breached.

The man, Nathaniel Hope, fell over it and stood between the king and the pageant folk. Murmurs and shouts rose. Even the guards seemed momentarily paralysed, unsure of themselves. Nervous in the direct sight of the king, they must have thought the sudden irruption meant his Majesty was just about to receive a spontaneous and unplanned protestation of love and loyalty from a loving subject, as the old queen had frequently arranged. The canopy above the king wobbled.

A pistol is the thing.
He's had it.

28

Hope stood before the false king, amidst the cries of the demonic. Devils stood everywhere around him now, cheering and murmuring and cursing and laughing. And yet there was the king, astride a pale horse, and his name that sat on him was Death, and Hell followed with him, and power was given unto them over the fourth part of the earth, to kill with sword, and with hunger, and with death, and with beasts of the earth.

He could feel his lips moving and he could hear the words of revelation, but they did not seem to be coming from him. The king, his face a mask of fear and anger, melted like a tallow candle and then reformed. He shone with gold. Was he on fire already?

Hope's head dipped and swam. The scene sank deeper into the swirling seas of his mind.

But I have a mission, he thought.

He raised his torch to the bag of powder fastened around his neck but there was no flame. There was no torch. It was as though he had imagined it.

Sharp pain caught him in the lower back, and he fell to his knees. He looked up and there was the king again, this time smiling, turning his head from side to side, and waving a hand. At me? wondered Hope.

No. At the demons and devils who were wrestling him to the ground. Lifting him off his feet. Making him fly.

He looked at them, felt their knuckles press into his armpit. 'Angela!' he screamed. 'Go home! Run!'

And then the devils laughed again. He turned sly eyes to them and yelped as he saw their faces. One of the creatures was the old queen, Elizabeth, who had visited him outside St Paul's. She was speaking to the other queen, Mary of Scotland, who had him under the other arm. 'To the Bedlam,' hissed the English queen to her Scottish cousin. 'Get him away from the king or we're all for it.'

The evil place.

'What's this round his neck? This, on the string?'

'Money?'

'Jesus – it's – I think it's gunpowder.'

'Christ. Here, throw it away. I'm not catching holy hell for letting that near the king.'

Hope swung his arms and legs wildly, earning a few more hard knuckle jabs. The physician's potion, he thought weakly. It had not brought him visions – he had always had visions – it made them real, gave them the weight of hard bone and flesh. And now they had him in their grasp.

'I'd like to go home,' he said, his vision fading as he flew. 'I'd like to see my wife and sons.'

29

I stood, transfixed, at the sight. Hope had launched himself over the railing directly before the king's horse, but he had commenced only to begin raving, waving his arms about his chest, shouting at people.

Two guards, finally awoken from their surprise, had realised, apparently, that this was no part of the pageant, nor even a subject desperate to speak to the king, but a common madcap. And they had forced him to the ground, before carting him off into the shadow of the great arch.

Where Cecil's men waited, I thought.

The king, I had to admit, had handled the brief affray remarkably well, affecting laughter at the unexpected fool and waving to the crowd to show that there was no problem. He had, however, spurred his horse on past the disappointed city men and their child actor, leaving them in his wake as he, his attendants, and the party of ladies which followed him passed through Fleet Street and continued on their way to Whitehall in a clatter of hooves and rising burst of music.

Where's Angela?

She was my best chance of finding David – for where else would she have to run to but their lodging house?

I nearly tumbled from my crate as the railings were forced down, the people again flooding the carpet to rip it apart. Regaining my footing, I looked out over them but could see no tumble of maidenly blonde hair. I cursed, clawing at my neck where the light ruffled collar of my shirt had gathered sweat. I began stumbling through the crowd, shouting her name, demanding if people had seen a blonde woman. Few paid heed – all were intent on discussing the king or retrieving their bloody gobbets of carpet.

As I wandered, a low rumble of laughter caught me. I moved towards it and found a crowd of prentice lads.

'Mad bitch is raving – hahaha! Ay, I'd tumble her.'

'I'm spoken for,' sniffed another.

'Oh, your little red-headed whore.'

A fist flew, and I stepped into the melee, breathing hard. The puncher was Nicholas Hopgood. 'Good job,' I said, patting him on the back. I would thank him later, I decided, and maybe learn to dislike him a little less. 'Have you seen a blonde woman?'

The boy who had been punched, and apparently bore no ill will for it, smirked, kneading his cheek. 'You mean the mad bitch?'

'What? Nicholas, what's he talking about?'

'I don't know, sir. Just got here.'

No – he is *useless.*

'Some bird drank herself daft. She's gone 'orf raving down Ludgate just now, screaming about angels and fire. Laughing like anything. Mad bitch.'

Pivoting, I took off for Ludgate Hill at a gallop, leaping over bending people, spent torches, small bonfires, and the assorted waste of hundreds of drunken Londoners. As I crossed over the Fleet Bridge, my heart hammering, I had a good view ahead of me and finally I could see a dot of yellow, bouncing in the distance, veering wildly.

Downhill. Towards the Thames.

I ran again, leaping in the air like a dancer occasionally, fearful of losing sight of her. My doublet came loose, buttons popping, until I must have looked as much a zany as the woman I was chasing.

Pausing again at the top of the hill, the hulk of St Paul's ahead of me, I thought I'd lost her. But no, she was still moving, still zigzagging, and I went on. She veered onto Thames Street, appearing to pick up her pace.

Does she know I'm after her?

Along the great thoroughfare I went, losing sight of her for certain this time, but continuing anyway. She was the only chance I had of finding David – that day at least. Baynard's Castle loomed up on my right, and I fell under the jagged shadow of its many triangular roofs. There were fewer people about here – just some carters and some city folk lighting celebratory bonfires with torches – and I asked a man who was filling a cart with old cloth about the woman who must have recently passed by.

He gave me a long look, smirked, and said, 'you should go up Bishopsgate Street, mate, and–'

'Not the fucking Bedlam – where did she go?'

His smile faded. 'No fear, no fear. She went down that way.' He gestured behind him. 'Drunk as a lord. Arms up as if she were bloody flying. What've they put in that wine over on Cheapside, eh?'

I didn't smile but kept moving, fresh waves of pain coursing up my legs. Ahead and on my right was the entrance to Queenhithe, the old dockyard. I knew where she was flying to. Back when I'd had a father who loved me – when I was a small child, before he had begun to despise me as a twisted creature of rotten lusts – he had enthralled me and Thomas with stories of the '88. Of the fireships the great Drake had set amongst the Spanish.

Interested in the battles of '88, for a spell, only. As he loved to know of all forms of death and dying.

I ran.

30

The flash was blinding, but mercifully it was not long lived. Gurney and David shielded their eyes from it. When it had faded, the door to the hold did not hang on its hinges, but had been taken off them, along with a fair chunk of the bulkhead.

'God be praised, we are free!' said the doctor, hope and fear mingling in his voice.

They had been brought the means to light the boy's gunpowder in the morning, as Hope had promised, and in return the leader of the Enlightened had been given his pouch of physick – enough henbane and its fellows to hopefully stop them doing whatever they were planning.

But not enough to kill, of course. The solemn oath taken by all physicians was unbreakable. It would be the hangman's job to deal with the creatures.

When we are off this ship, thought Gurney. He took David's hand. They had waited the best part of the day, until they could be sure Hope and Angela would be off in the City.

If the damned lunatic had done as he said he would and not concocted some other daft plan.

'We'll have to be quiet,' said David. 'They sleep just down there.'

Gurney laughed. 'A little late for that, my boy. That bang would have woken the dead far more than anything these fools have planned. How do we get topside?'

'To the light? Outside?'

'Yes.'

'Come on, before they come and get us.'

David began dragging him along the passageway. He hesitated a little as they drew near the door to the main deck – the room in which the sect apparently lived together, chanting, and feeding one another's frenzies. But there was no sound from inside it.

Suddenly, the old ship shuddered. And then it lurched to one side. Gurney collapsed into the bulkhead, David following and landing against him. The boy yelped like a whipped puppy.

'My God,' cried Gurney, 'we've sunk her. That powder!'

'Are we sinking?' The boy's question came calmly, and it steadied the doctor even as the deck drew level again.

'I don't think … No, I … By God, we're moving. They're sailing her.' Again, the *Crown Elizabeth* jolted, this time to port, and it took longer to steady her. 'Or trying to.'

'Where are we going?'

'We are going nowhere but home.' Horror coursed through him. 'Their powder! This ship must be laden with guns.'

'No. No, I heard them say the guns were in there. And all gone.'

Together, they opened the door to the deck and stepped into the reek of weeks, months, of waste and lunacy. Is this, thought Gurney, how they've been living? Buckets of God-knew-what lay tumbled, spilling their ordure to where it pooled and ran beneath the joins of the decking. Their old cooking pot was on its side. Dirty clothing – doublets, skirts, all the stuff of their former lives – lay in piles, flies buzzing around them.

The ship moved again.

'There,' said David, pulling the doctor along, kicking rubbish out of the way. He led them, both on unsteady legs, towards a pool of light which spilled in from above. Gurney blinked as he stepped into it, and then took David under the arms, lifting him past the ladder. The boy's legs dangled for a second as he gripped the edge of the upper deck. They kicked in the air and then were gone, his freckled face and mop of red hair replacing them. He reached down and helped Gurney up the rungs of the ladder.

Blinking in the sunlight, Gurney let his eyes adjust. To his left, he could see the expanse of the Thames, the other boats that had been the *Crown Elizabeth*'s fellow derelicts presumably gone off to the scrapyard already. To his right, the irregular skyline of London stood, smokier than he had ever seen it. Amidships, the sails were rigged and furled, holes and patches evident in the old cloth. He was still staring, wondering how to get them both off the ship, when singing caught his ear. He turned, and saw Angela dancing up the deck towards them, twirling with her arms outstretched. Her cap was gone, and her blonde hair flew in all directions.

Gurney moved to stand before David, but the boy stepped around him. 'We're going home,' he said.

She looked towards them, not seeing them. She must, Gurney realised, have taken the henbane – and probably more than she had been advised. 'Me too,' she said. 'Home to see my baby.'

'Where is Hope?'

'Gone to see the king.' She began humming. The ship moved again, and Gurney stepped to the side of the deck and looked over. Sweeps were sticking out of the oarlocks and they moved haphazardly, some digging into the water, other skating over it.

'Come, David,' said Gurney primly, taking the boy's hand again. They were edging around the woman when David shook his arm.

The doctor sighed. 'Please, Mary Glover. End this madness. Come with us.'

Fear crossed her face. 'What? Why? We must go. Nathaniel, we're moving. We'll kill them all and live.'

'Ay,' said a new voice. Gurney turned to see Amos's bald head emerge from the hatch, a tinderbox in one hand and a torch in the other. 'If Hope has failed it is for us to see the great city of sin burn. I will lead us to victory. Angela, come here.' She stepped over to him, smiling. 'Have you your pouch?'

'Hm? I hear angels singing. I hear Nathaniel.'

As Amos stepped across the open deck towards her, Gurney cast a look down towards David, who looked back. As one, they began shuffling away, their boots a bare whisper. And then Gurney halted, his eyes widening. 'No, Harry! Stop! David, don't look!' He grabbed the boy's head and forced it into his side.

Just as he did so, Amos touched the flame of his torch to the pouch around Angela's neck and then leapt backwards. It caught, fizzed, and then there was another flash, Gurney hugging David closer and both pushed back by the wave of heat. When it faded, her lovely face was gone, replaced with red and blackened meat. The smell hit a moment later – acrid and chemical, with the foulness of burnt pork at its base. She had given no cry, but the soft thud of her body hitting the deck announced her end.

Gurney stood for a moment, staring in horror, tears already beginning at the corners of his eyes.

'Sister Angela went first,' shouted Amos. 'She dwells now in the dust. She will awake and sing for joy. We will all follow.'

Amos threw the torch overboard and Gurney heard the brief splash and fizzle. And then the man was gone, back down the hatch, and the ship began moving again, lurching forward. There was another splash, louder, but the doctor remained standing, staring down at the corpse of one former patient murdered in his sight by another.

'Look! There's no way off.'

David's cry coincided with another crazy dip of the boat, this one nearly knocking Gurney off his feet. He turned, joining the boy at the ship's port side. Below them, the little bridge of rope and wood that formed the gangway to the jetty had broken off and fallen into the water as the ship began its passage out into the harbour. Amos, he supposed, must have been marshalling the drug-crazed Enlightened to a greater show of dexterity. 'We can't … perhaps we can hide on the ship and let them think us off it. And leave when they reach wherever they're sailing her. Without Hope they must mean to escape.'

'David!'

The voice rose from somewhere down on the docks. Gurney looked and saw a man he didn't know coming towards them, his arms pumping and his clothes falling apart. He, too, was carrying a torch.

Another one, thought Gurney – another madman with murder and destruction in his heart.

'Ned!' The boy turned, grinning. 'It's my brother! Ned Savage!'

'Throw him!' shouted the man from below. He looked at the torch he was carrying and then, standing back, launched it into the air and over their heads. It caught in the sails and its flame immediately began feeding. 'Quickly. There's powder enough on that ship to blow it to Scotland. Get off before they fire any guns.'

Gurney and David both moved, running along the edge of the deck as it began to creep away from the jetty below. They stopped when they were again level with Savage, and the doctor began to lower the boy amidships. Though it was only a small pinnace, she rode high in the water with most of her guts and organs stripped out; she was, thought Gurney, a corpse, post-mortem, being forced into animation. The drop was too great for a child. The man, Ned Savage, caught the boy and hugged him briefly, before setting him down. 'Dr Gurney?'

'I am.'

'Come, I'll catch you.'

Gurney did not jump, but sat on the edge of the deck, his legs hanging over the port side. 'I … I can't. I'll break my legs.'

'Good thing, then, that you're a physician.'

'I …' Gurney's words became a cry as the rocking ship jettisoned him, and he fell forward, landing on his rescuer. Behind him the screeching and splintering of wood pierced the air, followed by a rush of water, as the stern of the freewheeling *Crown Elizabeth* collided with one of the other jetties. Gurney rolled off of Savage, ignoring the grunts. 'You fool,' he hissed, 'you might have killed us. Throwing flames into a ship with powder in it.'

'It has to go down,' the man breathed. 'Now.'

'What? What are they planning? They rave madly.' But, as the words sank in, he thought he already knew. He scrambled to his feet, offering a hand to Savage.

'Fireship.'

'What?'

'Like in the '88. If they catch the high tide, and that thing so high in the water – it'll run right into London Bridge.'

'Look!' David's piping voice silenced them, and the trio turned to watch the Crown Elizabeth. The ship had escaped the square space of the dock and was making for the Thames proper. Its sails, though, were ablaze, and the mainmast collapsed, falling forward, catching the foremast. It, too, went up, tongues of red and orange foraging greedily. The ships wheeled in the water, almost managing a complete revolution, as the white caps of the navy waters resisted its crumbling hull. Sweeps spun wildly in every direction and the whole thing pitched and rolled to one side. It reached an angle of about 45 degrees to starboard and remained there for what seemed an eternity.

Bang.

The sound came from somewhere within the hull.

Bang-bang-bang.

Flames shot in a column upwards, some coming from portholes and others making new breaches. Water surged up and over the hull to meet them. More bangs followed, and suddenly the three watchers were joined by others come to see the show.

'What display is this?'

'Fireworks?'

'An old wreck lit up for to delight the king!'

They remained there for some time, watching the *Crown Elizabeth* torn apart between tide and flame. Eventually, only broken masts, water-animated sails, and a sliver of rotting hull remained. 'What a sight,' said Gurney, eventually, wiping sweat from his brow. 'There were people in there. Men and women, starved of their wits.'

Savage grunted. 'I think,' he said, 'the king will have need of you. He was frightened by a madman. Don't worry – the guards caught him. And the lord secretary Baron Essenden has been worried about you.'

Gurney gave him a long look but said nothing.

'Ned,' said David, shaking Savage's hand. 'I never had the plague. I had the gaol fever – the aryotitus. The doctor told me and he's a physician. So if you felt bad…' He looked at the wooden boards of the jetty, his face reddening. 'Just if. You don't got to.'

Savage grabbed the boy and swung him up onto his back. 'Jesus, that's a good thing to know. Would you tell your sister?'

David grasped thin white arms around his brother's neck. 'And – and I know what I wish to do when I'm a man.'

'Oh?' asked Savage. 'And what is that – and how much will this trade cost me?'

'A great deal,' said Gurney, exhaustion suddenly threatening to overcome him. He reached up and put a hand on the boy's back, patting it. 'He would be a physician, I think.'

'No,' said David, shaking his head. 'I wish to be an actor. Maybe in one of Mr Jonson's plays, like *Cynthia's Revels*.'

'Over my dead body,' said Savage.

Together, they began moving through the little crowd that had gathered on the dockside and left Queenhithe and the burning wreckage of the *Crown Elizabeth*.

Epilogue

We were sat in an upper gallery of the Curtain Theatre in Shoreditch, and quite a number we were too. Beside me were seated Faith and Nicholas Hopgood, the callow youth smiling far too much at her and she telling him to look down towards the stage, where the actors had finished their opening jig and already begun the performance. Their voices mingled with the crunch of nuts and occasional argument amongst those in the pit. The playhouses had been reawakened and they were crying out in their hunger for people and plays.

A disturbance behind us announced the arrival of our two late-coming friends.

'I apologise,' said Dr Gurney, easing his bulk along the bench, past tutting men and women who twisted their necks around him to continue watching the show. One of them hissed at him to be quiet, as Faith, Hopgood and I slid sideways to make room for him and his wife. Maud Gurney remained as painted as ever, her red lips defiant and her wide, lashless eyes rolling in wonder towards the stage.

'Mr Savage,' she said, ignoring the frowns and murmurs that rose behind her. 'We thank you for our new servants. The girl is such a sweet thing.' I inclined my head as she and her husband settled themselves in a ruffle of skirts and breeches. Gurney sat beside me, his wife on his other side.

'I have been,' he said, 'to the Bedlam.'

I said nothing. My eyes were on the stage, where a clown bounced about, drawing laughter. 'Oh lord,' he cried, 'the house is beset! Soldiers are as hot as fire, are ready to enter every hole about the house!' People laughed.

Dr Gurney, I knew, had been visiting Nathaniel Hope for months now, reporting to Cecil and King James on the man's ravings and necromantic powers, which he did not believe existed. It was, Gurney insisted, only some malady of the brain – a brain-sickness – that troubled him. And he knew of no way of remedying it. I did not give a damn. Frankly, I had said to the doctor that it was beyond me why he had not simply poisoned the whole pack of them – and properly too, to the death – the first night. That seemed only to horrify him.

'He will not live long,' said the doctor, his breath hot in my ear.

'Oh?'

'Yes. He thinks his friends, Mary, and that brute Harry Windham –

are with him in the cell. Speaking to him. I have given him something to stop their torments.'

'You said that there was no cure.'

'None other than by giving him into a gentle sleep.'

I turned to Gurney, but it was his turn to fix his gaze on the stage. *Good riddance.*

'Are we for supper together at a tavern after this?'

'No, doctor. Thank you but – some relations of mine from the north should arrive tonight. To be honoured by the king.' My brother Thomas, in fact, with Ann, were coming to lodge in the city. He would no doubt already be giving himself airs over the knighthood he hadn't earned and didn't deserve, but which Cecil had engineered as part of my payment for stopping Nathaniel Hope's band of lunatics from killing Gurney and crashing their powder-filled pinnace into London Bridge or wherever else they might have reached.

Sir Thomas Norton of Norfield, a £30 knight made by a greedy king.

'Please,' said Faith, leaning over Nicholas's lap towards me, 'be quiet, Ned. Or we might miss him.'

No chance of that. I had ensured David had been given a very good part.

'I should miss you,' simpered Hopgood, 'even unto sickness, if I didn't see you every day.'

Damn him.

Every time I began to think well of the lad, he would say some foolish thing that made me wish to puke. Still, he had encouraged Faith to live with me again, for several days of the week, so that she might be near her brother and I might not have to learn how to stuff eggs with herbs and butter myself. The rest she spent at his master's house, tending his wife. I did not like it much, but she was hardly a child.

'There he is!' she cried, rising.

Four players appeared below us, bearing a litter through the rear curtain. On it lounged David, his face painted so he could be seen in the pit and his red hair compounded with a similarly coloured hairpiece. A rich nightgown, with an imitation ermine cloak, was about his shoulders. I leapt up, grasping the railing before me, and cheered.

So too did the crowd, albeit for different reasons. Hurrahs flew like excited birds up to the open air, my own bouncing off the roof of our gallery.

'My God,' said Gurney. 'Here is resurrection for you. Queen

Elizabeth risen from the grave.'

'Don't tell the king,' I laughed, not taking my eyes from the stage.

'We are not pleased with your intrusion, lords. Is your haste such or your affairs so urgent, that suddenly, and at this time of night, you press on me, and will not stay till morn?' David's voice blended imperiousness with the high, clear song of youth and majesty, and pride slashed a grin across my face. Faith, too, was on her feet, waving a handkerchief in the air, and Hopgood was beating a tattoo on the railing. Gurney was clapping and his wife wiping the red paint from her mouth with a frown.

He's doing it.

At the counterfeit Queen Elizabeth's first words, in Thomas Heywood's play of her fight for the crown, the crowd roared its joy again and my own soared to meet it. There, in the theatre, was life after death indeed.

Author's Note

King James VI of Scotland was crowned James I of England, thereby uniting the crowns in a personal union, in Westminster Abbey alongside his wife, Anne (or Anna) of Denmark in July 1603. However, the ceremony was perforce a private one, which took place in pouring rain. The private nature of the ceremony was due not to adverse weather but to an intense outbreak of the plague which had followed hard on Elizabeth's death. It was during this outbreak that Bills of Mortality first began to appear nailed to church doors – although we can only guess at their accuracy. Further, James issues his 'Order for Plague' against the disease (also called 'the pestilence' or 'the pest'), including guidance on quarantine (six weeks) for infected households and the marks to be painted on the doors of sick houses. In researching the plague, I found Kira L. S. Newman's wonderfully titled article 'Shutt Up: Bubonic Plague and Quarantine in Early Modern England' (2009: *Journal of Social History*) useful. Critical also was the contemporary writer Thomas Dekker's *The Wonderfull Yeare*, 'wonderful' meaning shocking or full of surprises. From Dekker comes the great line regarding James's succession: 'Upon Thursday it was treason to cry God save king James of England, and upon Friday treason not to cry so'. Dekker also provided the lists of the herbs I described strewn about London's streets – although I find his claim that 'withered Hyacinthes, fatall Cipresse and Ewe' were 'thickly mingled with heapes of dead mens bones' to be a little dubious. Interestingly, the plague had and has a mortality rate of about 70-80% if untreated, and studies of the remains of those who contracted it in the period and survived indicate that they went on to have longer-than-average lifespans.

For the coronation itself, I used Sybil M. Jack's '"A Pattern for a King's Inauguration": The Coronation of James I in England' (2004: *Parergon*). Because of the plague outbreak, the theatres were shut for nearly a year and, more irritatingly for James, the public part of his coronation – the triumphal 'entry' into, or procession through, London had to be delayed until the following March, by which time the number of deaths had abated. For this procession, I found Caroline Bingham's biography, *James I of England* (1981: Weidenfeld & Nicolson) and the more recent 'Dekker's Accession Pageant for James I' (2009: *Early Theatre*) by Anne Lancashire great helps. From the latter I discovered that although James made his entry at Fenchurch Street, he had originally been expected to do so at Bishopsgate, and so he swapped hearing Dekker's pageant first for Ben Jonson's.

King James's appearances in the novel, I'm afraid, do not paint him in a particularly positive light. However, I find that much of his behaviour in real life doesn't do so either. He was, for example, a stout and vocal opponent of 'sodomy' – that ugly, catch-all term that embraced homosexual practices. This led many early biographers to conclude that his famous relationships with a succession of handsome men were chaste, perhaps even fatherly rather than sexual in nature. I find it more likely that he was simply a hypocrite. It was reported at the time, for example, that 'it is well known that the king of England fucks the duke of Buckingham' (a later favourite). Although that report can be questioned as biased, James's private letters to Buckingham refer to the duke as his 'wife'. Further, his kissing of Philip Herbert at his coronation in Westminster, as I've described it, is drawn from contemporary accounts and the king certainly fell slavishly in love with a number of prominent men. It is difficult to then believe that his warnings against sodomy were anything more than the monarch protesting too much. Rounding out James's pretty appalling real-life behaviour is the fact that, in his private letters, he referred to the wives of his boon companions, collectively, as 'the cunts'.

The king was, however, a published author, and his works include the famous *Daemonologie* (1599) which Savage reads (partly) in the novel. This is a marvellous read – though obviously not for the reasons the king intended. It is spooky, strange, and full of anecdotes, presented as absolutely real, that continue to enthral (my favourite being the supposed power of devils to reanimate corpses and have them creep through windows). James is also to be credited with drawing a clear line between the arts of astronomy and astrology, which did not yet exist for many of the period's scientists, who considered stargazing and study of the planets as inextricable from magic, conjuring, and fortune telling. The text is available freely online and in plenty of easy-to-read editions for purchase.

Amongst the other contemporary texts that I used are a couple of bibles – the *Bishops' Bible* and the *Geneva Bible*. Here, the *Textus Receptus Bible* website was invaluable, fully searchable, and with all original spellings intact. I retained these as I find that they give a nice flavour of the period.

Savage meets a number of real-life figures in the novel and reading up on them was one of the most interesting parts of the research for this book. Dr John Dee is best known as an Elizabethan magus, but he was still alive and kicking after the queen's death, although he had been rusticated to Manchester as warden of Christ's College. In including him, I leant heavily on Benjamin Woolley's fantastic *The Queen's Conjuror: The Science and Magic of Dr John Dee* (2001: Henry Holt & Co.). Dee trafficked throughout his life with those who claimed to be able to hear the voices of angels, and his overriding quest was to discover the 'celestial' language, or the language of the angels, that he thought was spoken in Paradise and by Adam and Eve before the fall. In doing so, he embarked on a number of dubious ventures, frequently involving crystal gazing, spiritualism, and, in the later stages of Elizabeth's reign, wife swapping. His interest in numerology (a term which did not exist in the period) is my own invention, but I've based it on his mathematical interests, studies, and early teaching practice. Mathematics, in the period, was another area of study which often crossed over into the realms of what we would now call magic (although in *Daemonologie* King James makes clear what he feels are the right and wrong types!). Dee returned from Manchester in around 1605 but would not find preferment under James. He died in the winter of 1608-9.

Simon Forman, another early modern physician of ill repute, I find to be an equally bizarre and intriguing figure. He is prized by scholars for the copious records he left recounting everyday life in Elizabethan and Jacobean London, including his frequent visits to the theatre (which helps date certain plays) and his insatiable sexual appetite. He appears in a number of novels, frequently as an antagonist, but his carefully-kept records of case files (something plenty of more legitimate and accomplished physicians didn't bother doing) has made him the protagonist of his own series of detective novels: *The Casebook of Dr Simon Forman* by Judith Cook. Cook has also written an excellent nonfiction biography, *Dr Simon Forman: A Most Notorious Physician* (2011: Vintage). There is no evidence that he visited the Holland's Leaguer brothel in Southwark, but the place was real enough and run by one Bess Holland, or Donna Britannica Hollandia, whom I came across in *Private Vices-Public Virtues: Bawdry in London from Elizabethan Times to the Regency* by E. J Burford and Joy Wotton (1995: Robert Hale Ltd.). From this book comes the wonderful description of the doctor as a 'an early Rasputin whose astral powers were as genuine as his medical degree'. Forman was indeed a plague survivor who treated himself, lancing the infamous buboes and taking, by his own claims, twenty-two weeks to fully recover. His diaries are worth reading if only for his bizarre cataloguing of his never-ending sexual exploits with his wife, his patients, married women, and maidservants. Dates and times of copulation are recorded in a manner business-like enough to make one of the 'whores' he routinely criticises blush. He died in late 1611, only to be posthumously involved in the Thomas Overbury poisoning scandal (the 'witch' Anne Turner and the murderous countess of Rochester having been his clients).

Savage's theatrical colleagues and contemporaries are all real. In addition to Jonson and Dekker, Thomas Heywood (author of *If You Know Not Me, You Know No Bodie*) was active in the period, and Shakespeare probably would have taken part in the king's coronation festivities, given that his company, the King's Men (formerly the Lord Chamberlain's Men) were given yards of red cloth and made grooms of the chamber at the time of the triumphal entry. Elizabeth really was resurrected on the stage as early as 1604, with Heywood's play published in 1605. So began a long history of cultural depictions of the queen, which are traced in *England's Elizabeth: An Afterlife in Fame and Fantasy* (2002: Oxford University Press) by Michael Dobson and Nicola Watson.

Another figure, though on the fringes of the theatrical world, is the Earl of Oxford. The earl really did travel through Italy in 1575, stood in judgment of Mary Queen of Scots (I've found no record of him physically present at her execution, but I am certain he would have sent witnesses) and thereafter is found outfitting ships against the Spanish Armada in 1588. He was, by most accounts, vain, manipulative, argumentative, and a keen patron of the arts, particularly verse and music. If readers have heard of him at all, it is probably via Rhys Ifans' portrayal in the picture *Anonymous* (2011: Dir Roland Emmerich). Prior to this he was largely known to students of the period for his killing of an undercook, his crossed words with Sir Philip Sidney, and his messy marriage to Anne Cecil (who died in 1588). He died in 1604, of unspecified causes.

And I do not think for one moment he wrote the works of Shakespeare.

Here, I think, I will have to say something about the strange, always intriguing, sometimes infuriating, occasionally funny 'authorship question'. In short, the argument, which was born, really, in the nineteenth century (and thus after hundreds of years of no one voicing doubts – and I do not count secret codes or alleged 'knowing winks' hidden in plain sight) runs thus: the author of the plays attributed to William Shakespeare were written by someone other than William Shakespeare of Stratford-upon-Avon. When the idea gained traction in the Victorian period, its earliest adherents were keen to prove that the plays were in fact penned by the celebrated lawyer and essayist, Robert Cecil's cousin Francis Bacon (and my favourite twentieth-century novelist, Daphne du Maurier, flirts with this theory in her two-part biography of the Bacon brothers, *The Golden Lads* and *The Winding Stair* [2007: Virago]). Baconians butted heads with Marlovians, who thought that Christopher Marlowe had faked his own death and written the plays whilst abroad. In the early twentieth century, J. Thomas Looney, a schoolmaster with an interest in the question, came across the Earl of Oxford (by then a largely forgotten Elizabethan courtier) and decided that his verses and his general biography made him a perfect candidate for the authorship of the Shakespeare canon. Only since then has Oxford developed a cult following amongst certain sections of those who don't think Shakespeare of Stratford wrote the plays. There is, however, no evidence that Oxford wrote them – certainly far less than there is that Shakespeare did.

At any rate, a whole host of famous names from the period have their supporters, from Queen Elizabeth dashing off *Hamlet* to the Earl of Derby being the secret author. No doubters of Shakespeare have suggested, to the best of my knowledge, that the plays were written by anyone other than a well-known figure; the only common bond between the disparate groups is that that well-known figure can't have been the glover's son from Warwickshire.

The biggest problem that doubters of Shakespeare have is the question 'why?'. Why should any writer of a body of works have them published pseudonymously using the name of an otherwise unimportant member of an acting company? One suggestion put forward is that there existed a stigma around putting material into print, with aristocrats considering it beneath them. This doesn't bear close scrutiny, given that King James himself was much published in print (although, being a hypocrite, his advice to his son was that a prince should not put their thoughts to the press). The idea of there being a stigma around the printed word seems to have been a later invention, as a staggering number of respectable works were printed in the period (not least bibles, works of devotion, and accounts of royal pageantry). Another suggestion is that the plays were politically dangerous and could bring trouble to the author – making a 'front man' necessary. Again, this is problematic in that plays went through the Revels Office, where they would be read and censored if deemed overly political (and the office staff and Revels Master would have to be convinced that the plays were written by the credited writer, unless they were in on a conspiracy). Indeed, doubters of Shakespeare must contend with the fact that that a significant number of people would have to have been involved in Oxford, or any other writer, producing a huge number of works as part of an elaborate con job. None of these people appear to have left any records of a coverup.

More recently, many of those who doubt that William Shakespeare wrote the plays have become less absolute about who they think did and instead begun to consider the idea of Shakespeare being an Alan Smithee-style front for various playwrights who wished to use a pseudonym for various reasons. Likewise, those who think William Shakespeare was indeed the author who is credited in the *First Folio* have, likewise, opened their minds to the collaborative nature of early modern writing, recognising the frenetic site of the playhouse as one of bouncing ideas and several collaborators (personally, I like to think of Shakespeare writing and then having his fellows in the company query and alter the language according to their interpretation of the characters). Perhaps this indicates a future rapprochement between those who hold to the orthodox view and those reasonable doubters who simply think something more complex and now forgotten was going on.

At any rate, the whole authorship question remains interesting and, though I don't subscribe to it, it has produced a lot of useful reappraisal of early modern theatrical practices and personalities from traditional, mainstream, and independent scholars (and a lot of addictive YouTube videos from ardent Oxfordians and conspiracy theorists). Oxford, in my opinion, led a crazy and bizarre enough life without trying to prove or disprove that he also pseudonymously penned the entire Shakespeare canon. For his life story, I would highly recommend Alan H. Nelson's *Monstrous Adversary: The Life of Edward de Vere, 17th Earl of Oxford* (2003: Liverpool University Press). Nelson's text is firmly in the 'Shakespeare wrote the works of Shakespeare' camp, and his biography is packed with contemporary documents relating to Oxford. In the opposite camp (and sadly no biographies of Oxford exist that don't have an agenda regarding the Shakespeare connection) there are *The Shakespeare Guide to Italy: Retracing the Bard's Unknown Travels* by Richard Paul Roe (2011: Harper Perennial) and the unambiguous if long winded *Shakespeare by Another Name: The Life of Edward de Vere, Earl of Oxford, the Man Who Was Shakespeare* (2005: Gotham Books). For an overview of the authorship question, I'd highly recommend James Shapiro's *Contested Will: Who Wrote Shakespeare?* (2011: Faber and Faber). To me, the best and most fruitful discussion question arising from this strange debate should not be 'who wrote the works of Shakespeare?' or even 'which famous person other than Shakespeare wrote the plays?' but 'how were early modern plays written?'

Finally, I'd like to thank all who have read this far. Once again, I've hugely enjoyed stepping back in time to early modern England and I hope that I've done the period justice. I hope, too, that Ned Savage will be back – especially given the momentous events which Robert Cecil was involved in over the years following the coronation. Savage has been lucky indeed to meet a number of famous Elizabethan and Jacobean personalities – but there are plenty more pounding the streets of London and the corridors of Whitehall. If you enjoyed this book – or if you didn't – I'd love to hear from you. I am on Twitter @Scrutineye and on Instagram @steven.veerapen.3. Thanks again!

Printed in Great Britain
by Amazon